I0648438

Quill's Barn

Quill's Barn

a novel

Willa Perrine

Quill's Barn
by
Willa Perrine

Copyright © 2009 by Willa Perrine

All Rights Reserved
No part of this book may be used or reproduced by any
means without prior written permission of the author.

Printed in the United States of America

First Edition

ISBN: 978-0-578-01936-9

Published in the United States by Willa Perrine

Quill's Barn *is a work of fiction. Any resemblance to actual person or persons living or dead is coincidental and not intended. Little Wood, Millennium, The Farm, and Trinity Hospital exist only in the mind of the author.*

Acknowledgements

I would like to thank the Writers Workshop of Chico Prime Timers for valuable comments on the work in progress.

*In particular, I am indebted to
Gary Briley, Clidean Dunn, Phyl Manning,
Nelson Ober, and Mike Sajben
for their discerning critical readings
of the manuscript.*

I wish to acknowledge Trent Stewart of the Iowa Writers Workshop for his encouraging critique of early chapters, and Michael McClintock for his enthusiasm and unerring eye for the right word.

I am grateful to Peter Perrine for technical assistance, to Lisa and Peter for their perceptive suggestions, and to Lucy Perrine for barn photos.

QUILL'S BARN

1. <u>Casey</u>

It was mid-March, 1950, and the snow was gone, the ground soggy, the trees stark and bare. For three days, rain had fallen stiletto-straight.

In the men's violent ward of the asylum known locally as The Farm, seven miles from the nearest village, the yellow ceiling and walls seemed to suck the last light from the lead-gray sky outside. Pinpoints of light from the buildings across the loop of driveway shimmered in the stream sluicing down the windows.

In the dayroom under banks of fluorescent lights, the inmates shuffled back and forth in their canvas slippers. Although the thermostat stood at a subtropical eighty degrees, most of the men wrapped themselves in their arms against the perceived cold. They paced, each following his own internal rhythm, what individual rhythm was left after the whittling-down of institutional life -- the measured round of feeding, sleeping, toileting, the twice-daily line-up for chloral hydrate or paraldehyde or Dilantin; the herding down the stairs and through the tunnel three times a day to their dining room. Their only respite from tedium was the week-day presence of student nurses from Pocatello and Boise, fresh and lively in their white wing-like caps and blue and white pinafores. The latest class of student nurses had left a week ago.

For now, the men were hibernating, locked away from the weather and every other peril of the world outside the asylum. Out there, they'd be up against loud voices jostling and pressing them to hurry, to speak, to produce, to account for themselves. Here, they were insulated, each accorded his own three-foot bubble of space. Behind these barred windows, they were safe.

Whatever had earned them a berth on Men's Violent, they soon became seasoned to the consequences of combative behavior. Most of the violence they did was to and within themselves (all but Howard in his cell, who would kill anything that moved). When the impulse boiled over, the attendants, big and burly, stepped in and deflected the blows.

Some attendants, like Schwartz, second in seniority, bore it with considerable grace and a paternal attitude. The youngest and newest attendant, Whitaker, waiting out the Korean War as a conscientious objector, believed in his bones in the basic goodness of people; he was still taking a few bruises. The head attendant, Casey, the biggest and burliest, had the lowest boiling point and a vindictive streak as well.

Schwartz was off duty today. Whitaker was keeping the peace between two men each trying to occupy the same space. Casey was lounging, a tightly coiled spring, in the doorway to the dayroom.

From inside the locked core of the nurses station, the top half of a Dutch door ratcheted open and the big nurse, Mrs. Carson, appeared in the window space. "Time for our medicine," she called out.

Casey snapped to attention and all but six men single-filed across the hall. Barred by Casey, the six remained in the dayroom, their heads and shoulders collapsing onto their chests. For them, the chloral hydrate, the paraldehyde and the Dilantin had lost effectiveness and only the unthinkable mercy of electroshock would restore each to equilibrium.

In white muslin bathrobes, they moved into a loose circle in a facsimile of mutual support. They were quiet except for one man who periodically flung out his arms and flipped his feet before hauling them in again, holding his arms to his sides and locking his knees, shuddering until the next spasm hit him. A gap opened in the circle to accommodate another man. They were waiting for Wizard and his escort, Mr. Wheeler, from the infirmary below, where Wizard was being treated for a self-inflicted urinary tract infection.

"Now keep an eye on the boys, Jimbo," Casey barked at Whitaker. He pushed off from the door frame, and strode into the nurse's station and sat down.

"Get your feet off my desk, Casey," said the big pear-shaped nurse.

Casey took his time swinging his legs around, letting her know he was only doing it because he was ready to. Like it was his own idea. He remained seated in her chair. She didn't argue. The nurses liked it better when he was not towering over them.

He grinned, watching her lumber over to the other side of the desk. She plopped herself down and started leafing through a sheaf of pharmacy forms. Miz Crack. She smelled like paraldehyde. She gave the medications, answered the phone, let him manage the men. In the staff apartments, she lived down the hall from him. When she was off duty, she'd knit and listen to religious music on the radio, and go to church suppers and rummage sales in town.

"Yes, Miz Crack," he said. Not her real name, which he didn't remember, hadn't paid any attention to, but his name for her, which she was not about to question because she guessed she wouldn't like the answer. He'd decided she was Miz Crack the first time she stood up and walked away from him with her skirt caught between her buttocks.

You had to call people something and it didn't take him very long to see what a person was all about, what their names ought to be. Real names didn't matter. His name was Keith Cochran, on file in Administration so they could write it on his paychecks. That was all he needed it for. They called him Casey, wrote it like that on the assignment sheets, but he was KC.

"Mrs. Chisholm is sending up a patient to go with our bunch to shock therapy," said the big nurse.

"That's fine, Miz Crack." Casey let a nasal note creep into his voice. "The boys are all pottied and ready to go. Jimbo's got them in the dayroom."

Down the hall the big door opened in a jangle of keys. He sucked in his stomach, marched into the corridor and took a stance, feet braced. A little man in Infirmary whites, the inmate "Frog" shuffled into the ward, stood with his chin on his chest. Behind him, his escort held open the door, key still in the lock, the rest of his arsenal dangling on the chain.

It was Healer, the only attendant who refused to wear white. Healer's khaki trousers and shirts were the same color as his skin and hair. Made his sharp blue eyes stand out. It was fine with Casey if The Great Healer wouldn't wear white; made it plain whose side he was on. Thought he was as good as the psychologists, even took classes with the student nurses.

Healer locked eyes with Casey. "Here he is," he said.

Casey held his ground, scraping two keys together. This was his territory. If Healer wouldn't come to him, then Frog would have to come in by himself.

"Come and get him," said Healer. "Mrs. Chisholm borrowed me from Men's Intermediate and I've got to get back."

Casey and the head nurse on Infirmary were buddies. He called her Miz Chisel and she just laughed that high-pitched whinny. She had powerful B.O., so you always knew where she was. Nobody could smell Casey. He was clean.

Miz Chisel was on the White side too. Said nobody but staff should wear white. Let the inmates wear military surplus drab.

What color you wore was important around here. You didn't touch anyone who wore white. Casey and Healer knocked heads over it one time. Healer said white was sacred and what that meant was, patients were sacred. That was about enough to make Casey throw up. Healer moved slow and easy and talked low; he said it kept the patients calm. *Patients.* They were patients for maybe half an hour after a session in Dr. Quill's shock room; otherwise they were inmates and that was that.

That wasn't Casey's only beef with Healer. He was too cozy with the night supervisor, Miz Quill, used to live across the hall from her and her daughter. By rights, she should have been nicer to him, Casey, when she first came here fifteen years ago. Fine-looking woman, obviously pregnant, a widow they said. Needed a man if ever a woman did, wouldn't give *him* the time of day. So what did she see in Healer? And then ten years later, along comes Dr. Quill, same name, and they act like they don't know each other.

Casey stood there facing down Healer until Miz Crack pushed past him. She walked with a broad base, shifting her weight from side to side, down the hall to get Frog.

"G'morning, Mr. Wheeler," she said to Healer, and then:

"Round up the rest of the men, Casey, and get along to the shock room. Don't keep Dr. Quill waiting."

Still smarting from Miz Crack pulling rank on him in front of Healer, Casey unlocked the door and let his boys out of the tunnel into the Clinic basement. Heads down, they shuffled past him in their frayed white canvas scuffs and white bathrobes. *Sacred.* Sacred sheep. They pretended they didn't know where they were going.

Jimbo brought up the rear. "You lock the door now," Casey told him in the same tone of voice Miz Crack had used on *him.* He knew he didn't need to tell Jimbo to lock the door.

Jimbo's sunburned moonface didn't change expression; he was used to being low man on the totem pole. He was about to close the door when the one Casey called Hawk grabbed the door jamb and hung on. Jimbo pried loose Hawk's fingers and slammed the door.

In the dim hall, the men crowded together, careful not to touch or look at each other. A stench of acid perspiration rose. Casey scraped his keys together; the friction made his fingers tingle with pleasure.

At four minutes after nine, bony Miz Frizzle walked in. Dr. Quill followed, looking neither right nor left. He unlocked the wide door to the shock room, threw it open and flipped the light switch. The walls flared yellow. "Let's have the first patient," he said.

He glanced up, raising his eyebrows as Casey strode in the door, wincing as if he expected him to bump his head. This happened every day.

In the hall, Casey grabbed Hawk, lifted him by the armpits, flicked off his white scuffs. "Okay, Hotshot. Show KC how brave you are," he said. He whisked him into the shock room and shut the door before the first of Hawk's screams could set off general pandemonium.

Casey and Jimbo pinned the little man on the table and strapped him down. Hawk twisted and flipped and lunged. Miz Frizzle, with her yellow skin and crisp dry hair, stood by with the electrodes. Dr. Quill daubed Hawk's temples with KY jelly and gestured to the nurse. She fixed the electrodes in place with a rubber strap.

Casey had asked her once if all that electricity sparking through the electrodes was what shriveled her skin and hair. She took it personally. "Oh yeah?" she flared. "Where'd you get that beetle brow?" What the heck, he was just being pleasant.

Contact jelly sucked the electrodes into Hawk's skin. Casey and Jimbo threw their weight onto his shoulders and knees. Miz Frizzle held a thick padded tongue blade between his jaws.

"Ready?" asked Dr. Quill.

Hawk collapsed suddenly, melting into the table top. A current of excitement raced through Casey. Dr. Quill set a dial and flipped the switch, counted under his breath -- one, two, three -- and flipped it off. Hawk stiffened and his back thrust up off the table, his body touching only at the head and heels. Casey and Jimbo hung on.

The convulsion broke up into shudders rippling through Hawk's legs and arms, now flopping like landed fish. His face was purple. Shudders ebbed to tremors, and he began snorting huge chunks of air, while his skin washed into lavender.

"Ah, that was a good one." Casey licked sweat off his lip.

Dr. Quill lifted his eyebrows. "It seems to be a good one for all," he murmured.

Casey wondered how much Dr. Quill knew about him. For that matter, *he* didn't know all that much about Dr. Quill.

Why worry? What was there to know about Dr. Quill? He was at least sixty. He didn't have a car, never left The Farm, never went into town -- Millennium. Didn't leave his apartment except to work and go walking out the reservoir road. He wasn't finding any fun out there.

Jimbo helped Casey lift Hawk onto the gurney, and they rolled him into the hallway to begin waking up. Heads turned away, trying hard not to see him.

"Okay, who's next? Don't keep KC waiting." Casey plucked up Frog, quivering and bleating and trying to shrink into the woodwork. Suddenly the little man darted free, planted his back to the wall. He fixed his eye on Casey, pointed his finger like a wand: "You. ... !"

Filth boiled out of Frog's mouth and anger rose into a knot in Casey's throat. "You think your nasty words will stop KC? When you gonna learn?"

Sticks and stones may break my bones, but names will never hurt me. That's what she had told Casey, that Sunday school teacher who washed out his mouth with soap. She'd done some other things too that maybe didn't turn out the way she expected. Didn't know who she was tangling with. He was thirteen then, but he was a man. He'd shown her and now he was going to show Frog. He and Dr. Quill were going to shock the filth right out of his head.

Casey stretched out his arm, beckoned with his finger: Come on, sinner. You don't like it, do you? Well, you brought it on yourself. Now you got to start over.

Casey didn't pull the little man in, not yet. He wanted him to know he'd lost, wanted him to sweat. Now Frog thought he had Casey backed off; he sucked the filth back into himself, mixed it up and shot it out again, teasing him with words and gestures.

Oh, was that what he was after, the fornicating sinner. Frog wouldn't know what to do with it if it was handed to him. Dirty words didn't make it happen. Casey knew how to get what he wanted without using dirty words. All he had to do was give a woman the eye, maybe a little sweet talk. Old maid or married, panting for it or playing hard to get. All but that Quill woman, that icicle. But that girl of hers, that Ellen, was coming right along.

His big hand closed around Frog's skinny wrist, jerked him stumbling into Casey's arms. Yeah, that girl of hers was going to be sweet, and wouldn't the Quill witch take him seriously then.

2. <u>Mrs. Quill</u>

The rain had stopped and the wind from the west was picking up. Mrs. Quill didn't know which she liked the least -- the wind or the rain. After all this time, seventeen years, mild weather was the one thing she still missed about Boise, sheltered in its basin.

In the driveway, she let herself into her grey Plymouth and put the key into the ignition. Her gaze swept the length of her house from the solitary square of fluorescent-lit kitchen window to the dark bedroom end. She was uneasy about leaving home tonight and she hoped it didn't look as if no one was here. Ellen hadn't returned from babysitting the youngest Swensons.

Motherhood as Mrs. Quill conceived it was not meshing well with work. A daytime job would solve the problem, but she had always liked the quiet and the lack of interference in night work. She rather liked sleeping in the daytime while Ellen was in school. She knew too that Ellen would worry less about being alone than she herself worried for her.

She turned on ignition and headlights, and maneuvered the car into the street.

She had thought it was the right thing to do -- moving from the staff apartments into this house on the edge of the hospital grounds. It seemed essential to provide a normal environment for Ellen. Even with Dr. Swenson's children for friends, what kind of social life could a girl have growing up in the shadow of an asylum? They had gained privacy but lost security. They had lost the comfort and company of Ynez, whose official address was Women's Intermediate Ward but who in fact had slept on Mrs. Quill's sofa for years. Ynez had tended Ellen since babyhood, while Mrs. Quill worked at night, and remained in the household when Ellen went to school. Now she spent most of the day working in the big hospital kitchen.

When Mrs. Quill had moved them into the house, Ynez came with them, but by the end of the first week she'd become restless. By the end of the second she was confining herself to tight spaces. Backing into corners, brushing elbows with Ellen.

A week ago, she returned to Intermediate, saying only that she missed living on the grounds and that Ellen is going on fifteen and is old enough to lock herself in at night.

Mrs. Quill couldn't understand Ynez's lack of loyalty. What more could she have done for her? That Ynez, unlike most long-term inmates, still had her teeth and was free of TB she owed at least in part to Mrs. Quill's intervention.

After she found Ynez here fifteen years ago, in 1935, and then secured her own employment, Mrs. Quill's first action was to arrange grounds privileges for Ynez and start proceedings for her release from the institution, an effort she abandoned when she learned that the legal action could become a matter of record in Little Wood, where they both had lived. Neither she nor Ynez wanted their whereabouts common knowledge. Ynez, who was not accustomed to being at liberty anyway, was happy just to have the freedom to come and go.

And now the house: Mrs. Quill had taken pains to find a place with a well-equipped kitchen and a garden and a porch, and more space than they'd had before, a bedroom for each of them. She'd thought Ynez would love it and she was astonished that Ynez wanted so much to live on the grounds that she was willing to go back to Intermediate. Why hadn't Ynez told her before and spared them the move?

Ynez's answer had been vague and Mrs. Quill wondered if the move simply gave Ynez the excuse to make the break she had been wanting for some time. Was she bored with them? Ynez said simply, "Ellen doesn't need me any more."

Now, most of all, Mrs. Quill missed Ynez, but she was surprised to feel nostalgic even for the old nurses with the thick, stiff waistlines that seemed to go with institutional nursing and the honorific "Mrs." though they were no more "Mrs." than she was herself -- Mrs. Chisholm and Mrs. Frickes and even Mrs. Carson with her pungent aura of paraldehyde and the religious music blaring on her radio every evening.

And it had been nice to have Mr. Wheeler in the next apartment, a good neighbor whose brand of paternalism she could tolerate, coming as it did with no strings attached. She had liked having a man in her life, but neighbor was as close as she wanted to get. She rarely saw him now and she wouldn't try for more -- the relationship would be ... different.

Although Mr. Wheeler looked young, with an unlined face and clear blue eyes in contrast with his ecru skin and hair, he'd been here before Mrs. Quill, and his direct, unblinking gaze and immobile expression were more ageless than youthful. That he had been a minister she felt certain. She could imagine his appeal as a preacher, the touch of theatricality that could transfix you, although his voice was not sonorous, as she would expect a successful preacher's to be, but thin and nasal, a little unpleasant and oddly stirring. He had a way of standing very still, until you began to wonder if he was all right, and only when he had your nervous attention did he begin to speak. And then he would lead up to a point and pause, and you'd feel that the next word would shatter every idea you'd ever had, shock you out of your silliness, and when he delivered the word, it was in almost a whisper. His style of speech charged his ordinary discourse with an electricity that made you realize how much of life is extraordinary and you'd feel chastened for taking it for granted, from the weather to the baseball games to an inmate's behavior. She had the sense that preaching was now, for some unspeakable reason, an indulgence he must deny himself.

Often in the evening she had heard his strap fall -- slap/snap -- and sometimes she heard a whimper, choked as if he didn't want to make a sound but couldn't help it. When Ellen was a baby, he'd liked to hold her and he had never gotten out of the habit of laying his hand on her head -- his baptismal reflex, perhaps. Once, a small voice inside had asked Mrs. Quill: Do you want a man who scourges himself to handle your child? And she had answered silently: Yes, I do. She didn't know why she trusted Mr. Wheeler, but she did.

Even his conviction that if she would have peace she must put her trust in God did not raise her hackles. When they gave up the apartment, and then Ynez left them and he had an inkling of Mrs. Quill's distress, he had said to her in his thin and nasal voice, "There is a reason. Have faith and it will be revealed to you."

She conceded that life would be simpler if she could invoke a higher authority as an answer to everything. She wouldn't have to do this endless sifting and sorting and re-examining her values. She'd know as clean as reflex what was right and important, but that seemed like an easy way out that she hadn't earned.

She guessed she was a nonbeliever but not an unbeliever, or maybe it was the other way around. What she did believe in was the moon and the stars and forever, and lava-rock and soil and cold, and water and ice and steam, and solid and lightning and ashes. When she was a child in Boise, she had believed in kitchens and sunshine and warm laps, and then her mother died in childbirth and she believed in the dark and in hiding places and in the gooseflesh on her arms when Cousin Malcolm ran his fingers up her scalp at the back of her neck, and then Cousin Malcolm went away and she'd learned to believe in secrets and in excellence in school, though her schoolmates hated her for it, until she grew out of those years and went to work for Uncle Amos. Uncle Amos did not believe in God; he believed in pharmacy. So she came to believe in powders and tinctures and roots, and mortars and pestles, and sorting and classifying and dusting, and cooking stews in the back of the shop and in wearing white, and then Uncle Amos died of influenza and her aunts and her stepmother too, and her father nearly. What her father believed in was money and pleasure, and when he recovered, and his appetites too, and she realized what he had in mind for her, she packed the black valise and carried it barking her ankle in the night to her first refuge, Trinity Hospital three blocks away.

She was twenty-five then. She didn't believe in running away from her problems, but she'd never have become a nurse if she hadn't needed to run away. At eighteen just out of school, she hadn't given nursing a second thought. Her name was Mercy then, a burden laid upon her by her father, but a name alone didn't qualify one to work with the sick and disabled and dying: You were supposed to be maternal and generous and cheerful and God-fearing, and by consensus of her stepmother and her brothers, she was selfish and eccentric. Secretive and unloving. She'd known it was true -- when her mother died and Cousin Malcolm went away, her generosity and cheer shriveled into a cinder until she went to work for Uncle Amos.

Trinity Hospital had been a self-contained world a mere three blocks from her family's homes, so cloistered that she would live and apprentice and work there for thirteen years without being found. When she asked for sanctuary, they took her in, although she was not generous and cheerful and tender-hearted. Instead, she was focused and disciplined and seasoned, and she did believe in seeing what was needed and providing it, and in making no mistakes, and she came to believe in blood and excreta and vomitus, and in the quick slice of the scalpel and the dance of bedside procedures and the sanctity of the medicine keys. And she believed in wounds visible and invisible and in healing and dying, and in the stricken who suffered their wounds and their cures and their dying, and who believed the cures even as they were dying and didn't doubt that God and their doctors were infallible.

Mercy had not been looking for anything better in life. She felt absurd out of uniform and believed so little in money that she'd kept her earnings hidden in plain sight in a large talcum can on her dresser in her room with a door she never locked. When she had been at Trinity Hospital for thirteen years, a wealthy woman dying of cancer had put her life in Mercy's hands. She asked for death, and Mercy helped her, responsibly and subversively, as the situation required. Mercy gained nothing tangible from the dignified, managed death of Mrs. Winstead, only an awakening to the possibility of a universal truth beyond conventional wisdom, and so she'd left Trinity Hospital, taking a train half across Idaho to Little Wood, where the convergence of willows and river and village signaled a settling place.

In Little Wood, she had believed in belonging and in the smell of birth and the sight of Dr. Flower's white hair setting off sparks under the dome light. She called herself Mary and she'd learned to believe in the sisterhood of women, until they betrayed her with their foolish ideas and a dose of scopolamine. So that when Leonard, one of the husbands and her friend, had said to her, "You can't save them, Mary, save yourself," it was easy to believe him, and she believed him that strange night all the way to Ellen, who has her father's eyes and triangular chin.

The Farm out of Millennium had been her third taking of sanctuary, and now and evermore she believed in Ellen, who didn't know she was a Macpherson and a Thorel, but believed she was a Quill, and didn't ask questions and seemed to think she was immortal. But Mrs. Quill believed there was a mortal vulnerability to the hours after midnight: When the sun goes down, the natural laws of daylight are suspended. How else to explain that when your eyes adapt to the dark, what you see is not normal, not real? There is no depth and no shadow; everything is uniformly illuminated. You can't see an object if you focus on it, if you look at it straight on. It's not the world as it exists in daylight, but a kind of reflection of that world.

She knew the scientific explanation for this phenomenon -- rods and cones and all that, but she could never quite accept the germ theory of disease either, or the miracle of x-ray or the beneficence of electroshock. She did not insist on being rational, if it felt right. She didn't believe in the existence of God or the infallibility of doctors, neither of which had been demonstrated to her. And she still didn't believe in money, although she accorded it a conditional respect, since as sure as the earth turns, today's twilight is tomorrow's dayspring, and you can't know what stretches beyond the horizon.

She guessed that what happens may not depend on whether you believe in it. This was what she knew: That her daughter was young but not as young as she was yesterday and younger than she would be tomorrow. That Ellen was fourteen and that when Ynez was fourteen, she was a mother mute and mad and a refugee in Dr. Flower's kitchen. No wonder Ynez thought Ellen was old enough to lock herself in at night.

Mrs. Quill eased the car into a parking space in front of the administration building, flicked off the ignition and the lights, and stared out the window at the shapes that slowly emerged from the dark. Here I am, she thought, with more space than I need and more alone than I want to be, and feeling sorry for myself.

She'd work it out. She got out of the car and set out, a damp breeze lifting her hair. Beyond the roadside elms, the darkened building gave way to the larger ones of brick, lodging nine hundred or so wards of the state, and the old, two-story, wooden admissions ward on the periphery. The sidewalk led her past the nursing office, in the administration building. No one would care if she turned on all the lights for company and kept her uniform clean, drinking coffee or reading or napping by the telephone all night. But that was not her idea of how to do her job and so, the office was just her mailbox and, sometimes, desk space while she researched in Records. She continued on to C Building, which housed the infirmary on the ground floor and the violent wards above. On the third floor, Men's Violent was dimmed down for the night, but Women's Violent on second was still bright.

Inside Infirmary, the nurses' station was quiet, the night staff making rounds. The evening supervisor's report lay on the desk. Mrs. Quill reached for it, then withdrew her hand, picked up the phone and dialed. Ellen answered; the older Swensons had just gotten home from the basketball game.

"I don't want you letting yourself into an empty house," said Mrs. Quill. "Please ask Mrs. Swenson to keep you there overnight." Bless Julie Swenson -- she'd understand.

The deed done, she was absurdly pleased with herself. She breezed through the evening supervisor's report, then checked the transfer rosters. Here was where the night's work would be. The new transfers and the backsliders would have their wards in an uproar, Women's Violent in particular. Recalling their bright lights, she flipped quickly to their roster, read it, pursed her lips: Wouldn't you know -- it was Alma.

Alma, old maid schools superintendent and part-time auxiliary volunteer in Mrs. Quill's past life as head nurse of the Little Wood Municipal Hospital, had appeared at The Farm two years ago, in 1948. Near blind and stunned and querulous, when she got her bearings she was up to her old shenanigans, managing and manipulating. Her stay on the admissions ward was brief; she was assessed as unlikely to improve and was assigned to Women's Intermediate. If she had found a niche and settled in peaceably the way most derelicts and castoffs did, she wouldn't have come to Mrs. Quill's attention or Mrs. Quill to hers, but on the third evening, bored and boxed in, she'd lashed out first with her tongue and then, thrilled with the spectacle she was creating, with her feet. She was transferred, at the change of shift, to Women's Violent. There she sat stonily in the dayroom while a bed was made up for her in an isolation room.

When Mrs. Quill came through on her early night round with only a fleeting glance at the small gray dumpling of a woman in the dayroom, she'd paused at the door to the nurses' station to exchange greetings with the head attendant, Mrs. Brunt, who was coming out. With Mrs. Quill's first words, there was a stirring behind her, and then a voice she didn't at first recognize uttered a name that raised the hair on her arms.

"Mercy?"

She took a closer look at the apparition in the shapeless white nightgown and fraying scuffs -- long hair springing and draggling out of a familiar, sculpted roll of hair, and two sets of eyebrows above tortoise-shell-rimmed glasses. That fine, long nose and mournful slope of cheek. Despite aging and the institutional garb, it had to be Alma. In Mrs. Quill's confusion at being discovered, one thought stood out: How did Alma manage to keep the forbidden hairpins for her artful twist of hair? A *chignon*, she used to call it.

"Mercy!" Alma said again.

"This is the transfer from Intermediate," said Mrs. Brunt. "Created quite a ruckus over there but she's all tuckered out now. Alma Duffy. You just sit tight for a minute, dear, and they'll have you in bed in a jiffy."

Mrs. Quill had been pretty sure that wasn't going to be the end of it, and it wasn't. In the two years Alma had been here, she had refused to acknowledge herself an inmate and had corrupted every ward she'd been assigned to. Most inmates were incompetent or deluded or hallucinating, but Alma was not out of touch with reality. Her only incompetence was blindness, her only lapse in judgement, aside from a passion for ancient religions and pagan rituals, an unwise trust in the goodwill of her relatives. Most inmates settled into some kind of accommodation to their circumstances. Alma had not reached that level of quiet misery. Now, irregularly, unpredictably, she shook up Women's Intermediate, and then she was strait-jacketed for escort by an attendant through the tunnel to Women's Violent where she'd spend a night or two or three, being returned to her home ward before she could incite this ward to frenzy. On these occasions, she cried out for Mercy, until Mrs. Quill on her first round sequestered herself with Alma in her little padded cell.

Now, Mrs. Quill tucked the supervisor's report onto a clipboard, let herself out of Infirmary, and took the stairs one flight up. Unlocking the door to Women's Violent, she felt a familiar wave of heat roll up from the back of her knees. "Every half hour on the dot," she muttered. "I could set my watch by these hot flashes." On a good night they didn't leave her shivering. This had been going on for five years, after the doctor in Pocatello assured her they'd last only a few months. What did a man know? Heat washed over her and she drew herself up tall and took a deep breath. Sometimes, if she concentrated, she could meet the flushes head-on.

She opened the door. There, key advanced, stood Casey Cochran looking surprised. Then he lifted his heels to loom over her, smirking.

She froze him with a look. "Are you pulling a double tonight, Casey?"

"I'm just bringing the boys and girls back to the wards after the dance at the rec center." He rocked back on his heels, scraped two of his keys together. He had nearly as many keys as she had, giving him almost equal power if not authority.

"At eleven o'clock? The patients should have been in bed an hour ago."

His grin hadn't changed and he didn't look a day older than the first time she'd seen him. In spite of his size and muscle, he looked unhealthy, his skin as pale as if he lived under a rock. She liked to think that when he was off duty he crawled into a damp hole in the old tunnel and hibernated until time to go to work again. She didn't turn her back when Casey was around.

He strode off in his black rubber-soled shoes, his knees springing.

The heat dissolved into perspiration; the feeling of power dissipated. This is how women pay for the flowering of youth, she thought; this is what beauty comes to.

As she locked the door into C-3 behind her, the wail began: "Mercy! Mercy! Mercy!" Alma was waiting for her.

Mrs. Quill knew no one would suspect that Alma was calling her name; all the same, she winced. This had happened before. In a moment the attendant would approach her, mimicking, "'Mercy! Mercy! Mercy!' You'd think we were torturing her."

Outside the door to one of the locked solitary rooms, a clutch of women scattered, cackling and catcalling. Three of the women tried to insinuate themselves inside as Mrs. Quill let herself into Alma's cell.

Alma was getting herself ready for bed. Mrs. Quill knew that Alma knew that she was here, and she knew that Alma would pretend she didn't know until she was finished with what she was doing. Alma had managed by ingratiation or blackmail to hang onto the appurtenances of her former public self, and now she slipped her corset out from under her nightgown and tucked it under her pillow with her dentures and eyeglasses, then delicately wiped the powder off her face with the sheet. Mrs. Quill watched, fascinated, as Alma slipped under the top sheet and closed her eyes, lips moving silently. *Now I lay me down to sleep I pray the Lord my soul to keep if I should die before I wake I pray the Lord my soul to take.* For all Alma's pagan pretensions, her childlike trust was Protestant.

Alma opened her eyes and turned her blind gaze in Mrs. Quill's direction. As usual, she had two sets of eyebrows, one set natural, the other drawn on with a pencil that Alma could no longer see to guide but that vanity wouldn't let her give up.

"So you're Mrs. Quill now," she said. "Mrs. Q they call you. It took me a long time to figure out your name. I thought it was Mrs. Cue, C-u-e. It's strange to think of you as a Mrs. Somebody. Do you really have a husband? I don't recall what your last name used to be. You were just Mary to me. I know I'm not supposed to call you Mercy, but I thought it would get your attention."

"What seems to be the problem, Alma?" Mrs. Quill said. "What kind of trouble are you in now?"

"Do you have a husband?" Alma persisted. "It's not Dr. Quill. I imagine you're wondering how I know about him. I'm not going to tell you. I have my connections."

Mrs. Quill was unimpressed with Alma's "connections," since she didn't even know that Mrs. Quill had a daughter -- and there were women who had been here long enough to remember, including the trio at the door.

"I know things about many people you've probably never given the time of day to," said Alma.

Mrs. Quill resisted the temptation to respond. She *was* curious about Dr. Quill. When they'd first met in staff meeting, he hadn't commented on the coincidence of their sharing an uncommon surname, nor on the possibility that they might be related, didn't ask where she had come from. Because then she might ask where *he* came from. One didn't ask such questions on The Farm: No one exiled himself to a place like this without a reason.

He had been here just five years. Their paths intersected only at the weekly staff meetings and occasionally in the dining room at breakfast when she worked overtime. She kept him at a distance and he called her Mrs. Quill very distinctly, firmly, as if it were a different name from his own, unfamiliar, as if he had to think to remember it.

Mrs. Quill was sure his name was an alias, the same way he'd know hers was an alias, if he thought about it. Like her, he'd have come into town from the west, his train passing, as hers had ten years earlier, the crossing outside Pocatello, stopping to take on water. She'd stared at the side of a barn for five minutes before she saw what the sign was trying to tell her. Quill's Feed, the sign said. *Quill.*

There wasn't a Quill in the phone book -- she checked before she signed her name to her new bank account, to be sure there would be no one trying to claim her for a cousin. Quill's Feed? The sign on that barn must be a hundred years old and Dr. Fugitive Quill was just another pitiful human being on a dead-end track.

A snuffling and rustling announced that the women in the doorway were making themselves at home. Clarissa and Eloise and Rochelle. Their shapeless nightgowns were their only concession to sleep. Women's Violent was a non-stop slumber party.

Rochelle stood just inside the door, face flushed, eyes glassy. She looked soft as putty. Mrs. Quill had seen that look on Rochelle's face, the time she'd been standing in a warm shower for twenty minutes and wouldn't get out until they turned off the water.

Eloise, a smooth-faced, gray-haired wisp, approached Mrs. Quill, tacking to the left and then to the right, sneaking up on her by degrees. Finally, she faced her off-center and peeked at her out of the corner of her eye. "You. Are. Eliminated. With. Courtesy," she said.

"Thank you, Eloise," said Mrs. Quill. Eloise zigzagged back to the wall.

"Who's that?" said Alma.

Clarissa oozed over to Alma's bed, the tails of her Posey belt draped over her arm like a bridal train. She rarely got violent any more, but the restraint reassured her, got her through the night. It didn't immobilize her. If she wanted to get up and prowl, she knew how to untie it.

She grabbed Mrs. Quill's hand, turned it over and spat luxuriantly into her palm. Mrs. Quill glanced sharply at her hand, then relaxed. Not sputum, just spittle. Clarissa's last chest x-ray was clear, finally, after two years on Streptomycin. Mrs. Quill felt a rush of affection for her, a sweet-tempered sprite and one of her successes.

Clarissa gazed into the frothy pool in Mrs. Quill's hand as if studying her reflection. "Wipe your lips, Clarissa," said Mrs. Quill. "You're drooling. No, not on my uniform. Here, use a tissue."

Alma cocked her head to one side and then the other. She still had some peripheral vision. "Get them out of here," she shrieked, sweeping them away with flicks of her hand. "Get these lunatics out of here! Shoo! Shoo! Shoo!"

"They're just being friendly, Alma."

"Friendly! The Three Graces. A Trio of Harpies. They're horrible, horrible."

"Watch your manners. Please, ladies, Alma and I need to talk." Mrs. Quill turned her back on them and when she looked again the three were gone. "How did you get in trouble this time, Alma? I'm beginning to think you get yourself sent over here every once in a while so you can have a private room."

A smirk rippled across Alma's face.

"Alma, I've got work to do. What is it this time?"

"I was observing my devotions to Hecate; it's dark of the moon. It's my time to be crazy." Her voice was plaintive.

"Come on, Alma. They don't put you on Women's Violent for having crazy ideas. You were causing a disturbance."

"I'm having hot flashes. Maybe I was wrong about Our Mother. A benevolent goddess wouldn't condemn us to hot flashes. I'll bet you have hot flashes too." Mrs. Quill didn't respond and Alma turned over, punched the pillow. "Well, it's Ynez. She acts so superior because she gets to go out and work in the kitchen. She offends me. She ignores me, turns up her nose. She won't talk to me."

"Why would you expect her to talk to you? Ynez doesn't talk to anyone." Hand in pocket, Mrs. Quill crossed her fingers. Hardly anyone. "She hasn't said a word for thirty-five years."

"Well, I know that. But surely she could make an exception in my case. After all, in this whole *sanitarium*, we're the only *residents* from Little Wood. And she's known me for fifty years. She could talk if she wanted to. She's not crazy. She's no crazier than I am."

Probably less, Mrs. Quill thought. Certainly smarter. "Ynez keeps out of trouble. She's not snubbing you. After all these years her vocal cords have probably atrophied." Which was not quite true. When something needed to be said, Ynez said it.

Mrs. Quill remembered a morning fifteen years ago, three months after she found Ynez here, like herself a fugitive from Little Wood. In the mammoth basement kitchen where Mrs. Quill was having breakfast before going home for her day's sleep, she'd realized Ynez was staring at her. Ynez's lips parted and the words came out like the cranking up of a rusty machine, cracking into a two-note chord. "You're pregnant. How?" And stared at Mrs. Quill until she told her how. And *how* might be why Ynez now didn't feel obligated to her.

"What did you do to Ynez?" Mrs. Quill asked Alma.

"I didn't do anything to her. Pushed her a little bit maybe."

"Hmmm."

Alma glanced at her sidelong. "I suppose you think I can't hurt you. Everyone thinks I'm crazy as a bedbug. Since that's what I'm doing here. Who would believe that fifteen years ago you and I were friends in Little Wood? I can't tell anyone where you wound up without telling on myself too. I can't do you any harm. Talk to me." Alma was pleading now. "We were friends. Don't treat me like an inmate."

Mrs. Quill felt a tug of sympathy for her. It couldn't be easy for her to have no power to wield, no means of controlling people. But she had potential for setting off a bigger catastrophe. Alma was a loose wire, sparks flying in every direction.

"All right, I hit Ynez. Even that didn't get a word out of her, but everyone else started squawking for the nurse. And they brought me over here and I had to wait out in the dayroom for an hour and a half while they put everyone else to bed." Alma's voice was rich with indignation. "Everyone but Rochelle. She was sitting in the dayroom with that obnoxious Casey."

"Casey? An hour and a half? How do you know that, Alma? You can't see."

"I can't see but I can hear. She's a mouth-breather. She sighs. He refers to himself in the third person. He scrapes his keys together. He came up behind me, scraping his keys, and pushed me into the dayroom. He said, 'Git along, girlie. Don't stand in the middle of the doorway.'" Alma hesitated. "And I said to him, 'How dare you patronize me, young man!'"

Mrs. Quill smiled. Once a schoolteacher, always a schoolteacher. "Behave yourself tonight," she said, "and I'll try to have you moved back to Intermediate in the morning. And the first thing you do is apologize to Ynez."

"You always did like her better than me."

A muscular blonde attendant with scowl creases between her eyebrows and long wavy bangs that rolled up at the ends, Mrs. Brunt opened the door to the nurses' station for Mrs. Quill with her little crystal pool of spittle. "Evening, Mrs. Q," she said.

"Let me wash my hands and I'll be on my way," said Mrs. Quill.

"You can stay here all night if you want to. The girls behave themselves when you're around."

Mrs. Quill picked up the soap, turned on the tap. "What was Casey doing here?"

"Said he was bringing Rochelle back from the dance. But the dance was over two hours before. I don't know what he was hanging around for."

Mrs. Quill couldn't imagine that Mrs. Brunt didn't know what Casey was hanging around for, or the way he "protected" every female he sniffed out, from nurses to wives to inmates if the staff couldn't stay one jump ahead of him. "Does Rochelle have dance privileges now?"

"Surprised me too. She was so excited she wouldn't settle down. She was hanging onto a rag of paper like it was a dance program. Wouldn't let go of it."

"I wonder how she got dance privileges." Mrs. Quill ratcheted down a length of paper towel and tore it off.

The attendant said nothing, reminding Mrs. Quill that Mrs. Brunt had been here longer even than she had, when there hadn't been an RN on duty after sundown. No one could believe Mrs. Quill actually wanted to work nights. There had been some hard feelings at first among the long-term attendants, who were used to being the top dogs and wanted it no other way. But they came around, most of them. Those who didn't left. Mrs. Brunt stayed, but sometimes the attendants' common lot was stronger than the call to conscience.

"That new attendant was here a few minutes ago," said Mrs. Brunt after a moment. "Don't know his name. Nice young man. Cute cleft chin and freckles. Could be the boy next door."

Mrs. Quill dried her hands, crumpled the wet paper towel and tossed it into the wastebasket, picked up her papers and headed for the door. She knew his name, this employee who seemed to want to avoid her. Rex McFall. She had been following in his wake for three weeks. Every ward she entered he had just left. She had been told that he introduced himself as attendant-at-large, working wherever he was needed, and as a courier. But there *was* no attendant-at-large. On occasion, she had glimpsed him close enough to identify his horn-rimmed glasses and thatch of dark brown hair.

This morning she'd gotten a good look at him. After getting off duty too late to see Ellen before she left for school, she'd gone to breakfast in the employee dining room. Just ahead of her in line, two men were making the kind of shop talk --

"passive-aggressive," "oral-dependent," -- that along with their unshined shoes and shaggy hair identified them as the psychologists. The taller one glanced over his shoulder at her, and she recognized Dr. Matthew Ryder. The other, following his colleague's gaze, turned to face her for a moment before he whipped his head around. But not before she'd gotten a closeup view of horn-rims, cleft chin, boy-next-door freckles.

Like the rest of the personnel with modern ideas, whom Dr. Swenson called The Upstarts, Rex McFall had an office in the Admissions building, alien territory where they policed their own problems and resented traditional solutions and intrusions. Mrs. Quill didn't feel welcome there, but it was high time she had a little talk with Dr. Rex McFall.

3. <u>Rex</u>

Damn. She nearly caught him this time. Was there no way to get away from the woman? Mrs. Quill seemed to be everywhere at once.

In the tunnel, Rex locked the door behind him and stood with his back to it, breathing hard. He was tempted to take refuge in his office, but the office was for his daytime identity.

He wondered if she had recognized him at breakfast this morning. At staff meeting on Thursday mornings he was careful to keep a low profile so she wouldn't have reason to remember him. They were on different sides of the fence. She was Old Guard, inmate-oriented, part of the asylum: Clinic, Intermediate and Violent. He worked with new admissions while they were still called patients, curable. She was Nature versus his Nurture. Behavior control versus therapy. No reason their paths should cross. She wouldn't have recognized him: She didn't know him.

Well, back to Intermediate. No point hanging around Women's Violent. He should have known when he saw Alma's name on the transfer roster that Mrs. Quill would head right over there.

He pushed himself away from the door and descended into the tunnel, which he liked to think of as Preconscious. His footfalls echoed softly on the concrete. Aureoles of light from overhead fixtures stretched out and overlapped on the yellow ceiling and wall. Institutional Yellow. Was yellow supposed to be uplifting?

At the intersection to the old Building B tunnel a damp rush of air hit him. No longer in use, that tunnel was low-ceilinged, shallow and dripping. It smelled like a swamp. A large wooden sign propped on a sawhorse advising "Danger Do Not Enter" blocked the way. The sign didn't discourage anyone determined to use the tunnel.

Away behind him the door to Women's Violent opened and closed and Rex could hear someone approaching. A stride long enough to overtake him so easily could belong only to

Casey. What the hell was Casey doing here this time of night? The hair rose on the back of Rex's neck.

Aboveground, Rex would have been tempted to sneer at Casey's heavy reptilian brow, the implied lack of intellect. He suspected that Casey was borderline endocrine. But now Casey made Rex remember all the times in high school when the baseball dropped between his hands in outfield, all the locker room humiliations. His own 170 IQ was no help to him in the tunnel. What was the IQ anyway? Just a talent for taking a certain kind of test. It had no correlation with achievement or survival skills. Arthur, the patient who played the piano for the dances, was off the scale on Stanford-Binet but tore his hair over the Wechsler-Bellevue, where even giving him the benefit of the doubt he rated only 110. Rex hadn't told him his score, of course, but the kid knew he hadn't measured up to his own expectations. He was in such a frenzy that Rex put off the Rorschach for a couple of days and then the kid wouldn't speak to him, just glanced at the cards one after another and kept shaking his head.

Casey's IQ? Probably 90 on the Stanford-Binet, higher on the Wechsler-Bellevue.

Casey passed Rex, sponge soles squishing, knees springing. His grin said he could flatten Rex with one swipe of his hand.

Okay, thought Rex, it's a tossup on intelligence but I'll bet I've got more keys than you have.

Keys were power. Rex had more keys than he was entitled to as a psychologist. He couldn't do this study without the clanking artillery that was the mark of the attendant. From his original ration -- keys to his office, the records room, the classrooms and library -- few enough to carry in his pocket, his collection had grown to include all the wards and nurses' stations, and hydrotherapy and the shock room. He even had a key to the narcotics cabinet on Admissions.

At first he'd acquired keys one at a time. Whenever he had to give tests in another building, he'd borrow a key, run it down to the shop in the basement of Intermediate before he returned it. But yesterday morning, a bonanza had fallen into his lap.

In his office, he'd been trying to work on his patient assessments. At the near end of the hall a couple of alcoholics were letting off steam with a raucous game of pingpong. Rex could diagnose them by the varied inflections of their horseplay, their creative insults. Psychotics and other patients dysfunctional enough to be hospitalized had no such wealth of squawks and catcalls. Their displays were monotone, stereotyped, repetitive. They worked hard at "spontaneity."

The alcoholics could be troublemakers. They didn't learn from experience, were not burdened by conscience. They corrupted other patients, charmed them into subversive schemes that came to a bad end. On the outside, they'd go on a tear, get picked up by the law, come in to dry out for the thirty-day stretch that was the alternative to a jail sentence, then go out and do it all over again. They were incurable but they had more fun. They *were* more fun.

The game was an uneven contest. The younger man, Driscoll, blond and tanned and sculpted in t-shirt and bluejeans, crouched, leaped and swooped in an exhilarated muscular dance. The last serve, he captured the ball, teased it into a sustained dribble before slamming it back across the net, ricocheting it off the wall before the older man, Johnson, could blink. Johnson laid down his paddle, covered his head in mock defense and backed away from the table with an amiable, "I know when I've been licked."

"Hey there, Doc," said Driscoll. "Grab a paddle. I'm just getting warmed up."

Rex had been tempted; he was pretty good himself and it was obvious he wasn't going to get any work done there. But he had to have his assessments ready for the review board Thursday morning, so he'd picked up his folders and headed for the treatment room next door to the nurses' station. It was locked. The RN, Sarah, was on her way down the hall, almost out the door when he caught up with her to make his request. She started to retrace her steps, changed her mind, unhooked her entire keyring from her belt and thrust it into his hand.

"Here," she said, "let yourself in and hang onto these until I get back. I'm going to lunch."

After she was out of sight, he'd made a fast trip to the basement tool shop, where he stood first on one foot and then the other, stealing nervous glances at his watch while the artisan, a shiny-pated deaf-mute, tapped and filed away at his vise.

He returned the keys too late for lunch in the dining room, but he was so pleased with his *coup* that he decided to celebrate with a double BLT in the canteen. Rex recognized the cook from the intermediate ward. "BLT with double bacon," Rex told him.

Beneath his starched chef's hat, the cook's face froze, his eyes, nose and mouth drawing in on themselves, as close to a scowl as Rex had ever seen on an inmate. Starched Hat looked over Rex's head as if at some invisible screen, reading off the formula for a BLT: "Bacon, lettuce, and tomato sandwich: Bottom slice of bread. One tablespoon of mayonnaise. Three slices of tomato. Three slices of bacon. One piece of lettuce. One slice of bread on top. Fifty cents."

That prompter tape, thought Rex; he's organic, with an obsessive-compulsive overlay. "Look," he said. "Two BLT's: two slices of bread spread with two tablespoons of mayonnaise, six slices of tomato, six slices of bacon, two pieces of lettuce, two more slices of bread. Comes to one dollar. Right?" The inmate was watching Rex's lips. Rex went on: "Take away one slice of bread, one tablespoon of mayonnaise, three slices of tomato, one piece of lettuce, one slice of bread. Seventy cents, okay?" The starched chef's hat bobbed in assent.

He understood. It just took a simple explanation. Obsessives like explanation. Rex had the bit in his teeth now. "You charge ten cents for the bread, ten cents for the tomato, ten cents for the mayonnaise, ten cents for the lettuce. Twenty cents for double bacon, but we'll make it thirty. You get a bonus, okay?"

Something rippled across Starched Hat's face. He looked cross-eyed and his face set again. "Six slices of bacon is two BLT's. One dollar."

Watching Starched Hat at the grill, Rex had hoped he wouldn't overcook the bacon. He probably had a formula for that too. Obsessive-compulsive.

Rex didn't like putting patients into pigeonholes except as it helped him screen those he could most likely help. Psychotic, organic, or merely neurotic, they were all in it together. As a small society, which was how Rex liked to think of them, they were interdependent. Nothing could happen to one that didn't ripple outward and affect them all. Usually, he reserved diagnoses for lunch table sport with Matthew Ryder. Staff were fair game. When they ran out of stuffed shirts to cut down to size, Rex and Matthew dissected each other's psyches.

Matthew's sharpest thrust was, Rex was compulsive. Rex answered, too fast, "I'm not compulsive, I'm orderly. Order is beautiful, adaptive, satisfying. Compulsiveness is chaotic and enslaving." Only later did it occur to him that Matthew too was compulsive. For that matter, what was wrong with compulsive? Try and get through graduate school without it.

Starched Hat brought Rex two BLT's on two plates, set them down and held out his hand for the money. Rex shrugged, gave him his dollar. Starched Hat took back one sandwich and disassembled it. He removed the top slice of bread, the tomato slices, the piece of lettuce, and the bottom slice of bread, leaving three slices of bacon which he held out for Rex to pluck off the plate. Then he carried the second sandwich minus bacon to the grill where, back turned to Rex, he ate it.

When am I going to learn to shut up while I'm ahead?

Rex knew he had a problem. He couldn't let go when he'd attained his objective. He wanted to savor his successes instead of using them as stepping stones to bigger successes. Any day now, Matthew would be labeling him anal-retentive -- absorbed in self-analysis, his own psyche the source of endless fascination. Matthew called it a form of mental masturbation.

Rex conceded he could be a little bit compulsive. That's how he got into this business -- he was neurotic and looking for a cure. He hadn't solved his own neurosis but it had provided him with a profession.

So why couldn't he be satisfied with the practice of his profession instead of pursuing these odd notions? Matthew didn't know about this latest excursion, this participant observation of life in an asylum. Rex didn't want Matthew to find out because he would insist on knowing what he was looking for, and Rex didn't *know* what he was looking for. Oh, he had some vague idea that the answers to some nasty conflicts would be found in the interactions between patients -- or inmates -- and staff. And you couldn't find out who was doing what to whom by asking. People would tell you what they thought you wanted to hear. They would tell you what they wanted to think, what they wanted you to hear. To know what was really going on, you must observe people in their natural setting behaving unselfconsciously.

No, he wasn't looking for anything specific. He was looking for what was there. He wouldn't know what was there until it revealed itself to him. Unacceptable, Matthew would say. You must have a hypothesis, he would say; that was the psychological method. Our business, he'd say, besides training our interns, is psychotherapy. If the inmates are not susceptible to psychological treatment, then we stay away from them. They are nothing to do with us.

Rex wondered why Matthew bothered with him. Well, he knew the answer to that. Matthew's wife Gilda's answer, paraphrased from Sartre: On The Farm, as in Hell, one has few people among whom to choose friends. Rex was the only person around here Matthew could talk to on the same level. Restless, intellectual Gilda, too, needed someone to talk to and Rex was in the middle. Most of all, Matthew wanted Rex close by, where he could keep an eye on him.

Now, Rex came to with a start. He realized he had been standing in front of the door to Women's Intermediate for some moments, in a lather of indecision. The heart was gone out of the evening if Alma was not there. Alma, the little old blind woman with all the querulous eyebrows. She wouldn't hear the word "asylum"; she insisted this place was a sanitarium. When he had first seen her in Admissions, she'd looked in the direction of his voice and reached for his hand. "Hermes?" she cried, and he thought it the most refreshing nonsense he had heard from a psychotic. Then she said, "Hermes, you will be my guide in this labyrinth," and he knew she was in the wrong place.

Alma called the tunnel system the River Styx, the entry to Hades. Rex preferred a Freudian metaphor: Above ground was Conscious, the main tunnel Preconscious, access to the shadow world of the Unconscious, which was analogous to the older dank tunnel from which primordial slime he liked to imagine Casey had slithered.

Rex had seen that Alma would be one of those patients who wouldn't be "cured" within the thirty days allowed to a potentially curable, dischargeable new admission. This lady was a reject. Rejects went on to rock out their days on Intermediate. No longer patients, but inmates.

To his surprise, she hadn't lasted even a month on Admissions. One morning in her second week, she was gone. His inquiries at Administration met a stone wall, so he'd gone over their heads to Dr. Swenson, who himself had made the decision. Not Admissions material, Swenson said; not curable. That sounded to Rex like instructions from her family. Alma was not psychotic. Eccentric, yes, but if being eccentric was grounds for incarceration, God help us all. No, her only fault was getting old and being single. Even her money hadn't protected her.

Though her doting parents had left her well off, she'd worked for thirty years as county schools superintendent just because she liked it, until a nephew wormed his way into her confidence and her bank account. Here, she had told her sad story to everyone who seemed sympathetic, anyone who would listen, and then shriveled in despair as they pulled away. After all, she was crazy, wasn't she? She was here, she was crazy by definition.

Then she'd told Rex and he believed her.

They'd gotten to know each other well enough that he could kid her about being crazy. "I'm not crazy, am I?" she said to him once.

"You're not crazy," he answered, "just weird."

Her eyebrows, all of them, shot up. "Weird can keep you from despair."

He was momentarily taken aback. She was right, of course, but ungrammatical for her school-teacherly sensibilities. Ungrammatical but somehow more true, more metrical. She was not a slave to form. She created language. That was not crazy. He wondered if she knew she had double eyebrows.

Weird *could* keep you from despair. Taking action, making a decision, being angry or weird was better than being helpless. Rex knew about despair.

Alma was a treasure. She'd be a wonderful case history but he was jealous of her, wanted to keep her for himself. He was half in love with this little old lady. He wished she were twenty years younger, but he couldn't tell her so. Instead, he said once, "You make me wish I were twenty years older."

Twenty years. Would he really give up twenty years of his life for a woman? In some ways, this was the best of it -- a meeting of minds. Never consummated, never quenched. No torture, no betrayal. None of the daily torture and small betrayals of being in love with Gilda. How many years of his life, of his love, was he giving up right now, staying where he was?

He reached out and thumped the yellow metal door, which reassured him with a dull echo. He was not going to see Alma tonight. He was not going to see Gilda tonight. Might as well go home and go to bed. Get up in the morning and meet the new crop of student nurses with a clean shave and clear eyes. Not that he absolutely had to. He didn't have to lecture; Matthew was meeting the first class. Still, he liked to be around to see them. He enjoyed the incredulous farm-fresh faces. He put his key into the lock.

4. LeahNell

In the twilight, LeahNell and Cleo and Melba stood on the sooty brick platform, their suitcases and boxes stacked around them, while the train chuffed away from the depot. A tumbleweed scuttled with the wind down the middle of the track and came to a stop against a flatcar. Sand scurried past on both sides. This was it: Millennium.

Inside the depot, a hooded bulb burned over a desk. Under his green eyeshade, the agent squinted at the rumpled trio while he mulled over their questions. "Taxi closed up shop at sundown," he said. "The state hospital? You want to go out to The Farm?" He scratched his chin. "Maybe I could raise the taxi."

He reached for his telephone, an old upright with a receiver that dropped into a loop. As the girls reached the door, he called after them, "He'll be over soon's he's finished his supper."

While the dusk deepened, the girls sat outside on their suitcases. "It's going to be too dark to see anything," said LeahNell. "What did he call it -- the farm?"

The agent came out of the depot, slamming the door behind him. "Don't s'pose nobody'll walk off with the place while I have supper," he said. He sauntered down the street and turned in under a neon light flashing "Pool" alternately with "Olympia."

LeahNell's stomach was beginning to cramp. "They said we'd be there in time for supper." She loosened her belt a notch. "I'm supposed to eat every two hours."

Melba, her cornsilk hair electric under the streetlight, stretched her lanky body and basked like a lizard on a rock in the noonday sun. "They didn't come by train," she said. "Marjorie drove her boyfriend's car. Kept it here the whole three months."

Cleo took a last long drag on her cigarette and tossed it into the gutter. "I don't know how she does it. 'One of my many boyfriends just happened to have this car sitting around...,'" she said in falsetto. "It's unbelievable. And she's still a virgin. Or so she claims."

"I'm a virgin," said Melba.

"We all know you're a virgin, Melba."

"So's LeahNell."

A wave of claustrophobia washed over LeahNell. It had to do with last night's dream, which she couldn't remember.

"Yeah, but she doesn't brag about it," said Cleo. She leaned back and crossed her round cheerleader's legs, arched her back, thrusting out her breasts. "I don't care what the place looks like. I want to see the psychology interns."

"Yeah," said Melba.

A car pulled up at the curb, "taxi" sign sputtering into life. A man eased out, his belly straining a red buffalo-plaid shirt. "You little ladies need to be go out to The Farm?" He belched, a redolence of onions and beer. "Two dollars. In advance."

While the girls pooled their dimes and quarters, he loaded their bags and boxes into the cab. Cleo held her pose for a moment for him to appreciate, then sashayed around and claimed the front seat where she settled herself and sat humming and twisting one of her pink kewpie-doll curls around her finger. LeahNell and Melba sat in back.

The few blocks of Main Street became country lane and after a while, at a turn in the road, massive stone gateposts loomed and without slowing, the driver zipped between them. Against the deep violet spring sky, naked, spidery tree branches overhung the long driveway. At the end, several three-story buildings blazed with lights, setting off one unlit, anonymous mass in front. The driver stopped his cab in front of the gloomy structure. "Here we are. This-yere's the 'ministration building." He opened his door and got out.

"We need to go to the student nurses' dormitory," said LeahNell.

"I don't take nobody no farther than the 'ministration building."

"But there's no one there. Where is the dorm?"

"This is as far as I go." He began pulling out luggage.

Cleo clutched his arm. "Please! Wait! Help us! We'll make it worth your while ..."

Whatever the hell does she mean by that? LeahNell thought. First thing you know she'll have a date with him, although he's obviously married, and drag in his friends for Melba and me, to give her an excuse to go park in some cornfield like before and gave me the worst night of my life -- well, the second worst night -- because she wound up in the hospital with poison ivy on her back and I had to take care of the newborns all by myself. Or that night on TableRock where everyone was pretending they just wanted to see the city lights, and that yokel wouldn't keep his hands to himself and I walked all the way back to Trinity and was late late late, and guess who got grounded ... No thank you, Cleo.

From the sidewalk, two young men were approaching. LeahNell sprang out of the taxi and flagged them down. As one, they responded in flattened tenor, almost treble, voices: "Sure, we know where the student nurses live."

That they wore identical blue shirts and brown trousers and their hair slicked down and parted in the middle gave her only a second's pause. They loaded up with luggage and led off around the 'ministration building. The taxi sped off. So much for Millennium.

Beyond the buildings visible from the road, spotlights illuminated a small, two-story square of whitewashed lava rock with bars on its large windows.

"Careful now." The leader pointed to the end of the pavement. A line of boards made a trail across the muddy yard. "Yeah, be careful," echoed his partner. "Today's the first time in two weeks it wasn't raining."

"Yeah, it's real wet." The pair stood nodding and grinning from the girls to each other and back again.

At the door, under the yard light, the young men set down their burdens, pushed a doorbell and disappeared into the dark.

The door seemed to open by itself, then a small pale woman came into focus and stood aside to let them in. In the sudden light and warmth and enclosing walls, LeahNell, Cleo and Melba babbled, about the town and the taxi driver and the muddy yard. The woman waited, focusing her eyes level with their throats. Is she blind? LeahNell wondered. Is she our housemother?

In a monotone the woman volunteered that the other students had chosen the first-floor rooms. She helped the girls carry their things to the landing of the second floor. "You can take any of the rooms up here you want."

They were standing in the middle of a large open area with kitchen facilities on one side, barred windows all around. Thick walls were whitewashed, like the outside of the building. Large, colorful woven rugs warmed the painted concrete floors. "It looks ... Mediterranean," said LeahNell.

"This is just beautiful!" Cleo gushed. "The rugs are so pretty!"

Some weight shifted in the woman's face, not exactly a smile. "They make them in occupational therapy," she said. "This used to be the women's violent ward."

The girls looked at each other. "Two real nice guys showed us the way from the taxi stop," said LeahNell.

"Jep and Ollie," said the woman. "They've lived here about twenty-five years, and they've been waiting all day for the new student nurses." Then she recited: "The door's locked after ten when the outdoor lights are turned off. You can stay out as late as you want if you check out a key. There's sandwiches and milk in the refrigerator."

The wind wailed and whistled around the corner of the building. "Does the wind blow all the time?" LeahNell asked. "Are you our housemother?"

The woman's face went blank for a moment. "Unless it's raining. You need both hands to hang onto your skirt." She glided down the broad steps, the girls staring after her.

"Weird," said Cleo.

"Sandwiches and milk," said LeahNell, but Cleo and Melba were headed down the corridor, and she followed.

Each cell measured about six by ten feet, with a large barred window at its long end. LeahNell chose one on the south side, to catch the sun. A bed along one wall faced a wardrobe at its foot. On the other wall, a kneehole desk and chair and a chest of drawers left only an arc of space for the door to open, with a two-foot strip of floor covered by a green, blue, and orange rag rug. The room was snug and safe. LeahNell sighed and felt the hunch going out of her shoulders.

Later, while Melba was singing off-key in the shower and Cleo was away downstairs chatting with the girls from Pocatello, LeahNell turned off the lamp light and raised the Venetian blind. Through the barred window, moonlight flooded her room. She sat in the deep window-well, hugging her knees to her chin, skirt tucked around her feet. Food was a soft weight in her stomach.

Of all the people she could have come here with, why, she wondered, did she have to draw Cleo? All Cleo could think about was boys and sex, and who was a virgin and who wasn't and who was lying about it, and how of all their class only Melba and LeahNell were virgins, and of course Cleo'd blurt it out in front of God and everyone, and then assume that LeahNell was blushing because she's a prude -- since she won't even go to the bathroom if anyone is in earshot, and she laughs too loud at all their jokes. LeahNell guessed that if she told them she wasn't a virgin they'd all die laughing. No one would believe it. Floyd probably didn't think she was capable of it. But Floyd didn't know her as well as he thought he did. Well, that made two of them. *She* didn't know herself as well as she'd thought she did.

For a whole year, it had been easy not to think about it. There hadn't been time; the workload and the overtime were inhuman, and then her appendix had ruptured and she'd spent a month in the hospital, still not thinking about it, just letting herself be sick. And then she'd gone back to work and there was the ulcer. But today she'd had nothing to do but think, on the train from one side of Idaho to the other, while she pretended to nap. Or what passed for thinking about it, her mind circling, teasing at the edge of *what* had happened, backing off and circling in again on *why*.

Why was easier. It had to do with trying to be grown up in the world of grownups. You are no longer girls, Miss Wintergreen had told them the very first day; you are young women. But it also had to do with drinking, trying to belong, and failing that, trying to make the best of being different. Not using makeup, not having cut her hair, although it meant stuffing her hair into a net in uniform. Of the years of ballet class showing in the way she moved. And succeeding too well, because she had stood out.

And it wasn't that she wanted to shake off her parents' influence; she believed in what she'd been taught. She believed that anything worth doing was worth doing well, and she cared less about being pretty or popular than about knowing everything that could be known. And she believed in chastity. But somewhere, there had been a fork in what had seemed like a straight road and she'd taken -- chosen? -- the wrong way.

The hard truth was, she'd been flattered and foolish and she hadn't listened to that small voice inside reminding her that principles were for all time and now was no different and she was no exception, and she had dismissed all the cues that this was not right, because she thought she had entered a larger world where it was time to put aside childish attitudes.

The truth was, she'd gotten too big for her britches and flirted with Dr. Reamer, misinterpreted his motives at every turn being puffed up at her success at attracting him, had gone with him to his apartment, and even when she'd realized it wasn't a party she'd trusted him, and when he mixed her a drink, even though she knew he'd been spiking her punch at the dance, she'd accepted it and she drank it.

So all right, there were other things too, things she hadn't understood. She was playing out of her league, and a moment had come when she thought she was floating, but she was on her back and he was between her knees and then she was torn and bleeding. And it had not been for love.

Oh yes, she had survived but living was a puzzle that had to be fitted together piece by piece, and what good times there were arrived without warning and left the same way, as if she'd slipped the track into some parallel life. She watched herself through her days and with people, and she could see that she must look quite normal, but her heart wasn't in it.

And now she just wanted to finish what she'd started and go home to Floyd and safety and playing duets with Daddy on Grandmother's old Steinway, and she hoped her heart would be in it.

She watched the lights from the other buildings. Just last night in Boise -- was it only last night? -- one of her classmates,

Sparrow, who'd been here for the winter quarter, had sat on her bed watching her pack and told her, wide-eyed, that the inmates didn't sleep at all when there was a full moon, but rattled the bars and howled. It sounded like the sort of thing old-timers would tell newcomers and then laugh at them behind their backs. LeahNell didn't believe it but still, gooseflesh crept up her arms. Now the only sound was the wind, and LeahNell guessed she was as much a lunatic as the others, sitting moonstruck in her window-well. "God," she whispered, "are you out there?"

There were no empty tables. Cleo led them into the dining room and gravitated toward a round table where two men, youngish and carelessly jacketed and tied, were engaged in earnest discussion that didn't stop when the girls set down their trays. Cleo took the chair beside the taller of the two men, leaned across him to set the sugar bowl beyond her sitting reach. "'Scuse me," she said. The men didn't look up.

A woman with pencil-arched eyebrows brought a pitcher of milk and a pot of coffee. She filled the girls' cups and warmed those of the men.

"What royal service," said LeahNell. "They don't treat us like this at Trinity." Last night she had dreamed the old women's violent ward was an island in the center of a deep clear pond. This morning, she felt quick and clear-headed.

With a switch of her shoulders, the woman turned and took the coffeepot to the next table.

The taller of the men looked up and his ice-blue eyes challenged LeahNell. "Inmates make adequate, if robotic, waitresses," he said. "And cooks. And laundrymen. Plumbers. Electricians and farmers. Even clerks."

He punctured the air with his fork as he spoke. "We the professional staff are surrounded and sustained by inmates. We are outnumbered, an island of pampered elites. We must be grateful and respectful, or the incarcerated -- who are in control anyway -- will organize and rise up against us. We could all be slaughtered in our sleep." He locked eyes with her.

He can't be an inmate, she thought; this is the staff dining room.

"You're wondering if I'm a patient," he prompted. "A

paranoid schizophrenic, with reality organized around my logically impeccable delusional system. Not so. I'm secure in my marginal madness. I don't need to conceal it. You'll find that the insane hide behind their eyes, twist their hands behind their backs, shuffle in single-file."

Whoever he was, he obviously knew they were new students. Did he think he had to perform for them? "I'm LeahNell Thorel," she said. "From Trinity Hospital in Boise."

He nodded, looking over her shoulder, and turned back to his companion. Cleo nudged LeahNell's toe and mouthed: What a prick! She glanced meaningfully at a nearby table.

LeahNell's face was burning, but there was something she wanted to know. "Our housemother -- she doesn't look anyone in the eye."

The man looked at her with some interest now. "Opal Owens? Yes, she's one, in a roundabout way. She was an attendant in your building when it was Women's Violent, but she came up through the ranks. After they shocked all the silliness and much of the life out of her about thirty years ago, she was deemed harmless enough to be a caretaker. The meek shall inherit the earth. This corner of it anyway." He looked away. "M'name's Matthew. No nicknames, please. The quiet one over here is Rex."

The Quiet One had large limpid eyes, freckles and a dimpled chin. He gazed soulfully into the eyes of each girl as she gave her name. Melba smirked and Cleo wiggled.

"Did you say thirty years ago?" LeahNell said. "That makes her about fifty."

"Closer to sixty. Doesn't look it, does she?"

"She told us Jep and Ollie have been here twenty-five years. They don't look much older than me."

"The institutional look. We call it the Shangri-La Syndrome. The thin air on these heights of isolation. After the initial misery, they just stop connecting. No grief, no anger -- no lines or wrinkles. And they live nearly forever."

He stood up. "Welcome to The Farm. Come, Rex. Duty calls."

LeahNell watched them leave. Matthew and Rex. No last names. No nicknames please. She glanced around the dining room at all the white uniforms. "Somehow they don't look like the nurses at Trinity," she said. "But I guess anyone who's being waited on is staff."

"They walk like they've got boards up their backs," said Melba.

"Brooms stuck up their asses." Cleo twisted a pink curl around her finger. "That cute cleft chin! He can eat crackers in my bed any time!"

From the dining room building they took the tunnel, following a female attendant with a flock of shuffling inmates all leaning into the same unseen wind. "They look like a chain gang," said Melba. They reminded LeahNell of a Rivera painting; all they needed was sombreros.

She had heard about these tunnels. Through them, a few attendants could herd enormous numbers of inmates to meals and work assignments and to electroshock. Only clinical staff had keys to the tunnels, but long-term "residents" knew of at least one secret entrance. This new tunnel, well-lit and paved, intersected old, dim, damp, shallow tunnels that were supposed to have been closed.

"Sparrow told me some attendants still use the old tunnels," said LeahNell. "She said, watch out for the attendant called Casey."

The thought of an underground passage -- a labyrinth -- sent a delicious shiver up her spine. She had seen *Gaslight* three times, *Spellbound* four. Any of these inmates could be released from their hundred-year slumber by persistent and loving detective work.

Matthew No-Nicknames-Please was Dr. Ryder. He was fifteen minutes late for the first lecture in abnormal psychology. He tossed his jacket onto a desk, missing LeahNell by mere inches. He slouched over the lectern, ice-blue eyes fixed on the door while, for thirty minutes, he discussed Charcot, Mesmer, ..., then dismissed his subject with a wave of his hand.

"Don't take notes," he said.

"Now he tells us," muttered Melba.

"Our library is just down the hall. It's all in the books. Read them." He picked up his jacket. "Don't tell yourself you're going to help other people understand themselves. A dozen interns a year pass through here bleating about how they want to help other people. Malarkey! They're in this business because they don't know who *they* are. Most nurses are in the nurturing business because of their own dependency needs. Or their need to control."

Dependency needs? LeahNell thought she had more of an independency need. She'd have to think about that. Maybe this was the kind of work for her. Psychiatric nurse? Why go only halfway? Why not psychologist? She wondered what her father would think of Dr. Ryder. Daddy would understand but not approve of any of this. He'd rather she'd never left Little Wood, but she couldn't go nowhere after high school and there'd been no money for college, the art major she had aimed for.

Scowling, Dr. Ryder scanned the puzzled faces. "Don't try to see yourselves in our patients," he said. "They are not like you. They're specimens in cages, on display. They have nothing to do with real life. And this isn't 'Gaslight' or 'Spellbound.' Mental illness isn't romantic."

LeahNell hoped he wouldn't notice the flush sweeping her face.

"Over the next three months, I'm going to develop each theory as a comprehensive model that appears to defy argument. When I've persuaded you it's the gospel truth, I'll bring it down like a house of cards. You're going to fear and detest me. I won't give you anything you can depend on."

"Then what are we doing here?" Melba twitched and smirked.

He eyed her with a nasty grin. "If I don't see some evidence that you can think for yourself, you get an F in this course." He pushed himself away from the lectern. At the door, he said over his shoulder, "Dr. McFall will meet this class tomorrow."

The door closed behind him. "Wow," said LeahNell.

"If he thinks he's not crazy, he's kidding himself," said Melba.

"I hate him already," said Cleo. "I was hoping we'd have class with the interns."

It was patients' dance night. Keys in jangling bouquets from their belts, attendants stood at the door and around the recreation hall. Female patients lined up on one side and stared across the hall at the male patients, most of whom stared at the floor, faces sunk into their chests. The student nurses danced with the male patients and pretended not to notice the psychology interns, who were ignoring them, dancing with the women.

A young man, hair slicked back in a pompadour, face glossy with effort, attacked the piano keys with clench-jawed determination. He embroidered his work with trills and arpeggios without inflection, and his music surged and stuttered. Another patient, his thatch of brown hair bobbing, thumped out rhythm on snares, cymbals and triangle with a dissonant effect, like two radio stations playing simultaneously. "Alexander's Ragtime Band," "Tennessee Waltz" and "Sentimental Journey" shared the same martial fervor.

Jep and Ollie were here on the sidelines, beaming and swaying, close as shadows to a tall, well-built attendant whose electric blue eyes contrasted with the monochrome of his light khaki clothes and skin and hair. Cleo and Melba went to them, hands outstretched, but Jep and Ollie shrank back.

"Oh no," said one. "We don't ..."

"... dance," said the other, "and Mr. Wheeler here says we don't ..."

"... have to."

Cleo went on to find a partner, but Melba got into their rhythm, swaying and smirking her smirk that passed for a smile.

LeahNell danced with one man after another. They mutely pushed her around the floor or stood immobile until she led them off. One inmate, at the end of a dance, found his voice. "You think I'm harmless, don't you?" he said, and then went on to Cleo.

The next man in line said quickly, "Don't worry about him, Ma'am. He says that to all the girls. My name's William, Ma'am. May I have this dance?"

William was the first to look her in the eye, the first to stand up straight and pick up his feet. She would have taken him for an employee except that he wore no belt. Broad-shouldered and wide-browed, he studied her through thick glasses, and, oddly, she didn't feel stared at.

At ten o'clock, piano player and drummer stood up and bowed. The attendants herded their charges into segregated lines and began marching them out the door. The patients eased into their leaning shuffle. The only holdout was a young woman with a flushed face and moist, dreamy eyes who swayed as though she was still hearing the music. LeahNell felt a rush of sympathy -- she too could hear music long after it ended.

Then a gigantic attendant with an enormous array of keys took the young woman by the arm. "Dance is over, Rochelle," he said. "Be a nice girl and come with Casey."

Not now, thought LeahNell; don't spoil her evening.

Rochelle planted her feet, chin jutting, elbows out. As LeahNell watched, the khaki-dressed attendant, Mr. Wheeler, left Jep and Ollie and approached.

Casey whipped his head around. "This is none of your business, Healer," he said. "She's not on Intermediate any more. She belongs to Violent."

Rochelle seemed torn between Casey and the electric blue gaze of Mr. Wheeler. Finally, she went with Casey, who was stroking her arm and saying, "Come on, Rochelle. Come with Casey. We don't want to have to call Dr. Quill."

5. Dr. Quill

Sometimes Friday's treatment didn't hold Hawk until Monday, so here he was snarling and fettered, with the attendant Schwartz from Men's Violent looking maternal and forebearing. "Helluva way to spend a Sunday afternoon," said Schwartz by way of apology for calling Dr. Quill on a weekend.

Dr. Quill shrugged, trying to remember what it felt like to have better things to do on a Sunday, trying to imagine feeling at home in his studio apartment in the staff residence. When he was sick of his own company within his four walls, he'd walk along the reservoir road. He didn't have a car. He never went into town, into Millennium.

Whitaker was tagging along, hanging back. The moonfaced attendant always came into the shock room looking as if he were about to cry. He and Schwartz were a couple of melancholy worrywarts. Dr. Quill doubted that they missed Casey, who as senior attendant didn't work on Sunday. Casey made fun of Whitaker and, about once a week, would tell him not to wet his pants.

Nor did Dr. Quill miss Casey, who was a long-time hanger-on from the administration before Dr. Swenson's and a major impediment to modernizing inmate care. Early on, Dr. Quill had raised the issue, which Ronald Swenson had dismissed with a flick of his hand. "Casey keeps the inmates in line and the tedious details off my desk. If his methods are a little primitive, they're effective -- people don't cross him twice. You know yourself a sharp instrument cuts clean. I'd have to hire half a dozen to replace him. Complaints of sexual misbehavior? Consider the source."

The sources? Nurses and female attendants, low on the pecking order. Inmates, no "credible" witnesses.

The clinic nurse didn't work Sundays either, so today the team was one short. Whitaker was all right. He held the tongue blade, did what needed to be done. And after Dr. Quill threw the switch, counted time, and turned it off, he himself restrained Hawk's legs, a job below his station on week days.

Later, while Schwartz and Whitaker returned to Men's Violent with Hawk shambling along between them, Dr. Quill locked up the shock room and headed down the hall toward the tunnel.

The basement was a different reality from above ground, where a map would show buildings with sidewalks and the street between them. Underground was like the inside of a beehive or an ant hill, a grid of tunnels intersecting other tunnels, opening into clusters of cells. In this cluster, called Clinic, he passed Dentist, X-Ray, and Insulin Therapy, all dark.

He could hear some kind of ruckus going on in Hydrotherapy. What the hell? He hadn't authorized treatment for anyone today, and if Mrs. Chisholm was opening up the place at her own discretion, she was going to hear about it.

He threw open the door onto a scene like a Roman bath. Three barefoot girls in blue-jeans were soaking their feet in the whirlpool, four more were shrieking and skidding in the needle spray flashing hot and cold. What the hell. They couldn't be patients -- they were *laughing*. They looked almost ... normal. He stood there perplexed. No one paid him any attention.

Suddenly, one of them, a slender imp with a wet rag of hair straggling over one shoulder, glanced at him and waved. "Come in," she called. "We're having a picnic. We're sailing."

Waxed paper sandwich wrappers floated around her feet and a yeasty aroma of beer suffused the air. A searing sensation drew his attention to his left arm and he found that his shirt sleeve was dripping. He whipped his head around in time to see a kewpie-doll-faced girl with pink hair finger-deflecting the needle spray in his direction.

"Cut it out, Cleo," said a girl in a skimpy halter top. She scooped up water in a sandwich paper and dumped it on Kewpie Doll-Face.

The imp was perched on the side of the whirlpool. "Come on in," she said again. "Take off your shoes and roll up your pantlegs."

Take off my ...? Roll up ... Who the hell do you think you are? What the hell are you doing in my territory?

"You'll like it." She smiled, and "fetching" was the word that leaped to his mind.

Dr. Quill took off his shoes, rolled up his pantlegs, and sat next to the imp on the edge of the whirlpool. Too late he discovered he had sat on a wet spot. "So," he said. "You're having a picnic. Who let you in here?"

A hush fell and the imp's eyes opened wide. She stared at him so frankly he knew she was about to tell a lie. "The door was unlocked," she said.

"You know you're trespassing, don't you? This room is open only for scheduled treatments. Who are you?"

She giggled, almost a whinny, and studied him for a moment before she said, "We're students."

"Student what?" he said. "We train attendants and psychology students ..." He knew perfectly well student what, but he wanted to hear her say it.

"We're student nurses." She gestured to a lanky frizzle-head across the whirlpool and to the kewpie doll holding the needle-spray. "Melba and Cleo. We're from Trinity in Boise." She indicated the halter-top girl. "Patsy here and the others are from Pocatello."

So this was the latest batch, was it. They'd sashay into Electroshock one of these mornings all agog, as if they owned the place, as if everything was being done for their benefit, thirsty for the sensational -- which he would provide them -- and it wouldn't even shake them up. They had strong stomachs, these farm girls. They had cut their teeth on bawling cattle and barnyard smells and middle of the night birthings and cowshit on their shoes. Now they were vomited on, and they swabbed pustulent excrescences and wallowed in bedsores. Nothing fazed them, and at first he'd liked that about the warrior women bursting with good health and bloodthirst, and the way they seemed like conspirators with him in this nasty but necessary business. But after a while, when he'd begun to see how impersonal it was, how it wasn't him they conspired with but the position he held, the switch he pulled, how they had no feeling either for the man or woman on the table, just a lump of flesh about to be jolted for their entertainment, then he began to slip over the edge from executioner to advocate.

Maybe he was just getting old. Even after a sweet, clean shave and a brisk shower, within minutes in their presence he would feel moldering and sour of breath.

He looked at each of them in turn, said dryly, "Well, aren't you cute as kittens." It came out less biting than he'd intended. He wondered if the warm water was turning his brain to mush. "Evidently, you've getting the red carpet treatment. Including, if I'm not mistaken, several bottles of beer."

"Oh no, we're just intoxicated on our freedom. My name's LeahNell," the imp said, as if he'd asked. "This place is a non-stop holiday. We don't have any responsibilities. We can associate with anyone we please. We're being coddled. And cultivated and counseled. We have permission to be crazy. If we did this at Trinity we'd be campused for three months."

Kewpie Doll Cleo sat down on the other side of him, extended her crimson-nailed toes into the water, peered over her shoulder. "She should know," she said. "She was campused for three months. It was my fault." She smiled and paused to give him a chance to ask why, and then blinked and went on: "Do you work here?"

"My name's Quill. You could say I work here."

"Are you an attendant?"

Was he an attendant? Did he look like an attendant? Would they all snap to attention if he told them he was a doctor? "It's complicated," he said. "Tell me about coddling and cultivating and counseling."

The frizzle-head called Melba shrugged and rolled her shoulders. "That's what Leah calls it. She likes big words -- her father's a teacher."

He studied Leah, or LeahNell, she called herself. Her face was flushed, her eyes glassy; and she had an on-stage expression of determined cheer. He would bet the big words were the beer talking. He wondered what she was like when she was not drinking. She wore tied at the midriff a blue shirt he recognized as World War II surplus. One side was sopping and clung to her bra, revealing the stitching pattern, which spiralled into a point like the armor of a Wagnerian soprano.

Suddenly, his penis throbbed into life. He froze with the unexpectedness, the uninvitedness of pleasure. He hadn't had an erection in over five years. "Is this what they feed you for Sunday dinner?" he asked, distracted. "Sandwiches? That's not exactly coddling." *Cool down and get the hell out of here.*

"This is our supper. We had dinner at Dr. Swenson's with his family... you know? ... the head of the hospital."

Dr. Quill suppressed a snort. He had been subjected to Sunday dinner at Dr. Swenson's once. Just once.

Kewpie Doll Cleo struck a pose, arms wide. "The snobs at Caldwell High should see me now. Eating dinner at a doctor's house."

"They live on the hospital grounds," LeahNell said in a confidential tone. "He's got six children." She paused, looking puzzled. "The oldest is sixteen. They're all two and a half years apart and they all look alike. They look just like him. He looks just like Mrs. Swenson."

Melba the frizzle-top smirked, rolled her shoulders and twitched. "They've got two maids ... inmates. They stuffed us with food. Leah said they were fattening us up for someone's oven, but I knew we were being screened for babysitters. I don't like kids. I stuck out my tongue at the little one."

Two of the Pocatello girls, each chunky as a dumpling, glanced at each other with contrived modesty. "We got the job."

"Congratulations," said Dr. Quill. *Congratulations on getting a plum that will console you evenings while the other girls are out having a good time.* "Did Dr. Swenson talk all afternoon about Freud?"

"Oh, you've been there too," said Cleo. "They're sure free and easy with the booze around here. Not Dr. Swenson. He's the only one so far who hasn't given us any. Friday, Miss Hunter -- the nursing instructor? -- had us all over for tea. That's what she called it. Can you see me drinking tea?"

No, she sure as hell didn't act like a tea drinker. Dr. Quill murmured a generic response and she went on, "We all wore dresses and nylons and heels and I kept telling myself, Cleo, you *will* act like a lady. So we're simpering around and sticking out our little fingers and sipping tea and eating these dainty little sandwiches, and *she* pops the top on a bottle of cognac and pours everyone a chaser and pretty soon we're all sitting on the floor with our shoes off and laughing it up and calling her Imogene."

"You called her Imogene," said one of the Pocatello dumplings. "I didn't."

"Yeah, but I noticed you had your glass out every time she came around with the bottle," said Patsy. She leaned back on her elbow then, and one breast slid into the neck opening of her halter. Dr. Quill looked away.

LeahNell took in a sharp breath as if to speak. He waited, but she sat back.

"Of course, you young ladies are all of legal age," he said.

"Some of us are, some of us aren't." Melba smirked and rolled her shoulders. "That's never stopped us. Leah's got an ulcer. She's not supposed to drink."

LeahNell flashed her a look that said, Tattletale! "One little drink isn't going to hurt me," she said.

"You're asking for trouble," said Dr. Quill. "Quit before you start vomiting blood."

For a moment, she looked almost sober.

He stopped himself before he could say, I know what I'm talking about; I've been there.

Enough altruism for the day. Time to go.

What a weird interlude. Faerie folk. And get a load of him -- horny old man. She liked big words. He knew some. Maybe she'd like to swap a few over ... Stop that. She was twenty only by a stretch of the imagination; she was pert, but she was a virgin, not an appropriate target. Why couldn't he get it up for someone his own age? Mrs. Quill, for example. She was still a succulent dish when he'd come here. He'd looked at her and thought his concupiscent thoughts and then put her down cynically: Don't hump the help, he would say to himself. That was his excuse but he knew then and he knew now that it was only an excuse. And anyway, a nurse, even a supervisor, might be "the help" in any other hospital, but at The Farm, Mrs. Quill outranked him in seniority and authority and respect too. If he tried to pull rank on her, she could squash him like a bug. By now, she was probably a stringy old bird. Apparently the only flesh that would do it for him was the kind that sprang back when you touched it.

Mrs. Quill indeed. The minute he'd heard the name, he knew she was a fraud. Because *his* name really was Quill.

In Boise five years ago, just divorced and stripped of his assets, he'd been hitting the bottle pretty hard and had had only the good sense to stop driving. When he was called to the hospital one night, he wasn't worried about delivering the baby; he figured that after all those years his hands were on automatic pilot. But the confusion of the charge nurse running both delivery rooms, only loosely supervising the student nurse who was pouring ether for him, compounded his own incompetence, and in the resulting patch job the mother exsanguinated. *Say it straight: bled to death.* He'd taken a cab back to his studio apartment, where he drank himself into a stupor, vomited all over the place, then did it all over again. Finally, he pumped himself full of vitamins and got on the next train, disembarked in Little Wood halfway across the state, and checked into the Colonial Hotel for three weeks until, with the help of a bartender whose name was Wellcome, he was thoroughly detoxified.

The way it happened was, after ten days, feeling just enough better to be getting bored and antsy, he'd gone into the Nebraska Bar telling himself he'd just hobnob with the locals for a little while. He hadn't reckoned on the seductive sweet and sour and smoky poolhall fragrance that engulfed him the instant he closed the screen door behind him. He went on in a trance and fumbled for words for the big, hearty face across the bar. "I guess a beer will do it."

"Pabst? Oly?" The bartender waited.

Dr. Quill hesitated. He was not a beer drinker. He felt the bartender's eyes piercing the smoke and the gloom, taking in the web of capillaries blooming on his cheeks and intuiting those on his barrel belly and thin arms. Dr. Quill vacillated and the bartender took the leap. "We've got CocaCola," he said.

Dr. Quill opened his mouth to tell the man to mind his own business and bring him a beer -- any brand, but something about the way the man was holding his breath held him back. "Coke," he said.

He listened to the balls clacking under the canopy of smoke over the pool table and watched the men, mostly Basques, chalking their cues and waiting their turns. The bartender popped the top off a CocaCola, set it on the bar. "Name's Wellcome," he said, and didn't take offense when Dr. Quill reciprocated with only a nod.

It got to be a routine: fresh-squeezed orange juice, two eggs and hashbrowns and link sausages and a mountain of toast and strawberry jam and two or three cups of strong coffee at the Manhattan Café every morning; then a long walk out the railroad track and a sunbath in the park with sleeves rolled up and collar open; a sandwich in the Boston Cafe; a Coke and silent communion with Wellcome while they watched the Basques tilting at the table; back to the Manhattan for a salad and mashed potatoes and chicken-fried steak and apple pie, or lemon meringue or cherry; winding up the day in the Nebraska Bar. His belly shrank and he got his color back; he began cultivating his mustache, white and luxuriant and silky.

"I used to be sheriff," Wellcome once told him. He didn't say so, but Dr. Quill knew he'd been a drinker; the Sign of the Spider was on him too.

"I'm a doctor," said Dr. Quill. "Don't know if that's 'used to be.'" He was going to have to figure out pretty soon if he could still ply his trade, here, or anywhere.

"This town's had trouble hanging onto a good doctor," said Wellcome. "The first one came with the railroad in '83. Our last doctor found better compensation in Gooding."

With his bar towel he swabbed at an old stain on the counter. "In between, early on, a good man came into town, eked out a living helping folks who couldn't pay. Built a hospital ... Long story. Ten years ago, the hospital burned down. Accident. The doctor died getting people out."

He continued prodding the stain, his face sagging with sorrow. "A few people disappeared. His nurse, couple of others. Some folks said she skipped town. She didn't." He hesitated long enough for Dr. Quill to hope he would tell what he knew.

"Left a lot of sad, miserable folks here. That was a bad year more ways than one. No snow. It rained, it froze, tore up the highway. Pile-ups on 93. Fires. I didn't start drinking right away. Not until after the next election cleared out the regulars at the courthouse and I was out of a job. Among other things. But you don't want to hear about all that."

Well, yes, Dr. Quill did want to hear about all that, but it couldn't be easy for Wellcome to talk about. Give the man time. And there would be time. The village, Little Wood, felt like a good fit.

But on the night of VE Day, after he'd watched the high school kids' snake dance from outside the bar and turned to go back inside, he saw down the street, crossing from the depot to the Wood River Hotel, a familiar face. Not a new familiar face. An old familiar face. And the next morning, he was on the train again, headed for The Farm at Millennium.

All the way to the far side of the state, he wondered if he needed another name. When the train stopped to take on water at a crossing beyond Pocatello, he'd sat for fifteen minutes staring at the side of that barn, beat-up and falling-down but still hawking its message probably fifty years old: "Quill's Feed." Its permanence admonished him, and he knew he was stuck with it. And that's how he knew that *Mrs.* Quill came into Millennium from the west, the same as he, and how that barn supplied her with a name while confirming his own.

So now he was the man who threw the switch, signed the orders to legitimize the paraldehyde and Dilantin the attendants were already giving, and tried to limit the damage Casey could do.

When he'd realized no one was coming after him, he relaxed and the nightmare came on in earnest. When he was alone, he ground his teeth and cursed, and beat himself where the bruises wouldn't show. When he was on duty, he counted the hours until he could be alone to punish himself some more. Finally the self-hatred gave way to a deep hunger for atonement. One night, he'd started cleaning his floor with a toothbrush. The next day, a Saturday, he called the taxi from town and went into Millennium, where he bought two dozen toothbrushes. After a month of scrubbing his floor and every surface he could reach standing on a chair, he began to resent his punishment and finally to rebel against it. Then he was able to invest himself doggedly in his work.

He could do some real good around here if only he dared. His duties included doing physicals on new admissions and checking out the ones who left. The alcoholics always came back and when they did, he'd examine them again and prescribe the usual vitamins. And then he had to step back and keep his mouth shut while those assholes Ryder and McFall tried to cure them with psychotherapy, which he knew wouldn't work. Only another alcoholic could help them, as Wellcome had helped him -- someone who knew exactly what they were going through, who they knew wouldn't put up with their excuses or let them down. But he couldn't do it without the news getting around, and then he'd be out and what good would he be to them then?

He didn't want to jeopardize his safety for LeahNell, but he could keep an eye on her. He wondered how much he could tell her before she'd blow the whistle on him.

Monday morning, the nursing students were just ahead of him in the line for breakfast. They were chattering, most of them, like magpies. Melba Frizzletop's instant recognition turned to puzzlement as she tried to assimilate his yesterday face with today's white lab coat and the insignia stethoscope looping out of his pocket. Behind him, Mrs. Chisholm, Clinic head nurse, chirped, "Good morning, Dr. Quill," and the entire group except for one pulled together in a knot, as if huddling together against rain. Leah, or LeahNell, stayed apart and seemed not to have heard anything or seen him, so he was surprised when she said, "I've decided to take your advice."

The imp had turned into a gnome. Her mop of hair was coiled and netted; her face now was pale and small and closed, with the look that says that nothing in the world can match in importance the floods and quakes and famines and ambushes going on in the twisting and turnings of her internal landscape.

"Decided" to take his advice, had she? Had a bad night, did she? Well, it would pass and then she'd give it another try. They always did.

6. LeahNell

Last weekend, Melba and two of the girls from Pocatello had been invited to Matthew Ryder's for dinner. Tonight was LeahNell's turn, with Cleo and Patsy. Dr. Ryder would pick them up at their dorm, which, for the small chill it sent down her spine, LeahNell still liked to think of as the old Women's Violent. Another happy family dinner. LeahNell hoped they'd be more interesting than the Swensons, but, yes, happy. That was all she wanted, really. If everyone else was happy, maybe there was hope for her.

At five-thirty sharp, Dr. Ryder arrived in his army surplus Jeep, in which he drove them, all jolting and hanging on like rodeo riders to his two-story house. They stepped down into the spring-muddy driveway.

"I have fetched the young ladies," he called out to the woman who watched their approach from the front door.

Ash blond, short and compact, wearing a simple black jersey dress threadbare at the wrists, Mrs. Ryder lifted to her lips a cigarette in a black onyx holder, her cheeks sucking into hollows.

"Come in," she said without letting go the smoke. "I am Gilda." She pronounced it "Zheelda." Wth her back against the screen door, she held it open for them.

Inside, Dr. McFall was leafing through a small book, his freckled, cleft-chinned face creasing into a grin. He got to his feet while they trooped into the house. LeahNell glanced at the little book. *The Lonely Ones,* it was called, by William Steig. Her scalp prickled.

"Rex, you are here," said Dr. Ryder. "Did you creep in by the back door?"

This was the way LeahNell's brother and his friends talked to each other, jabbing with words. She thought Dr. McFall would jostle him back, but he merely looked reproachful and said, "You invited me."

"So I did, so I did," said Dr. Ryder. "Well, you nearly weren't invited. Gilda said no. It was I who said we couldn't do without you."

That sounded to LeahNell like Gilda wasn't all that crazy about Dr. McFall. Gilda didn't say a word, just put out her cigarette and went to the kitchen.

Cleo and Patsy almost knocked each other down. "Dr. McFall!" they said in chorus.

"First names, please," he said. "I'm Rex." He looked to Dr. Ryder. "Matthew?"

"God, yes. First names, by all means."

Cleo and Patsy claimed the chairs bracketing Dr. McFall -- Rex. Cleo had on a short skirt that showed off her cheerleader legs and Patsy was about to pop right out of a tight pink sweater.

Dr. Ryder -- Matthew -- slouched his long frame into a chair. "I must have extended the invitation to Rex in a moment of unguarded altruism and logorrhea," he said. "I am clearly a supernumerary."

LeahNell gasped with envy -- the big words came so easily to him. He glanced at her, then at the chair beside him. Not exactly an invitation, but it was the only empty chair. She sat on the edge, and he went back to watching Rex with the other girls.

Patsy and Cleo liked to talk about themselves, but LeahNell couldn't seem to open her mouth without telling more about herself than she wanted, and she certainly didn't intend to say anything she hadn't had a chance to think about first. Patsy had said more than once that Dr. Ryder had a mean mouth, and LeahNell was glad he didn't have her in his sights.

She drank in the aroma from the kitchen -- cinnamon and cloves, something citrusy, and scents she couldn't identify: one pleasantly barnyardy and another ... saturating, pungent but sweet and warm. It reminded her of something from a long time ago that she couldn't put a name to, but made her want to breathe deep. She didn't quite dare breach the closed door to the kitchen, and soon enough, it opened to a loaded teacart. Swiftly, Gilda put dinner on the table, dinner like nothing her mother ever cooked -- no meat or potatoes or gravy or boiled vegetables, but a salad with blue cheese in a large wooden bowl, a steaming casserole, and long loaves of hot bread sliced through and garlic-buttered.

Patsy and Cleo ran away with the table conversation, which suited LeahNell just fine. She had never understood how other people could talk and eat at the same time. She could eat or she could talk, but not both, and there was no question what she wanted to do now. Somewhere into the apple pie, of which she'd shamelessly accepted a second helping, she failed to laugh with the others and realized she'd been savoring when she should have been listening.

Pay attention. No wonder she couldn't figure out what was going on. Still, if she listened only to what they said, she missed the way they said it. Sometimes, what they *did* didn't come out like what they said.

Like: When Gilda cleared the table after dinner, she reached for the empty casserole dish and Matthew laid his hand on her rump as if she were his horse or his dog. "Mighty fine clambake, Maw," he said, and Rex kind of jumped and took an absolutely gargantuan drag on his cigarette, and when he let go the smoke, it hung there under the light in a canopy over the table.

"That is a foul habit, Rex," Matthew said. "And you seemed like such a clean-cut American boy." He was grinning, but his eyebrows were knotted.

Then Gilda popped a cigarette between her lips and touched it to Rex's cigarette between *his* lips and sent a puff of smoke melting into his canopy. She was simply lighting her cigarette with his cigarette. People did it all the time; why did it seem to mean much more?

Now, after dinner, they were all in the living room sprawling in chairs while Matthew fussed with green and brown glass bottles and stoppered crockery, like a minister preparing communion. Patsy and Cleo took the little purple glasses of liqueur he handed them. LeahNell said no thank you to crème de menthe, no thank you to Drambuie, and no thank you even to Benedictine, though it tasted like terpin hydrate with codeine, her favorite cough prescription. Matthew raised one eyebrow but let it pass. Which she was glad of because she was still regretting tea and cognac at Miss Imogene Hunter's.

All this coddling and cultivating and counseling was fun and made her feel special, something she hadn't felt since she left home, but they encouraged you to indulge yourself, and then you had the bellyache and the hangover, so it was not like being a child with parents anticipating your impulses and stopping you before you hurt yourself. Or talked too much. And sometimes she had the distinct impression that they were all studying her, like some laboratory animal. When Miss Hunter had said, "Don't depend on men to fulfill you -- you'll end up drudges, passive-aggressive. Go out and do your own moving and shaking," LeahNell had been so surprised that without thinking she said, "Oh, Miss Hunter, teach me how to be self-sufficient." Which she couldn't really mean, could she? Since she was going to go back to Little Wood and marry Floyd.

Just now, Rex had asked, "What's the order of the evening? Charades? Confessions?" and right away, Matthew fixed his ice-blue eyes on LeahNell.

"We haven't heard a word from you," he said. "Give us a dissertation in twenty-five words or less on how you like The Farm."

"Um, it's not what I expected," she said, and then rushed on before he could ask what she'd expected, before she could tell him she felt as if she were under some kind of spell. "For the past two and a half years, we've had to do ... everything. Trinity Hospital couldn't run without us and now, all of a sudden, the nurses here don't trust us with medications or keys, much less responsibility for a patient, as if they think we don't know anything. We don't have to work nights or evenings or split shifts or weekends. We get every weekend off. We can stay up and stay out as late as we want. We get away with murder, and no one criticizes us. Everyone is polite. It's like a rest cure."

"Which is as it should be," said Rex. "Our business is to provide an atmosphere in which one can cure oneself."

"That may be your idea and Miss Hunter's," said Patsy, "but I just finished my two weeks on Infirmary. The RN's there know exactly what we're good for. I had to do all the old scut work and restrain patients for the dentist and the x-ray technician and electroshock. Just wait until you have your turn, Leah. You'll feel right at home, whether you like it or not."

"Electroshock? Restrain them?"

"Yeah, it's no big deal."

Something about Patsy's lighting her cigarette with theatrical, swooping gestures made LeahNell think Patsy was not telling the whole truth.

"I'm waiting." Matthew stared at LeahNell.

"Waiting?"

"I requested a dissertation on how you like The Farm, and all I get is a lot of shop talk. No shop talk in this house."

What to say? She thought of the labyrinth of tunnels and the wind that never stopped blowing and her dream last night of the moon following her through a swamp smelling of over-ripe fruit rotting into the ooze that squeezed up between her toes, and how the dream didn't feel all that different from daytime. She wouldn't tell him that, but she would allow that The Farm was exotic.

"It feels like the other end of the rabbit hole." Well, that was stupid. "I mean, like walking through a mirror." Worse and worse.

He waited. "Don't hold back. No spectators. You are not permitted to look before you leap. Nothing ventured, nothing lost."

"Come on, Matthew," said Gilda. "You know what she means. Alice in Wonderland."

"Don't put words in her mouth, Gilda. Let her speak for herself. Did you love Lewis Carroll's tender yarn?"

This seemed pretty harmless. "It terrified me," said LeahNell. "The teacher read it to us the year I was seven. I had nightmares. The baby that turned into a pig and ran away squealing. ... "

"Splendid. Everyone hush. Testimonial time. Were you afraid you'd turn into a pig?" He put down his cordial glass, and while she watched, fascinated, the liquid around the rim coalesced, elongated into a teardrop and slid down the side of the glass. He leaned back and propped his elbows on the arms of the chair, fingertips together. She wondered if this was his therapy posture. "Come, dear. Plunge in," he said, but then his rogue left eyebrow sprang up and suddenly she felt secretive again.

She blushed and stammered, "I just think it's not a children's story at all."

"Exactly," said Gilda. "Now, how about ..."

Matthew shook his head. "You may not turn this into a literary discussion. These are my students. Come now, my dear; don't be superficial. Confess to some hideously diminishing trauma."

Everyone was watching her. Suddenly, LeahNell could see what was needed: Be a good sport; it's only a game.

"One day, the teacher opened the book and I burst into tears. I was taken out of the room. I spent that period every day reading in the library. The other kids made fun of me for months. Always, just when I'd think they'd forgotten, someone would say, 'Oink, oink,' and it would start all over again." She sat back smiling foolishly, feeling inordinately pleased with herself.

"Same thing happens here, to patients, all the time," murmured Rex.

"Well done," said Matthew. "A tearjerker. A classic drama ..."

"Greek tragedy," said Gilda, fingering her black onyx cigarette holder.

"Complete with moral," said Matthew. "I'm sure you find this institution full of such illusions and transformations. Lasting stigmata? Oh yes, nightmares. We'll talk about the dreams another time."

Oh no we won't, thought LeahNell; he is not getting any confessions out of me. No true confessions, anyway.

"Patsy is putting you on about electroshock," said Matthew. "'No big deal,' she says. It is a big deal. It's what this place is all about."

"Actually, you don't have to help or even see it," said Cleo. "Miss Hunter told us it's voluntary."

"So don't do it," said Rex. "Spare yourselves the spectacle."

"I disagree," Matthew said. "Are you just putting in your time? How can we talk about the evils of the status quo if you don't know what they are?

"Who's next? Gilda, you fed these peasants too well. They are all somnolent."

"Then can we have a literary discussion?" said Gilda. She accepted a cigarette from Rex, her back arching as she twisted toward the flame licking out from his lighter.

"It's your turn, Gilda. We haven't heard from you in lightyears. How little we know of you, fair spouse and earth mother. Everyone, look at Gilda -- her face is radiant as the moon. She's a silence to be interpreted."

This kind of talk made LeahNell uneasy. Gilda sprang out of her chair. "Rex, would you like a little fresh air?"

"All right, all right, let's not break up the party," said Matthew. "Rex, why don't you instruct our students in the Nature Versus Nurture war that rends the fabric of this institution."

He stood and stretched, then brought out the liqueurs. "Come on. Musical chairs." His smile pulled his face into long creases and showed his teeth.

Everyone stood and stretched, and resettled in new combinations. Rex was now sitting between Patsy and LeahNell. He looked at LeahNell. "You're not drinking," he said. "You're probably the only one of us with a clear head."

If Melba were here, she'd blurt out: *LeahNell's got an ulcer. She's not supposed to drink.* But she was not here, so LeahNell could say it herself. "I had an ulcer. They say it's cured, but it's like a reflex." Rex was nice; she didn't mind telling him.

"An ulcer." Rex looked interested. "More grist for Matthew's mill. Another testimonial another time."

Well, that wasn't so smart. "Nature Versus Nurture," she said quickly. "Is that the difference between electroshock and providing an atmosphere in which. . . ?"

"... one can cure oneself? We don't have to talk about that. It was just a way for Matthew to change the subject."

"I know," she said. "But I've been wondering." Rex looked surprised, and after a moment, she said, "Most of the time, it feels like a rest cure. But sometimes some people ... a few people -- attendants and RNs ... well, not all the attendants, Casey mostly, not all the RNs ... They seem to resent us. When they want us to think *they* think we're not looking, they sneer, and talk around us as if we're not there. They herd the patients like animals or criminals or imbeciles ..."

"They are ignorant," said Rex. "There's a lot of ignorance around. When I was a kid, the scoutmaster told us we'd go insane if we masturbated."

Her mind clenched in alarm. He couldn't talk like that in mixed company, could he? She glanced around the room. Evidently, he could. Not a ripple, no raised eyebrows. Cleo and Patsy's faces expressed studied blandness. She guessed she'd better get used to it. It was clinical, like discussing menstruation or emesis or excreta in the chart room. Rex wouldn't talk so freely if he didn't consider them on his level.

"Most people," Rex went on, "call this an *asylum*; our charges are called *inmates*; they are *insane*. Insanity is a life sentence. No one gets well and they have to be controlled. Hydrotherapy, restraints, sedation with pills and foul liquids. Does anything brand someone insane as fast as the stench of paraldehyde? And electroshock ... They think they're modern here because they don't use metrazol any more. We ...," he indicated all the present company, "... like to think we're enlightened. We want to follow a different approach."

Matthew loomed over them with his coffee and Drambuie, then folded his lanky frame into a chair so fast that coffee leaped onto his trousers. He whisked it off. "Spare us the classroom post-mortems, Rex. When I suggested a topic of conversation, I didn't expect to be taken literally." He looked hard at LeahNell.

Rex shrugged. "Our tools are talk, talk, and talk. We must listen all day. That's why we talk so much after hours. What's your pleasure, Matthew? What shall we talk about now?"

"You may talk about whatever you please. I don't have an agenda." Matthew stared into his coffee cup.

It felt as if the conversation had gasped its last breath. Rex and Gilda were rolling their eyes at each other; Cleo was twirling a curl and Patsy yawned.

Cleo crossed her legs above the knee. Her skirt slithered upward. "Dr. Swenson calls you upstarts," she said.

Which LeahNell knew was true, but was Cleo trying to get them all thrown out? But Rex shot Cleo a smile, as if he approved of her smart-ass remark.

"He does, does he," said Matthew. "Sour grapes. The old mossback can't stand it that we're getting people out of here. He'd have you think this institution is self-sustaining. He'll tell you the farm and the shop and the sewing room are paying its way. Truth is, The Farm is a drain on public funds. Too many bodies are not carrying their own weight; the back wards are stacked with people rocking and staring out their lives."

"Matthew's hypothesis is, they never die," said Rex.

Patsy leaned close to Rex. Her arm brushed his shoulder and stuck there for a moment like a nail drawn to a magnet. Supposed to look like an accident, thought LeahNell. Now Cleo's leg was visible to the lacy edge of her panties. Rex coughed and plucked Patsy's hand from his inner arm.

"You're wasting your time, sirens," Matthew said. "You can't seduce Rex; he's a psychologist. When a pretty girl walks into the room, he watches everyone else." Cleo blushed. Patsy didn't.

Rex went on as if nothing had happened. "The Old Guard, the mossbacks, are embedded in the system. The old inmates too; they know how to live with it. They're secure and there are no surprises. If things changed, they'd get reshuffled and have to learn new routines, and maybe the top dogs won't be on top any more."

The Old Guard: Dr. Swenson, Dr. Quill...? LeahNell liked Dr. Quill. The attendants were all right, most of them, all but Casey. The RNs she didn't know by name, except for the night supervisor, Mrs. Quill, same name as Dr. Quill, but Miss Hunter said they're not related. Mrs. Quill was nice. LeahNell had seen her at breakfast a few times, and once, she'd walked with LeahNell on her way to class. Mrs. Quill might be a Mossback, but LeahNell was not going to hold that against her.

"And then there are territorial claims," Rex said. "Inmate territory and patient territory. Our patients pretty much own the rec hall but they're tight as piano wire when they go to Clinic for insulin or hydrotherapy. They don't want the place to rub off on them."

"Dr. Quill doesn't like to go on the Admissions ward," said LeahNell. "He does physical exams without saying a word to anyone but the patients." Without looking right or left, and without speaking even to her.

"We don't care much for the wards, either."

"Mossback Territory?" LeahNell sneaked a peek at Matthew and was rewarded with a lift of his eyebrow.

"Mossback Territory. We keep our backs to the wall," said Rex. "Ours is Maverick Territory."

Matthew swirled his Drambuie and slapped the little glass into his palm. "What rubbish," he said. "Where do you get this sociological drivel? You're a psychologist, damn it. This is not psychology. No wonder you can't get a teaching position."

Not nice. LeahNell wondered if Rex ever felt like punching Matthew in the nose. Gilda rolled her eyes; she looked tired, like a mother of small boys just holding on until their bedtime.

"I was offered a job at Pocatello last year," said Rex softly. "Here is another observation: The Mossbacks are so worried about how hard it is to tell some of our patients from the caretakers, they bend over backward being professional. They don't smile; they make fetishes of their eyeglasses and their starched caps and insignia. Some suggest that patients and inmates shouldn't be allowed to wear white."

Matthew seemed to accept that well enough.

"Maybe it's my imagination," said LeahNell, "but some inmates act pretty normal among themselves, but they put on a show of symptoms when staff members come around."

Rex sat bolt upright. "Ah."

Matthew groaned. "Now you've done it. I'd hoped we could get through an evening without that notion surfacing."

"Well, there's a tall, thin woman who dresses in black," said LeahNell. "She goes up to people and says, very staccato, 'You are eliminated with courtesy.' You. Are. ... And another woman, who drools and smiles, and Miss Hunter says is a hopeless hebephrenic. This morning, these two were sitting on a bench outside doing something with a stick. One of them would poke the stick in the dirt and then the other would take the stick and poke it in the dirt and hand it back. They were talking to each other. I couldn't hear what they said. As I passed them, the woman in black stood and said to me, 'You. Are. Eliminated.

With. Courtesy.' And the other woman giggled and jerked and hid her face in her coat. I peeked at the place in the dirt where they were poking the stick. They'd been playing TicTacToe."

Cleo sighed loudly and reached for her drink. Patsy stood up and stretched, thrusting her breasts within inches of Rex's face. "I suppose the little girls' room is upstairs?" No one looked at her and she sat down.

LeahNell went on: "The other day outside the infirmary, the inmate they call Frog was following the head nurse, Mrs. Chisholm, mimicking the way she walks rigid as a pole, until she turned around and almost caught him and he went right back to bobbing around with his knees bent."

"See, what did I tell you?" said Rex.

"So? What are you trying to say? I don't see the significance." Matthew glanced at LeahNell, then spoke to his liqueur glass. "Look. Rex fancies himself a breacher of taboos and great mysteries. He actually insinuated himself onto the wards as an attendant in order to be a participant observer, as he quaintly puts it, of patient life. He's trying to explain mental disease in social terms. Don't encourage him."

Rex's face pinked up. "Maybe it's not orthodox psychology, but it's a helluva good hobby. She's right, you know. Quite a few patients are capable of normal behavior."

He steepled his fingers under his chin, looked sage. "They manifest their greatest degree of the pathological behavior they've been shaped into as the basis for their particular diagnoses when they are in the presence of those persons who are responsible for making and defending those diagnoses."

Silence fell as everyone sorted it out.

Matthew got there first. "That's a variation on what LeahNell said. You are making three outrageous assumptions. You suggest that patients are molded into certain diagnostic categories. You suggest that they cooperate with this and reward us by perpetuating their own statuses as incompetents and classless persons. You say they are capable of normal behavior. Now I ask you, would a normal person allow others to carry out a life sentence on him? Don't be an ass, Rex."

"I did not say they were normal. I said that some are capable of normal behavior. Please allow me the difference.

What is normal? Normal behavior is nothing more than socially accepted role-playing, not rocking the boat. Any good mimic can do it."

Gilda sighed. Matthew waited. LeahNell held her breath.

"As to their reasons, my 'sociological' method does not reveal this to me, but I can make some educated guesses. Security. Freedom from hunger and violence. Not having to answer for their behavior -- a good trade-off. And they are exploited. They do allow it. They compensate: their behavior preserves the status quo. They mock the caretakers behind their backs, make us look like puffed-up fools. They are putting one over on us. The inmates are pulling the strings. You say yourself the inmates are in control; we depend on them for the necessities of daily life."

"What you're describing is nothing more than passive-aggression," said Matthew. "Why the hell can't you employ respectable psychological terms?"

"Why don't I confound and mystify, aggrandize myself with jargon? Call it passive-aggression if you want; I'm telling you how it works. Inmates exchange success for security and a place to retire from the world. Success is hard work. These people don't have to compete any more."

Matthew's expression seemed to be softening.

Rex went on: "We have few monasteries, no poorhouses. Maybe we're doing a disservice urging opportunities and the 'good life' on everyone. Are we only trying to relieve our own guilt when we try to close the asylums? These people could be on the streets. Maybe we should leave them their sanctuaries."

Matthew slumped onto his spine and jammed his hands into his pockets. "Christ," he said. "You were beginning to make sense."

Rex studied Matthew. "Which brings it home. What are we doing here? How do you account for us?"

Rex fell silent, peering at Matthew. Gilda was as still as a bird being invisible.

Suddenly, without any idea what told her so, LeahNell was certain this was a performance. They'd had this argument before. Was it part of the curriculum?

Matthew stood and scowled at Patsy and Cleo nodding

in their chairs, and at LeahNell. "On your feet, ladies," he said. "Rex is going to pour you into his chariot and convey you to your residence."

He bowed in front of Rex, who smiled slightly. "I walked," he said.

"Take mine." Matthew opened his arms wide. "You may drive my grand vehicle. After all, I went and got them."

Gilda stood up. "I'll take them home," she said.

"My dear, you'll do no such thing," said Matthew. "Why deny Rex the pleasure? Why should you leave the comfort of home and husband?"

"I'll take them all home." Gilda held out her hand for the car keys while Matthew opened his mouth, closed it, and his eyebrows lifted, one at a time and then both together. He pulled the key ring out of his pants pocket and dropped it into Gilda's hand.

Whatever was at stake, Gilda had won, but what, wondered LeahNell, had she won? Why did it matter who took who home?

Matthew made a fuss of helping the girls into their coats. Gilda and Rex put on their own coats, not looking at each other. They were silent, in the front seat of the Jeep, all the way to the old Women's Violent, and Gilda waited in the idling car while Rex walked Cleo, Patsy and LeahNell to the door in the damp spring night.

The door closed behind them and the girls stood in the entry hall. LeahNell halted on the first stair step when she saw that Cleo and Patsy were looking at each other, eyebrows raised, Cleo mouthing a silent "Oh."

"What does 'Oh' mean?" LeahNell drew back her foot. "They're more interesting than Swensons, and we finally had some intelligent conversation."

Patsy shot her a blank look. "His being a psychologist isn't the only reason we can't seduce Rex," she said. "There's another, and that's Gilda."

"What are you talking about?" said LeahNell.

"He's getting into her pants," said Patsy.

"Yeah," said Cleo.

"Oh, you two. You've got a one-track mind."

She wouldn't believe it for a minute. Patsy and Cleo *looked* for sex everywhere. Matthew and Gilda and Rex were intellectuals. They had better things to think about.

LeahNell had better things to think about too. She and her classmates were invited to participate in the Friday night seminars with the psychology interns at the Ryders', a development welcomed by the girls, but regarded with suspicion and condescension by the young men.

On Sunday night, one of the psych interns, Hopkins, announced after a big powwow in the dining room that the best way to resolve residual hostility was to sublimate it in play. LeahNell went along with him and the others as far as Three-Deep on the lawn outside the old Women's Violent at twilight on Monday, and with parading in sheet sarongs and lipstick tattoos through the rec hall during the patients' dance on Wednesday. On Thursday night, she drew the line at splitting off into couples and grappling in the bushes after dark.

The game was Kick-the-Can and LeahNell was It. Everyone disappeared and no one came Home to kick the can, and she was left listening to giggles and whispers in the deepening dusk. She retreated to her cell in the old Women's Violent and sat in her deep window well hugging her knees to her chest, and watched the waning moon spring above the cottonwoods behind Intermediate.

Later, Cleo poked her face, plundered of lipstick and whisker-burned, around the door on her way to her own room. "You must be arrested in the latency stage," she said, which was the way she was talking now that she was shining up to one of the interns. "Of course, you have Floyd waiting for you at home, but don't you think you should have some fun before you settle down?"

LeahNell wanted only to go back to Little Wood with what remained of her virtue. She was not just putting in her time. She would close the Venetian blind against the moonlight and read: Freud, James, Fromm, Horney, and as many pages of Jung as she could focus on. Right now, she would write a letter to Floyd.

But what to say? He had it in his legalistic mind that her exotic experiences at Trinity and "the insane asylum" were the arbitrary prescription of some board of functionaries in the State House. Not relevant to real life -- the job she'd have at Gooding Hospital just to tide them over until the babies started coming. She'd tried to share what she was seeing and learning and sometimes enduring, but he had told her kindly that medicine and hospitals weren't the sort of thing he was interested in. Which had made her feel lonely and dislocated, because she hadn't wanted him to be interested, but just to hear her. She could have talked to Daddy, but he'd have said, "You don't have to let people treat you like that. Come home."

She could tell Floyd that she'd been to dinner at a doctor's house and he'd be impressed, but a Ph.D., even two Ph.D.s, of psychology would rate little more than a shrug.

Still, she tried to write her letter, and when her mind wandered, she summoned up Floyd's face: his eyes, which for some reason were hardest of all. Blue, she told herself, and prominent; long eyelashes darker than his lank, light brown hair; blunt medium-size nose; round face cheekier even than hers. She guessed he would be handsome when he was older. The other girls thought he was handsome now, because he was over six feet tall. And when she had conjured up each of his features separately, she took a deep breath, clenched her elbows to her sides and tightened all her muscles and sphincters, screwed her eyelids shut and concentrated, and so brought him all together for the complete image, which lasted as long as she could hold her breath. She had never played Three-Deep or Kick-the-Can with Floyd.

After a while, the door downstairs slammed shut and the footsteps on the stairs turned into Melba in her doorway.

Melba was under the spell of The Farm. She wore purple Chen Yu nail polish, and now that it was officially spring, she had taken to wearing a peasant blouse. The stiffest wind didn't raise gooseflesh on her lizard skin. She let her blouse slip off one shoulder. One day, when Miss Hunter told her that her bra strap was showing, Melba had smirked her smirk that passed for a smile and shrugged her blouse up all of half an inch.

"Evans is a lousy kisser," she said now, poking at the imagined disarray of her electric hair. "Anyway, why should I confine myself to one guy when I can have four?" She didn't wait for LeahNell's answer, but turned and stalked down the hall to her room.

What Melba was talking about was, Jep and Ollie and Whitaker, the moon-faced attendant from Men's Violent, and Mr. Wheeler, the charge attendant from Intermediate. All together, they escorted her from dining room to canteen to rec room and every other place they were permitted to be with a student nurse. LeahNell didn't know what they saw in each other, but maybe it had started with the baseball game.

Every afternoon when classes were over, an old baseball bat and a ball fraying at the seam were hauled out of the rec room, and the patients with grounds privileges and the attendants, with the exception of Casey, lined up to play ball against the psych interns and the student nurses in the open grassy field beyond the old Women's Violent. The game would go on until suppertime.

After the second game, Ollie seconded by Jep said the teams should have names.

LeahNell was fascinated by Jepson and Oliver. When they seemed unsure of themselves, they'd tuck their thumbs inside their fists. They never actually held hands, but often, they'd hold onto opposite ends of the same object -- Jep left-handed and Ollie right-handed, or go through the same motions simultaneously. When Ollie went up to bat, Jep would pick up a stick and a rock and toss the rock up and swing the stick as Patsy pitched the ball Ollie's way. Then when Ollie's bat connected, Jep's stick would connect; and when Ollie missed, Jep missed. They were as likely to cheer the other team as their own. When anyone hit the ball, they'd watch its soaring trajectory and yip as one, "C'mon team!"

"C'mon team," muttered Clarence, who wore a starched chef's hat in the canteen. He would swing an imaginary bat, and when he himself was up, he'd swing a real bat and mutter, "C'mon team," at each of Patsy's strikes that whistled past his shoulder. And when he struck out, he'd lay down the bat across the leaky sandbag that served as home plate so that there was not a tenth of an inch more space on one side of the bag than on the other, and stalk back to his unmowed tuft of fescue and pick up his imaginary bat. "C'mon, team."

"C'mon, team!" cheered Jep and Ollie.

"Hey, don't cheer for the other side," said Whitaker. "Cheer for our team. Cheer for us."

"A team is a team," said Ollie.

"A team is a team," said Jep "Two teams ..."

"... is two teams. Teams have ..."

"... names. There's no difference unless ..."

"... they have names. Different names. One name ..."

"... for one team, another name for another team. You can't be a ..."

"... different team without a different name. Right, Mr. Wheeler?"

"Sounds reasonable to me," said Mr. Wheeler, in his immaculate monotone uniform. He was still wearing his khaki tie, although he had rolled up his sleeves. Mr. Wheeler never seemed to sweat.

Everyone else had agreed and everyone had a favorite animal mascot and there was no majority.

Nature Versus Nurture? thought LeahNell. "How about the Mavericks and the Mossbacks?"

Their instant approval didn't surprise her, but there seemed to be a lesson somewhere, although she didn't know what it was, in the attendants and the inmates choosing to be Mavericks, leaving Mossbacks to the psych interns and the nurses, among them Melba.

But when Melba rejected Evans she abandoned her team too, to play with Jep and Ollie and Whitaker and Mr. Wheeler on the Mavericks, and that left the Mossbacks one short.

"We have an imbalance here," Mr. Wheeler said. "I wonder if we could recruit Casey."

It fell to Whitaker, who worked with him, to approach Casey, who soundly rebuffed him for no good reason, but Whitaker guessed that baseball was one thing he did better than Casey.

A patient named Driscoll took Melba's place.

7. <u>KC</u>

When Jimbo had the men grouped in the hall, Casey strode into their ranks, wedging them into two columns around him. He unlocked and threw open the door to the shower room and in they went, their footfalls echoing off the yellow tiled walls and floor. He slammed the door, opened the control panel and turned on the water, which burst out of the seven shower heads. While the water warmed, the men shucked their clothes and dropped them into a round cloth hamper. Most stood shivering and hugging themselves. A few were immobile, and one of those, Hawk, when prodded, threw his elbows outward and, his eyes darting about, whipped his spread fingers in an arc.

Casey and Jimbo leaned back against the wall, eyes on the men under the showers. Casey liked the steam rising around the men's white bodies and the smell of the shower room, a clean sulfur smell after the sweet stench of paraldehyde out on the floor. He was glad he'd gotten Rochelle out of Women's Violent. He didn't like her smelling like paraldehyde.

Now and again he urged one of the men to move the soap a little faster and don't miss the important parts, the ears and the neck. And get the soap out of the hair, and not just a swipe down the front but the privates too and between the toes, though none of the men could stand on one foot without teetering.

Hawk, who had been transferred from Intermediate to Violent, EST failing to make him quit spitting and throwing his food, liked to wait until Jimbo's back was turned and then splash him. Now he took aim, one thing electroshock hadn't messed up.

The back of Jimbo's trousers wouldn't be dry before noon. When was Jimbo going to learn not to turn his back on an inmate? One time, he got a shoeful and the sole squished for two days. What a pansy. Wanted him, Casey, to come out and play ballgames with the rest of the staff. What a waste of time.

Frog was through with his shower first. His shoulders drooping, his little bowlegs springing and his toes splayed over the tiles, he waited for Jimbo to hand him a towel, which he accepted with a nod of his head.

Casey was proud of Frog. Wasn't long ago Frog spent his days jerking off, or trying to, and crying over his limp penis, and Casey, because he couldn't knock him around for it as he'd have liked to, had to find a reason for Dr. Quill to shock him to his senses.

In their weekly confab in Miz Crack's office, Casey had thought hard about Frog, looking for the words Dr. Quill would need to hear. "Jerking himself off" wasn't the way to put it -- he'd tried that once before and Dr. Quill said, don't deny them their simple pleasures. Which was one place Casey and Dr. Quill parted company. Casey read Miz Crack's weekly ward reports, looking for some good words. "Abusing himself" seemed to put the right twist on it. He decided not to mention shock. Let Dr. Quill figure that out.

"Frog abuses himself," said Casey.

"Abuses himself?" said Dr. Quill. "He masturbates? We don't punish inmates for masturbating." He stared at Casey, and Casey let it go by because Dr. Quill was pulling rank on him.

Masturbation? Was that what Miz Crack meant? Casey hated big words. Why didn't people just say what they meant?

"Or do you mean flagellation?" Dr. Quill said. "Does he hit himself?"

"Yeah," said Casey, "all the time, night and day. And he cries."

He cries. Those were the words that got Dr. Quill.

"Night and day?"

"Night and day."

Yeah, you had to have the right words and Casey'd found the right words, and then three times a week -- Monday, Wednesday, Friday for a month -- he'd prodded Frog into the EST line and afterward herded him stumbling back to the ward, until he didn't jerk off any more. He still cried, rocked and cried, but Casey didn't tell Dr. Quill, because he'd got Frog where he wanted him, he'd got him trained. Frog was a good boy now, didn't throw his filthy language around like he used to, didn't diddle his little froggy even in the shower. Casey felt a kind of affection for Frog, like he'd raised him. And a fond contempt for Dr. Quill because he'd put one over on him. Casey felt big and generous. Everybody's father. That Rochelle sure leaned on him.

The men were dried and dressed and out in the hall, shuffling toward the dayroom to the straight-back chairs lined up against the walls under the bare barred windows. Jimbo flushed the suds down the big drain in the middle of the floor.

"Let's go get Howard," said Casey.

Howard had his turn last, after everyone else was out of the shower room. You put Howard in the shower with a bunch of other inmates, you had someone dead before you know it's happened. Now there was an animal. And was he fast. Casey recalled the last time they took Howard to a dance, ten, fifteen years ago. Piano was playing and William was singing something about harbor lights and all of a sudden Howard was on top of this little woman, Casey didn't remember her name, but hadn't forgotten her big soft tits or the way they flattened out across her chest inside her dress ripped from neck to crotch by the time they got to her and the way her head flopped back when they tried to lift her. The dead surprise on her face.

That Howard had a wire shorted out somewhere. He saw the sweet stuff, he wanted to kill it.

That was the last time they let Howard out of his cell, and that was when they stopped letting the inmates dance with each other. Now, the men danced with the nurses in their white uniforms. Wearing white wouldn't stop Howard. Casey could just see that tight-ass little number, the student that wanted to see Howard's pictures the other day -- her face'd go all red or maybe white and she'd squeak, "I beg your pardon!" or maybe, "How dare you!" Like Casey's old Sunday school teacher did the first time he stuck his finger down the front of her dress after the way he could see all the way to her waist when she leaned over him and the way she straddled the piano stool playing "The Old Rugged Cross" and "Beulah Land." That's what she'd said: "How dare you!" He'd smiled and mumbled something. He hadn't even said anything really but she thought he did and she called him dirty and washed out his mouth with soap.

He'd let her do it. He was only eleven, big as a man and had fuzz on his cheeks, but he was afraid of her. She had some kind of power, she could call up angels nobody else could see and she could tell you exactly how many rays shone out of Jesus's halo and what shade of blue his eyes were because she'd seen them, she'd seen him -- Him -- and so he'd let her do it to him. Wash out his mouth with soap.

But the next time, he was thirteen and she wanted it, he knew she wanted it, though she was hollering at him to stop, that she was going to put him in jail, and he didn't stop, though he already knew what the inside of a jail looked like because that's why he was going to Sunday school in the first place.

He'd gotten a little girl from the neighboring farm to come into old Quill's barn with him and it turned out the old bitch across the road was watching and by the time she and the kid's mother caught him, he had all her clothes off. The judge had called him a heathen and sentenced him to two years of Sunday school at the Methodist church. The Sunday school teacher was the preacher's wife, and she was maybe the best time he'd had and it was the way he liked it now.

He wasn't comfortable with a woman until he'd had her. Sometimes though, the closest he could get was by looking through her clothes. Clothes didn't stop Casey's eyes. He could peel a woman down to her skin layer by layer. He could see through all the ways women tried to hide and the ways they tried to trick you. He could tell a girdle by the one hump instead of two and the roll of flesh above the waist, and a padded bra by how it was round all over and the way it didn't move with the body. And he was pretty sure Miz Crack didn't wear underpants.

He didn't like women to flirt with him, let him know he could have them -- he knew he could have them and it was more fun if he got to persuade them. What excited him most was when they couldn't stand him. Those were the ones that were worth going after. They'd get the blood roaring in his ears and his throat tightening and the heat spreading through his groin, but he didn't let on because that was half the game, not letting them know, and all he could do was grind his keys together and watch and wait. Sooner or later they'd come around. One way or another. Sometimes one way, sometimes the other.

What it was with Rochelle was, she was as sweet after as she was before, she was still bursting with it. He'd taken her to the canteen yesterday, bought her a Coke, and then back to

Women's Intermediate through the tunnel. When he turned her into the old tunnel, she'd balked at first, but he let her know it was all right, he'd take care of her.

He liked to stand them up, but the old tunnel wasn't high enough. He had to walk bent-kneed or he'd bang his head. The best he could do was a high spot without any puddles, but he'd have liked it darker. And maybe if he'd been standing up, he'd have paid more attention. Because when he was through, he sat up and at the end of the tunnel, there was that sissy pair Jep and Ollie staring for all they were worth. 'Course, their brains were so fried they didn't know what they were looking at. He didn't have to worry about them. They make one peep, he knew what to do about it.

Still, he didn't like anyone watching him. It was like they were getting some of that sweet stuff too and Casey doesn't share.

8. LeahNell

Stella was a patient of Rex's and the only exception to the rule that at the end of one month, patients were either discharged or moved to another ward as inmates. Stella had been on Admissions for half a year.

In her mid-twenties, she was educated and articulate, and she prickled with independence. As if that weren't enough to set her apart from her company of merely average psychoneurotics and melancholics and character-disordereds, she was an inch taller than LeahNell and had a full mane of wavy golden hair, longer than LeahNell's, high cheek bones and a high-arched aristocratic nose. She had a room to herself and her shower at seven-thirty sharp every evening and first dibs at the pingpong paddles. Every Monday, Wednesday, and Friday afternoon promptly at three, she was admitted for an hour to Dr. McFall's office, where she glanced past the closing door with a tight little smile at anyone who might be passing by. All of this LeahNell could forgive her if she would talk to her, tell her what it was like to *be* Stella. But the only words Stella would waste on anyone except, apparently, Rex were that she didn't waste words where they didn't count.

LeahNell had spent three weeks on Admissions, her first rotation. It came to an end and she expected that was the last she'd see of Stella, except maybe at the ball games.

LeahNell's introduction to Men's Violent came from Cleo, who was just ending her rotation there. At lunch, they were several at a table, including Matthew. Cleo had parked her tray and sat down.

"Leah, you're going to love Men's Violent," she said. "They have an inmate's been there thirty-five years. They keep him in a locked cell because every time he gets out he kills someone. With his bare hands. He strangles them. Casey told me all about it. He's little but so strong that once he gets his hands around your throat, it takes at least two men to pull him off. He just hangs on like a bulldog and growls. He killed a woman at a patients' dance and they haven't let him out of his cell without an attendant for ten years."

Enthralled, she gazed into the distance and then added, "What you'll like, Leah, since you used to be an art student, they let him have crayons and he's drawn pictures over every inch of his cell. Beautiful pictures. He never speaks a word and he's perfectly meek but they say he reaches out to the world through his art. He's a genius. How do you like that?"

"Oh, yeah. Howard," Matthew muttered.

"Is he a genius?" asked LeahNell.

Matthew shrugged. "I'm not qualified to comment. You see and tell me."

"Howard's art? Everyone who comes up here asks about him," said Mrs. Carson, the big, pear-shaped nurse on Men's Violent. "He's our star patient. I guess you can go in and take a look. He's pretty good right now."

In the dayroom, two attendants were leaning against the wall. "Casey," Mrs. Carson said briskly to the bigger one, "Miss Thorel wants to see Howard's pictures. Take her down there, will you. Mind you don't leave her alone with him."

Casey pried himself loose, swaggered ahead of LeahNell down the hall. With a great clatter of the keys chained to his belt, he threw open the door to a cell and addressed the occupant. "Brought you a visitor, Howard. Little lady wants to see your pictures. Still flapping that magazine, are you?"

To LeahNell he said in a normal conversational tone, "He don't talk, he don't read, he don't do nothing but sit here and flap that magazine back and forth all day. He's harmless. Just don't let him get between you and the door." Then Casey flashed a death's-head grin and walked out.

LeahNell gazed into the cell. The same size as her own room, it contained only a narrow steel-frame bed and a pot in one corner. A little man sat on the edge of the bed, flipping a magazine over and back, swish-slap, swish-slap. Pale and bland, unmoving as a mannequin, he stared at her.

He was quiet all right, but LeahNell thought he was not docile. Most inmates never looked you in the eye. She greeted him, then moved slowly to examine his illustrations, being careful not to step on them and murmuring a kind of lullaby of appreciation to the tempo of the swish-slap.

The images made no sense to her. A single, unbroken line of convolutions resembling loops of intestine formed a web over every inch of the room, enclosing it. *Swish-slap*. Where the crayon line came to the bottom of the door, it continued across the floor to the other side, imprisoning the door. Nothing was left to chance, no room to breathe. *Swish-slap*. It reminded her of a cardiogram, a direct transposition of neuron to paper. The work of a soul reaching out for human recognition? Maybe the vapor from a brain fried by electroshock. She shuddered.

Behind her, the swishing stopped. She turned around. The man stood up, still gazing at her, unblinking.

"Thank you," she murmured, then slowly backed out the doorway. Leaning on the wall outside, Casey flashed his grin, then pushed away and slammed the door shut.

LeahNell didn't last out the week on Men's Violent.

She was surprised to see William, from the patients' dance, here on the violent ward. Perfectly groomed within the limits of his status, he carried himself as if he were well-dressed. Typically, the admission sheet on his chart was not legible, and the record of his transfer from Intermediate was not dated.

She knew that paranoid schizophrenics could be logical and rational, even persuasive. Still, her conviction grew that he was as normal as she and a virtual prisoner. She couldn't detect a shred of delusional thinking in his speech. He wasn't even getting medication. While the other men lined up for chloral hydrate, Dilantin or paraldehyde, William worked on financial records from the administration building.

One morning, she walked by the nurse's office, where William was scanning the bulletin board nearby. Without turning his head, he said in a low, measured voice, "I know that you are Betty. It was clever of you to lose weight and change the color of your hair. It's an effective disguise. I understand that you have come to help me. I am working on a plan. I will not tell you the details because they might torture you. It is safer if only I know. Wait. When the time is right, I will take you away with me."

He walked away before LeahNell could respond.

The head nurse had gone to the pharmacy; later she was busy with a transfer. The morning passed and with it the opportunity to report the incident. At lunch, LeahNell told her classmates, who thought it hilarious. By the time their instructor, athletic, iron-gray-haired Imogene Hunter, joined them, it had become burlesque. Half-way onto her chair, Imogene reversed her descent and went straight to the table where the clinical nurses were eating.

When she returned, she said, "Well, it's all too bad. William was doing so well. There was a nurse here three years ago whom you resemble, LeahNell. He was convinced they were married and that she was here against her will. He told her about his escape plan, and she tried to talk him out of it. He decided she'd been brainwashed. He made secret arrangements. I don't recall the details, but he very nearly succeeded in kidnapping her. When he was found out, she left and he was put on Men's Violent, where he's been ever since."

"There's nothing in his chart," protested LeahNell.

"They keep poor accounts on the wards. The files in the adminstration building would record the incident, but to see them requires almost an act of God." Miss Hunter smiled wryly. "Dr. Swenson of course will let you see it."

"What will happen to him -- William?"

"Not much. Increased surveillance. Mainly, they will not let you back on the ward. Where would you like to spend the rest of this rotation?"

Her new assignment was Infirmary/Clinic where, true to Patsy's prediction, she felt right at home whether she liked it or not. She didn't like it. She spent the mornings feeding and bathing and dodging fingernails and feces and sputum. By the time she finished, it was time to start feeding again. It was like her first year of training, without the bullying of head-nurses, to which she was no longer susceptible.

Most of the patients were bedbound, old and sick or catatonics so frozen they had to be tube-fed. Every disease she had seen on the medical floor at Trinity was here, mostly untreated. The head nurse, Mrs. Chisholm, claimed that inmates wouldn't cooperate.

LeahNell had noticed that most of the inmates had no

teeth. On Clinic, it didn't take long to find out why. One Thursday a month, a dentist came out from town, and all the inmates with cavities, toothaches or impacted teeth lined up in the basement to be treated. On Dentist Day, Mrs. Chisholm sent LeahNell to work in the clinic, telling her only, "Everyone gets the same treatment, which at least is democratic." LeahNell was pretty sure that what was going to happen she was not going to like.

Downstairs, she waited in the corridor. Melba's friend Whitaker brought two men from the violent ward, snappish and grumbling. They fell silent when joined by Mr. Wheeler and his charge from Men's Intermediate. The two men sidled over to Mr. Wheeler and nudged their way into space at each side of him, and without complaint, the displaced inmate from Intermediate moved behind with Whitaker.

When the door opened, all that LeahNell could see was the regulation dentist's chair, a table with instruments and rolls of gauze.

Mr. Wheeler had been studying her and seemed to come to an unspoken conclusion. He went inside with his man, closing the door behind him. Then as the morning wore on, the inmates disappeared into the room one by one, door opening only wide enough to admit them and release into the hall a sweet pungency of ether.

A very exclusive club, she thought; do they think I've never seen blood? But when the door finally opened wide and the inmates stumbled out reeking of ether and the hot, metallic scent of blood, with bandages tied around their heads and under their chins, and their bleeding jaws clamped over the gauze packing their now toothless chops, then she was grateful to Mr. Wheeler for taking her for a lady. Lunch was out of the question; her stomach lurched at the smell of food.

Second Thursday was X-Ray Day, not an idle exercise, according to Matthew: tuberculosis was still prevalent among long-termers. LeahNell didn't plan to spare herself the spectacle of electroshock, but she was not going to hold inmates for their chest x-rays. For some idiosyncratic reason, she did not fear TB, but she figured that in her first year of nursing school, having given total care to bedbound women with pelvic radium implants, and carrying their bedpans and emesis basins, she had gotten enough radiation to last her a lifetime. So she gritted her teeth and found a reason why a particular clenched-up catatonic needed a complete bedbath and a pedicure and a shampoo. She "missed" finishing in time for x-ray duty.

The third week featured treatments, beginning with Hydrotherapy. In the hot, steamy tubroom, LeahNell was as stuporous as the patients, dragging herself around to check water temperatures and giving sips of water to one after another head lolling above its canvas tub cover. She reminded herself that she was in Mossback Territory; that this was the asylum and these were inmates.

She moved on, with higher hopes, to Insulin Therapy. Surely a treatment called Insulin Shock would be interesting. But the RN smelled sour and looked stringy and her hair was limp -- just like the patients', whose response to the insulin that LeahNell administered early every morning was nothing she could perceive beyond perhaps a shiver and a twitch of eyelids and two hours of inattention. LeahNell preferred the sharing and extraversion of the talking cure that Matthew and Rex worked, something she could hear and see and ... identify with. She could hardly wait to get outside the stale, windowless maze of the Clinic basement hive, which was gloomy in spite of the relentless yellow walls.

Outdoors, she relished the daylight and the locust trees with their shadows squarely centered along the walks in the noonday sun, the gusty wind blowing little squall clouds over with their occasional fitful, sunshiny rains.

Unexpectedly, one of the insulin patients was Stella, whose beauty was diminished by the effects of insulin. After being revived by orange juice, she shook off her lethargy quickly each morning and waited, clenching and unclenching her fists, until LeahNell could walk her back to Admissions.

One morning when Stella seemed more approachable than usual, LeahNell asked her, "What does insulin therapy feel like? How does it make you feel? I'd really like to know."

"Then why don't you try it yourself?" Stella laughed her brittle laugh.

So there! I should have seen that coming, thought

LeahNell. They walked on in silence then until, rounding the corner with the admissions building before them, Stella said in a rush, "It's a kind of infantile retreat. A benign suspension of normal rhythms and demands and sensations. It's an invitation to float and dream. Listen to the lapping and sighs and the whistles and coos inside ..."

Stella glared at LeahNell as if she had hoped to catch her laughing at her. "Do you think I'm crazy?"

Did LeahNell think Stella was crazy? We-ell, ... What was Stella doing here? "Of course not. That doesn't sound crazy. It sounds like poetry."

"Well, I do write poetry. And a lot of other things. I worked for a newspaper until ... I suppose you know I'm an alcoholic. They think I may be schizophrenic too. Isn't that a riot?"

Stella glanced sidelong at LeahNell. "I told you about insulin. Tell me about electroshock. Come on -- turn-about."

"I don't know anything about electroshock. I haven't seen it." Which LeahNell was thankful for, because she was not sure she wanted to describe something that could happen to Stella, a patient.

"Well, I'm here to experience everything," said Stella. "And tell the world about it. I'll let you know." She arched an eyebrow. "And you're trying too hard if you think I don't sound crazy. I'm going to blow the lid off crazy around here."

Having been reminded of electroshock, with just one day to go in Clinic, LeahNell signed up and presented herself the next morning at nine o'clock outside the Shock Room. Inmates assembled in the hall, shuffling in their frayed canvas slippers, looking down at their feet, sometimes clinging to the door frame of the entry. An eerie silence contrasted with the trembling chins, the jerky hand movements shrieking apprehension, reminding LeahNell of a movie with a defective sound track.

At four minutes after nine, a nurse three paces behind him, Dr. Quill walked in looking neither right nor left. He unlocked and opened the door to the Shock Room and flipped the switch that lit the four yellow walls to a blinding intensity. He beckoned LeahNell inside and motioned past her to the attendants, Casey and Whitaker. As she went by him into the room, Melba's friend Whitaker glanced at her with a mixture of recognition and shame, as if this was not the kind of place he liked to run into people he knew.

In the hall, Casey lifted a quivering little man by the armpits. "Okay, Hotshot," said Casey, "set a good example for everybody. Show them how brave you are." To Whitaker with a jerk of his head: "Come on, Moonface." They whisked the man inside and shut the door, pinned him onto the table and strapped him in place.

LeahNell pressed her ears shut, resuming the defective sound track and with it a feeling of unreality as the inmate flipped, twisted and lunged against the straps, his mouth opening and shutting silently. Then she recalled Matthew's admonition: "Don't spare yourself," and was ashamed. She let her hands fall away from her ears.

Dr. Quill daubed the man's temples with jelly, and he gasped and was quiet. It's cold, LeahNell thought; the jelly is cold and it's shocked him silent.

Dr. Quill gestured to the nurse. Mrs. Frickes, a woman with yellow skin and crisp dry hair, fixed electrodes in place with a rubber strap. Contact jelly sucked the electrodes into the skin. Whitaker and Casey, long-armed and heavy-browed, threw their weight onto the shoulders and knees. The little man was boardlike and staring as Mrs. Frickes nudged open his mouth for the thickly padded tongue blade.

"Ready?" said Dr. Quill. As if he heard the cue he had been waiting for -- God's bidding -- the little man relaxed into the table top and the attendants stepped away from him. In the brief expectant hush, Dr. Quill set a dial and flipped a switch, counted under his breath, one, two, three, and flipped it off. The little man stiffened and his back thrust up off the table, his body touching only at the head and heels. With LeahNell holding his feet, Casey and Whitaker's combined weight barely kept him on the table. This at least was familiar. She had seen a patient in convulsions.

The inhuman arching broke up into shudders, rippling through the legs and arms now flopping like fish out of water, and then faded away in tremors. The man's face was purple.

"Ah, that was a good one." Casey grinned. Dr. Quill's eyebrows lifted.

"He isn't breathing," said LeahNell.

"He will," said Dr. Quill, and immediately the man snorted in a huge chunk of air, and then another and another. The purple paled into lavender and the snorting eased into a deep snore, and then the man was slid onto a stretcher and rolled out into the hallway to begin waking up to all the faces trying not to see him.

The air reeked of the acid, rancid pungence of nervous sweat. "Okay, who's next?" Casey didn't wait for an answer but plucked the nearest of the unfortunates, all quivering and bleating and trying to shrink into the woodwork.

Hoping to slip out the door, LeahNell was caught in the bottleneck of the stretcher being returned and the next inmate being pulled in. She found herself again holding feet and looking up into Casey's eternal grin. "Seen one, seen 'em all," he said.

The next... victim was a woman who went under hitting and scratching, and left like the two men before her, pale and blue, eyes still rolling when her lids were pulled back. LeahNell placed herself at one end of the woman's stretcher and escaped into the hallway. There she spent the rest of the morning keeping patients from swallowing their tongues and drowning in their own secretions. They looked like vegetating organisms, and LeahNell tried to remember they were human. The odor of urine grew strong.

Finally, it was over; the inmates, staring vacantly, were herded back to their wards. LeahNell hung back from following them.

Drying his hands on a towel, Dr. Quill came out of the Shock Room. His white mustache drooped at the corners. He looked her in the eye for the first time that morning.

"Do you know that patients ask for it?" he said. "They think they die and are reborn into a new life. It has a modicum of truth, I suppose." He looked away. "A new life minus a few brain cells."

LeahNell was numb; her voice came in a croak. "Miss Hunter told us electroshock isn't painful."

For a moment, Dr. Quill's expression was like that of

Whitaker when he'd recognized her two hours ago: ashamed, as if this wasn't the kind of place he liked to see people he knew.

Dr. Quill recovered. "As far as we can know," he said. "From the instant the current hits, they remember nothing. But something that isn't quite pain ... maybe everything coming suddenly to a standstill ... Some residual of that sensation ... I've thought about it. But I don't know. I don't think it is pain they are afraid of."

"Casey is so rough with them ..."

"They have to be restrained to prevent compression fractures."

That was not what she meant; she believed he knew it. "He corners them," she said. "They're trapped. They don't have a choice."

She didn't expect an answer; she just wanted Dr. Quill to know how she felt. She wanted to get away from here.

"You're pale," said Dr. Quill. "Go get some lunch. I know you think you're not hungry, but believe me, you'll feel better."

"I'll never be able to eat," she said. "Food would taste like cardboard."

In the dining room, she sat at a table alone, and to her shame, her salivary juices sprang like sap from a tree, and the food on her tray tasted like roast pork and mashed potatoes and gravy, and peas and carrots and chocolate pudding and milk.

Matthew Ryder on his way out leaned over her shoulder and said in a low voice that she was to come early and alone to seminar and have dinner with him and Gilda and Rex.

9. <u>Mrs. Quill</u>

Morning came with a rare summer drizzle that Mrs. Quill hoped would lift by the time she'd had breakfast, since her umbrella was in her car. On her way through the tunnel, she made a detour to the kitchen, just to say hello. There was more she'd like to say to Ynez, but hello would have to do for now.

Even hello might be more than Ynez wanted to hear. Though fluent in English and Spanish, as well as her native Basque, Ynez had an antipathy for the spoken word that she hadn't given up when her mental balance was restored. It had something to do with having being lied to.

According to Ynez, what was important didn't need to be said. But it seemed to Mrs. Quill that complex transactions -- technical information, where to find things, when to do what -- must be explicit. There is no body language for tomorrow or a mile away. Nor of the words that draw people together, tell them where they stand with each other.

Ynez would say that silence makes it possible for people to put up with each other, that words make them hate each other and hate themselves. Words can kill.

Mrs. Quill could see some truth to that. Certainly, too many words had passed between the two of them. She regretted the words with which she herself, fifteen years ago, had revealed that she was pregnant by Leonard Thorel. It was not the illegitimacy that Ynez disapproved; she had borne a child and refused to marry the father. Nor did Ynez care that Leonard was married, since in her opinion Olive was a ninny who deserved whatever she got. But the words that would have let Ynez know that Leonard was her half-brother hadn't been spoken until she was thirteen and as promised to him as a thirteen-year-old can be, and she had never gotten over it.

Mrs. Quill didn't know what else she could have done. A lie would have served only until Ynez could see Ellen's likeness to Leonard and to Ynez herself. Mrs. Quill couldn't have lied in any case. According to her precepts, lying was prohibited among intimates and allowable with others only in extremity and by omission. By her precepts, one faced up to what one had done, hoped for mercy and took the consequences. So she had said the awful words and watched her hope of friendship with Ynez slip away. And then, overestimating Ynez's capacity for forgiveness, Mrs. Quill had welcomed her into her small household, welcomed her devotion to the baby.

The arrangement couldn't have provided Ynez better opportunity for revenge. During the early years, the balance favored Mrs. Quill, who took breaks during her night's work to nurse and cuddle her infant. Putting aside dignity and uttering gibberish, she rejoiced in Ellen's growing capacity for speech, for humanity, for she believed that human beings were not born but made. By accumulation, in close relationship.

Ynez would say, had said, that what was important between two people could be said with the eyes. Ynez rarely looked at Mrs. Quill, or anyone, and it was easy to assume she was paying no attention. But her occasional, wide open gaze made it obvious that she hadn't missed a thing. Sometimes it seemed to Mrs. Quill that Ellen should know Ynez was her aunt and that she, Ellen, had a father who didn't know she existed and a sister, LeahNell. Then Ynez would turn that gaze on Mrs. Quill and she would hold her tongue, and the accumulating silences tilted the balance.

Mrs. Quill recalled that in Little Wood she had liked to help in the kitchen and in the garden, for the simple pleasure of being close to Ynez. She had thought it charming that Leonard would sit in wordless communication with Ynez, he perched on a sawhorse in the hospital garden while she tied up beans. Mrs. Quill had been delighted to see Leonard's five year old daughter LeahNell sitting at Ynez's feet gathering up the perfect spirals of Ynez's potato parings, the two of them exchanging glances and messages without making a sound. Those séances had not seemed unnatural.

But with Ellen, Ynez's caretaking became overtaking, and the day came when Ellen in her mother's arms reached out to Ynez. Daily, Mrs. Quill came upon her daughter and Ynez silently communicating matters of great significance for each other and no other, and then a hollow ache began to grow in her. There was a word for what Mrs. Quill felt then, felt yet, an ugly word for an ugly, self-diminishing feeling, and it was Jealousy.

Sometimes, she wondered if she was imagining things. Ellen was simply a private person, as private as she herself, and seemed happy to remain so. But oh! Ynez could penetrate that privacy.

And now, despite the breach and Ynez's choosing to return to the intermediate ward, Mrs. Quill felt responsible for her.

Under the pipe-and-conduit-girded ceiling she went on to the fork of the yellow tube of tunnel. On the left were the inmate dining rooms. She turned right. Outfitted in stainless steel from refrigerator wall to steaming vats to smoking grills, the kitchen looked more clinical than any examining room or surgery or autoclave room Mrs. Quill had ever seen. Even the aromas of coffee and sausage and baking bread were sanitized.

Among the cooks at their various stations, Ynez seemed dwarfed by the armament of pots and kettles, the arsenal of cleavers and spatulas and ladles. At a long table, wearing a white butcher's apron over her daisy-print dress, she was wielding a paring knife, slicing green onions several at a time and discarding roots and withered ends into a rolling tripod bucket at her feet. Mrs. Quill approached and stopped at the end of the counter. The little Basque woman glanced up, acknowledged Mrs. Quill with a nod and turned her attention back to her work. Her fingers lingered a moment on the onions before she swept them into a stainless steel bowl and scooped up another handful.

In her lisping contralto, she spent her words quickly, answering Mrs. Quill's questions before she could ask them: "I'm doing all right. My bed is near a window and the mattress is okay. The other women don't keep me awake."

"Let me know if you need anything." Mrs. Quill could think of nothing more to say.

A faint, unfamiliar flush suffused Ynez's cheeks and she turned away. It didn't look like a hot flash.

Mrs. Quill said goodbye and got as far as the door before a convoy of portable steel kitchens on their way to and from the infirmary tunnel blocked her way. While she waited, she studied Ynez across the great, steaming engine of a kitchen. Something about her had changed. Mrs. Quill doubted that Ynez had hot flashes. She seemed too vital, too uncompromised. She was still trim and graceful. Certainly, she had not lost her touch with food, a skill approaching sorcery. When Mrs. Quill detected a piquancy of garlic in the institutional scrambled eggs, she knew where it had come from.

She darted through a break in the convoy, only to retreat from another wave propelled by inmates focused on the thrust through the passage to the kitchen. She was in Ynez's line of vision and would have made comedy of her entrapment. But Ynez didn't look up from cupping a tomato in her hand, caressing it, before she took up a knife to slice it.

Across the traffic, Mr. Wheeler entered from the tunnel. He waved and Mrs. Quill waved back. The last of the caravan had come through the door, lining up bumper to bumper like a miniature freight train against the back wall of the kitchen.

At the top of the stairs, Mrs. Quill let herself into the hall to Staff Dining. The night nurses from Admissions were in line in front of her, lively young women with their second wind for the breakfast social hour after their all-night vigil, their hair and makeup freshened.

Makeup. Lipstick. Ynez was wearing lipstick.

Ynez had never worn makeup before. With a primping gesture, she'd poked fun at other women and their vanity. But there she had been, in the kitchen, with a cupid's bow artfully contoured in a shade of orange-red that vibrated against her honey-gold complexion. Nothing else had changed; it was not a complete makeover, but to Mrs. Quill's mind, something more specific. Lipstick was a beacon, a signal. The languor of Ynez's movements, the way her fingers lingered on the onion and cupped the tomato told Mrs. Quill the signal had been received. Ynez had a boyfriend.

Ynez, who'd scorned men for forty years. Ynez, fifty-three years old, although she didn't look it. Ynez, an inmate.

But who could it be? What inmate -- if he was an inmate -- was normal enough to engage Ynez's interest and intact enough to return it?

Oh yes, the little romances happened: Clarence, who wore the chef's hat and made hamburgers and rootbeer floats in the canteen, whose brain was shorted out by congenital syphilis, would circulate between the counter and a seat at a corner table where a lanky, red-haired schizophrenic woman waited out his duty hours sipping lemon coke after lemon coke, which he paid for out of his wage. And there was the occasional pregnancy, ignored -- because what could you do about it? -- until it was so imminent that something had to be done, arrangements made, with disruptive outside contacts. Staff would put off acknowledging a rogue pregnancy in the hope the problem would disappear by some natural process. And sometimes something natural, or unnatural, did occur, the problem go away, and everyone would take a deep breath and forget about it, except for the little niggling wonder: who's next and how did this happen in the first place?

Out of the corner of her eye, Mrs. Quill noticed Mr. Wheeler in the doorway to the hall. What was he was doing here when his shift had already begun? She recalled his admonition a few months ago: "There is a reason. Have faith and it will be revealed to you." Was *this* what was to be revealed to her -- that Ynez had a boyfriend?

She knew better than to take it for granted, but it had never occurred to her that inmates, mind and body sundered by electroshock and drugs, could be capable of more than the ecstasies of puppy love. What opportunities could they have? Even those with grounds privileges were confined to open areas and daylight hours.

She guessed the possibilities were limited only by the scope of her own imagination. Anything free people might do after ten p.m. could be done as well in the daytime, and it was an easy wander off the baseball field to the farm road and the acres of towering cornstalks and beanfields. There were the tales of the old tunnels, which were supposedly sealed off. Yes, for a couple of highly motivated inmates, conception might be unlikely but it was not impossible.

Maybe it was not an inmate. The tales of the tunnels included whispers and asides about Casey. Not only staff, but inmates too would testify, often garbled and incoherent but specific as to person. Just last year, Clarissa had wandered the ward with an anguished stare. When she could get someone's attention, her message was a gasp and the name "Casey," followed by a silence and then a deep breath and a torrent of words. Nurse after nurse and attendant after attendant patted her on the arm and discounted her distress as a figment of her involutional melancholia. Mrs. Quill would not have dismissed Clarissa's or any story, but she worked at night and things got to her by hearsay and long after the fact.

She hoped to God it wasn't Casey. Surely Ynez had that much sense.

Breakfast tray in hand, Mrs. Quill paused in the entry to the staff dining room and glanced around. The tables were empty except for the night nurses at the far end, and one other. There, Dr. Rex McFall's eyes met hers and locked briefly. He was with Dr. Ryder, and she hesitated. Then a hot flash surged up from her feet, and she told herself, *He's here, you're here; Dr. Ryder can fend for himself.*

The flush rose as she headed for their table. There were four chairs, one covered with a leather-elbowed corduroy jacket, evidently Dr. McFall's, since he was in shirtsleeves.

Rex McFall's eyebrows rose in alarm and his dimples vanished.

"Good morning, Dr. McFall," she said, setting down her tray. She pulled out the empty chair and sat down while he mumbled a generic response.

"Good morning," said Dr. Ryder, stage-hearty.

Her face and neck burning, she spied his glass of water, untouched. She reached for it. "May I?"

"Everything I have is yours," said Dr. Ryder.

Inexplicable female behavior. At the moment, she didn't care what they thought. She drank and set down the glass, but held onto it with both hands. "Dr. McFall, I've been looking for you," she said.

The reappearance of one cheek dimple -- *For little ol' me?* -- made it easy for her to be nonequivocal. "When can we talk?"

"Your place or mine? Office, that is."

She thought fast; she wanted the advantage of her own territory but the nursing office would be bustling by the time she got through breakfast.

"Why not right now?" said Dr. Ryder. He had bolted the

last of his oatmeal. "What better time? Neutral territory."

He got to his feet, picked up his cup of coffee, jostled Rex McFall and muttered an aside meant to be heard: "Ha ha. Caught. Ignominiously found out."

Dr. McFall glowered at his colleague's retreating back, then glanced at his own sausage and scrambled eggs and biscuits sorrowfully, as if they had soured on the plate. He picked up his fork. "What can I do for you." It was not a question.

"I don't see how you do it." Mrs. Quill let go the glass and spooned her grapefruit.

Halfway to his mouth, his forkful of eggs jerked. "Do what?"

Her grapefruit was pink and ripe and sweet. "Look so fresh in the mornings after you've been circulating the wards all night." She eased her spoon into the next segment. "But you're young. I certainly couldn't."

He was silent for a moment, masticating egg, spearing sausage. "I don't see how you can do *that* -- eat grapefruit without squirting it in your eye."

"Patience," she said. "Finesse." He had handed her the advantage; she wondered if he realized it. "So much for how. Tell me why. Why you do it."

"You mean, why does a Ph.D. in psychology pretend to be a lowly attendant to the absurd and incompetent, leaving the comfort of home and friends and a reasonable bedtime to prowl the wards at night?"

"Something like that."

"What difference does it make?"

"The difference is, from midnight until eight in the morning I'm responsible for this entire hospital. I must know who's working for me, and they must be accountable for their actions. I don't want things going on that I don't know about. I don't want my good work sabotaged. Whether these inmates are absurd and incompetent is beside the point. Their welfare is our responsibility. I'm asking you to account for yourself."

"The psychology department is independent of the custodial staff. I'm not employed by the nursing office."

"In presenting yourself as an attendant you claim to be our employee. And you are somehow getting into places you shouldn't have access to. I have a pretty good idea how. What I want to know is why. What are you up to?"

"What am I up to." He nudged his plate aside, placed his hands palms down on the table as if to push away. He hesitated, then centered his coffee in front of him and leaned back in his chair. "I'm trying to figure out how things work. Not how it's supposed to work or how you think it works, but what actually happens. Who does what to whom."

"What do you mean? You've been here -- what? Two years? Three? You know the routine. There is no mystery."

"Then you tell me. How does the system work? Who does what to whom?"

She opened her mouth, closed it. "Be specific," she said finally. "Or, assuming that how things work is not as simple as it looks, what is the problem? What are you trying to fix?" She had a pretty good idea: They might have the title Doctor, but psychologists had no authority over lesser personnel, no authority beyond the classroom and the admissions ward. To get into wards other than Admissions, they had to check out a key or call ahead. That surely rankled.

He reached into the pocket of his jacket on the chair and withdrew a pack of cigarettes and a book of matches. "There are inmates I -- we think we can help," he said. "We want to be available to all inmates, not just new admissions and the few selected by the review board."

"We? Are you acting alone or is Dr. Ryder in this too?"

"I'm acting in behalf of the psychology department."

She pushed aside her grapefruit rind, poured milk onto her oatmeal, stirred in raisins and a shake of salt. "That was not my question."

"That's my answer." He tapped a cigarette on the table and tore out a match from the matchbook, which said "Olympia" in green letters on a red and white background. "As things stand, if certain staff have a personal grudge against certain inmates, they can bring influence to bear on their freedom and their access to therapy. When we go onto the wards or make inquiries, we hit a stone wall. What is this stone wall? What's the open-sesame? That's what I want to know."

She knew that stone wall. Even with the autonomy of

night work, she was aware of an undertow of resistance. In the weekly staff meetings and review, she felt asphyxiated by the clamor of administration, nursing, social services, everyone jostling for the least advantage, advancing territorial lines inch by inch. "We may not be as different as you think," she said.

"Oh, I think we are more different than we appear." He tapped the cigarette again. "We sit around a table together at Staff and we nod and smile and exchange pleasantries, but from the word *Go* you have a different concept of what it means to be human and why some fall by the wayside and what to do for them -- or in your case, what to do *to* them, to straighten them out, control them, stack them out of sight ..."

"Whereas you. ..."

"... try to do *for* them and then get out of their way while they help themselves."

He put the cigarette to his lips and lit it. He doused the match in his water glass and plucked a shred of tobacco from his lip. "I always put the wrong end in my mouth," he muttered. He looked around for an ash tray and, seeing none, propped the cigarette on his saucer, where it slowly snuffed itself out while he turned the Olympia matchbook over and over.

"May I remind you that until a few years ago, there was no psychology department," said Mrs. Quill. "Life was a whole lot simpler then. We understood each other. We knew what to expect, once the inmates got used to being here."

"You mean, once you got them broken in, or broke their spirit."

"That's a harsh assessment. The system did work, for most. For the rest, all we had was padded cells, restraints and hydrotherapy. Medication ... "

"... and metrazol and electroshock. Can't you imagine what it would be like to be dumped into a place like this and abandoned? With everyone around you in the same fix, it's bedlam and it feeds on itself. Of course you get out of control. Freezing up or acting bizarre are only the mildest possibilities. These people are not so much crazy as fragile."

She was surprised at his passion. Only minutes ago he'd been calling them absurd and incompetent.

"Granted it wasn't perfect," she said. "We didn't have enough staff to be flexible or to give them special attention. We did the best we could."

"On Admissions, we do have the staff, and our nurses are trained in psychiatry. Our patients have peace and quiet and someone to talk to, and they don't languish for days and weeks waiting for someone to do something for them. They don't have to mix with inmates; they're segregated from all that. They're going home. Most of them."

"Give us a little credit, please. Our old director, before the war, had no psychiatric training. Dr. Swenson has made real progress ..."

"Dr. Swenson is only superficially knowledgeable about psychodynamic theory, and less of psychotherapy ..."

"If you want my sympathy, please respect the fact that Dr. Swenson is a friend of mine."

Dr. McFall tucked in his chin. "Sorry. I got a little carried away."

"Dr. Swenson is open to new ideas and he brought you in. And it's worked pretty well, except ... for some reason we don't mesh. We should appreciate you and we do -- most of us, most of the time -- but we don't understand you and you look down your noses at us. ..." Her voice trailed off.

"...You resent us and keep us isolated and throw red herrings across our way every chance you get ..."

"... Instead of doing things above-board, you sneak around and spy on us, like an undercover agent, and ..."

"Participant observer. I'm a participant observer."

"Why didn't you bring your idea to Staff? Why didn't you do this legitimately?"

"Why didn't I ask permission? Because I didn't want to give Dr. Swenson a chance to say no. I didn't want a committee telling me how to do it." He sank back against his chair. "I didn't think it was anyone else's business."

The dining room had emptied and the waitress began removing their dishes onto a cart. Dr. McFall hung onto his coffee. Mrs. Quill kept hers also and handed over her oatmeal bowl, not quite empty. The waitress retreated and Rex McFall sighed heavily. "We don't send all of them home."

Mrs. Quill waited.

"We can't help all of them in their first thirty days. If we can't pull them together enough to face a staff review, that becomes their failure and they're not prepared for what happens, and *then* they're terrified and lost and abandoned. It may not be bedlam but it's failure. And they still have to learn how to get along, and we're not available to help them any more. I don't know exactly what happens then, but for some reason, they apparently decompensate pretty fast."

Mrs. Quill sat up straight. She knew what happened; she'd seen it time and again. "You want to know what happens to a patient who gets back-warded? Let me tell you. The first time she goes to a dance, she's eager to see her old friends from Admissions, but they want nothing to do with her. Because to acknowledge any connection means it could happen to them too. That first dance often precipitates a psychotic episode, and then there's no going back."

She remembered how Rochelle, newly transferred to Intermediate, kept her end of her room awake with her preparations a day in advance of the dance -- laying out her clothes, rolling her hair on curlers, chattering happily. How the next night when Mrs. Quill came on duty, Rochelle was strapped into a Posey belt, in seclusion, bloodied by her own teeth and fingernails, and scheduled for a series of electroshock.

"Maybe we're doing patients no favor, letting them think themselves a cut above the inmates," said Dr. McFall.

Now they were leaning together, elbows propped on the table. "There is an inmate named Rochelle," said Mrs. Quill. "She's been here for three years, on Intermediate, sometimes on Violent, in and out of seclusion. Recently, she has improved enough to be on the grounds with supervision and go to the dances."

"I've seen her around. Pretty woman. Full lips, wide cheekbones, kind of a post-coital flush ..." He caught himself. "... A dreamy expression. Unusual in that she still has her teeth. But not all of her cerebral connections. Doesn't talk much ..."

"That's Rochelle."

"... Ask her a question, any question, and thirty seconds and several shifts of visual focus later, she will mouth a word or two, sigh and say, 'I guess.'"

She told him about Rochelle. "There's an attendant called Casey. I doubt that he's welcome on your ward, so maybe you don't know him."

"Oh, I know Casey, all right. And I hear the rumors, if they are rumors. He hangs around the canteen. Fortunately, the patients on Admissions are safe." He looked at Mrs. Quill, eyebrows raised. "Unless and until they graduate to a ward."

"Working nights, I miss a lot of what goes on in the daytime, but my ... sources tell me that the canteen is where Casey picks his prey, keeps track of them."

"We should put our sources together and keep track of *him*." Dr. McFall reached into his jacket pocket, and as he pulled out the cigarette pack, the jacket slid to the floor. He dropped the cigarettes, snatched for them and the jacket, which up-ended and spilled out his collection of keys. "Hell, spit and damn," he muttered. He rehung the jacket, parked the keys on the table, and took out a cigarette.

Mrs. Quill held out her hand. He looked at it, then down at his keys. "Let me see," she said. He put the keys into her hand.

Among the large, pronged keys to the wards was a dainty one that she recognized as the key to a medicine closet. "This one you have no reasonable use for," she said.

She popped the chain, removed the key and pocketed it, then squeezed the chain together again and laid it on the table. Then she sat back, eyeing the rest of the keys, and picked up her coffee cup.

He watched her for a moment, then lit the cigarette. "There is a patient, an inmate ... I'll always think of her as a patient ... on Intermediate, Alma Duffy, who says you two are from the same town. Little Wood, I think she said."

Mrs. Quill stopped in mid-sip. For a decrepit old lady confined to a ward, Alma was certainly making herself known. It had been a vain hope that no one would take her seriously. Mrs. Quill had been reckoning without Rex McFall.

He was gazing at her thoughtfully. "I'd like to take Miss Duffy off the ward occasionally, give her a little outing," he said. "I know I can't do it without going through channels. I'd like your help." He drained his cup and snuffed out the cigarette, and pocketed the remaining keys.

She felt lightheaded, fatigue catching up with her, but also a sensation like a change in the direction of the wind.

"If you want to pass for an attendant," she said, "you should get yourself a decent key chain. That little pop-chain will fall apart any time someone snatches at it."

They left the dining room, and down the hall, the student nurses in a cluster outside the classroom greeted Dr. McFall in a fugue and counterpoint of birdcalls. One of the students stood apart, waiting as he and Mrs. Quill approached. Still and slender, with a thick swatch of hair bound in a net below her nurse's cap, the girl was a dark-haired, brown-eyed image of Ellen.

"Mrs. Quill, here's someone you should meet," said Dr. McFall. "LeahNell Thorel, from Little Wood."

"Thank you, I've already had the pleasure."

Indeed she had. She liked to welcome the new girls and let them know who she was.

When this group arrived, three weeks ago, she had hesitated, struck by the familiar look of LeahNell, who with her dark hair had a night and day resemblance to Ellen. It had never occurred to Mrs. Quill that Leonard's other, legitimate, daughter might train to be a nurse.

Her first impulse had been to turn away, go home for breakfast, avoid the dining room for the next three months. She'd seen the folly of that: LeahNell wouldn't recognize her -- she was only five years old when Mrs. Quill left Little Wood, and she'd known her as Mary Macpherson. So Mrs. Quill had set down her tray at one table and had gone to the students' table to extend her welcome. She'd pretended that no one name or face was more distinctive than another, and was amused by Cleo Weaver ("My name's Cleopa(y)tra Weaver -- no kidding! But everyone calls me Cleo ...") while acutely aware of LeahNell Thorel in her peripheral visual field.

After that, it had been easier and one morning she fell in with the girl after breakfast when they were headed in the same direction, Mrs. Quill to the parking lot and LeahNell to class. They hadn't far to go but they'd taken their time. Lightheaded after working all night, Mrs. Quill was grateful for LeahNell's easy small talk: She, LeahNell, was the world's slowest eater and the other girls had gone on ahead. ... Was Mrs. Quill glad to be going home and to bed? ... She herself liked nights, her favorite shift.

Relieved of the need to talk, Mrs. Quill had studied LeahNell, marveled at the resemblances and the differences. Like Leonard, she was slender and long-limbed, with his long, pointed chin and the squint lines at the corners of his eyes. Her voice echoed Leonard's oboe undertones, his reflective pauses. Not much evidence of Olive, except in her darker coloring.

LeahNell said The Farm was much nicer than she'd been led to expect. Almost the first thing she had done was to look up someone she knew from Little Wood.

"It was so strange and sad to find Miss Alma Duffy old and blind and just sitting in the dayroom. She used to be schools superintendent and she taught me classics in high school. She has changed so much. But she's not as different as she looks. She recognized my voice and we had a visit like old times and ...," LeahNell's voice became hushed, "... Miss Duffy isn't crazy. Not a bit."

A mixed pleasure it had been, getting acquainted with LeahNell. And now, when the girl focused on Dr. McFall and gave her only the briefest acknowledgement, Mrs. Quill didn't know whether to feel slighted, or relieved to be, for a while at least, saved from being ignominiously found out.

10. <u>Mrs. Quill</u>

Mr. Wheeler was waiting for her at the curb.

As she approached, he walked toward her fixing her with his startling eyes, turquoise in the brilliant sunlight, the drizzle having blown away. He gave only a nod in greeting before he began to address her unspoken question.

"Oliver and Jepson have come to me with an alarming, hideous story. Why such evil visited itself upon them is beyond my understanding."

Mrs. Quill was quite talked out for the morning and she had hoped she was on her way home to bed. Under the shade of a locust tree, she snuggled her cape around her and listened.

"I hardly know where to begin," said Mr. Wheeler in a voice meant not to carry beyond the two of them. "It's not a story for a lady's ears, but something must be done and I'm not sure that Dr. Swenson is inclined to take testimony from inmates seriously."

She waited.

"It seems that Jepson and Oliver have been witness to a brutal ... assault upon a female patient. In the old tunnel." He looked away, an unfamiliar flush flooding his neck. "I'm sorry, Ma'am. I truly wish there were anyone else I could trust with the matter."

Her skin prickled with gooseflesh. "You're quite right to come to me. Anything that concerns a patient is my concern. Please, tell me what *is* the matter." Rather, she thought, confirm my suspicion that Casey was the perpetrator.

"We hear rumors of this sort of thing, of course, but now we have a witness -- two witnesses... themselves victims, I fear, to have had to bear such a sight... and I know them well and I will vouch for their truthfulness..."

"Please, Mr. Wheeler. Was it Casey? I see. And the woman ...?"

"They said it was Rochelle. You remember she was on Women's Violent for some years and had recently transferred to

Intermediate. I'm not sure how that came about. I couldn't find anyone who seemed to know. Just that she'd been pretty steady for a while. But surely a transfer has to be approved in Review."

With a sinking feeling, she realized no such move had gone through Review. "Exactly what did Jep and Ollie tell you?"

"You know how they go back and forth a while before they get synchronized and start to make sense. It finally came out they were taking the old tunnel, where they knew they weren't supposed to be, and they heard someone coming and they hid. Or, ... no, they heard some commotion and they hid until they could see what was going on. ... Let me think a moment." He closed his eyes, held his hand over his forehead.

Poor Mr. Wheeler, she thought. This was more than he could handle, maybe too close to home. She realized she had no idea of the nature of his secret shame. "I need to hear it from Jep and Ollie," she said. "Right now."

He winced, nodded. "They're at work in the kitchen, but I'll bring them."

She found a quiet room upstairs in the administration building, and pretty soon the three came trudging up the walk, Mr. Wheeler in the middle and, flanking him, Jep and Ollie in their blue shirts and brown trousers, their hair parted in the middle and slicked down. It seemed to her that the only times they were separated without losing their equilibrium was when Mr. Wheeler was doing the separating. A balance wheel, a pole star was what he was.

But when she closed the door in the little room, Jep and Ollie took adjacent seats, elbows touching on the arm rest, facing Mrs. Quill.

"Mrs. Quill, you know Jepson and Oliver, don't you?" said Mr. Wheeler.

They didn't wait to be acknowledged.

"Yes, Ma'am, Jepson Frohmarkel, Jr., that's me," and, "Oliver Slade, that's me," they said in their flat treble voices.

"But when Casey says *Jepanollie!* we know who he's talking to, and we pay attention. 'Jepanollie!' he hollers at us down the tunnel. But this time we keep running. Because we saw ..."

"Slow down, Oliver," said Mr. Wheeler. "You're getting

ahead of yourself."

Jep and Ollie scratched their foreheads, Jep with his left hand, Ollie with his right.

"Here's a chair, Mr. Wheeler," said Mrs. Quill. "Start over, Ollie, Jep," she said. "Take your time."

They looked at each other and Ollie nodded slightly, then began. "Jep and Ollie, we like the old tunnels because down here it's quiet. No voices coming between us, mixing us up about where Jepson begins and ends and where Oliver ends and begins. They call us ..."

"... Tweedledum and Tweedledee, and they say that neither one of us ever goes to the toilet without the other. That's mostly true because what else can you do when they lock the doors and take everybody in all together before breakfast and after breakfast and before lunch and after lunch and before supper and after supper and before bed ..."

"... and no times in between and they lock the door again so you better be careful not to drink too much."

"They say we finish sentences for each other and that's mostly true too because how many sentences do they let in this place when all we do is sleep and go to the toilet and eat and work in the kitchen and help the student nurses and talk to the psychology boys? We know all the words they'll let us have and if Oliver says half of them, that leaves the other half for Jepson. Isn't that right, Oliver?"

"That's right, Jepson. And they say that looking at us they can't tell us one from the other, and maybe that's true because that Dr. Quill with his radio dial and telephone wires and that altar he lays you on and ..."

"... everybody's praying before he plugs you in and you make the trip to heaven and back, or maybe hell, you can't be sure which because they take your thoughts when you go in and they don't give them back to you until you ..."

Mr. Wheeler looked at his watch.

"... wake up and one thing about electricity is, it peels off all the knobs and snags a little here and a little there until you're even, so sure we look alike."

"But tell Mrs. Quill what happened in the tunnel."

"They're doing fine, Mr. Wheeler. Please go on."

"We're not Casey's boys anymore," said Jep. "When they got us ..."

"... pared down and paired off, they let Mr. Wheeler take us back to his ward. He's our attendant now. We do what he tells us and he takes care of us. We don't have to listen to Casey except when we're in the ..."

"... tunnel and he's in the tunnel and there's no one else there, to keep him from stretching out his arms and clapping our heads together. Sure Rochelle was there but she couldn't stop him. The only way you can stop Casey's arms is run. So we ran. Because we saw."

"What we saw was ..."

"What we saw ..."

"And they say we can't leave The Farm because we work side by side and what ..."

"... restaurant is going to hire both of us to do the same job? They want a cook and they want a dishwasher. We figure the dishes have to be washed and they have to be ..."

"What we saw ..."

"... dried and that's two half-jobs, right? And food has to be washed and cut up and it ..."

"... has to be grilled or fried and that's four quarter-jobs, right? So Jepson has a half- ..."

"... job and two quarter-jobs and Oliver has two quarter-jobs and a half-job, right? And that's ..."

"... two whole jobs for Jepson and Oliver. So who says we can't ...? Her hair was ..."

"When we see her hair we think it's a dragon but even in the old tunnel there's no such thing as a dragon so we guess..."

"... it's snakes. Big snakes and medium-size snakes and a lot of little snakes. All twisting and coiling and whipping around. But we didn't hear any..."

"... hissing and rattling, which is about all the noise a snake can make, snakes don't grunt and snakes ..."

Mr. Wheeler sprang from his chair. "Now watch your language. Be careful how you talk to a lady."

"... don't cry. And we see this big snake a-rutting ..."

"Oliver! Stop this right now."

"It's all right, Mr. Wheeler. Please sit down."

"... and a-humping on her, and she a-twisting and crying. And when he's through, he rolls off and she slithers into the tiniest little ball against the wall and ..."

"... cries. And she's Rochelle. And he stands up."

"That Casey. He."

"And we've got to tell Mr. Wheeler."

Wound down, Jep and Ollie looked at each other and sighed. Mission accomplished.

Mr. Wheeler's face was red and he seemed shrunken. "Thank you, Jepson, Oliver. You've done a good service. If Mrs. Quill has no questions, you may go back to work."

"We did right, Oliver."

"You bet, Jepson."

They stood up and left without a backward glance.

Mr. Wheeler was still seated, his hands palms up on the armrests as if in supplication. "What are we going to do, Mrs. Quill?"

"Oh, Mr. Wheeler." She took a deep breath. "I don't know how much good Dr. Swenson will do, but that's where I'll have to start."

In spite of the claim of loyalty she'd made earlier to Rex McFall, she had to admit to herself that Ronald Swenson was flawed. He called Casey a necessary evil and that evil hadn't hit him close to home. Unlike most of the staff, Dr. Swenson wasn't a fugitive in any sense. He was here because he wanted to be here. He liked the autonomy, the simplicity and implied safety of the rural life. Perhaps most of all he liked being in charge.

"I guess all we can do is the best we can."

Mr. Wheeler glanced at her and she guessed he thought she'd lost her bearings.

"For a start," she said, "Casey takes every weekend off, which, of course, he is entitled to as head attendant of his ward. You're head attendant of your ward and as far as I know, you've never taken a Sunday off."

He sat up straight. "I ..."

"I know."

She did know. It had to do with denying himself any association with his former calling. "But now we need you free to stay close to Casey. Can you do it?"

"I can. And I will." He looked grim and focused.

She swallowed her nursely impulse to ask him to keep her informed. He would, of course, being Mr. Wheeler.

She had to tell Dr. Swenson. He was entitled -- he was *obliged* -- to know what was going on. And if anything further went wrong, ... She couldn't *not* tell him.

He would drag his heels; he'd invoke the democratic process, if he didn't table it outright. She foresaw weeks of haggling at staff meeting, or civilly and formally confronting Casey, giving him every opportunity to deny, to lie. And, because Casey would be next to impossible to replace, perhaps admonishing him, and then looking the other way. She wished she could go to Dr. Swenson with not a problem but a solution, even a *fait accompli*.

She was bone-tired. She'd have to sleep on it. If she could sleep. One thing was clear: It was Dr. Swenson's business to deal with Casey. *She* would take care of Rochelle.

11. <u>Rex</u>

Rex knew that he should feel guilty about what he was doing, but he and Gilda had fallen in love and it had nothing to do with Matthew. Who would never understand.

Matthew considered himself open-minded, enlightened, permissive, but in truth, his postures were absurdly traditional. Didactic therapy hadn't solved his need to control. "Talk about whatever you please," he had said on the night of the last dinner party; "I have no agenda." Hah, thought Rex; talk about passive-aggressive.

Rex and Gilda were now hoping to persuade Matthew -- without giving themselves away, of course -- that they needed a fourth person to square their threesome, a triangle in more ways than Matthew knew. Because three's a crowd -- someone is always on the outside looking in. That was Matthew, and they didn't want him to know it.

There were good reasons for a foursome. The pair is the primary social unit in our society, so a quartet would look more normal in public appearances -- the ballgames, the occasional movie in Millennium... And they needed input to keep them from getting stale. This student, LeahNell, was intelligent enough not to bore them, and she was housebroken; she wouldn't embarrass them. She wasn't afraid of Matthew and his daunting intellect and viper tongue. Rex dared to hope she'd even turn Matthew's head.

She's perfect, Rex told himself. Lonely but choosy. She's repressed, so our Hot Young Bloods put her off. She likes older men; she thinks we're safe, and she's an intellectual snob.

He and Matthew, a pair of psychologists on the other side of thirty-five, were made to order for her. Perhaps most important, she didn't have the frame of reference to know how to interpret what she might see.

LeahNell would have Rex's vote for no other reason than the way she'd waded through Hopkins' bullshit the other night. Hopkins! Rex wondered if *he* had been that callow and presumptuous as a graduate student. He was afraid he had been.

Except for the fact that Hopkins had only two expressions, mouth wide open or a heavy-lidded, full-lipped pout, Rex had hardly noticed him until that Friday night two weeks ago when the interns walked into Matthew's house for their weekly seminar and the girls were already there. Hopkins had squawked, "No fair!" or words to that effect. Matthew pointed out that the young ladies were excellent subjects for study and told him to go soak his head. Words to that effect. Hopkins sulked the rest of the evening, recovering when it was time to escort the young ladies home.

The following Sunday, Rex and Matthew and Gilda had gone to the hospital dining room for supper. At the adjacent large, round table the six student nurses greeted them and then went on with their meal.

In marched the interns with their trays, crowding into the girls' table. They paid Rex and Matthew no attention, their cue for the Elders to ignore them. The usual adolescent conversation ensued but pretty soon, Hopkins was sprawling into the center of the table, his elbows edging out Francis on one side and Evans on the other.

"In social psychology," said Hopkins, "we'd put us on a space diagram."

So far, so good, thought Rex; he's a pedantic ass, but at least he's thinking psychology and talking psychology, which is what he's supposed to be doing here.

"On this diagram, we'd be three dots in a straight line," Hopkins said, "you nurses on one end, Matthew and Rex on the other end, and we interns in the middle ... "

Not so, thought Rex, but let's see where he's taking it.

"... To get to them you'd have to go through us. In the natural order of things. They did an end run and now you're in the middle ... " Hopkins caught himself. *"They're* in the middle. We'd be better off with a triangle. No sense fighting each other for the next two months."

Pretty transparent, thought Rex, and LeahNell hadn't let Hopkins get away with it. "Correction, please," she said. *"You'd* be better off."

"Yeah," said Patsy. "What's in it for us?"

Hopkins surely knew the Elders were at the next table, but that didn't stop him. Matthew had told each class that The Farm was only a testing ground for practicing what they learned in school, and Hopkins took him at his word. He went around with his mouth a-flap, and when he bruised someone, he'd say, "This is a laboratory, not real life. We're here to make mistakes. Your feelings, my feelings are not important." So Rex knew that Hopkins would turn this situation to his advantage.

"We'd all have more fun if we pooled our resources," said Hopkins.

"What resources?" said Patsy. "Besides equal access to Rex and Matthew?" *Touché.*

Patsy too was aware that the Elders were at the next table, but she was a brazen hussy, which was part of her charm. Everyone else gave Rex and Matthew a nervous glance, and LeahNell blushed. She would.

Hopkins pouted until he had everyone's attention, then said, "Gossip, professional wisdom, the pleasure of each other's company?"

They'd shaken hands across the table all around. Peace. An alliance of sorts. Not that the Elders had seen any more of them than before. The other "resources" seemed to have taken precedence. They made a show of sniping at each other in the dining room, but Matthew said he saw them on the grounds in the evenings, more or less all together right after supper, then in pairs when it started to get dark. Having gotten their collective foot in the door, the Young Bloods now wanted it both ways: take the girls into the bushes after dark, but keep them out of the seminar evenings.

This arrangement seemed to please some of the girls too; the next Friday night, LeahNell and Cleo were the only girls who accepted the invitation to join Matthew and Gilda and Rex, with the interns.

Gilda had broached the subject of a fourth person, but Matthew was noncommittal and for a while, it was an awkward evening. LeahNell was no help; she sat in a corner and leafed through *The Lonely Ones.* Not a smile. Rex wondered if she had no sense of humor.

Cleo had been working on her personal style. She carried her chin in the air and spouted "transference" and "empathy" and "projection" and the like every chance she got. She now wore horn-rimmed glasses, and Rex took the liberty of looking through the lenses to confirm his suspicion that they were clear glass. He flattered himself that she was trying to impress him until he saw that she was conspicuously avoiding eye-contact with the solemn and scholarly Francis, of all people. If she could convert him to her frisky approach to life, it would be an improvement, Rex thought; but that evening, Francis dared nothing beyond sneaking a peek at her when he thought no one was looking.

As usual, the Young Bloods aired their traumas, flaunted their weaknesses and incompetencies -- they actually enjoyed having them pointed out to them. Masochism wasn't a pre-requisite for learning to be a therapist that Rex knew of, but it seemed to come with the territory. LeahNell with her need for concealment and saving face was almost refreshing.

Finally, it seemed that Hopkins couldn't stand her nose in a book, her silence any longer. "I can't decide whether you're narcissistic or neurotic," he told her.

She ignored him.

He tried to draw her out about the trauma he supposed caused her ulcer. He asked questions she answered with other questions. He pleaded: "Don't you understand that I'm trying to help you?"

"You are very helpful," she said. "I'm in training to be... um, an enigma."

Oho, thought Rex; she's got a mean streak after all.

"Is that why you're so standoffish about our games?" Hopkins flashed, therapeutic posture forgotten.

She flashed right back at him, "I like the kiddie games -- Kick-the-Can and Three-Deep -- just fine, but I don't care for the games in the bushes."

"You're repressed," he said. "You're inhibited. ...."

Evans, a young man with an earnest case of acne, interrupted before Hopkins could add that ultimate putdown, "frigid," which would permit Hopkins to deny that she found him resistible.

"Your inhibitions will cost you health and peace of mind," Evans said, attempting to fix her with his version of a hypnotic stare. "You must learn to let go, give way to your impulses. It is healthy to express your feelings and desires, and unnatural to suppress them."

Cleo switched her head around and peered at him. "Not where we come from. Where we come from, natural feelings and desires will get you in trouble. My natural feelings and desires got LeahNell campused."

Evans looked at Cleo with interest, then returned to staring at LeahNell. "I am willing and able to help you," he said. His eyebrows were leaping like a villain's in a melodrama.

Matthew was scowling hard to suppress a grin. Gilda's lips were twitching, and Rex could hardly stay in his chair.

LeahNell smiled at Evans, eyebrow tilted. "Thank you, Father Sigmund," she said softly.

Rex's ribs ached with silent laughter. Matthew kind of snuffled into his hands as he sat rocking, his shoulders heaving.

Gilda and Rex exchanged glances: *We've got him.*

Now it was Friday night again, seminar night, and the Elders invited LeahNell to dinner, alone. Rex and Gilda had let Matthew think it was his idea, to treat LeahNell to "the real" Matthew and Gilda and Rex, interrupting each other without apology, padding around in their stocking feet.

LeahNell wasted no time taking off her shoes, and they took their time with dessert (Gilda's strudel ... *What a fantastic woman!*). All were sated and domestic when the doorbell rang, announcing the arrival of the seminar group.

With Cleo, the interns filed in and at first gaped at LeahNell and then made a show of ignoring her while they turned up their gems of free-association, mostly pre-scripted and rehearsed, for the scrutiny of the Elders.

But Matthew wanted to talk business. "Jep and Ollie braved the staff meeting today to make their pitch for new baseball equipment," he said. "They made a good pitch and gave a creditable account of themselves. Even Dr. Swenson was impressed. Looks like the ... what do you call the teams? ... Mavericks and Mossbacks will be subsidized. Francis, you look like a good little boy sitting on his potty. Tell me, how did it happen that those two made the request instead of you?"

Francis was straddling the piano stool, his back arched. "They don't want anyone to know yet, but they're talking about getting out. We thought it might help their case if they were more visible, if the staff could see how well they're doing before they apply for discharge."

"You've been working with them without consulting anyone?" said Matthew. "What the hell do you think you're doing? All you know about them is the little you can find in the records and their own skewed testimonials. Are they talking about leaving together?"

Francis looked surprised. "Yes. Why?"

"Just that this is nothing new. If *one* of them came to Review, I'd take it seriously. If I saw them apart and functioning, I might think they could make it. But neither of them ever goes to the bathroom without the other. Why do you think we call them Tweedledum and Tweedledee? How do you think they're going to make it on the outside? They'd be ridiculed and discredited wherever they went. Who'd even give them a job? What could they do?"

Francis threw up his hands. "Same as they do here."

"What do they do here?" said LeahNell. She was leaning into being at home, nesting in the easy chair with her sock feet curled under her.

"Kitchen," said Hopkins. "That level job would be easy to find. It's not as if they were professionals."

Matthew shook his head. "This is history repeating itself. The trouble with you kids is lack of longevity. You're wet behind the ears; you think everything that happens here is happening for the first time. You identify with the patients. Your understanding is superficial. You are so imbued with the need to be saviors and revolutionize the system that you can't see beyond the ends of your noses. You can see the similarities, but you can't see the differences. Jep and Ollie have been here for twenty-five years. They look like boys with their smooth skins and toothy grins, but they're in the neighborhood of fifty years old. They're old enough to be your fathers. Can you see either one holding up fatherhood?"

"Goddammit, Ryder, you tell us to be open-minded." Hopkins looked as if he was about to cry. "You say, think of them as patients and not inmates. Cultivate normality."

Matthew struggled for the last word, gave it up. He shoved his hands into his pockets and slumped in his chair. "All right. Sorry. But don't be surprised at what happens."

"Are they homosexual?" asked Cleo. Something funny was going on with Cleo tonight. She'd been sitting there not only quietly but as though she were far away. Rex wondered if she was making any headway with Francis.

"No, no." Matthew sounded tired. "Neither is capable of sexual interest. Drugs and electroshock render them as neutral as cheese sandwiches."

"Really?" said LeahNell. "Then why is everyone so ... um, obsessed with sex?"

"Counter-phobic bravado. Pretending to be competent where people most fear the lack of it. Competition. Actually, if leers and invitations were accepted, almost everyone in this institution, patients and curers alike, would run like rabbits ..."

Speak for yourself, Matthew, thought Rex.

"... Present company excepted, of course."

Cleo stood and beckoned urgently to LeahNell, who unraveled her tucked-in unshod feet and followed her up the stairs to the bathroom. *Girlish confidences?*

Matthew having riled them up and Rex personifying the benign if absent-minded therapist, the interns lapsed into free-association. Until Matthew interrupted. "What is it with all of you? Here you are, masochistically picking at your psychic sores, taking turns at mental masturbation. You pretend to listen to each other, but all the time you're thinking about how to present your next disclosure."

LeahNell and Cleo came back down the stairs. Cleo looked happier. She sat down by Francis, and LeahNell sank back into the big chair and tucked her feet under her.

"Well, doesn't everyone?" Hopkins smirked.

"This is not conversation. Do I recall that you desire to become therapists? You're not listening; you're talking past each other. Self-aggrandizing, pompous pricks leaning on jargon and wallowing in self-importance."

"I've had it up to here with you, Ryder." Hopkins' voice cracked. "You've got a chip on your shoulder. First you castigate us for how we handle the patients, then you ridicule our... manhood." Florid gestures. "There's no pleasing you. What's the matter, aren't you getting enough? You take your pick of the student nurses ... Is LeahNell sleeping with you? Is she sleeping with McFall too? Maybe you've got a *menage `a quatre* going ..."

Francis gripped the seat of the piano stool; Evans pushed back in his chair and braced his feet. Rex watched LeahNell. How would she take this? Her expression was one of determined blasé.

"Whoa," said Matthew. "Let's not get carried away. Do they teach you that in French 101 nowadays?"

Francis stood up. "I think we'd better go. We've worn out our welcome." He was towering over LeahNell. "Come on; we'll get you home safely."

Rex held his breath. Show-your-colors-time. Would she preserve her reputation and risk her edge with the Elders?

"No, thank you," she said. "I'll take my chances."

Cleo and the Young Bloods left, and Rex and Matthew sank back in their chairs. "The master puppeteers have done it again," said Gilda.

Rex lit a cigarette. "Dr. Ryder's Confrontation 101. I thought my face would split when that young squirt called your bluff on Jep and Ollie."

"And how they did seethe and foam about LeahNell, fueling and festering it into a great orgy. Where do they get these ideas?" Matthew was peeling the foil from a bottle of Benedictine. "Four glasses, LeahNell? No? Three it is. They are learning too much too young. Their education is making of them a generation of *voyeurs. Menage `a quatre,* indeed. I'd never even heard that phrase until I was thirty. The foreclosure of innocence advances year by year. Soon they will be chewing pornography for teething biscuits."

"They'll all hate you," LeahNell ventured. "They'll never come back."

"Hate me tonight, grudge me tomorrow. They need me, to complete their internships. They must have windmills to tilt at.

They'll be back, and it will be as though tonight didn't happen. Being an apprentice at life is never having to apologize." He pointed his glass at LeahNell. "For all our permissiveness, we are not here to be loved. We are here to do a job, to help these callow, spoon-fed youth think for themselves. We are all role-playing."

LeahNell looked ... what? Disappointed? Wondering if this included her?

Matthew held out his arms, peering over an imaginary baton. "Rex is straight man, advocate and intercessor to my villain. Gilda is all grace and beauty, the restoring mother. Her presence is all that stands between us and mayhem and murder. Allows us to sustain a higher level of tension, more productive manipulation." He spread his arms and raised his elbows. He looked like a monstrous bird of prey.

Oh, come off it, Matthew, thought Rex; your audience has gone home. He glanced at Gilda, prepared to share a rolling of eyes, and was startled to see that she was rapt and engaged. Did she *like* Matthew's posturing? Was he performing for her? A spasm of unease rippled through Rex. His cigarette jerked, tipping off a quarter-inch of ash.

"We must design a role for you, fair LeahNell," said Matthew. "Tonight you are pawn, spoils to be coveted. Sides are drawn. We must find something more. How shall we use you?"

Little does he know. Rex put aside his doubts.

"We have our assignment," said Matthew. He switched on the phonograph. "While it simmers, let us be transported on wings of euphonia. What will you have? Ravel? 'Bolero?' Too obvious. Tchaikovsky? Maudlin. Rachmaninoff?"

"Oh, yes," said LeahNell.

"Oh, no. Thanatoptic, an erotic celebration of death. Ah. Khachaturian. Here we are. To the carpet, everyone."

He held the needle delicately and set it on the record, turned off all but one lamp, and stretched out on the floor, an old routine. Rex put out his cigarette and followed, and Gilda came next. LeahNell hesitated, then unfurled out of the chair and slid to the floor. The music swelled.

"Close your eyes," Matthew told LeahNell. "Don't spy on people at their private devotions. Just listen. Free associate.

Let the music do what it will."

LeahNell blushed and closed her eyes. A moment later, she was popping up again. "That's 'Sabre Dance.' That's been on the jukeboxes for two years."

Bad timing. Rex was stroking the bottom of Gilda's foot, which was arching in response like a stretching cat.

LeahNell closed her eyes again and Rex guessed she was too naïve to make anything of it, but he knew he'd have to be more careful. How could he know for sure that Matthew's eyes were shut tight? Better keep his hands to himself.

The next band would be "Ayshe." For all its thunder, "Sabre Dance" was no more than a prelude to the most sensuous, compelling music Rex had ever heard. "Ayshe" commanded him to stop thinking, a tough assignment for it was music to make love by.

And as "Ayshe" came to an end, Matthew called an end to the evening. "Go!" he said, "And be happy..." His eyes flashed from Rex to LeahNell, his left eyebrow springing, and he ushered them out the door like the dog he was, claiming his territory. Rex was ready to howl at the moon with frustration and longing.

12. <u>LeahNell</u>

"Saber Dance" was over. LeahNell held her breath and waited for what would come next. Everyone else was silent too and then Gilda said, "Now."

It was a simple melody, but kind of wild and sweet and pulsing. It flooded LeahNell's senses like the taste of chocolate. Eyes closed, she could feel how she'd dance with it, her head tossing like a flower in the wind, her body rippling and arching like nothing Miss Olga ever taught her.

The music ebbed and flowed out of the pit of her belly, liquid with warmth. Her arms twitched with wanting to lift and fall; her feet flexed, poised to sweep into languid pirouettes and sinuous patterns across the floor. Suddenly, she thought of one warm night in Boise.

Odd that she'd recall it now -- this music reminded her not so much of swimming and then running, as she had done -- as it did of the way it made her feel: awake and shivery at first and then heavy and melting inside.

The melody faded away, almost letting her go. Then it rocked up again from somewhere deep and pulled her under. Now it *was* like swimming, and it was like the wind and the man's hand raising her hair off her neck and sending small thrills down her spine. Gooseflesh springing on her arms.

She had wondered if it wasn't just a dream. Sometimes she wished she hadn't run away, but things had taken a bad turn at the last. She guessed she had had a narrow escape.

When the music ended, its throbbing signature left her restless and thirsty for more. "What was that?" she asked. Her voice felt drowned.

"'Ayshe'," said Matthew from a long way away, his voice husky. "This is the ballet *Gayne*."

They lay on the carpet, the four of them, listening to the needle rasp on the inner groove until Matthew got up and lifted it off the record. "What shall we hear now?" he said. "Your pleasure."

"Nothing," said Gilda. "After 'Ayshe,' anything else would be anticlimactic." Her eyelids drooped, and she stood up moving like a sleepwalker.

"Then I deem the evening ended," said Matthew. "Up and away, both of you. Go forth and be happy."

He meant her -- LeahNell -- and Rex. But Rex seemed glued to the floor, as he looked from Gilda to Matthew to LeahNell, and back to Gilda again. Gilda looked away. Rex stood up. Matthew helped LeahNell into her jacket and swept open the door. "So you're quitting our company, leaving us to our connubial devices. To the winner all, eh, Rex?"

The door closed behind them. It had happened so fast. LeahNell wasn't ready for the evening to end. It seemed as if there should be something more, although she didn't know of what. She stood in the wet grass, straining to hear the music from the other side of the door.

"Ayshe" was once more swelling into the night. Rex took LeahNell by the hand and led her to his car. They rode silently, and when they reached the whitewashed old Women's Violent, he turned off the ignition and sat there looking straight ahead. LeahNell knew she should get out of the car, but she was glued to her seat watching him as he swallowed hard, tears filling his eyes.

It's not a game, she thought. He's in love with Gilda.

He turned and took LeahNell's head gently between his hands and rotated it straight ahead to face the windshield.

Oh, yes. What had Matthew told her? "Don't spy on people at their private... " Rex was being nice about it. Matthew would tell her off.

They sat in his car for some minutes, the only sound his occasional swallow. "Bastard!" he said suddenly. "His idea of foreplay is lying on the carpet and playing that music. All he has to do now is open her knees."

He got out of the car then and came around to open LeahNell's door and walk her across the bright-lit yard. "I shouldn't have said that. That's no way to talk to you. I'd forgotten you were there."

Not very flattering. Would have hurt her feelings if she were attracted to him, as she thought she ought to be, wished she were, because he was everything she considered perfect in a man for her. He was intellectual and nice-looking, sensitive and kind, and he listened. But something was missing. Cynical though he was, Matthew was more appealing. Of course, she wasn't really interested in anyone but Floyd. But whole days went by now when she didn't think about Floyd.

It was past midnight. She let herself into the darkened old Women's Violent with a key, and by the light of the moon, she climbed the stairs to her six by ten foot cell. The door to Cleo's room opened, and Cleo peeked out and leaned on the door frame, tousled and tugging the hem of her baby-doll pajamas.

"You didn't pick up your mail today," she said. "You got a letter. From Floyd. I put it on your bed." She followed LeahNell into her room. "Why don't you turn on a light?"

"I can see," said LeahNell. She could see the white envelope on her pillow, with the familiar scrawl crowding the margins. "Hope I didn't wake you."

She started peeling off her clothes, sandals first, then the dark red belt she had thought was so daring with her light rose skirt, until Gilda's black jersey dress with the threadbare wrists made her despair of ever growing up.

"I was waiting up for you," said Cleo. "Wanted you to know Francis and I know you're not sleeping with Matthew or Rex ..." She paused for a moment. "... Or Gilda."

Was *that* what *menage `a quatre* meant? LeahNell stepped out of her skirt and petticoat, and pulled the peasant blouse over her head.

"... And the rest of the boys were just showing off."

Cleo shifted from one foot to another, but LeahNell didn't invite her to sit. This was as far as she was going to undress. She didn't parade around in the nude like some of the other girls.

"Thanks, Cleo. It doesn't matter what they think."

Matthew and Gilda and Rex were more interesting. She hoped they'd invite her again. She hoped she hadn't said anything too stupid. She had blushed a couple of times, but she couldn't help that.

"Well, nighty night," said Cleo. "Sleep tight. Don't let the bedbugs bite."

If they do, take a shoe and knock them black and blue.

LeahNell closed the door behind Cleo and pulled her pajamas out of the drawer. She slipped off her bra straps and put on the pajama top, then unhooked the back of the bra, pulled it out from under. She glanced at the letter on her pillow and turned it face down before she stepped out of her panties and into the pajama bottom.

In her narrow bed, she held the letter loosely, propped herself on her pillow. In a moment, she would turn on the lamp and read the letter.

She knew Cleo was wondering about her, but she was not going to explain herself. What did you tell someone you'd double-dated with, who had gotten you grounded because *she* wasn't ready to come in out of a cornfield in time for lights out, and then spent the next three days in the infirmary with poison ivy on her back?

And what did you tell her when she didn't know you betrayed her, sort of, and even though she didn't know, she still called the cops, just to make an issue of it?

Cleo had been strange tonight at seminar. She looked as if she hadn't slept for a week. She'd had a few gulps of beer and then nudged LeahNell and led her up the stairs to the bathroom, where she shut the door behind them and plopped down on the toilet lid. Her eyes filled with tears. "Leah, I'm just beside myself," she said.

She *is* beside herself, LeahNell had thought. There were two of her: Cleo seated and Cleo reflected in the mirror under the bright, hot light. Be serious, LeahNell told herself; Cleo's in distress.

"I just don't know what to do," said Cleo. "I'm so in love with Francis, but he makes me feel bad. He's religious and so ... serious. He talks about mortal sin and ..." She gulped. "We finally made love. We couldn't help it. It was the most heavenly thing that's ever happened to me. He said it was for him too, but afterward he made me pray with him and beg forgiveness. Can you imagine me down on my knees begging forgiveness?"

LeahNell couldn't.

"And that's the way it goes. He can't stay away from

me, but he stares at me, won't touch me until he can't stand it anymore. It's absolutely wonderful and it's absolutely hell. Is this what love is like? It's awful. I can't think straight. I can't eat, I can't sleep, I wouldn't care if the hospital burned down. What am I gonna do?"

She seemed to want an answer. "I don't know," was all LeahNell could say.

Cleo rocked and the toilet seat creaked. "He calls me his temptress, his Delilah. Isn't that romantic? I feel bad about there being so many others. They didn't mean anything to me -- not like this. It was just a friendly thing to do. But I didn't know it could be like this, and how I wish he'd been the only one."

"Have you told him about the others?"

"Oh, yes. You don't keep secrets from someone you love. We've told each other everything."

How much "everything" could Francis have to tell? "I know that's what everyone says," said LeahNell, "but, ... I don't know. It just seems to me you need to keep some things to yourself."

She couldn't imagine confiding her own... lapse to anyone. She could hardly believe it herself. What had possessed her to think that Victor Reamer would be interested in a second year nursing student for her mind? Call me Vic, he had told her. That was a year and a half ago, and now she hardly cringed when she remembered him in the scrub room (when she could finally speak to him again without crying), not looking at her, speaking to the suds forming a meringue on his knuckles. "Hell, you were a nurse," he said. No, she would never again trust anyone that much.

"What if you quarrel?" she said to Cleo. "You will, sometime. It'll be the first thing he thinks of." Her advice was straight out of her mother's mouth -- she herself would never need it. She had reclaimed her... integrity. Never, never again.

"Oh, no, he'd never be so unkind," said Cleo. "He loves me. He says I didn't know I was doing wrong -- like a child -- and he forgives me. I can atone for it."

"How?"

"With prayer. I do hope he won't want me to quit smoking." Cleo sat up straight and crossed her cheerleader legs.

She pulled her silver cigarette case and lighter out of her pocket and squinted into the mirror, watching herself light up. "I guess I'm going to have to behave myself. You can help me. I'm sorry I used to make fun of you."

She glanced at LeahNell through the haze from her first draw. "I guess you didn't know I called the cops on you that time we went swimming at Dr. Fiddler's."

No surprise. "Why?" LeahNell wondered if Cleo would be sorry tomorrow that she confessed tonight.

Cleo shrugged. "I didn't have a date, and it looked like you were going to wind up with the man. Dr. Ambrose. It was so unfair when you weren't even interested. I always wanted to fuck a doctor."

"Cleo!"

"And now I guess I never will. F... oh, you're such a prude, Leah. But Francis is going to get his Ph.D., so I guess I better learn to talk like a lady. A psychologist is almost a doctor, isn't he?"

LeahNell knew it was Cleo who called the cops. And if Cleo hadn't, what would have happened?   Would she have stayed with him, run from him until she got tired and let him overcome her, and then gone upstairs with him?   She couldn't imagine herself letting go like that, but she had had such strange dreams ever since it happened. She didn't know what got into her that night.

Often, she didn't know what got into her. Sometimes, at Trinity, she had to wander, break free of the other girls and the white walls and the rules, and the smells of Dermafresh and Phenol disguising everything natural. Or, she couldn't sleep and her hands were restless and she was afraid of where they might go, and then she'd get out of bed and dress, or just put on her raincoat over her pajamas, and her moccasins, or maybe she'd go barefoot.

At Trinity, she'd hoist herself to her window by stepping onto the radiator pipe, and unlock the screen and slither out, leaving her window open just a finger. She'd walk and walk and walk, with the wind lifting her hair off her neck. Sometimes down to Julia Davis Park, but most often around the big old houses on Warm Springs Boulevard, sometimes on the sidewalks, just as often in the yards when the lights were out, from tree to tree and in the shrubbery up close to the houses and among the flowers and around the pools -- the houses that had pools. She never knew what she was looking for, but the swimming pools fascinated her.

It was water, deep water, that drew her. She wanted to slip into the water at night and feel it wash around her and into her and through her and lift her hair away from her scalp in the way that made her tingle all over. Swimming made her feel as if she were sinking into her own body and levitating. Only then could she trust her body not to let her down.

She intended to swim in one of those pools sometime, but it was a pleasure she'd put off, honing her anticipation to a keen edge, waiting for the right moment, a signal, a magical juxtaposition of forces. Until the morning Cleo burst into her room and snatched off her sheet, she couldn't imagine who the agent would be or how she would recognize the moment.

She could still see Cleo in her panties and bra, blue ones that day, knuckling out her cigarette in her cold cream jar.

"My gawd, you sack rat," Cleo had said. "You going to sleep your life away?" She teased the sheet near LeahNell's groping fingers. "Why don't you sleep in the raw like the rest of us do? It's so much cooler."

"Go away," said LeahNell, curling onto her side. "I work nights, remember? I sleep in the daytime."

"This is your weekend off. You can sleep tonight but not too early. It's going to be a lovely warm night and the moon is full." Cleo sat down on LeahNell's bed and gave back the sheet. "I don't have anything to do tonight." She sounded pitiful.

Saturday night without a date. For Cleo that was big trouble. She was too broke for a movie and LeahNell wouldn't go to Franco's Bar, and so they compromised on swimming. LeahNell knew where the pools were, and those with natural hot water. Knew one where they were not likely to be caught, the house having been converted from home to office when Dr. Fiddler moved up to Whitney Bench.

Cleo didn't ask how LeahNell knew about the pool. She just said, "Let's do it."

But Cleo had gotten cold feet after all. To begin with, she brought a bottle and was offended when LeahNell wouldn't drink too, although she knew LeahNell couldn't. Her excuse for the bottle was, she'd mentioned the plan to Melba, and Melba said Dr. Fiddler had an apartment upstairs which he was renting to the new internist.

"Name's Ambrose or something," said Cleo.

LeahNell had seen him around the medical floor, but she wasn't going to let him scare her out of a quiet swim. "Melba's got the wrong house," she said. "I tell you there's no one there."

But when they arrived, well after sundown, three open windows on the back corner upstairs were softly orange, and sheer curtains fluttered in and out. They had let themselves into the walled yard at one of the two side gates and skirted the lawn, threading their way around the large granite house through dense Douglas firs and lilacs. The trees opened like a forest glade onto the large, lipped rectangle of pool containing and reflecting the night sky.

Cleo said she wouldn't go into the pool until it was dark upstairs, and LeahNell realized that meant she might not swim at all. Under the canopy of firs, Cleo took out a Camel and lit it, and tucked the rest of the pack into her swim top between her breasts. She peeled back the top of a narrow brown bag, unscrewed a lid and tilted the bottle to her lips.

LeahNell didn't want to think where Cleo had gotten a bottle when she didn't have money for a movie. "No mixer?" she said.

"Yeah, I wish I had some potato chips."

LeahNell watched the rising moon and played with the fireflies until finally the upstairs light went out. Cleo took a long drag on her cigarette. "Imagine going to bed at eleven o'clock on a Saturday night. Most doctors would have more dates than they could handle."

"We don't know that's who it is. And maybe he has a ladyfriend up there."

"I've seen him," Cleo said. "He's short and he wears horn-rims. I wouldn't give him a second look if I didn't know he was a doctor."

LeahNell got to her feet, stepped out of her moccasins

and picked up her towel. She wanted to play in the water until her fingers dimpled. "I came to swim," she said. "I'm going in." She dropped the towel at the pool's edge, dipped her fingers and watched the ripples spread and shimmer under the moon.

In she slid at the deep end, gasping as the cold water washed up over her stomach, and then she lay back, taking in the night murmurs and perfumes. She could feel her hair lift and float around her head. After a while, she turned over in the water, and as she lifted her arm to stroke, a clanging like a thousand Oriental gongs jarred her alert.

She started up out of the water just as Cleo shrieked and leaped to her feet and charged across the lawn like a frenzied scarecrow. "Jesus Christ, Leah!" she screamed.

As LeahNell was pulling herself out of the pool, Cleo reached the gate, shook it, slammed and pounded. LeahNell snatched up her towel.

A scraping sound near the house sent her bolting for the gate. "It's jammed," she squeaked, and pulled Cleo away. "Over the wall."

Cleo swung her legs across. LeahNell's feet slipped, without a niche to give her a foothold. She could hear the slap of Cleo's feet down the sidewalk and then it was quiet. She let go of the wall. She would pick up her moccasins and go out the gate on the other side of the house. She turned around.

A man separated from the shadow of the house, his own shadow too big, she thought, to be Dr. Ambrose. *Forget the moccasins.*

She darted back into the yard, headed for the cover of trees. The man came after her. Close behind, between her and the house, he would reach the other gate before she could. She zigzagged, hoping he would change his course. He cut her off in mid-trajectory. She backtracked and tried again.

Suddenly, she was exhilarated as a moth flying at a lightbulb. It was a game, touch-tag, or three-deep, her favorite childhood pastime. She had liked to lure even the biggest of the boys into cornering her, let them tag her, and then tag them back before they could get out of her range.

She could see now that this man was not as big as he'd looked, but lean and fast. She almost laughed as he crouched to spring after her whichever way she might go. The moon at his back threw his face into shadow, and then his silence reminded her that she was a trespasser and he wasn't a playmate.

It became a contest of endurance. Beginning to tire, she feinted in one direction, then struck out in the other. Her wet hair slapped across her cheek. She barely slipped out of his grasp and gasped at how fast he had seen what she was up to. She plunged into shadow, running a darkened course around the periphery of the yard, still too far from either gate but under cover. She molded herself to the side of a tree, where she could watch him and glide around it when he passed close to her, twigs snapping under his feet and shadows casting shifting patterns across his face. Her chest ached with the need for air.

He spoke, in a conversational tone. "I thought you were alone," he said. "I was watching the moon come up and I saw you in the pool with your hair floating around you. I didn't mean to scare you. That damn cute dinner bell of Mrs. Fiddler's. I run into it every time I come down the stairs."

He sounded so reasonable.

"Let's stop playing games. It's fun but I'm tired. I think I know you. You're a student nurse, aren't you? I'm not going to tell on you. I just want to know who you are."

Maybe, but she was excited, and that scared her. She stayed where she was. If he would give up and go back where he came from, she would find her moccasins and go home. Soon. She didn't relish the idea of trying to keep warm outside all night.

"Then again," he murmured as if to himself, "maybe this hermit is hallucinating."

Laughter bubbled up in her throat. She would catch her breath, then show herself, fling her arms out dramatically, and lead him another merry chase. Peter Rabbit, lippity, lippity. But he turned and walked away.

She saw him cross the lawn near the pool and disappear into the shadow of the house. She waited, counting for a sense of time, and studied the leaves that waxed in the moonlight. She took her first deep breath in what seemed like hours and stepped out of the shadows.

She didn't hear him, but a slight fanning of the air raised

the hairs on her arms in the split-second before he gripped them from behind and spun her around. It wasn't quite like dancing; her bare feet wouldn't slide. Stalled in a left-hand dosey-do, her dancing partner was barefoot too, wearing jeans and a shirt open at the neck. He blinked and his eyebrows lifted in recognition.

She did know him and not just from the medical floor. He'd played the piano one morning in the nurses' parlor and she, just off duty and boggy with fatigue, had stood in the doorway until she almost fell over. Ravel. Debussy.

The wail of a siren ruptured the night air, grew louder homing in, and choked off as a car crunched to a stop out in the street. Doors opened and slammed. Heavy footfalls approached the gate.

"What the hell?" He snapped his head around. "Come on," he said, and pulled her back into the Douglas firs. They scrambled into the shelter and she dropped to her knees, rolling behind the curtain of branches. She was breathing hard against his neck when the gate clanged open. He smelled of allspice. They shrank together as the beam of a flashlight scanned the ground a few feet away. She wondered why, with such a bright moon, they needed a flashlight.

Here was help if she wanted it. But would the police return her to Trinity Hall, turn her over to the housemother? Would they even believe her? She hadn't called out, and their tangle of arms and legs was... compromising. The light beam moved on, and she could see the two policemen tramp around to the other side of the house.

The man felt long and smooth. He lifted his head and looked down at her. A lock of hair fell over his forehead. If I pushed his hair out of his face, she thought, he would kiss me. She flushed, warm with confusion. Did she want to get away from him or didn't she? Suddenly, he froze, his eyebrows lifting, and he doubled up as he pulled away from her. But not before she felt him rising and swelling, straining toward her.

"Don't do that," she cried. "I don't even know your first name." As if it were a matter of etiquette, as if it were important.

She thought it might be, but she couldn't remember why. She leaned up on her elbow and in one swift movement he pulled her down, rolling her back. His hand circled her wrist, pinning it to the earth. Her skin prickled, guarding itself with gooseflesh. He let go and ran his fingertips lightly up her scalp at the back of her neck. She gasped and arched with the shock, tilting her face and closing the distance between their mouths. She could feel herself molding to him like mercury running into crevices.

Too soon, he lifted himself away from her and sat up. "It's Nick," he said. His voice sounded rusty. "My name's Nick."

She felt so good it couldn't be right. She sprang to her feet and scrambled, running for the gate, hearing him call after her, "I don't know *your* name."

Her body felt too warm and slow for running and her legs ached. Even so, when the policemen rounded the front corner of the house and gave lumbering chase, she lost them once she was across the boulevard.

Working nights in obstetrics, she'd had no fear, or hope, of meeting him again. She did wonder if her moccasins were still under the tree.

Floyd's letter slipped from her hands and off the bed onto the orange and blue and green rag rug from Occupational Therapy. She left it there. She would read it in the morning. She slid down on her pillow and closed her eyes to shut out the moon's light, but slowly it crept under her eyelids.

She drifted into sleep, following the moon through long shadows. Its light shifted too fast to warm. The wind moaned through trailing branches, not brisk enough to free them from the water in this swamp smelling of fruit, over-ripe and rotting into the ooze that was neither plant nor animal but something in between.

Somewhere out there, something waited for her, if she could move softly and not change the balance.

13. Dr. Quill

Staff meeting came to a grudging halt and Dr. Quill was out the door before the inevitable exhortation to participate in a patient-staff event could reach his ears. He maintained his fiction of ignorance of the weekly, Sunday evening ball game until the invitation sneaked up on him in the person of the imp-gnome student nurse LeahNell.

Just ahead of him in the lunch line on Friday, she turned around and said to him, as though they were already engaged in conversation, "The Mavericks and the Mossbacks are playing ball again Sunday after supper. Our team is the Mossbacks. Would you come see us play?" It was so precisely articulated that he knew she'd turned it over in her mind until she got it just right.

She turned away before he could acknowledge her, say yea or nay. He wouldn't go, of course.

As usual, Sunday supper was early, five o'clock, just an extended snack, the mid-day meal having been the traditional gorge, featuring baked ham this time. Sundays were one day of the week he half regretted not having a driver's license, a car, a movie ticket. He supposed there was a movie house in Millennium. Even tiny Little Wood had had a movie theatre, with an ice cream parlor next door.

He remembered the homey rattle and aroma of fresh popcorn before the early show and between the two shows; the back-row line-up of high school couples, prim and self-conscious before the lights went out, then muffled-giggling and heavy-breathing in the dark; the firefly glow of cigarettes; the usherette's cone of light guiding late arrivers to seats; the ripple of sh-h-hs before everyone settled into the larger-than-life unfolding on the screen. It would almost be worth the trouble.

He left the dining hall and meandered down the locust-shaded walk toward the staff apartments. Amid cottonwoods, the ballfield lay to the south, and there, trickles of patients and inmates and students and staff were converging, dispersing onto the grass or into the dusty field. What the hell, it was an improvement on his own four walls. He took that path, made a beeline for a small circle of shade set apart from the milling clusters of people.

Folding himself to sit upon the tuft of fescue, he was nudged out of balance and caught himself on one hand. He glanced up to see Clarence the soda-jerk glowering at him as he eased his red-haired schizophrenic girlfriend -- of such long tenure on The Farm that Dr. Quill had no occasion to know her name -- into the coveted spot. Owned it, did they?

He picked himself up feeling foolish and looked around. From the overlapping shade of three large cotton-woods nearby, Dr. Swenson amid his *ménage* of look-alike stairstep kids and look-alike wife called out, "Over here, Angus." Dr. Quill was so astonished to hear his first name aloud that he followed the summons.

Around the center of tubs and picnic hampers, they were flipping out blankets, gray and laundered into felted stiffness. It appeared that they expected multitudes. "Won't you join us for supper?" said Mrs. Swenson. Jewell? Julie.

He declined as gracefully as he could muster, and sat down Indian fashion on the fringe of the circle, on the east side so the shade would hold as the sun went down. Still, she continued to cast her net of hospitality over him.

The oldest boy had staked out a blanket between Dr. Quill and the eastern-most cottonwood, marking his territory with his jacket and a pair of ice chests. While the boy toted hampers and bags from the Swensons' station wagon at the curb, the oldest girl moved one of the ice chests.

"Leave it alone," the boy barked. The girl shoved it back into place and plumped herself down beside it.

The other kids parked on Dr. Quill's blanket. With six other blankets, why were they crowding so close to him? He considered that the time might have come to shave off his avuncular mustache.

Under the central cottonwood, Dr. Swenson settled his large, lean frame and took out a can of Prince Albert and his pipe, making a ceremony of filling it and tamping it down.

"These are our children," said Mrs. Swenson, proud as a

farm wife lining up entries for the state fair. The Swenson kids were all spare and large-boned, blond and wide-set blue-eyed. Fortunately, they in no way reminded him of his own children, of whom he could not bear to think.

She nodded toward the oldest boy. "Our son Richard. He's going to go to medical school. Stanford."

Richard rolled his eyes. "Mo-om. We don't know until they accept me. I've still got two years of high school." The oldest girl was eyeing him while she nudged the ice chest out of her way. "Leave it alone, Roach," he said.

"Mo-om, he called me Roach."

"Richard is sixteen," said Mrs. Swenson. "Rowena is thirteen and a half. Reginald is eleven; Rosalind is eight and a half; Roland is six; Rita is three and a half. Maybe you noticed all their names begin with R."

Yes, he'd noticed.

"I want to sit there," said Rowena.

"You can't," said Richard. "I'm saving it."

"For El-len," said Rowena.

"What if I am?"

"The boys were born in June and the girls were born in December ...," said Mrs. Swenson.

Let me guess, Dr. Quill replied silently; Papa Swenson -- *Ronald* -- was born in June and you were born in December.

"I aimed for June tenth and December twentieth, but no one came close."

"Well, my dear, I don't expect you to be perfect," said Dr. Swenson.

Dr. Quill would have bet that he did indeed expect her to be perfect, and that she was and they both knew it.

"Roland will start school in September and Rita is my last baby bird in the nest."

Which Dr. Quill guessed meant she was in menopause. He was beginning to feel claustrophobic.

"Here's Becky and Elspeth," squealed the middle girl. "You came, you came to our picnic."

The two dumpling girls from the hydrotherapy romp, winners of the babysitter audition, were moving in on them.

"Well, but we have to play ball," said the larger of the

two. She plumped herself down next to Dr. Quill. "Remember us? We're the baby-sitters."

They began to explain the names and ages. "I know," he said. He was trying to decide whether to move or just go home when Mrs. Quill and her young daughter reached the oasis of blankets. From bad to worse? He'd wait and see.

Before they'd vacated their apartment, he would see them at supper in the dining room, Mrs. Quill out of uniform, still skirted. Today, she carried a light blue sweater, wore sandals and a blouse tucked into belted gray slacks, which she was still slim enough to wear well. The girl was smaller than her mother, colt-like in early adolescence, and, like the other kids, she wore shorts. He wondered what it was like for a kid to grow up on the fringes of an institution. He supposed she went to school in town; did the other kids set her apart, make fun of her?

Dr. Swenson unraveled his long frame and offered Mrs. Quill his place, starting a round of reseating reminiscent of musical chairs. Richard abandoned his place by the big ice chest and pioneered a new site on the other side of Dr. Quill for himself and the girl. Mrs. Quill moved into Richard's old space, among the kids.

"Reginald has a big crush on Becky," Rowena/Roach announced to no one in particular.

Reginald, kid number three, flushed. "Do not," he said. Said she: "Do so."

Richard and Mrs. Quill's young daughter were silent, not looking at each other. The boy's ears were cherry-red, but Ellen looked serene. Dr. Quill could scarcely take his eyes off her. She looked eerily familiar.

The girl had never made much impression upon him. She seemed to shade into the woodwork and she could sit absolutely still longer than anyone he'd ever known. He had never heard her speak. She watched and listened, seeming not dull or passive, but focused on absorbing knowledge and energy until she knew enough to get it exactly right. Which seemed a little sad; taking a risk and winning, taking a risk and losing was a rough ride but your wins and your losses belonged to you. Her reluctance to put herself on the line seemed to him a character flaw. Not unlike his own. It was too late for him, but she was young enough to weather the bumps.

Still, she reminded him of someone.

She turned and caught him staring. He looked away. He liked to have a puzzle, and the solution would come to him as all his answers did -- at four o'clock in the morning.

The picnic hampers had been opened and an aromatic *pot-pourri* of fried chicken, potato salad, tomato aspic, and potato chips filled Dr. Quill's nostrils. The emergence of the meal, which he had declined to share, was a good excuse for him to turn his back and watch the players warming up.

The baby-sitters got up from the blanket and headed for home plate. Clarence left his lady love on their tuft of fescue and followed his team -- a few patients and inmates, and the attendants Whitaker, Schwartz and Mr. Wheeler. The Mavericks, apparently.

It was not clear what variety of ballgame they were going to play, since they were using a baseball with a softball bat. Dr. Quill guessed it didn't matter much -- the three bases were pillows; the only player with a mask and chest protector was, inexplicably, the first baseman. Only the catcher wore a mitt; and there didn't seem to be an umpire.

Dr. Quill knew the two patients from Stella's series of insulin therapy and from doing their admission physicals, in Driscoll's case repeatedly. What an improbable pair they were in a place like this -- golden-haired, bronze-tanned, graceful creatures, surely blessed by some malevolent providence. A waste of perfection. At present, they were the only alcoholics on Admissions. Driscoll made no bones about his status, calling himself, with a watchful air of mischief, a non-practicing alcoholic, which was true for the month on Admissions and four to six weeks after he was sprung. Until he'd get careless or over-confident or bored. Or just in the wrong company. The cycle would begin again. Once, last year, he was out for five months and Matthew Ryder was boasting "Cure!" when back he came. The revolving door.

Stella was another story -- a narcissist spending a lot of her daddy's money trying, for some reason unfathomable to Dr. Quill, to convince herself that she was schizophrenic, perhaps to absolve herself of responsibility for her condition. Until her habit made her unemployable, she'd worked as a reporter for the *Boise Statesman*; now she would have the other patients understand that she was here on an undercover story.

Driscoll liked to describe himself as an undiscovered, uncompensated novelist, and together he and Stella put out a ward newsletter whenever they could set aside their territorial disputes long enough to cooperate.

One thing Dr. Quill had to say for them: they were the only patients who would breach the patient-inmate barrier. The others from their ward huddled together across the field.

Schwartz was catcher and Driscoll was on the pitcher's mound. Whitaker, Stella, and Melba Frizzletop from the hydro-therapy picnic were on the bases. Odd, Dr. Quill thought: Melba was a student nurse; what was she doing on the opposing team?

Mr. Wheeler played shortstop; Jepson and Oliver and Clarence were outfield. As far as Dr. Quill knew, Clarence had been here close to forever, born to an inmate with a syphilitic dementia. Jepson and Oliver were here when Dr. Quill arrived, and they hadn't changed a bit. Still looked like teenagers, except for Oliver's cratered brow, and still warbled like castrati. They hadn't needed medication or electroshock for the past three years. The last occasion was etched in Dr. Quill's memory, associated as it was with Casey, who had for some minor infraction decided they were getting too big for their britches and put them in separate cells, where they clamorously went off their rockers. The truth was, together they were about the caliber of one good man, full of themselves and good cheer. Apart, each was less than half a man.

The student nurses and The Callow, Pimply Youth, as Dr. Quill liked to think of the psychologists in training, clustered around home plate. It seemed to be a foregone conclusion that they had first up, until Mr. Wheeler hailed his crew to home base. He tossed the bat to Patsy, who caught it in midair and held it out. Driscoll strode forward, wrapped his hand around the bat above Patsy's. She overtook it with her other hand. At the top of the bat, Driscoll performed some sleight-of-hand Dr. Quill could see coming and, ignoring the chorus of boos and protests, the Mavericks were up. Patsy stomped to the pitcher's mound, and Driscoll tossed the bat to Schwartz, and raised his fist to the sky. "Let's play ball."

"C'mon, team," cheered Oliver and Jepson in their treble voices.

"Batter up!" On the first pitch, Schwartz popped a fly between first and second bases. Cleo zoomed in and caught it, and Schwartz was out.

"'Ray, team," sang Oliver and Jepson.

Driscoll swaggered over to the plate and sent Patsy's fast ball to the other side of the student nurses' dormitory. While Driscoll rounded the bases with show-off ease, LeahNell and one of the Pimply Youth chased the ball. LeahNell got there first, but her throw landed short. The intern snatched it up and delivered it into Patsy's hands as Driscoll crossed home plate.

Patsy took it easy on Whitaker. Her balls were slow enough that the wind carried them off course, and he made it to first base. But then, as if she'd been hoarding it, she wound up and threw Frizzletop three strikes before the girl knew they'd gone by.

A little animosity there. Dr. Quill wondered what the story was.

Stella made it to first on a walk. Mr. Wheeler, a crack ballplayer, sent a long one far enough to get him to second.

On the blanket to Dr. Quill's left, there was a series of pops -- soda bottles being uncapped. On his right, Matthew and Mrs. Ryder had arrived with four canvas folding chairs. They unfolded two chairs just in front of Clarence's girlfriend on her tuft of grass. They sat down, Dr. Ryder's gaze sweeping the assembly and Mrs. Ryder looking into the field.

The red-haired inmate sprang to her feet and tapped Mrs. Ryder on the shoulder, then planted herself in front of the new arrival, their faces almost nose to nose. She flapped her arms. "Re-move," she said.

Mrs. Ryder jerked back her head. "What? Matthew, what does she want?"

"You're sitting in front of her, my dear. She can't see the ballgame. She would like you to re-move your exquisite carcass."

Re-move. It was the first word Dr. Quill had heard Red Hair, supposedly mute, speak. He wasn't surprised. Most of these people had a word or two when the situation demanded. He turned back to the ball game.

" 'Ray, team," cheered Jepson and Oliver, jumping up and down. Schwartz called Jepson to home plate and the two inmates stepped up to the plate together. Patsy held the ball and turned to Schwartz.

Good old Schwartz. To Dr. Quill's mind, Schwartz was the ideal attendant, literal-minded perhaps, but reasonable and kindly and dependable. He seemed content with his job and his life.

With Schwartz, they got it sorted out. Oliver stayed put at home plate, while Jepson stepped back and picked up a stone with his right hand and something Dr. Quill couldn't see with his left hand.

Patsy lofted the ball to Oliver at waist height. Jepson tossed his stone into the air and, along with Oliver, swung his imaginary bat, tossing it as Oliver connected with the ball. Then they were running, Oliver first, Jepson close behind. Each got a foot on the pillow that was first base. Whitaker made it home, and Mr. Wheeler to third. Schwartz called Jepson to come back to take his turn, but Jepson wouldn't. Far as he was concerned, he'd already hit his ball.

From her new position near him, Mrs. Ryder's voice filtered back to Dr. Quill: "Where is Rex? ... just because it's Sunday ... care a bit about baseball, Matthew?"

And Matthew's reply: "No, my dear, I am not bored."

"... But you're not paying attention. Must you be a psychologist every minute?"

That question nearly caused Dr. Quill to look around to see what Matthew Ryder was up to.

Her stage whisper pricked up Dr. Quill's ears. "... Here he is at last. Look at the little apparition he is squiring about. Are we supposed to take this seriously?"

That was irresistible. Dr. Quill turned around to gawk.

Dr. McFall was unfolding the remaining chairs, with some damage to his thumb, and easing his guest into the seat next to Mrs. Ryder. The Little Apparition, which she was indeed with her double eyebrows and her useless eyeglasses and her gray hair springing loose from an elaborate knot, was Alma

Duffy from Intermediate.

Mrs. Ryder endured her introduction with an ironic formal handshake, but Dr. Ryder leaped to his feet and exuded Southern gentlemanly charm, which Dr. Quill thought was certainly not native to him, but which instantly called forth the Southern lady in Miss Duffy. She murmured and lifted her chin to turn her classic profile to full advantage.

No end of surprises. Dr. Quill turned back to the ball game. Clarence was at bat, bent forward from the hips, stiff-kneed, as Patsy's pitches whistled past him. He walked, but Elspeth sailed the ball to the intern Hopkins, who hauled back his arm with a menacing look on his face.

When on orientation, the interns had toured Clinic, and Dr. Quill had taken them around and shown them the treatment options. Hopkins of the heavy-lidded eyes and thrusting lower lip had been as conspicuously bored as he could dramatize, slouching into every room, leaning in the doorway, focusing on the ceiling, until they got to the electroshock room. There he came to life, marched in ahead of the rest, stood rapping his fist on the treatment table, and fixed Dr. Quill with a show-me stare.

When Dr. Quill had finished his spiel, Hopkins cleared his throat, opened his mouth. "So this is where ...," was as far as he got before his classmate, the pale, intense Francis with the horn-rimmed glasses, nudged him and muttered, "Knock it off, Hopkins."

"Don't be so anal-retentive," said Hopkins.

Subsequently Francis, unlike the others, acknowledged Dr. Quill when their paths crossed, soberly looking him in the eye and nodding.

Now, Hopkins teased the ball back and forth with the intern on second, trapping Jepson and Oliver. Three outs, or four, depending on how you counted.

The Mavericks took their stations as the Mossbacks headed for home plate. Driscoll had no such charity as Patsy and a stinging hard pitch besides, and he laid them waste as they came up to bat: Elspeth, then Patsy, then Hopkins.

Stella rushed in from third base and threw her arms around Driscoll, planted a kiss squarely on his lips while he stood stiff-armed. Oliver and Jepson jumped up and down until

Mr. Wheeler stepped between them and laid his hands upon their shoulders.

Patsy marched to the pitcher's mound with ball in hand, blood in her eye. But Mrs. Swenson had been standing at blanket's edge, waving and calling, "Cookies and soft drinks!" And the Mavericks were ready for a break.

"Refreshments!" In they swarmed. Driscoll and Patsy led the pack, skidding to a stop mere feet away from Dr. Quill, and from the Ryders, who'd begun evacuation maneuvers.

To the babysitters, family retainers, fell the job of distributing cookies. Between the two of them, they served all the ballplayers, Becky fueling up first with two peanut-butter cookies and then topping those off with one for about every two she gave away, and Elspeth making a quick pass with her box and then retiring to do serious munching.

Mrs. Swenson shrugged, refilled one box, and handed it to LeahNell, who had come from the field by way of the Ryders quartet. The girl surveyed the group on the blankets and circled around to Clarence, who had helped himself to two bottles of Dr. Pepper and retreated to his lady love on their grassy turf. He filled his baseball cap with cookies and turned away. LeahNell moved on to the Ryder party where, bending over Alma Duffy, her back was turned to Dr. Quill and their exchange lost to him.

He fell to watching the patterns people drifted into: who was comfortable with whom, or currently attracted to, or cultivating. The nurses and interns were a central, pulsing body, a colonial organism with other individuals attaching and breaking away.

The kewpie-doll Cleo and Francis were molded together about as close as they could be without actually touching. Like Oliver and Jepson, when one moved, the other moved too.

Synchronized as chorus-girls, Oliver and Jepson were eating cookies and drinking Orange Crush. Dr. Quill wondered what a diagram of their neural wiring would look like. The pair plus Whitaker and Mr. Wheeler were a familiar quartet, now surrounding Melba Frizzletop. Dr. Quill guessed that explained Melba's team switch.

Driscoll drifted from group to group, never alighting to stay, and soon Dr. Quill saw that Driscoll was being pursued.

He'd pause and take one draught from his bottle of Pepsi, and Stella would appear at his elbow. He would move on, muscle in somewhere, and Stella would pop up at his side. He'd pick up and go again.

Even as he chided himself for taking sides, Dr. Quill felt a tug of sympathy for the man. And a twinge of shame that he could, if he would, help him in a more substantial way than merely providing haven from a predatory woman.

He could, he should. But he would not risk revealing how much he and Driscoll had in common.

What the hell. What did he have to lose? His privacy, his pride, his edge of superiority... So? His job? Could it cost him his job? He wasn't the only fugitive at The Farm. Wheeler's past transgression seemed only to reinforce his moral authority. Ah, but Mr. Wheeler was an attendant.

His shame now was less for his long-ago malpractice than for the way it unmanned him. Dr. Quill straightened out his legs. *Old man, you've been sitting in one place too long.*

At home on the ward and on the ballfield, in this crowd Schwartz wandered about as though lost. Now he hunkered beside Dr. Quill, paying his respects.

Dr. Quill cast about for an opener. He knew that Mrs. Schwartz was head attendant on the women's long-term ward. "You and your wife are locals, aren't you?"

"Yes. Neither of us has ever been out of Idaho. I grew up on a farm out near the railroad. Next to the place with that old, falling-down barn." Schwartz glanced at Dr. Quill, was silent for a moment. "Family died out years ago, down to one old-maid daughter, if she's still alive. I don't recall the name. Wasn't Quill. Used to wonder if you had any connection to them, though it seemed unlikely."

Dr. Quill agreed that it wasn't likely. "Interesting, though." And, finally, only interesting. He might have been distressed if Schwartz had told him that five years ago. And maybe that was why Schwartz hadn't.

Here came LeahNell, dropping to her knees in front of them and holding out her box. "Cookies. Peanut butter and chocolate."

He hesitated. He wouldn't go as far as chocolate to be

agreeable, but settled for peanut butter. Schwartz took one of each, got to his feet and moseyed on.

She lifted out a deep dark chocolate cookie, sat back on her heels and nibbled silently, concentrating. Dr. Quill recalled his reflexive, initial assessment of her as an alcoholic, on the occasion of the hydrotherapy romp. He reckoned he'd been wrong about her, and too quick to make judgment based on his own, narrow experience. Those psychologists had a word for that: projection. Ascribing one's own attributes to someone else.

A minor commotion drew their attention. Jepson and Oliver were holding court. Between the two of them, they were asking one girl after another: "Will you miss us ... " "... when we're gone?"

Whatever that meant. It was news to Dr. Quill.

When she could get in a word, Cleo said, "We'll be gone before you are."

Said Melba, "I'm coming back after graduation. If you're not here, I'll miss you."

"I'm coming back after graduation too," said LeahNell softly. She got to her feet in a fluid move straight out of a ballet class, then offered her box again and circulated back to her classmates.

Having demolished everything in sight, the ballplayers were gone as fast as they'd descended, back to the field, taking with them their scent of dust and sweat and leather.

The direction of the wind had changed, and the fringe groups moved inward for shelter. The Ryder group abandoned their chairs, and Dr. Quill found himself helping Alma Duffy onto the blanket. He was astonished to see Mrs. Quill rise from the ground in one long lovely unfolding, and he was smitten, he hoped temporarily. Absurdly, he wondered if she ever went to a Sunday night movie.

When everyone got sorted out, Ellen and Mrs. Quill sat on his left with Richard just beyond, Alma Duffy on his right, the remaining Ryder party behind him.

He could hear Mrs. Ryder muttering to Rex McFall, "Aren't you the scintillating presence tonight? Never a dull moment." And his bitter reply: "She's my guest, dammit."

The lady sounded pretty possessive, Dr. Quill thought.

Having lost his cherished spot next to Ellen, Richard thumped one fist over and over into the palm of his hand. Dr. Quill too was restless. The game he'd come to watch was now routine, punctuated only by the occasional crack of ball and bat, or a cheer from under the central cottonwood where Mrs. Swenson was actually watching the game.

The evening's promise now seemed to lie with these souls around him, so close he could see their chests rise and fall, hear them breathe, and distinguish between the musky scent of Mrs. Ryder and the faint lilac mist of Mrs. Quill.

Mrs. Quill laid her hand on Ellen's arm and directed her glance beyond the blanket. There, regal of bearing and unmoving as a rock, a dainty, dark-haired woman in a red-embroidered white peasant skirt and blouse perched near a spray of field grass. Dr. Quill had the impression she'd been there for a while.

Ellen made a small move as if to get up, then sat back and turned to her mother. In Mrs. Quill's face Dr. Quill read the reception of a question, then a barely perceptible shake of her head. Both turned to look at the woman. "She looks nice, doesn't she?" said Mrs. Quill softly, and Ellen nodded.

As if he'd come to a long-pondered decision, Richard got to his feet, threw off his sweater, and bounded off to do battle on the ball field. The four youngest Swensons followed and chased each other around the outfield. Rowena/Roach stood in front of Ellen long enough sing-song, "Richard is mad at you."

A metallic sound, familiar but out of place, alerted Dr. Quill to another presence. He scanned the area, locating Casey a tree away scraping his keys together. The big man's face was in the canopy's deep shade.

Just as Dr. Quill identified the friction of Casey's keys, Alma Duffy spoke. "Casey is here."

"How do you know that?" asked Dr. Quill, even as he realized that she knew the way he knew.

"I may be blind, young man," she said, "but I am not deaf."

The expression on Mrs. Quill's face was a wonder to behold -- a mixture of attention and amusement and ... fright? She seemed to be holding her breath.

In the midst of all these women looking from one to the other, Dr. Quill felt it absurdly incumbent upon him to play host. "Mrs. Quill, Ellen, this is Miss Duffy. Miss Duffy, ..."

"Thank you, I know Mrs. Quill," said Alma Duffy, "but I haven't made the acquaintance of the young lady beside you."

Now the look of fright was real but fleeting, overtaken by a slump into resignation. Mrs. Quill drew a breath. "This is my daughter Ellen."

After a silence of significant length, Alma Duffy said only, "You have a daughter."

Dr. Quill wondered what he had missed, tried to sort it out. Did these women know each other? Well, certainly they knew each other, since Alma Duffy created enough havoc wherever she went that Mrs. Quill could hardly miss her. But both women bristled with unnatural tension, and Dr. Quill thought that of the two of them, the nurse had the most to lose by the association.

He thought back on what he knew about Alma Duffy, which wasn't much. He'd been called to do her physical and history. She'd been lofty and intellectual, but pleased with his patience and his willingness to listen. He considered her mental aberration to be situational and temporary. He didn't expect to see her again and told her as much. He was surprised then to see her ten days later on Clinic for hydrotherapy, from Intermediate.

Now she fidgeted beside him. "What is Casey doing? He makes me nervous."

Casey's attention seemed focused on their little group. Hoping for an invitation to join them? Surely not. On closer examination, the man appeared to be looking straight at Dr. Quill himself. Or almost at him. The object of his attention was Ellen.

Dr. Quill was rallying his muscles to hoist him up and carry him over there when a curious thing happened.

LeahNell and Mr. Wheeler had come in from the field, and Wheeler went directly to Casey's side and parked himself between Casey and his view of Ellen. Neither moved or spoke for what must have been a full minute, and then Casey strode off toward the residence hall, his knees springing, and Mr. Wheeler returned to the field.

Dr. Quill turned to see what impression this had made

upon his neighbors, but their eyes were on LeahNell, who was saying to Alma Duffy, "... I'm sitting out. I'm not much of a ballplayer. My mind wanders."

"Well, good, then," said Alma Duffy. "You may sit by me and we'll talk."

LeahNell dropped to her knees and then they were all in a circle, the women in that peculiarly graceful, feminine posture -- feet tucked to the side, weight on one hip, leaning on one hand.

Dr. Quill was surrounded by women. It was pleasant, particularly since no one seemed to expect anything of him.

Mrs. Quill appeared to be in a state of suspended animation, barely breathing between lips slightly parted, wide-eyed looking from LeahNell to Ellen and back again. It fell to Miss Duffy to introduce to each other the girls she could not see. And Dr. Quill's puzzle would not have to wait, after all, until four a.m. for a solution.

Except for the wing-like eyebrows, a widow's peak, and fair coloring, Ellen in no way resembled her mother. Even the gray of their eyes was different, Mrs. Quill's the kind of gray he thought of as grey -- English and serene. Ellen's eyes were darker, sharper. In all other aspects, she was the spit and image of the girl sitting across from her, from the triangular chin to the squint lines at the corners of the eyes, from the small, square hands to the ectomorphic musculature.

Mrs. Quill's daughter Ellen she might be, but she had a father too, and Dr. Quill would bet he could pick him out in a crowd. He wouldn't be surprised to see his like at a Basque festival dancing the jota, eating chorizos, tossing down whiskey neat.

To thicken the plot, both girls spoke with a cadence of reflective pauses, in voices like woodwinds. This Dr. Quill could hear now, because suddenly Ellen was talking.

LeahNell was a student nurse? Ellen wanted to hear all about it. What was it like -- nurses' training? Did she help deliver babies? Assist with surgery? Was the blood awful ...?

The Ryder group behind Dr. Quill grew quiet, and Rex McFall insinuated himself into the circle of women. "How are you doing?" he said to Alma Duffy. "Are you getting tired? We can go any time you like."

"No, no," she said, a faint edge of panic in her voice. She moved aside to admit all three of the Ryder party into the company. "I... we ... have just made the acquaintance of Ellen, Mrs. ... Mrs. Quill's daughter. This is Dr. McFall, who was kind enough to bring me here for an outing."

"And Mrs. Quill was kind enough to arrange it," said Rex McFall. Alma Duffy's eyebrows, all four of them, leaped.

With scarcely a break in momentum, LeahNell and Ellen continued. "What's Boise like? ..."

"What's it like? Well, it's the capital, you know, and when you drive into town, you kind of, um, sweep around the depot and look down the valley, and there it is -- the Capitol dome -- at the end of the boulevard. There are trees everywhere. But you know that. You must have seen it."

"I've never been there."

"We went through on the train," murmured Ellen's mother. "I showed you the Capitol building."

"But that's not like seeing it," said LeahNell. "Boise is worth a vacation. There's the campus, and the hospitals, and Julia Davis Park. The Egyptian Theater, and all the mansions on Harrison and Warm Springs ... Come to Boise and I'll show you around." She hesitated. "This summer. Since I'll be coming back here after graduation."

"That's very gracious of you. We'll see what we can do," said Mrs. Quill, in what seemed to Dr. Quill a dismissive tone. She was holding her breath again; the look of discomfort had returned.

Interesting, thought Dr. Quill. He had his own reasons to avoid Boise.

"Oh yes, please," said Ellen. "Where did you grow up? Your hometown ...?"

"Little Wood," said LeahNell.

Alma Duffy had been sitting back with a smile that grew broader by the minute. Now she said, "I can't tell which of you is talking unless I listen to what you're saying."

Silence fell while everyone tried to sort it out, and Dr. Quill wondered if his earlier assessment of her was in error and they'd been right to keep her here.

She amended quickly: "They sound so much alike that
...," but the damage to her credibility had been done and the
others had moved on, the Little Apparition not to be taken
seriously.

"I grew up in Little Wood. Have you been there?"

"I've never really been anywhere," said Ellen.

Mrs. Quill made a helpless kind of gesture, lifting her
hands palm up. "We've been through on the train. We... I ...
we're not very adventurous. We just get on the train once a year
and go. Salt Lake City. Seattle. We stayed in Santa Fe ..."

"But you used to live in Little Wood," said Alma Duffy.

"You lived in Little Wood?" Ellen and LeahNell said
together. "When?" asked LeahNell. "Did you know my ...?"

"Yes," said Mrs. Quill, her hands tightly clasped in her
lap. "I lived in Little Wood. A long time ago."

Dr. Quill wished for the sky to open. Anything to stop
this stripping off, layer by layer, of whatever it was she wanted
to keep to herself. "I used to live in Boise," he found himself
saying, to his horror.

It was enough. In the ensuing murmurs, Alma Duffy's
next remark went almost unnoticed. "But your name wasn't Mrs.
Quill when you lived in Little Wood."

The sun had gone down behind the trees and the game
was breaking up. Julie Swenson brought forth another box of
cookies and called everyone in for a parting snack. Whitaker and
Schwartz rounded up Jepson and Oliver. Mr. Wheeler and the
Frizzletop helped Alma Duffy to her feet. She glanced in Rex
McFall's direction and he went quickly to her side. "I'll walk her
back," he said.

"We're going that way," said Mr. Wheeler.

"I brought her; I'll see her home," said Dr. McFall,
edging out the Frizzletop. "She's my date."

Dosey-do, thought Dr. Quill.

Miss Duffy cast the psychologist a smile as he and Mr.
Wheeler took their places, one on each side, to guide her on the
walk across the grass to Intermediate, where the windows blazed
with sunset.

Mrs. Ryder sucked in her breath and rolled her eyes.
"We'll expect you at the house later, Rex," she called after them.

"And you too, of course," she said to Leahnell, and turned away without waiting for a reply.

As if undecided, LeahNell watched her classmates and the interns heading en masse in the direction of the canteen, then she and Ellen drifted out of earshot, still talking.

Driscoll went straight to Mrs. Swenson, bowed low, sweeping his baseball cap to the ground, and declined the cookies but accepted two Pepsis. He turned around and there was Stella, brushing him with her breast and holding out her hand for a Pepsi. He hung onto the colas and walked away, leaving her staring after him, hands on her hips.

"Horny little twitch, isn't she?" said Matthew Ryder, unexpectedly close to Dr. Quill's ear.

Dr. Quill glanced at him, then away. "Sex may be what she is offering," he said, "but sex is not what she wants in exchange."

Dr. Ryder leaned away to focus on him. "She's Rex's patient," he said. "Driscoll is mine. What do you think she wants?"

Dr. Quill considered his position. He could drop the matter right here, but he'd made one strike for Mrs. Quill and the ball was again in his mitt. Why not chance another, for Driscoll? "An alcohol pipeline," he said.

"My colleague might balk at such an assessment, but I would entertain the notion. Maybe you know something we don't."

They watched Driscoll approach the spray of field grass where the little dark-haired woman in the peasant skirt and blouse, still as a rock, was waiting. Holding the colas in one hand, with the other he helped her to her tiny feet, which Dr. Quill could now see were fitted with huaraches. Driscoll handed her a Pepsi, and they set off toward the farm road, each looking away, as if they didn't know each other.

Perhaps he had underestimated Driscoll, thought Dr. Quill, but he feared for the woman, whoever she was. He got to his feet as Mrs. Quill stood up in one seamless move and picked up her sweater.

She looked at him, looked away. "Do you know who the man is?" she asked.

He told her. "And who is the woman?"

"She's from Intermediate ...," she began.

"That's Ynez," said Mrs. Swenson, nesting the empty cookie boxes. "She works in the hospital kitchen. She made the fried chicken and the cookies, but she wouldn't come to our picnic."

Mrs. Quill apparently had nothing to add and Dr. Quill tried to think of a way to keep the subject alive, whether for the sake of her story, which she probably wouldn't want to tell him, or some wild notion of telling her his own. Surely it wasn't for the sake of her grace and slimness and long legs.

He was sorting it out when Mrs. Swenson asked, "Is she mute?"

Mrs. Quill hesitated. "Only intentionally." She paused. "I think that if any words pass between them, it is Driscoll who speaks them."

Dr. Quill could see that was all she was going to say. Still, she seemed in no hurry to move away from him and took her time putting on her sweater.

14. <u>Mrs. Quill</u>

Getting Rochelle out of harm's way had been easier than Mrs. Quill had anticipated. After the testimony of Oliver and Jepson, she had turned her reluctant feet down the hall to Dr. Swenson's office. She knocked. There was no response and the door was locked.

In the business manager's office, Mrs. Stone, a woman with blond, tightly permed hair and a bland, unblinking gaze, informed her that Dr. Swenson was gone for the day.

"To Boise," she said. "He'll be back in time for the staff meeting tomorrow. If you have a business matter, I can handle it. No? I suppose Dr. Quill is second in command. Or if it's a question for the social worker ..."

How like Ronald Swenson, thought Mrs. Quill, not to delegate, not cede an inch of his authority. He'd never even designated a nursing superintendent, leaving ward matters to the shift supervisors, directly accountable to him.

Mrs. Quill guessed she herself was as senior as any, and on the basis of her longevity and moral conviction, she'd set out for Women's Intermediate, where she gave the head nurse the briefest possible account of Rochelle's situation. The less Mrs. Doyle knew, the less she could pass on to Casey when he came calling.

Mrs. Quill personally escorted Rochelle to Women's Violent. In the dayroom, Rochelle eased into the company of her old roommates, ethereal Clarissa and stiff-necked Eloise. Mrs. Quill proceeded to the nurses' station and gave the head nurse, Mrs. Moody, a detailed account of the rape in the old tunnel.

She considered whether a locked ward alone would be sufficient security. "Let's keep Rochelle out of the dayroom," she said. "Put her in a cell at the end of the hall." She glanced out at Rochelle and her cronies -- Alma's "trio of harpies" -- murmuring together by the window. "You needn't lock the door, but keep her name off the roster. Let no one from off the ward go down that hall."

Mrs. Moody nodded. She'd had her own problems with Casey.

From there, Mrs. Quill had gone home to bed at last, waking later than usual, Ellen having come home from school and let herself in quietly, going about her homework without disturbing her mother.

The next morning was Friday staff meeting. Mrs. Quill was first to arrive in the long, narrow conference room behind the business office. She took a seat with her back to the window, three chairs away from the head of the table, where Dr. Swenson would preside. She sat quietly while the others filed in: the ward head nurses; the daytime nursing supervisor, to whom Mrs. Quill had an hour ago given morning report; the evening supervisor, yawning; Dr. Quill at the lower end of the table. Dr. Ryder and Dr. McFall slouched in with their sheaves of papers, Rex McFall plucking a shred of tobacco from his lip.

When everyone was settled and waiting expectantly, Dr. Swenson arrived with the business manager, Mrs. Stone, and Mr. Peters, the social worker, falling in behind him. Dr. Swenson eased his large, spare frame into the one padded armchair, and proceeded to fill his pipe and light it with the match provided by Mr. Peters. The performance was observed in silence by the captive audience.

Mrs. Stone cleared her throat and offered a summary of the financial status of the institution. She noted the anonymous donation of baseball equipment to be delivered the next week, and followed with a report on the week's output from the fields and dairy and Occupational Therapy's sewing room and rug loom.

Mr. Peters read a letter from the father of Admissions patient Stella inquiring about the prospects for continuing her incarceration. Mr. Peters returned the letter to its envelope and slid it across the table to Dr. McFall, Stella's therapist.

Then came the ward reports from one head nurse after another, until only Women's Intermediate and Women's Violent remained. With a glance at Mrs. Quill, Mrs. Doyle recounted in a plaintive tone Rochelle's removal from her ward that very morning. Dr. Swenson jotted a few words in his notebook. Mrs. Moody confirmed Rochelle's arrival at the violent ward and gave what Mrs. Quill considered with admiration a creative description of distress.

"And under whose authority was this transfer made?" demanded Dr. Swenson, and then it was up to Mrs. Quill. Her account of the attack on Rochelle had advanced only to the naming of Casey when Dr. Swenson smiled at her kindly and said, "Let's talk about it later, shall we, Mrs. Quill?"

She looked around the table. Dr. Quill gave her a quick nod, then lowered his gaze. Mrs. Moody met her eyes with a barely perceptible shrug. Mrs. Doyle studied her fingernails. As one, Drs. McFall and Ryder looked at Dr. Swenson, laid down their pens, and glanced at Mrs. Quill, Rex McFall with a tilted eyebrow that recalled her defense of Dr. Swenson a week ago.

The meeting ended. Dr. Quill was first out the door as Dr. Swenson reminded the assemblage of the weekly Sunday evening ballgame, urging all to attend and support this staff-inmate mixer.

In the hall, Mrs. Quill and Dr. Swenson were a wedge for the others to pass around. When the hall was emptied, he said merely, "Mrs. Quill, I appreciate your concern for our charges, but we have only the questionable testimony of two long-term inmates who can't function unless they can support each other, and possibly concoct these fictions between them. The alleged victim has a long history of emotional complaint, much of it a figment of her imagination."

"The alleged villain has a long history of ..."

"I don't question your judgment in taking her to Women's Violent before she could cause problems with the other inmates." He drew his pipe out of one pocket, a can of Prince Albert from another. "Go home and get some sleep," he said, not unkindly. "And remember the ballgame Sunday evening."

It was only what she had expected, but she couldn't continue to shrug off her deepening doubt about Dr. Swenson's integrity. She hoped it wouldn't cost her friendship with Julie.

She almost hadn't gone to the ballgame, thinking that Ellen could go with the Swensons, but it developed that their station wagon would be loaded with food. So it made sense that if she would have to drive Ellen to the ballfield, she might as well stay for the game and Julie Swenson's picnic.

If only she had stayed away. Or if Ellen hadn't been there. Or LeahNell. Or, especially *or Alma*. If any one of that disastrous combination had been missing, LeahNell's three months at The Farm could have passed with no more than a possible acquaintance, without anyone's ever noticing how much the two girls had in common. Even if they had met, ... If, if, if.

And what on earth had possessed Rex McFall to bring Alma to the ballgame? Mrs. Quill herself had facilitated the outing without considering the consequences!

As things stood, who knew what Ellen might suspect, with her habit of waiting and watching, keeping her perceptions to herself? To say nothing of the speculation and conclusions she and LeahNell ...

At that, Mrs. Quill had been lucky. Whatever malign Providence had brought the four of them together was surely neutralized by Dr. Quill's intervention in her behalf. He must have known what he was doing. She was certain that like her and many others, he'd come to The Farm under a cloud. He was a doctor and could be traced. And maybe, just maybe, his name really was Quill.

He'd been almost invisible to her at the ballgame until his sudden revelation that he'd lived in Boise, not so startling in itself, because probably a quarter of the population of the state of Idaho had lived at some time in Boise, but because it came at some cost to him. She had perceived his fleeting discomfort after he spoke, a barely noticeable withdrawal, his shoulders hunching slightly, his chin tucking in.

Even so, some damage had been done; an accounting for was due. Alma would have to be brought around somehow. Her being an inmate compromised her credibility, but to date that had never stopped her from making mischief for her own ends, her own entertainment. Mrs. Quill shuddered recalling Alma's peccadilloes in Little Wood.

Pre-emptive disclosure was called for, and not merely to clear the air. Mrs. Quill knew she had to take responsibility. First things first, she must speak with Ellen.

There was little chance though of serious talk. When

Ellen was not with LeahNell, she was talking *about* LeahNell. And, Ellen had turned into a chatterbox.

"There's something I must tell you, Ellen," said Mrs. Quill on Wednesday afternoon, when her daughter arrived home from school. "We need to talk."

"Is it all right if I go to LeahNell's after school?"

"Please. This is important."

"Yes, but... Can I?"

"When? Tomorrow?"

"Yes, tomorrow, and ... Instead of getting off the bus here, I'd get off at the Farm road with the other kids. She'll be out of class then and we'll go to her room."

"Honey, LeahNell is six years older than you. She's an adult. She doesn't want to spend her time with ..."

"Mom, she invited me."

"Of course you may, but there's something I need to tell you. It's about LeahNell ..."

"Isn't she interesting? She knows so much. We have a lot to talk about."

"That's what I want to tell you."

"And we'll all have dinner together and then I'll come home with you. She goes to a seminar in the evening. And then she has to study. And so do I."

Is this the talk I want to have with Ellen?

She considered. Whether Ellen knew LeahNell was her sister likely wouldn't change their wanting to be together. Could lend an unnatural imperative to their friendship, to say nothing of curdling Ellen's regard for her mother.

There was no reason the two girls shouldn't be friends, spend time together if they wanted to. And if LeahNell did in fact tire of Ellen and drift away, it would not be the last -- and perhaps not the first -- rejection Ellen would meet.

What if they did pool their impressions, compare personal histories, come to conclusions? It might already have happened. Certainly, she herself had supplied ample evidence. She had lived in Little Wood; she had known LeahNell's parents; and she hadn't been Mrs. Quill then. What she hadn't uttered herself, Alma had blurted out.

Had either Ellen or LeahNell perceived their physical

similarities? Had anyone else? The clues were there and Alma, at least, had fitted them together.

Yes, Mrs. Quill and Ellen needed to talk, not to lead Ellen's judgment of her mother, but in the natural flow of events.

By the time Saturday came around, Ellen and LeahNell were studying together, either at LeahNell's dorm or at home with Mrs. Quill, and playing ball with the Mossbacks. Sunday at noon, Mrs. Quill and the two girls were in the dinner line-up just ahead of Dr. Quill. Ellen and LeahNell had their heads together, whispering, and then LeahNell turned around and invited Dr. Quill to eat with them at the table they had staked out in a corner away from the student nurse and psychology crowd.

He watched with a smile spreading beneath his silky white mustache as they wheedled like a pair of six-year-olds, and by the time LeahNell said, "Pretty please?" he had given way.

Mrs. Quill felt her face pinking up as Dr. Quill held a chair for her. He sat across from her and focused on the girls and their chatter.

Mrs. Quill had made a case with Ellen for eating at home. Cooking in their own kitchen was the point of having their own house, wasn't it? It was true that Ynez would have been doing the cooking, as well as occupying the third bedroom, in her absence now spare. But eating at home meant time away from LeahNell, so evening after evening, there they were, the four of them, in a quasi-family group having dinner. The girls would call out to Dr. Quill as they filed into the dining room, or the three of them would be seated, Ellen and LeahNell flanking Mrs. Quill, leaving an open space, and here he would come, murmuring, "May I?"

Mrs. Quill was annoyed with herself for being pleased. And then they would ignore each other, he and Mrs. Quill, their eyes on the girls.

More and more, their chatter centered around life in Little Wood, featuring names familiar to Mrs. Quill, now linked in surprising ways. She found herself listening to parts of her own history played back to her through someone else's experience. Standing outside herself, rehearsing and trying on events to see if they fit. Then something would prick up her ears, like LeahNell's mention of Dr. Flower and the hospital burning down, as though she were reading from a news article, as if she had had no part in it. Or ... no recollection. Was it possible she didn't remember?

Dr. Quill listened with more apparent interest than she would have expected him to have in a rural crossroads village, and she reflected that his passage to Millennium from Boise would have taken him through Little Wood, with a stop for a train to take on water, long enough for passengers to stroll the park and have a meal at the Manhattan. Her own stopover from Boise had lasted three years. How long had Dr. Quill lingered?

One evening, the two girls signaled each other across the table like the conspirators they were, and LeahNell said, "One, two, three ..."

They launched into song in their blended woodwindy voices, and the hair stood up on Mrs. Quill's arms.

The tune scaled up and down a span of just five notes, three notes up, three down, three up again and a hop at the top, like a little adventure, or like a sheepherder stepping over a stile in the winter pastures east of Little Wood. Mrs. Quill had heard it first, years ago, as a wheedling, mournful air played on a crude willow flute, and then again one day in a sheepwagon, in a rollicking tempo from a mouthharp, while outside the sky opened and rain drummed on the canvas roof.

Mary Macpherson she had been called then; it was her mother's name. The old Basque sheep boss Salvador taught her the words to the song, in their exotic ancient tongue, syllable by syllable, until she could sing it without flaw, and only then told her what the words meant. Salvador, with his leathery, angular face and deep-set, squinty eyes, who, it turned out, was Leonard Thorel's father.

She'd wondered later if Leonard knew. The only clue was a remark he'd made. "I've never liked going to the boarding house. Salvador's wife has a way of looking at me that makes me feel as welcome as a carbuncle."

Song finished, the girls, flushed with accomplishment, sat back and Dr. Quill applauded.

"Where did you hear... learn that song?" Mrs. Quill asked.

"Ellen taught it to me," said LeahNell.

Ellen blushed and said, "Ynez used to sing it to me."

"Did she tell you what the words meant?"

Ellen shook her head and waited. It registered on Mrs. Quill that Ellen seemed not surprised that her mother might know the song.

"It's a silly song. About a truck carrying fourteen fat women playing trombones."

"I wonder if Daddy knows it," said LeahNell. "I'll sing it for him when I get home." She hesitated, and she and Ellen exchanged glances. "Just for Daddy. My mother wouldn't be interested."

So.

No, Olive wouldn't be interested in the *song*. And what would Leonard say? Mrs. Quill imagined that Leonard might look with surprise at his daughter and say, "I haven't heard that song in fifteen ..."

No, he'd say, "That's the first time I've heard you sing that since you were five years old." Because Mrs. Quill knew that LeahNell hadn't just learned the song here at The Farm. She was singing it by the time she was three. She sang it with the sheepherders that afternoon seventeen years ago on Galena Summit.

She had liked being Mary Macpherson.

She recalled Leonard, one summer day, perched on a sawhorse in the hospital side yard in Little Wood, absently rubbing an ink stain on the knuckle of his right second finger. The stain reminded her that he was a teacher, an English teacher. He was so humble that she couldn't imagine him a stern taskmaster. She had asked him how he got the high school boys' attention.

"Attention? The first week, the athletes like to loom over me." He shrugged. "I let them. They come around."

He spoke of the mountains, or the hills, as the locals called them, grazing country for his mother's sheep ranch. "Nowhere else," he said, "can you breathe so deep, feel such peace." Later, "Have you ever been in a sheep camp?"

She had not.

"Olive won't go. She likes the mountains and camping

in a tent and gathering wildflowers and cooking over an open fire. But she doesn't like the sheep camps. Thousands of sheep, the smell, the dust. She doesn't like the sheepherders looking at her strangely and then ignoring her, speaking in a language she doesn't understand."

"Do you speak Basque?"

"Only a little. I speak through Salvador mainly, what needs to be said. I sing a few songs I don't know the meaning of, and I can swear. The men like that."

He stood up. "If you'd like to see a sheep camp, I'm going up Thursday morning. The sheep are on Galena Summit, beyond Ketchum... "

And on that Thursday, wearing a pair of laced-up boots borrowed from Olive, she had ridden with Leonard, three-year-old LeahNell between them, in the dark green Lincoln into the hills, away from the water tower, the ballpark, the railroad tracks, the river, leaving behind even Dr. Flower's Almshouse.

The road ascended northward through mile upon mile of sagebrush dotted with lava formations and patches of tumbleweeds, which in March would dry and blow loose in the first spring gale, and earn their name -- tumbling like acrobats by the thousands in great traffic-stopping tidal waves across the prairie, down the highways and the railroad tracks, inciting the town's children -- young and old -- to caper after them.

"Rain over Fairfield," Leonard remarked, pointing to the western horizon, where sunlight bounced off a gray sheet falling vertically from a dark billow of clouds.

Brush began to give way to mountain aspen and pine, and beyond Hailey and Ketchum, the car left a trail of dust ruffles on gravel. Not a single vehicle appeared to challenge their claim to the center of the road. Clouds moved fast overhead, changing shape as they advanced, shadows plunging the road into twilight for a long moment before sunlight and blue sky reasserted itself.

She had forgotten how delicious it was to ride with a man, with the countryside rolling by and the rhythm of companionable silences, each of them lapsing into thought until random impressions coalesced into speech again.

Rocks appeared in the gravel surface and the ribbon of

road fell away behind them as Leonard finessed the auto around a series of hairpin turns. On the passenger side, Mary reflexively scooted away from the window view of the long drop into the valley. She glanced at Leonard, hoping he wouldn't feel that she was crowding him, but if he had noticed anything amiss he gave no indication. LeahNell put down her doll and clung to Mary.

As the elevation increased, tree life grew sparse, and on a mountain slope in the distance, Mary could distinguish a sea of sheep from sagebrush only by their creeping advance. Across a mountain meadow, a grove of aspen appeared and the roadbed smoothed out. Leonard let the auto roll to a stop into the midst of the trees, where a lone sheepwagon, its canvas top bellying out over the wood box bottom, a crooked, capped stove pipe rising out the top, sheltered from the sun and the wind. An icebox and a woodstack flanked the steps to the open-hatched door, and a battered, mud-spattered pickup was parked just beyond.

At first it seemed there was no one there, but then two figures in rough, faded blue shirts and pants and wear-warped boots -- the sheep boss, Salvador, and the sheepherder, a smaller, rounder, younger man -- emerged from around the far end of the sheepwagon, advancing to make them welcome. Bear hugs for Leonard, a lift to Salvador's shoulders for three-year-old LeahNell, and solemn bows for Mary. She stepped back then and stretched to shake off her stiffness from the long ride. Her first deep breath of crisp, thin mountain air made her nearly dizzy with exhilaration.

While the men talked business in phrases of English and Basque, LeahNell stroked the fleece of the lamb that was the sheepherder's special pet. Mary ambled around the grove admiring the white-barked aspens and the flickering highlights of their dainty round leaves that quaked a kind of rustling tinkle in the slightest breeze. Odd images and symbols were incised in the white bark of many of the trees.

Footsteps crunched dry leaves behind her and the men were at her side.

"Admiring our tree carvings, eh?" said Salvador.

"I wouldn't examine them too closely if I were you," Leonard said, then added mysteriously: "The sheepherder's life is a lonely one."

His words were spoken in an unfamiliar -- for him, insinuating cadence, as if he were speaking Basque, and his left eyebrow tilted whimsically. She had never before seen him in a state of whimsy.

He had unbuttoned his collar and rolled up the sleeves of his shirt, which was loosened and bloused around his waist. He stood with his feet braced, fists on his hips, elbows jutting. He needed only a beret to pass for one of the men who hung around Salvador's boarding house.

The young sheepherder had been ogling Mary, and now spoke at some length to Leonard, then stood aside and resumed staring.

Leonard turned to Mary. "He is mesmerized by your pale hair. He said, among other things, that if he had known you were coming, he'd have shaved."

Leonard might not speak much Basque, she thought, but he certainly understands it.

He continued: "Also, he wants to know if you like Rocky Mountain oysters. You don't know about Rocky Mountain oysters? Just as well." And then as an afterthought: "We are invited to share lunch with them."

With LeahNell in the bed of the truck, the men leaned on the tailgate, passing a wineskin back and forth among them. Mary perched in the driver's seat with the door open, her feet on the running board. After their sheepherders' lunch of bread and fresh cheese and boiled coffee, supplemented with apricots from Ynez's orchard, Mary drowsed a little and gazed at the rolling sea of sheep grazing on the slopes above the aspen grove. The men had fallen silent, and the only sounds were the steady insect thrum and the distant bark of a dog warning an errant lamb back into the fold.

The sudden agitation of aspen leaves that Mary had thought so musical signaled the onset of rain, which descended in a torrent. Salvador grabbed LeahNell and herded everyone to shelter. "Inside the sheepwagon, get in the wagon. Move!"

Mary was first into the narrow aisle inside. Her eyes adjusted to the dim light that revealed a rough-wool-blanketed bed built into and across the far end, with an underbed drawer, an overbed shelf, hooks for clothing, and a clothesline. On one side, a rough table with a bench faced, on the other side, the woodstove, which heated the wagon and the water for a small basin sunk into a wash cabinet, and baked the herder's sourdough bread and beans.

The sheepwagon reeked of wood smoke, pine sap, and wet wool. Fermenting tobacco, rancid bacon grease. And... maleness. Mary found the scent not unpleasant.

With a sweeping gesture, the sheepherder indicated that his home was theirs. LeahNell claimed the bed. Salvador persuaded her to share with him and the herder, leaving Mary and Leonard to crowd onto the bench. LeahNell bounced, and squealed when the springs protested. No one tried to rein her in.

From a can with an unintelligible label, Salvador rolled a cigarette of a dark, slightly sour substance with the texture of mincemeat. He licked the length of the paper, twisted the ends and lit it with a match, sucked in a deep breath, then passed it across the rough table to Leonard.

Leonard drew a long draft and peered at Mary through the haze as he offered her the cigarette. She began to shake her head, but the corner of his lip lifted in a lopsided smile and his left eyebrow tilted. She looked him squarely in the eye, put the cigarette to her lips and drew a breath. Though she gasped and coughed until the tears came, the men applauded. The sheepherder drew his mouthharp from his pocket and began to play.

Later, after the squall had passed, the sheepmen said their goodbyes with the same fervor as their welcome. Mary was accorded kisses on both cheeks. With Leonard at the wheel, Mary on the passenger side, LeahNell again between them, they began the trek back to Little Wood. The car swayed gently negotiating the rough roadbed. Soon LeahNell's eyelids began to droop and then with a sigh, she slid her head into Mary's lap.

At the lower end of the hairpin turns, Leonard pulled the car off the road facing south and shifted into neutral. He disengaged the clutch, and set the brake. Through the dusty windshield, the valley floor spread out below them.

Car trouble? Or a last look at the view?

Their glances met for an instant before, swiftly, Leonard

turned and leaned across the wheel and LeahNell's limp body, and took Mary's head between his hands and kissed her full upon the mouth. It was over before she could stop herself from kissing him back.

They rode silently then, Mary's mind blissfully empty of thought. As they slowed for the curve in the road leading into Little Wood, Leonard steered with one hand while he buttoned his collar, rolled down his shirtsleeves, and fastened them.

For the next two years, Mary would almost forget that Leonard was anything other than a sober, buttoned-up school-teacher and husband of Olive and father of LeahNell.

Mrs. Quill came out of her reverie and gazed around the table at three pairs of eyes focused on her. She realized that LeahNell had just spoken to her. "Excuse me?"

"My father and Dr. Flower were related somehow, weren't they? My mother said Daddy looked like Dr. Flower."

Mrs. Quill pulled herself up straight and peered at LeahNell sidelong, quizzical.

LeahNell rushed on: "She thought perhaps you and Dr. Flower were secretly married."

Mrs. Quill saw that both girls were looking at her rapt and expectant, lips slightly parted. They wanted something from her, or ... They seemed to be offering her something ... and were waiting for her to accept. But why here and now? Couldn't it wait until Dr. Quill had gone?

Then she saw what they were up to. The presence of Dr. Quill was essential. The scamps were playing Cupid. They had conjured a fictional relationship that would make a respectable woman of her, that would give Ellen a legitimate father.

She didn't know whether to laugh or protest. She would not explain, or confirm -- not here, not yet -- what they seemed already to have figured out, but neither would she compound the lie of omission with an outright falsehood.

"No, LeahNell," she said, "your father looked nothing like Dr. Flower." And Olive, though devious, would never have said so.

Mrs. Quill had a fleeting image of Dr. Flower with his white hair electric under the surgical light that caught the gold flecks of his astonishing turquoise eyes. "And Dr. Flower was a generation older than I." *And he was in love, LeahNell, with your grandmother*.

LeahNell's eyebrows knotted with perplexity.

Mrs. Quill's voice softened. "Do you remember his ring? The stone was a rare agate the color of his eyes. Turquoise."

LeahNell gasped and pulled back. *"His...?* I still have a ring," she said. "I didn't know it was ... At home. I left it at home so it wouldn't get lost."

"He asked me to give it to you. Before the fire. And when the fire broke out and we were getting all the patients outside, you were taking a nap." *Five years old.* Mrs. Quill took a deep breath. "I found you, carried you downstairs and outside. But he... Dr. Flower... was still looking for you, calling your name. When the ... when the fire cut off the stairway."

She couldn't go on, remembering how she had pounded Sheriff Wellcome's chest as he held her to keep her from going back inside.

They sat there, Mrs. Quill, Ellen, LeahNell, Dr. Quill, staring at their unfinished desserts, and then as one, they pushed back their chairs and single-filed out into the early evening, Dr. Quill holding doors, tenderly handing Mrs. Quill and Ellen into the gray Plymouth, and silently walking LeahNell to the old Women's Violent.

At eleven-thirty, having received the evening report, Mrs. Quill surveyed the ward rosters. As expected, Rochelle's name was not listed on Women's Violent. But Alma's name leaped out at her.

What had Alma done this time to be downgraded to Violent? Why would she risk Rex McFall's investment in her rehabilitation? Mrs. Quill tucked the report book under her arm and set out for Women's Violent.

Inside, she glanced down the hall -- all dark and quiet, not what she'd expected with Alma in residence. The night attendant, Mrs. Brunt, greeted Mrs. Quill at the nurses station, then said, "Guess who is waiting for you in the dayroom."

In the farthest corner of the dim-lit dayroom out of earshot of the nurses' station, Alma waited, blind eyes turned to

Mrs. Quill's approach.

"Alma, it isn't necessary to get yourself deported to Women's Violent when you want to talk with me. I make rounds of all the wards. And now you lose your grounds privilege."

Alma smiled slightly. "I'm not here on your account." She hesitated. "Grounds privilege? I'll get it back."

"Don't be too sure. Privileges aren't given lightly. You have to earn them and use them responsibly. Dr. McFall and I will have to do some fast talking at staff meeting to convince them you haven't relapsed."

Assuming Alma *hadn't* relapsed into meddling and theatrics. "So why are you here? What did you do?"

"I didn't do anything. Mrs. Moody let me come with Rochelle."

"Stay here, Alma. I'll be right back."

In the bright light of the nurses station, Mrs. Quill flipped back page after page of the day nurses' accounts until she found, ten days earlier, what she was looking for.

Mrs. Doyle had made the sparsest entry possible of the transfer of two women, Rochelle and Alma, giving cause only for Rochelle. Mrs. Moody had indeed accepted Alma to Women's Violent and in the days following noted, in effect, that Alma held court in the dayroom, where the women gathered around listening to her words of wisdom. *Still the teacher, the ... sibyl.* The women followed her around, and Alma and her cronies sequestered themselves with Rochelle in her private cell. On Mrs. Moody's morning rounds, she would find Alma asleep on top of Rochelle's bed, cuddling Rochelle like a baby.

How did it happen that Alma had been on Women's Violent for ten days without her name appearing on the roster? *Guess who's waiting for you in the dayroom.*

Mrs. Quill closed the day book and returned to the dayroom. "Alma, what are you doing on this ward?"

"Rochelle needs me. We're taking care of her, Clarissa and Eloise and I. I go where I'm needed."

"Why does she need you? She's here only to keep Casey away from her." Mrs. Quill wondered, too late, whether she was giving Alma too much information, then realized that Alma knew at least as much as she did herself and probably more. *She goes? Where she's needed?*

"She misses him," said Alma.

"She misses *Casey*? After what he did to her?"

Yes, of course. How many people in Rochelle's life had given her even a kind word? Mrs. Quill shifted her report book to her other arm. "You've achieved remarkable mobility between the wards. And now what?"

Alma turned her eyes to Mrs. Quill, opened her mouth to reply. From down the hall came a thin wail. "Rochelle is crying," she said. "I must go."

Alma rose and groped from chair to chair to the doorway. There she stopped and looked around. Softly she said, "Rochelle has morning sickness."

15: LeahNell

She hadn't read Floyd's letter the next morning after all, but set it on the dresser and opened it after breakfast two days later.

Following a formulaic opening ("Well, here I am again ..."), he had kindly advised her that he wouldn't be coming to Millennium to see her on his Memorial Day holiday as he'd promised, but had accepted an invitation to a stag weekend at the mountain lodge of a very important business prospect. He would attempt to meet her train when, in three weeks, it made its brief stop in Little Wood on her way back to Trinity. In any case, he would see her in Boise.

Her initial rush of relief was overtaken by annoyance that she let escalate into outrage because of the opportunity it provided her to justify taking the action she had been only fantasizing about to this point. Thrilled with her mounting resolve, she sat down at her desk, uncapped her grandmother's old green-marbled Sheaffer, filled it with fresh emerald ink, and in crisp, measured prose on Berkshire Bond, released Floyd from any and all commitment to her. She posted the letter at the drop box in the administration building and went on to her morning's work on Women's Violent, feeling light as a zephyr.

She had gotten over her surprise at seeing Alma Duffy there. Without being listed on the ward roster, that lady had for some mysterious reason been on the violent ward since the day after her outing at the ball game. This morning, as was her custom, Miss Duffy in the dayroom was surrounded by half a dozen women asking questions that varied from how to do long division to whether there was a god to what the nurse was thinking when she raised her eyebrows. Other women came and went. Wispy Clarissa gliding on tiptoe, stiff-necked Eloise with her refrain: "You. Are. Eliminated. With. Courtesy." The tight-clenched catatonic who flailed and kicked when her invisible three-foot territorial space was breached. And in the end room down the hall, Rochelle watched the coming and going through the six-inch square window of her cell.

On the sidewalk at lunch time, LeahNell was overtaken by Stella and her retinue of male patients, all on their way to the canteen. In response to LeahNell's greeting, Stella barely glanced at her, but tossed her glorious red-gold mane over her shoulder and turned away. She had just been granted another extension of tenure on the voluntary admissions ward.

The high spirits that had buoyed LeahNell all morning evaporated, and with her lunch tray she slouched downcast into the dining room. Rex hailed her from the corner table where he sat alone.

"Haven't seen much of you lately," he said. "Just off in the distance with the young lady who looks enough like you to be your sister."

She glanced at him. His expression betrayed no special knowledge. She guessed she must seem fickle. It had been so important to be one of the adults, and now she was ignoring her elders and her classmates -- who didn't appear to miss her -- in favor of someone she thought of as almost a kid sister.

Well, she *was* her kid sister. Or half-sister. No matter -- a sister was a sister, and LeahNell had always wanted one. And in truth, she hadn't missed Rex and Matthew and Gilda. Maybe Rex a little bit. Maybe Matthew a little. Being in the company of the three of them was wearing, since she had to guard her tongue every minute.

She guessed she ought to think before she spoke with other people too. She should have known better than try to link Mrs. Quill with Dr. Flower. For a childish moment, she'd wanted to clear Daddy of wrong-doing. In any case, she wouldn't see Ellen today until supper, Mrs. Quill having put a stop to the dailiness of their afternoons together.

"You're very quiet," said Rex. "Something wrong?"

"No, I'm fine," she said too quickly. "Well, I broke up with my boyfriend back home. Wrote him a letter this morning." She forked a chunk of lettuce, hoping to appear nonchalant.

"I didn't know you had a boyfriend." He eyed her reflectively. "And now you've cut him loose. I'll resist my impulse to inquire in my best therapeutic manner, 'And how do you feel about that?'" His dimple winked. She didn't respond and the dimple disappeared. "Seriously," he said. "Do you want to talk about it?"

"Not really. Well, maybe. I'm mixed up. I should feel happy about it. I did feel happy about it. I felt as if a hundred-pound weight had been taken off me, as if I could fly. Now I'm afraid I could just fly off into space. I'm not sure I can keep my feet on the ground." She put the forked lettuce on her plate, untasted.

He tilted back, slapped his matchbook on the edge of the table. "What a fantastic physical expression of a psychic state," he said. "You have the sense -- the experience of your emotions. I wish Stella could think like that, instead of those logical constructions -- those surgical dissections she thrusts between herself and her feelings." He fumbled in his pocket, brought out his cigarettes, turned the pack over and over, set it down.

Stunned, LeahNell stared at him. He was turning her tender, private feelings to his own impersonal, professional ends. Rejecting her. On top of the rejection she had already...

But *she* had cast out Floyd. Why was *she* feeling rejected? Because Stella's feelings were more important than hers? She wasn't jealous of Stella, of course. She felt *sorry* for poor messed-up, miserable, alcoholic Stella. She'd crawl into a hole before she'd be jealous of Stella.

Gorgeous, privileged, imperious Stella.

She wanted to crawl into a hole. "Rex, would you be my therapist?" she blurted.

"What? Your ..." He sat up straight. "No. I mean ... No. I can't be your therapist."

"You 'can't' be my therapist? Why not?"

"We know too much about each other. You know too much about me. Which gives you opportunity to shape the effect your words would have on me, makes you measure what you will tell me against how you want me to perceive it."

"Couldn't we go back to being friends after I finished therapy?"

"No. Doesn't work. Yes, it happens. But it shouldn't." He took out a cigarette, tapped it on the table. "Therapy is a lopsided relationship. A lopsided power relationship. For the patient, when it's over it should be over. You get your life back.

You go out and test what you've learned. The therapist gives up his power. Lets go. Clean break. You have to let the patient go."

"But... "

Rex put up his hand. "That kind of friendship is just another phase of the therapeutic process. The former patient exercises his new-found power to say no, like a two-year-old, to control the former therapist, and the former therapist continues to be the point of reference for reality, weighing in on every aspect of the patient's life."

"But after therapy, it's just another relationship ..."

"No, therapy is *the* relationship. It takes the place of reality. Everything that happens is seen through the lens of therapy. Everything that happens, that you do, that you think becomes fodder for the therapeutic session. How will the therapist interpret this? Do I want to tell the therapist that? Will he approve? You're never alone; the therapist is always with you looking over your shoulder. This does not change if you carry on as 'friends.' You feel independent, but it's an illusion. The therapist doesn't, shouldn't care about you beyond an impersonal business relationship. Yes, business. A contractual relationship. Of necessity. With a term and an end."

"People stay in analysis for years and years ..."

"Yes, and they are living an illusion. The analysand is unable to commit fully to another person, unable to become autonomous. The same thing is going on when therapist and patient maintain a fiction of friendship. You feel he is entitled to know everything. He is subtly exercising control, fostering dependency, however benign." He put away the cigarette.

"I wonder if I have a father fixation," she offered.

"Yes, I'd wonder that too." He laughed. "And if you do, you don't need to replace that fixation with a transference fixation. You need to get out and live. Take risks, make mistakes. Suffer maybe. Put yourself on the line." He leaned forward on his elbows and looked at her intently. "I don't want to be your therapist. I need you to be my friend."

"*You* need *me*?"

He settled back. "You don't need a therapist. You need a friend. I'm your friend. You're having a normal reaction to a life situation. You made a necessary decision. But nothing and nobody is all good or all bad, so of course you don't feel quite right about it. You've upset the status quo. You're not in the habit of taking risks. You're pretty buttoned-up. Which works for you most of the time."

Buttoned up? LeahNell thought she was pretty daring. She'd taken risks, a lot of risks, acted impulsively. Sometimes stupid-impulsively. "I'm not as buttoned up as you think I am," she said. "I'm not even a ..."

He glanced at her.

She stopped short of "virgin." "I'm not going to tell you unless you are my therapist."

He laughed. "What a manipulator. You just proved my point."

With his usual sheaf of papers tucked under one arm and clutching his lunch tray, Matthew approached their table, stopped in front of them and stood beaming from one to the other with what looked to LeahNell like approval. Was he hoping she and Rex had found each other?

"Am I interrupting something, I hope?" Matthew said. He lowered his tray.

"You're interrupting something," said Rex.

A flicker of satisfaction in Matthew's eyes confirmed LeahNell's suspicion. Matthew retreated to a table where the nurses from Admissions were starting on their desserts.

"The first time I've seen Matthew speechless," said Rex. "Tell me about your boyfriend? Ex-boyfriend. Where'd you meet him?"

"I grew up with him. I've always known him."

"You were playmates?"

"No. He's two years older. That's a lot when you're a kid. He's a partner now in his father's law office. In Little Wood." She hesitated. "And I don't know if Floyd was ever anybody's playmate."

"Are you attracted to him? Sexually attracted?"

LeahNell felt her jaw tighten and her voice came out a higher pitch. "No ..." She ducked her head.

"Is he sexually attracted to you?"

What a silly question. Didn't men always ...? She raised her head and looked at Rex with surprise. "You know, I don't think so. I think he's ... experienced ..."

No, Floyd wasn't that way about her, which was the *reason...* "... but with me, he's, um, paternal. Protective. Which I needed then." *Then. After. After Victor -- Dr. Reamer.*

"And you don't need him now ... "

Statement? Question? The flat word at the end left the choice up to her. "He's an only child. He wants to have a large family."

"Somehow, I don't see you mother to a slew of kids."

"I don't either. Now. I used to think it would be nice."

With a clatter of utensils, the nurses at Matthew's table stood and picked up their trays. In their wake, Matthew carried his coffee back to LeahNell and Rex, who had lapsed into silence.

"I perceive that my timing is immaculate," Matthew said. "How are things on Women's Violent, LeahNell?" He sat down.

She told them about finding Alma Duffy there. Rex looked first alarmed and then grim. "She's up to something," he said. "Why can't she learn to ask for help?"

"She seems to like Women's Violent," said LeahNell. "She's in no hurry to leave. She doesn't even mind the noise -- all that catcalling and screeching. She talks with the women. They talk to her. There's a woman they have to restrain or she'll take her pants off. She sits on the floor all day with her legs spread, in a ... a ..." How would Matthew put it? "... an attitude of ... sexual invitation, and makes obscene remarks at everyone. Alma Duffy speaks to her and for a few minutes the woman behaves herself. Alma's the only person she'll listen to."

For just a moment, even Matthew looked interested. She went on, "Why do the women behave so differently from men on a violent ward? The men are mostly quiet or just preachy."

"Excuse my indifference to your miswired inmates," said Matthew. "They are beyond the help of psychology. But doubtless Rex has a sociological insight for you."

"I do, actually," said Rex. "In Western society, men abhor religiosity but have greater sexual latitude, while women are forbidden free sexual expression. What is taboo is most likely to be flouted."

"That simple, eh?" said Matthew.

"More or less. Variations on the theme, of course. Would you like to explore them?"

"No. I have a loftier mission. This afternoon, I must lecture on Jung. You really should develop a taste for coffee, LeahNell. I expect you to be rapt and fully engaged. I depend on you to prod your sluggish classmates awake."

At loose ends after class, LeahNell followed the other girls into the canteen, where Clarence in his starched chef's hat scowled with concentration as he mixed fountain Cokes -- cherry for Cleo, lemon for Melba, chocolate-coffee-cream for LeahNell. On the lookout for her admirers -- Jep and Ollie, Whitaker and Mr. Wheeler, Melba's eyes were on the door.

"Floyd coming to visit this weekend?" asked Cleo.

LeahNell shook her head. "He changed his mind. He has something ... *important!* to do this weekend. I wrote him a letter, broke the engagement."

Cleo's jaw dropped. Melba twitched her shoulders and said, "It's about time. You weren't doing a thing for him. Well, you weren't. You're not the least little bit interested in settling down and having kids. High time you turned him loose so he can find someone who is."

Nonchalant. Be nonchalant.

Melba's quartet arrived, and she moved to another table with them. Then out the window, Cleo spied Francis and she was off. LeahNell made her Coke last another ten minutes while the white-hatted soda jerk glared at her. She stood then and sauntered out the door. *Not a care in the world.*

As she turned the corner to head for the old Women's Violent, Matthew's Jeep pulled up to the curb, Gilda at the wheel. At least, it seemed to be Gilda. With a faded blue scarf covering her hair, she wore sunglasses and an old sweater several sizes too large. She beckoned to LeahNell. "Hop in."

"Can I go change clothes?"

Gilda glanced at LeahNell's uniform and white shoes. "Hurry." She was slouched into the seat, gripping the steering wheel when LeahNell returned five minutes later, tucking her blouse into slacks.

"You look like an inmate," said LeahNell. She settled herself in the passenger seat. "Are you in disguise?"

Gilda turned on the ignition, put the Jeep in gear, and pulled away into the street. "Don't be pert. What have you been doing all afternoon?"

"Class ..., "

"Matthew?"

LeahNell nodded. "... and talking with Cleo and Melba."

Gilda turned the Jeep onto the farm road. "Let's give you a different afternoon, reconstruct it a little. Let's say you joined me for a long ride out to the reservoir. To see if it's warm enough for swimming." She glanced at LeahNell. "I need an alibi."

Rex? "What have *you* been doing this afternoon?" said LeahNell.

Gilda flashed her a sharp look. "Don't take advantage, young lady. This will be *your* picnic -- the farewell picnic at the resevoir. Let's go test the water."

"Matthew knows I was in class," said LeahNell. The Jeep was hot, as though it had been standing in the sun all afternoon. "This isn't the first time, is it?"

"Of course not. And to answer your next question, it won't be the last. Do you think me terribly immoral?"

"I don't know," said LeahNell. "I guess it isn't any of my business."

"I'm glad you realize that. I expect that's why we're such good friends."

Good friends? LeahNell mentally reviewed the lunch-time conversation with Rex in terms of what he had known he would be doing this afternoon while Matthew was otherwise engaged. Intrigue upon intrigue.

The barn flashed by, then the chicken coops and the tool yard, where a balding blue-denim-clad inmate hammered at an anvil. As they passed, a pair of mastiffs reclining in the shade of a stunted cottonwood sprang to their feet and, snarling, bolted after the Jeep. Their keeper shouted and the dogs slunk back into the yard.

"Haven't seen much of you lately," said Gilda. "What have you been up to?"

LeahNell considered. She didn't especially want to talk about Ellen. "Broke up with my boyfriend."

"We ... I never imagined you had a boyfriend."

LeahNell's antennae quivered. Rex had uttered those very words. "Who is 'we'?"

"Were you sleeping with him? You can tell Aunt Gilda everything."

"Wha-at? No. Does my having a boyfriend make a difference?" It was no longer a surprise to LeahNell that their association did not spring from affinity.

Gilda smiled. "Not now. It might have. I need you to keep Matthew entertained. He, of course, hopes you'll turn Rex's head."

"I guess you're pretty sure I'm no competition for either of them."

"What a bright little lady you are. I'll admit I don't want any competition."

"Isn't that kind of ... greedy?"

"Yes. No. This just makes for internal harmony. We all need some balance. You're using us too. We make you feel grownup and sophisticated. You're a smart girl -- there's no harm in using people when it's consented to."

"I don't use people. I'm not that kind of person."

"Of *course* not. You're just a selfless, benevolent humanitarian. You came here to learn about yourself, so listen to this: You're passive-aggressive and you want to know about life, but you want everyone else to make the mistakes so you can profit from them. Well, here's your chance. Make the most of it." Gilda turned her attention to the narrow, rutted road, stepped on the accelerator.

She hates me, thought LeahNell, flushed and fuming; she hates me, but at least Matthew and Rex like me. She nursed the idea. Then she remembered the night she had baited Hopkins and realized she could be mean. It was too much. She'd think about that later.

"Here we are. Let's test the water." Gilda pulled up onto a little rise and cut the engine. She thrust the keys into her handbag and pushed it under the seat. They got out of the Jeep and Gilda took off the sweater.

Water rippled and cattails leaned in the wind near the pond's edge where the ground was marshy. LeahNell took off her sandals and waded out to water deep enough for a reading. "It's cold but not heart-stopping," she said. "By the time the sun goes down, it might be almost warm."

"There's a high spot over there where we can build a fire and sunbathe. Here -- you can dry your feet on this." Gilda tossed LeahNell the sweater. "Tomorrow is the day. Can you get the word out? Just your classmates and the Young Bloo... the *interns*. No kids."

On impulse, LeahNell asked, "Why don't you and Matthew have children?"

"I can't. Or, we can't," Gilda said absently. "I don't know. Matthew says I can't. If you haven't heard him say it, you will. It's one of his stock speeches when we play 'Pin the Tail on Gilda.' Supposed to explain my restlessness, my infidelities ..."

"Does he talk about that? Does he know?" *What a strange marriage.*

"Oh yes. He knows."

"Then why do you need an alibi?"

"Because, little one, I may be a bitch, but I am not an unfeeling bitch." Gilda fumbled in her pocket, came up empty, looked toward the Jeep. *Cigarette.* "And, I want to keep doing it. Do you think he would sit still if he knew the very moment and place I was misbehaving?"

Sandals restored, LeahNell dropped the wet sweater behind the seat and got into the Jeep. Gilda followed, pulled out her handbag. Upside down.

An incredible number of items scampered off in every direction. Keys, cigarettes and black onyx holder, lighter, lipstick... LeahNell helped Gilda retrieve them. A rubber disk with a rolled edge sprang free from the tissue it had been wrapped in. LeahNell caught it, rewrapped it and handed it to Gilda before she realized the significance of Gilda's hard gaze.

"That's a diaphragm," said LeahNell.

"Give that here. Of course it's a diaphragm. But how would you know, Miss Innocence? Oh, yes -- nurses know all these things. Learned it in the classroom, of course." Gilda bit off each word and leaned her face so close to LeahNell's that it obscured everything else. "You keep your mouth shut. You don't mention this to a soul. Do you understand?"

LeahNell recoiled. Gilda sat up heavily, and restored her purse and her face to unrippled serenity.

After a few minutes, LeahNell said, "You know that I won't talk to anyone. But why do you need a diaphragm if you're sterile?"

Gilda tossed her head. "I'm not sterile. I don't want kids. Matthew doesn't really want kids. If he were faced with the reality of fatherhood, he'd fall apart. We'd fall apart. He likes to think he's being deprived. I'm just holding onto the reins."

She tipped a cigarette to her lighter, spoke through the haze of her first draw. "I'm not going to become one of those insipid women dedicating their bodies to the pleasure of men, waddling around sway-backed carrying babies. Shriveled breasts and stretch-marks. Hemorrhoids, varicose veins. And an empty head."

Her intensity was like a whip. LeahNell's nose tingled and her eyes stung with reflexive tears.

Gilda's tone softened a little. "I've got two brothers and four sisters. My brothers are braying jackasses. My sisters go on and on about movie stars and dates and hairdos, and are their tits big enough. Growing up was a twenty-year beauty contest, a race to see who could get married first. Now they compete with pregnancies. They don't care about children. They just breed."

She jammed the live end of the cigarette into the ashtray, ground it to a mash. "I could hardly wait to leave home, and I'm not giving up my freedom for a life like that."

They were silent for an interval, while LeahNell considered.

Her own mother had two children only. Her mother's friends had one or two, or three, except for a trio of spinsters which used to include Alma Duffy. And the minister's wife had five kids and gave piano lessons. Her mother's friends had gone to college and were sophisticated, or thought they were. LeahNell recalled being sworn to secrecy the time she came home early from school on one of their study club afternoons to see all the windows wide open and the ladies puffing delicately on cigarettes.

Her mother and her friends played bridge and gossiped, but they also had gardens and canned, helped at school and the clinic. Mrs. Perry kept the books for her husband's pharmacy. Mrs. Evans and her husband published the weekly newspaper, and the spinsters practically ran the County.

Gilda might have left home, but what did she do with her freedom? She didn't work and she didn't have friends.

"Why do I bother talking to you?" said Gilda. "What does a twenty-year-old virgin know?"

"This twenty-year-old is a nurse, and what I know is, most of what you're worrying about comes from gaining too much weight. And you don't have to waddle."

Gilda stared at the car keys in her hand, as if she had forgotten what they were for. "I haven't used it every single time. With either of them."

An image flitted through LeahNell's mind, Matthew unceremoniously ushering her and Rex out the door. "You haven't used what? The diaphragm?"

"Of course, the diaphragm. I might have to make a little trip. To Pocatello."

"What do you mean?"

"You're a bright girl -- figure it out." Gilda thrust the key into the ignition. "I've got to go into town and get some sodas and beer. Wieners. Potato chips. I'll drop you off so you can go to supper."

Her uniform lay where she had dropped it. She picked it up, removed the metal-shank buttons, emptied the pockets, laid pencil and bandage scissors on the desk, and was stuffing the uniform into the laundry bag when she realized that her pen was missing.

When had she last used it, the beautiful green-marbled Sheaffer with which her grandmother had daily penned letters and columns of figures in her elegant, spidery hand? LeahNell had filled the ink chamber that morning. When she changed her clothes, she'd tossed the uniform on her bed. Perhaps the pen had fallen out of her pocket then. She had taken notes from Matthew's lecture with a pencil.

A hands-and-knees search of the room revealed nothing. She must somehow have left the pen on Women's Violent. There was no chance to look for it -- she wouldn't be on duty tomorrow, Saturday. The day nurses had gone home and had the weekend off; the instructor, Imogene Hunter, had left for Pocatello. Oh, the terrible finality of Friday afternoon when the clockwork of the everyday world was suspended.

She sat on the bed and stared into the middle distance, trying to recall the sequence of events. She remembered how elated she'd felt all morning, until she bumped into Stella at noon, by which time the pen was surely gone, and the sudden sensation that the ground had fallen away under her. But no -- before then, she had written the letter to Floyd. Had her "freedom" made her careless, cost her her lucky charm, her rabbit's foot?

Wondering how her stomach could feel both hollow and heavy at the same time, she went on to supper, where her despair was perceived by Mrs. Quill, who gave her hope. She would not be working tonight, but would instigate a full search of Women's Violent.

By nine-thirty, she was able to call LeahNell with the news that her pen had been found and was in safe-keeping in the locked medicine cabinet. LeahNell could retrieve it in the morning.

So it was that after breakfast on Saturday, the day of the festivities at the reservoir, LeahNell was received in the nurses' station of Women's Violent and reunited with her talisman.

"We found it under Rochelle's pillow," said the relief nurse on duty. "I guess it was just too pretty for her to resist."

Equilibrium restored, LeahNell felt a flush of gratitude. "Oh, I probably put it down somewhere and forgot it. I'll go by on my way out and thank her for taking care of it for me."

Down the hall, she let herself into Rochelle's private cell. Rochelle was in her cot, face burrowed into her pillow with only her tumbled brown hair showing above the covers. LeahNell vacillated between waking her and waiting until Monday. Then she spied, on the floor under the bed, a spoon from the inmates' dining room, left behind perhaps from Rochelle's breakfast. LeahNell bent to pick it up, stopped her hand midway.

The bowl of the spoon overflowed with a liquid too dark and viscous to be Jello or even catsup. She snatched the blanket away from Rochelle, who lay on her side, eyes closed, chastely covered by her bloodied nightdress.

16. <u>Rex</u>

What a morning it had been.

After hearing from LeahNell that Alma was back on Women's Violent, apparently by her own design, Rex had, last night, phoned Mrs. Quill, who filled him in on Alma and her network, and her clandestine circumnavigation of the wards, not unlike his own nocturnal roaming. This morning, he had found Alma, in a shapeless white robe and canvas scuffs, in the day-room, surrounded by women.

The ladies had not been daunted by Rex's professional authority. Not until Alma dismissed them did they collectively depart, all but one clenched-up catatonic at the other end of the sofa. Rex pulled up a chair to face Alma. Head tilted, she appeared to be studying him from under her double eyebrows. He wondered if she had some peripheral vision after all.

"All right, Alma, what are you doing here?"

Silence. Finally she said, "You know the answer, Dr. McFall. Are you testing me?"

A new side of Alma, self-assured, almost defiant. Start over. "You're not totally blind, are you? Can you see, a little, in a bright light?"

"A little bit, if I don't look straight on. I can't read. I can't distinguish details. It takes so long to get an image in focus that I just don't bother. I haven't been trying to fool anyone, if that's what you're thinking."

Still looking sidelong, she leaned forward and touched his hand. "I need to stay here a few more days. For Rochelle. I'm sure you know she's pregnant."

"Stay here a few more days? Then what? Announce that you're all better now and expect them to let you go back to Intermediate? Until you think someone needs you again?"

"You sound angry. Are you disappointed in me?"

"What if they won't let you go?"

"They will. They need me."

"'They'? Are we even talking about the same people?

You've been pulling these shenanigans for so long that Dr. Swenson could come to the conclusion that you belong here. What of your network then?"

She withdrew her hand and sat back silent, apparently considering her potential losses. Finally, she said, "I wouldn't get my grounds privilege back, would I?"

"Alma, I don't doubt that you're doing a lot of good around here, that you're helping some patients -- inmates -- the rest of us don't connect with. But you don't have to do it this way. You'd be a lot more effective if you'd work with the system, instead of hatching these intrigues."

As he himself, by agreement with Mrs. Quill, was now required to do, taking some of the fun out of it. "I'm not asking you to quit doing what you are doing. I want you to do it better."

"Are you sure you're not embarrassed to be upstaged by a mere inmate, Dr. McFall?"

"Miss Duffy, I'm serious. We need you. I need you."

"Why are you calling me Miss Duffy all of a sudden?"

"Because you call me Dr. McFall. I can only call you Alma if you call me Rex."

She reached out, tapped him lightly on the knuckles. "'*I can call you Alma* only *if* ...',", she said. "Pardon this old schoolteacher. But you know I can't call you Rex. You're a doctor. I'm an inmate."

"That's what I'm trying to tell you. You don't have to be an inmate."

Her face went blank. "But that's what I'm doing here. I mean, where would I go? What would I do? No one wants me back in Little Wood."

"You could stay right here. Work here. On the staff. Live in the staff apartments."

"*Work* here -- doing what? Nobody would hire an old blind woman. I couldn't even babysit. And how would I get out of here?"

How indeed? "Right. First things first. You'll have to appear at the staff review. I will sponsor you."

With as much backup support as he could muster -- Matthew, Mrs. Quill, Dr. Quill. Sound out the Intermediate and Women's Violent nurses, who had probably been turning a blind eye to Alma's passages in and out of their wards.

Considering the way Dr. Swenson had stonewalled Mrs. Quill's attempt to have Casey censured, Rex guessed he'd do well to make an early, forthright appeal to that administrator, the better to avoid the appearance of sneaking around behind his back.

The big hurdle right now -- a purpose. When Alma was acknowledged mentally competent, they'd still have to have a proposal. There was ample precedent for former inmates becoming employees, but Rex couldn't conceive of a position a blind teacher could fill here. Certainly not attendant, very limited clerical. Alma would be wasted in any job of that level anyway.

The truth was, Rex wanted her for himself. He wanted her spooky wisdom, her eerie magnetic energy on tap for the psychology department, the humane psychology department he hoped would evolve out of the current, fledgling two-person partnership. The employee Rex wanted had no title, no job description.

He was turning over the possibilities in his mind when he heard the sound of running feet approaching in the hall and an urgent cry from a voice he knew.

"We've got to get Dr. Quill." LeahNell.

"Rochelle?" Alma sprang to her feet, swayed, caught herself against Rex's chair. She took off at a tottering half-run, surely kept aloft only by her own momentum, with Rex close behind her. She reached Rochelle's cell before Rex, who then could see only Alma leaning over Rochelle, holding her limp hand. He caught the acrid, metallic scent of blood, and reeled. He was no good here. Maybe he could help LeahNell.

As he rounded the corner to the nursing station, he could hear the clipped martial cadence of her voice, ten decibels louder than he'd ever heard it, as she barked into the phone: "An ice-pack? Is that all? ... Elevate the foot of her bed? This is no time for puny measures. She needs a doctor ... No, she needs a doctor *now*. I don't care if it *is* Saturday ... Yes, you go ahead and call the supervisor, while the patient bleeds to death. I'm going to find Dr. Quill."

She cut the connection, and then: "Switchboard? ... "

The door to the nursing station flew open and Rex

sagged against the wall, away from the onslaught of LeahNell emerging and muttering, "... *has to call the* supervisor, *through whom all calls to Dr. Swenson must go.* Ha!"

She glanced at Rex. He said weakly, "I'm no good in a situation like this. Is there something I can do?"

"Find Dr. Quill. He may be out of range of the switchboard." She sped past the two attendants herding the other women to the far end of the dayroom, her feet barely skimming the floor down the hall.

Could this be genteel, soft-voiced, graceful LeahNell? He guessed that with the low-pressure demands of life on The Farm, she had lapsed into a lower gear, normal for her, until shocked out of it. This situation was what she'd been trained for.

And Alma, resisting him this morning. These women had cores of pure, tempered steel. Unlike Gilda's molten warmth.

On the far side of the parking lot, he met Dr. Quill moving like a man half his age, grimly focused.

"Get a gurney," he told Rex, without a break in pace. "Clinic basement. Bring it up to Women's Violent."

Rex did as he was told, slower than he liked, having to figure out the mechanics of button-summoning the elevator while guiding a gurney with a mind of its own. He was beginning to wish that as a kid, he had put in more tagalong time with his father, a physician.

He was received at Rochelle's cell by Dr. Quill and LeahNell. Alma stood back while the ward attendants and Dr. Quill lifted Rochelle from the low cot up onto the gurney and fastened the cross straps. Alma applied the blanket to cover Rochelle, who was nonresponsive until Alma called her name and stroked her cheek. Rochelle's eyelids fluttered half open and she moaned. When the gurney began to roll out into the hall, she cried out. Alma took her hand and soothed her with lullaby sounds, walking alongside the gurney past the assembled, uncharacteristically silent and somber denizens of Women's Violent, all the way to the locked door of the ward. As they neared, the door opened to reveal Mrs. Quill dressed as for a night's work, though it was her weekend off.

Her sweeping glance took in the entourage, then paused

at the sight of Alma in her inmate's shapeless robe and canvas scuffs, poised to proceed out the door with the others. A silent question passed between Mrs. Quill and Dr. Quill, who answered with the barest perceptible nod. On they marched then, Dr. Quill steering from the head end of the gurney, LeahNell nimbly backing up with the toe end, Alma -- Miss Duffy! -- and Mrs. Quill flanking, and Rex bringing up the rear. Dr. Quill punched the elevator button, and they waited.

"Miss Duffy," he said, "you may stay with us -- her -- for a few minutes. Mrs. Quill will drip ether until Rochelle is asleep, and then you may wait outside with Dr. McFall until we finish. And then we shall see."

He paused. "LeahNell -- Miss Thorel, will you scrub in, please."

A few minutes later, Alma emerged from the surgery and sat down by Rex's side. They seemed to have run out of words. After a time, Alma stirred and sighed. "I was never much use in the operating room. Mary -- Mrs. Quill -- was the only nurse at Dr. Flower's mostly empty hospital. Ynez, who works in this kitchen now, was cook and housekeeper. My ladies' service club made the hospital our project for 1933. Mary trained us and for two years, until the fire, we staffed the hospital. That might have been the best time of my life, though I didn't know it.

"I didn't take it seriously then. I thought I was above all that blood and excreta, and I did some mischief. I am surely having my comeuppance."

"Have you had enough comeuppance?"

"Maybe. But I'm too old and infirm to start over. I've gotten used to the wards. I'm happy where I am." She slumped a little into her seat.

To Rex, she looked more resigned than happy. "If you could change anything, what would it be?"

"Oh, if I could only have a room of my own. And if Clarissa and Eloise could move off the violent ward. They haven't been a care in years. They don't need to be there."

That was all Rex needed to know. He sat up, stretched. "It's lunch time -- past lunch time. Let me take you to the canteen."

Alma shrank away. "I can't go outside, certainly not the canteen. I'm not dressed. I don't need lunch -- I can wait for supper. ..." Her voice trailed off.

"I'll go get our lunch. Trust me to order for you?"

"Trust me to be here when you come back?"

"BLT?" Did she know what a BLT was?

She smiled. "I had a BLT once. At the Manhattan. Bacon, lettuce, tomato. An elegant repast."

Elegant? She seemed to mean it.

Off to the canteen he went, and when he returned, with strawberry milkshakes and BLT's -- double bacon each -- she was still there. Enjoying his own lunch, he watched, fascinated, as she delicately lifted the top slice of bread and leaf of lettuce, set them aside on the plate while one at a time she ate each of the six slices of crisp bacon before restoring lettuce and bread to the sandwich and finishing it off.

Before long, the door opened and closed as Mrs. Quill came out, removing her surgical mask, her hair still tucked under the cap.

"She's going to be all right," she said. "We'll take her to a hospital -- Pocatello if they have a room. Dr. Swenson will let us use his station wagon, which I will drive. LeahNell is going to a picnic, and Dr. Quill will need someone to help him with Rochelle. Would you consent to come along, Alma?"

Alma's face was a study. Her double eyebrows bobbed and her lips were severely pursed, as if she were trying to quell a smile. Or a joyful whoop. She stood up and her voice quavered: "I must dress. My clothing is locked up in the ward. Also my cane."

Rex escorted her for the round trip to Women's Violent and back, then took his leave and set out for the canteen. There he was to have met Stella and her escorts, Evans and Hopkins, an hour ago, to drive out to the reservoir. He supposed they would be feverish with impatience at the prospect of waiting still longer for LeahNell.

Across the yard of the administration building, he saw Dr. Swenson exiting his station wagon. What an opportunity. Why not? He changed course and started to cross the yard, thought better of it, then changed his mind again and stopped thinking, to still the small voice advising prudence.

While Rex presented his case for Alma Duffy's discharge, withholding mention of the events of the morning, Dr. Swenson puffed on his pipe without a change in his bland expression, then held Rex's gaze for half a minute before he removed the pipe from his mouth. "Are you referring to the inmate you accompanied to the ball game?"

"She doesn't need to be in custody. She shouldn't be locked up She's intelligent and educated and could contribute a lot given half a chance ..."

"She's blind and doddering. A meddler and a ..."

"Which is not grounds for incarceration." Rex pushed on: "Let her dress like a lady, give her the latitude of a citizen and nothing in her behavior would mark her as incompetent ..."

"I have to disagree with you there. The remarks she made about knowing Mrs. Quill and their both living in Little Wood -- pulling stories out of her falling-down hairdo ..."

"But she did know Mrs. Quill in Little Wood. They were friends."

"I have only your word for that, Dr. McFall. I haven't heard it from Mrs. Quill, and until I do, which is exceedingly unlikely, it's a dead issue. Good day."

I have only begun to fight, thought Rex. Wait until he sees who's going to be riding in his station wagon.

He was tired. He'd done enough extraverting for one day. He considered driving his charges out to the picnic and going back to his apartment, but the thought of Gilda restored him. In the canteen, Evans and Hopkins hardly acknowledged his arrival or gave ear to his apology, but went on with baiting each other for Stella's entertainment.

Panting like puppies.

Stella stared at Rex and finally demanded, "Where's Driscoll?"

"I don't know. He's Matthew's patient."

In fact, Rex did know. He'd been there when Matthew extended the invitation to the picnic. Driscoll was interested, even flattered, until Matthew added that Jep and Ollie and Stella would also be in the party. At that point, Driscoll said no. Pressed for a reason, he said he didn't care to associate with Stella.

Matthew had watched Driscoll for a long moment, then said, "Rather spend the day with the little Spanish lady?"

Driscoll stiffened, turned away, and went off to play solo pingpong. The brittle sound of the ball ricocheting off the wall echoed as Rex and Matthew retreated.

Rex had his own reservations about the inclusion of Stella at the nurses' farewell picnic, but could hardly deny the precedent set by his own example in escorting Alma Duffy to the ballgame. Evans and Hopkins, both transparently smitten by Stella while claiming only therapeutic intentions, had insisted. Then of course, the invitation had to be extended to Jep and Ollie (with Whitaker and Mr. Wheeler), without whom Melba had declared *she* would not attend.

After the long morning indoors, the bright sky was blinding, but the wind was still. A fine day for a picnic.

All the way out to the reservoir, LeahNell in the front seat seemed withdrawn, even morose. Once only, she began to speak, then glanced at the three in the back seat and fell silent again.

In his usual pedantic style, Hopkins was holding forth: "... such that a partial enclosure or even a solid object forms a symbolic barrier that the mind perceives as real and complete, creating a private, inviolable space. Take, for example, this seat back, which separates the front seat space from our own. Unless we indicate open talk by raising our voices, it can be assumed that our conversation back here is exclusively among the three of us ..."

A signal for Rex to stop listening? Or that Hopkins was not to be held accountable for what he was about to say.

"Does that mean that we can talk about Dr. McFall as if he weren't here?" Stella's voice was throaty and lilting.

Stella on stage. Rex resisted the impulse to glance in the rearvew mirror at Evans and Hopkins flanking Stella, three heads together conspiratorially. Who was corrupting whom? Right now, Rex found it hard to care.

He tuned them out and went back to wondering how to

frame his job proposal for Alma. He was turning it around in his mind when, over a rise, the reservoir lay before them.

They were clearly the tail end of the party to arrive. Matthew's Jeep and Mr. Wheeler's station wagon were parked on the road end ramp. A camp fire had been laid but not lit; a battery radio blared Western music. Cartons and ice chests were out and opened, blankets spread, soda and beer bottles popped by the thirsty, and personal territories claimed. In the water beyond the cattails, Whitaker and Jep and Ollie, pant-legs rolled, were knee-deep splashing each other.

Carrying a magenta and green beach bag, Stella with Hopkins and Evans erupted from Rex's car and headed for the blankets. Turned away by Cleo and Francis on one, the trio elbowed in on Mr. Wheeler and Melba on another blanket and Patsy on a third.

The descending afternoon sun cast shadows from west-side willows and there, Gilda and Matthew sheltered.

As LeahNell and Rex approached, Matthew got to his feet. "Frying my epidermis on a blanket and swatting flies is not my idea of the way to spend my leisure. The ice is melting; the radio battery is running down. Where have you been? Dallying with this lissome lass is the only acceptable excuse."

Rex put out his hand in a staying motion. "Need to talk ..."

"Later. No shop talk on Saturdays. Tell it to Gilda if you must. But don't tell her anything you wouldn't tell me." Matthew looked around. "After a winnowing by defection of a couple of Our Boys and the drifting away of the baby sitters, this seems to be everybody. Now that Stella's here, I suppose we'll have to guard the beer.

"The prisoners are all accounted for," he announced in a stentorian voice. "Let the carnage begin."

He strode among the blankets, turning off the radio and admonishing all not to litter ("Empty bottles go in that carton ..."). Cleo and Francis made room on their blanket for LeahNell, who peeled off blouse and jeans down to an almond-green swimsuit.

Alone at last with Gilda, Rex drew his cigarette pack and matchbook from his chest pocket, and offered a cigarette to Gilda, who, to his surprise, refused it.

"Yes, where the hell have you been?" she said.

In what he thought was a reasonable, even gentle tone, he related the day's drama including Alma's part in it, her progress and his hopes for her. Met with silence, he looked to Gilda.

She was watching him through narrow eyes. Finally she said, "Well, I hope the two of you will be very happy together."

Stunned, Rex watched her rise to her feet, sandals oozing dirt with every sinking step, and make her way to the cache of sandwiches and potato chips that were to sustain them all until the fire was lit at sundown. He recalled her disapproval of Alma's presence at the ball game. Until now, he had considered it nothing more than a passing irritation, nothing to take personally. What had he said that upset her?

She seemed to expect him to know what she wanted without her having to tell him. Certainly, she had kept her silence, letting him talk himself unsuspecting into the trap. *Passive-aggressive.* But he would never dare say so. It was part of their unspoken covenant that no matter how outrageous her behavior, he didn't diagnose her the way he and Matthew did each other -- recreationally.

There was nothing for the pain now but the distance of the participant observer. Rex took a deep breath. Looked around. Opened his ears.

Supine and spread-eagled on a blanket, Hopkins droned away: "... ever notice that under some conditions we wear blinders? Here we are, practically nude and not an arm's length from each other, and custom demands that we pretend not to see all this bare, perspiring flesh. That's civilization."

"Sounds like sociology to me," growled Matthew. "You're sounding more like Rex every day. Watch it. You haven't even passed your prelims."

Stella's voice pealed like a bell: "Isn't it the truth. If I talked like that, they'd take me away for electroshock."

Out beyond the cattails, Ollie and Jep splashed after each other in an animated cartoon chase -- the Katzenjammer Kids --

wetting their rolled-up pantlegs. Chirping in their curiously flattened tenor, they were creatures from lightyears away imitating earthlings. The only way Rex could remember which was who was that Jep was the one who held his hands in fists with his thumbs inside.

The appearance of food from the ice chests, the whisper of sandwich wrappers and the crackle of Cellophane sounded a call, and with a whistle and a sweep of his arm, Mr. Wheeler hailed Whitaker and Jep and Ollie to shore. Soon, with a full paper plate, even Hopkins was silent. Rex knuckled his cigarette into the sand and arose and joined them. Gilda let him find his own sandwich while she filled two plates and sat down beside Matthew.

Rex considered what kind of statement he would make with his choice of a seat. Certainly he shouldn't give the appearance of a united front with Matthew or the interns. Wasn't the idea to dissolve social barriers? Patsy, who was likely to ignore him, was probably the safest bet, but he didn't want to be that close to Stella, on the same blanket. Under the circumstances, Jep and Ollie were the ideal partners, but they were already cozy with Melba, Mr. Wheeler, and Whitaker. At last, Rex cast his lot in with LeahNell, sitting apart from Cleo and Francis on their blanket.

As he sat down, he observed that Mr. Wheeler was studying LeahNell, as if undecided whether to speak to her. Rex wondered how much the man knew about the situation with Rochelle and Alma, and concluded probably quite a lot, though he'd been nowhere in evidence that morning. He was off duty besides, and might be in the dark about the latest development.

"... I suppose we have to break up early so you can get to church in the morning," Matthew was saying to Francis.

"No," said Francis without lifting his eyes from his ham-on-whole-wheat. "I don't go to church anymore."

"Indeed. What accounts for this state of affairs? I thought you were devout-and-devoted."

"I was. Now I'm a psychologist."

"I liked you better when you were religious. You've lost a certain sweetness."

"You mean I've lost my virginity."

"No, I mean you've lost your innocence. They are not necessarily the same thing."

There was an audible gasp from LeahNell, covered with a little laugh. Rex filed the gasp for future reference, wondered how he might facilitate disclosure later.

Hopkins took aim, tossed his second beer bottle onto the growing mound in the carton of empties and popped the top on another. "Have a beer, Ryder," he said.

"You know I am not a beer drinker," said Matthew. He was drinking Seven-Up. "It goes straight to the Reptilian Complex. Besides, someone has to remain sober."

Evans laid down his empty and nudged Hopkins into a huddle. They got to their feet and, thumbs in their Levis pockets, sauntered over to Patsy, who was eating a sandwich. Without preamble, they sat bracketing the girl, and Evans began nuzzling from her fingers up to her elbows.

"What low life-form has infested this place?" said Patsy. "Scat." She jerked her arm away.

Hopkins zeroed in on her neck, and shrieking and shoving, the three rolled on the blanket like puppies, bottles and sandwich flying. Connecting a slap to Hopkins' jaw, Patsy sprang to her feet, smoothed her hair and tucked in her blouse. "What is it with you two? Get a little brew into you and all you can think about is, 'Come into ze bushes wiz me, Babuschka'."

"What is it with *you*?" said Hopkins. "You weren't so cold in the bushes around the admissions building. Don't deny that I've enjoyed your corpus delicious."

"No, and it was damn poor judgment on my part, seeing it was the worst piece I ever had," she said to a round of gasps, murmurs, chortles and snickers. LeahNell shuddered and Mr. Wheeler eyed Ollie and Jep, both apparently oblivious.

"And since when," Patsy went on, "does one romp in the hay entitle you to general privileges? You don't own me, you sniveling adolescent. And you aren't likely to get it from anyone else if you don't learn some manners."

Matthew stepped into the breach. "Hopkins, lay off the beer. You too, Evans. And kindly consider the company you're in."

Hopkins sat straight-backed, holding his knees loosely with his arms. He stared at Patsy from under his brow; his full lower lip jutting gave him an aspect of unaccustomed dignity.

Gleeful malice had played across Stella's face as her head swiveled from one antagonist to another, and with a glance at Rex, she smiled at Hopkins and sat down next to him. He didn't move to make room for her but acknowledged her with the barest droop of his eyelids.

"In the bushes behind our building?" she said. "I had no idea there was any romance in this place. You all seemed so wrapped up in your intelligence tests and Rorschachs and analyzing everybody's behavior." She coiled her hair back behind her ear. "There's all this *talk* about sex. Everything we say seems to have sexual implications. And therapy ... I talk about my sexual experiences and feelings and ..." She arched her head away from Rex. "... my *therapist* ... acts as if it's about as seductive as a grocery list. There's just this constant drive to uncover trauma -- sexual trauma. I ask you, isn't that morbid? Not that I don't have sexual trauma ..." The pitch of her voice dropped a little, took on a fragile note. "Incest is bound to warp one's adjustment to life, isn't it?"

Rex almost shouted with outrage. The subject of sex came up in their sessions only when she initiated it, usually to avoid working through some challenge. With some effort, he kept his counsel. *I am a participant observer -- a potted palm.*

Evans looked at Stella like a moth blinded by the light. Hopkins leaned toward her and put a reassuring hand on her arm. "Incest? Really? God, how terrible." Stella rewarded him with a tiny brave smile.

Rex considered his investment in her. She was a patient by technicality only, a voluntary who signed herself back in at the end of every month instead of being transferred to a ward. Thus, she managed to keep herself in special circumstances, forestalling reality. That took money, her daddy's money. And his own role? He'd been dazzled by her beauty and so respectful of her intelligence and education that he'd rationalized her always being one step ahead of him and her talent for creating her own symptoms.

While he watched, the sun blinked green and dropped

below the horizon. A shadow fell over the reservoir, dousing the last light from the treetops, bringing a sudden chill to the air. The sunbathers groped for their clothes, and sweaters and shoes appeared. LeahNell pulled on her blouse and jeans. Stella retrieved hers from her magenta and green beach bag.

"Somebody light the fire," said Gilda. "Matthew, light the fire."

"Matthew, light the fire," chorused Patsy, Stella, Cleo, and Melba.

"Can't. Haven't a match. Has anybody got a match? Cigarette lighter?"

Rex handed him a match and the job was done, paper ignited, tinder sparking, dry brush flaring.

LeahNell tugged on Rex's sleeve and pointed over his shoulder to the moon, full and rising. He took out his pack of Camels and offered her one, which of course she declined, but was a good opener to the conversation he'd been wanting to have and that turned up more than he expected.

The radio put an end to discourse on the other side of the fire. Cleo and Francis, Stella and Hopkins, Melba and Whitaker danced to "The Tennessee Waltz," throwing long shadows into the night.

Others huddled on the blankets, singing snatches of the melody. Then the battery faded and "Begin the Beguine" ebbed to a whisper. Evans lifted his bottle and sang in a rich dark baritone, "'Drunk last night! Drunk the night before! Gonna get drunk ...'" Other voices in other colors chimed in with every drinking song they'd ever heard until, after an hour or so, the chorus splintered into couples -- Francis and Cleo, Melba and Whitaker -- or solitaries mesmerized by the embers of the bonfire. Jep and Ollie stretched their legs toward the fire, drawing away from Mr. Wheeler.

Before sundown, he'd been sitting beside the reclining Melba in a state of what looked to Rex like self-enforced relaxation. Some part of Mr. Wheeler seemed always to be on duty. Rex considered what he knew about him -- not much, not even his given name.

Indeed, his being known only as *Mister* Wheeler set him apart, in a higher class than attendant. He seemed never to perspire and even now there was not a wrinkle in his khaki shirt and pants. He still wore his everyday matching tie, all of which blended into his khaki skin and hair, the monochrome effect broken only by the brilliance of his blue eyes. He was tall and athletic, handsome in a distant way, curiously intense while serene, benign beyond human. What was he doing here on The Farm?

Though unmoving, he radiated restlessness, giving him an unexpected vulnerability. Rex took the chance. "Relaxing isn't easy for you, is it, Mr. Wheeler?"

He glanced at Rex, then away. "I'm wishing I could be in two places at once."

"It's your day off. Where would you rather be?"

"My responsibility for the safety of our inmates never takes a day off. I am always on call." He turned away. End of conversation.

Rex remembered why he had never warmed to him. *Sphinx. Sees all, hears all, knows all, tells nothing.* Mr. Wheeler's privacy be damned. "Were you a minister?"

Silence. Mr. Wheeler looked beyond Rex at LeahNell, who dropped her gaze.

"I was."

Rex searched his therapist's mind for a few words to keep the disclosure unfolding, found none.

LeahNell addressed Mr. Wheeler. "Did you know Rochelle almost bled to death this morning?"

"What happened?" Still affecting a relaxed posture, Mr. Wheeler was taut as a drawn bow, the arrow of his focus fixed on LeahNell while she recounted the happenings of the morning and the removal of Rochelle to the hospital in Pocatello.

"Mrs. Quill drove the car?" he asked, the rising pitch of his voice signaling distress. "Where's Ellen?"

"With the Swensons. She'll stay with them overnight, in case Mrs. Quill gets home late."

Mr. Wheeler's body now expressed what his words weren't allowed. His collapse into relief was almost comical. And a mystery. What was the nature of his concern for Ellen? Was this why he'd wished he could be two places at once?

Again Rex searched his therapeutic repertoire for phrases to elicit an answer, and again found none. Maybe *he* needed to take a day off. Yes, probably. But today wasn't the day. Evidently, it wasn't for Mr. Wheeler either.

"... a minister, yes. Full of fiery convictions and evangelical fervor. Convinced that I was the anointed, chosen to bring the sinners and doubters of the world to God, through the love of His only begotten Son." Mr. Wheeler was leaning in, speaking in a hushed tone, more to LeahNell than to Rex -- in fact, to him only as a courtesy.

Rex was mystified. How had LeahNell's feminine, unanalytical, reflexive sympathy accomplished what his own masculine competence could not? Was he overtrained? Had his training desensitized him? He could only admire the unspoiled wisdom of the unsophisticated, and concede that sometimes it took a disclosure to elicit disclosure.

Mr. Wheeler's chin dropped to his chest. "I gave no quarter. I ... " His finger traced a cross on the blanket. "I harangued a man to his grave."

In the campfire, wieners had been sizzling and marsh-mallows melting, blistering and browning, sometimes slipping from the spit into the flames. Now, Jep and Ollie approached, Ollie with a wiener on a stick and Jep with a marshmallow, and offered them to Mr. Wheeler, who thanked them but shook his head. His refusal apparently spoke for LeahNell and Rex also, for Jep and Ollie turned back to the fireside, taking their offerings with them.

After an interval, Mr. Wheeler resumed speaking in his curiously nasal voice. "I wanted to die myself. I implored The Lord to take me, but my petition was denied. The message was clear: I was to suffer a lifetime of atonement, and at last I found this place and it came to me that *here* I could take unto myself the plight of the miserable, the downtrodden ..." He stopped abruptly, as though he had just realized he was sermonizing. "I stayed."

Neither Rex nor LeahNell broke the silence, and the voices from the campfire reasserted themselves.

"C'mon, Ryder, have a beer. What, are you reforming or something?" Hopkins said, syllables slurring. "No bigger bore at a party. Do it on your own time."

He watched Matthew with a grim smile stretching his lips. "I've been diagnosing you, Ryder ..."

Yes, of course. He would.

"... and I conclude you're a plain old faker."

"Would you care to elaborate?"

Hopkins rocked side to side. "What's that bulge in your hip pocket? Nipping on the sly, are we? C'mon, share."

Matthew studied Hopkins as if he was trying to decide whether to let him get away with such insubordination. "My hip pocket is none of your business," he said.

Rex noted that Stella was following the exchange with glistening eyes. She would bear watching.

" 'Course, the amount of liquor you can hide away in a mere hip flask won't hold you all night. Where's your backup, Ryder? In the glove box? Under the hood?"

Say something, Matthew. Put the young squirt in his place: "My hood and glove box are none of your business," at the very least.

Matthew continued the silent stare and at last Hopkins turned away and looked away into the fire. Stella was studying her painted toenails, an innocent pastime that convinced Rex of the rightness of his suspicion. She looked at Matthew, running her pink tongue over her lips.

Matthew got up, stirred the fire and threw on the last load of dry sagebrush. The wind lifted the shower of sparks and carried them circling away. "We could use some good ole cowflops," he said. "Gilda, princess, why don't you organize an expedition and go out and find us some cowflops."

"Yes, my lord and master," said Gilda, and remained where she was.

Ollie and Jep leaped into the opportunity to please and went off into the moonlit countryside with Mr. Wheeler. Melba guarded Whitaker's beery slumber, his head in her lap.

From across the fire, Gilda was studying Rex. Ready to make up?

In a wave of restlessness, everyone was stirring all at once. Matthew rose to his feet and ambled into the willows, beyond the circle of firelight. Stella stood and slung her green and magenta beach bag over her shoulder and sauntered after Matthew, disappearing into the shadows only seconds after Rex caught sight of her. He sat up sharply.

Patsy arose and strode by headed in the opposite direction. As she approached, LeahNell raised her head and said, "Patsy, that was the bravest thing I ever heard."

Patsy barely glanced at her. "You do what you have to do."

"Did you see what I just saw?" said Rex. "And what's in her beach bag?"

"What? Who?" said LeahNell. "Stella? Just a sweater. Comb and lipstick. Really. I saw. She spilled the bag, and now she won't wear the sweater because it got dirty."

Swiftly, without rising above a crouch, Gilda scooted onto the blanket beside Rex. "Did you see that? She followed him. That was no coincidence."

"Maybe she's just looking for the ladies' room."

"Not a chance. Ladies to the right, beyond the cars, gents to the left."

"Matthew beware. Shall I go after them?"

Gilda shrugged, moved closer to him until he could feel her warmth. She seemed always to be warmer than he, as if her thermostat were set higher.

"Matthew can take care of himself," she said. "If he wants to."

Rex wasn't so sure, but if Stella caused trouble, she might have signed her own warrant. He drew cigarettes from his pocket, offered Gilda one, which again she turned down. Feeling vaguely rebuffed, he lit his own.

When the shriek came in on the wind, he realized he'd been waiting for it. A shriek of rage, it seemed to him. Stella burst into the circle of firelight, hair askew, blouse pulled out on one side, clutching her beach bag under one arm. Sobbing, she dropped to her knees, looked from one face to another.

Counting her witnesses, thought Rex in the instant before their eyes met. Count me out, he told her silently. Her gaze flicked quickly past him to light on Gilda, who leaned her way as if to take her in.

Stella reached out. "He... your husband... Dr. Ryder... "

"Am I being paged?" Out of the shadow, Matthew appeared, hands in his pockets. He looked down at Stella, who shrank away from him, then sprang to her feet and marched off on the moonpath to the right.

Such orchestrated exits and entrances... The firelit circle seemed to Rex like a stage; Hokpins, Evans, Patsy, Cleo, Melba the Greek chorus waiting for their cues.

"What was that all about?" Cleo.

"What did you do to her, Matthew?" Gilda.

"What did you do to her, Matthew?" The Greek chorus.

Matthew thrust his hands deeper into his pockets, stared hard at Gilda. "I didn't lay a finger on the vixen. She grabbed me and locked her luscious lips on mine and her fingers went exploring. I got to the goodies before she did. My hip flask and my virtue are intact."

"So you say."

"Stay out of it, Gilda. You don't know the woman."

"I know monkey business when I see it."

Now Mr. Wheeler emerged from the wings followed by Jep and Ollie staggering under stacks of what looked like giant pancakes, which they dumped onto the ground.

"Aren't Jep and Ollie going to smell like a bed of roses," remarked Patsy. "We have to ride home with them. They'll stink up the whole car."

"Sun-dried cowflops are essentially odorless," said Mr. Wheeler, "and they do make excellent fuel. They'll keep the fire going all night."

"You can stay here all night if you want to." Gilda was on her feet. "I'm going home."

"Sure thing," said Matthew. "First, we have to clean up and put out the fire."

"You clean up and put out the fire. Take me home, Rex. Now, please."

Mr. Wheeler looked at his watch. "It's after midnight. Oliver and Jepson must return to the ward."

"Stella needs to get back to Admissions," said Rex. "Where is she?" *Maybe she'll do us all a favor and throw herself into the reservoir.*

"Stella! Stella!" sang the Greek chorus.

Rex stepped out of the firelight onto the moonpath. Gents to the left, ladies to the right, beyond where the cars were parked. And there, Stella was visible emerging from around the Jeep. He backed off as she advanced. He didn't want to speak to her unless he had to.

Without ceremony, the party broke up. Whitaker helped Matthew snuff out the fire, then joined his friends packing themselves into Mr. Wheeler's station wagon, which led off in a puff of dust. Hopkins and Evans helped Stella, clutching her beach bag to her chest, into the back seat of Rex's car. Gilda took her place beside Rex in front, leaving LeahNell to ride with Matthew when he finished loading the Jeep.

Rex nudged his car up the soft surface of the ramp onto the road. At the persistent tattoo of the Jeep's horn, he slowed and peered into the rearview mirror at Matthew, who was waving urgently.

Rex put one foot on the clutch and braked, preparing to shift gears and back up.

"Don't stop!" said Gilda.

"Don't stop," echoed Stella.

Rex shifted into second and moved his brake foot to the accelerator, pressed it to the floor.

17. <u>LeahNell</u>

The company was getting sorted for the return trip. It looked as though LeahNell would trade off with Gilda, who wanted to go with Rex, having decided not to believe Matthew's version of the encounter with Stella. LeahNell would stay and help Matthew clean up the picnic site.

She didn't relish the idea of the bumpy ride back down the reservoir road with a full bladder, so she took the path to the right, from which Stella had returned. Gilda had provided a roll of toilet paper, but no one had thought to bring a flashlight. Luckily, there was a moon to show LeahNell the way to the open space in a circle of willows. One didn't have to stray very far from the campfire to find privacy.

Earlier, LeahNell had almost encountered one of the men. At the place where the path diverged, her eye had caught, to the left, an arc of liquid light, red, blue and green. She'd stopped for a moment in awe of its beauty, so unexpected. When she realized what it must be, she glanced about and no more than twelve feet away, from the edge of the stand of willows, Mr. Wheeler's stream made a rainbow arc in the lowering sunlight. He was apparently oblivious of her nearness. She sped onto the right-hand path out of sight.

Mr. Wheeler was so godlike, he seemed exempt from anything as carnal as urination, but it seemed fitting that it would manifest in every color of the spectrum, as if it were a sacrament. And later, when he confirmed that he had been a minister, she was not surprised.

Surprises there had been, among them amazement at herself. She had finally told someone. Over time, the trauma had dissolved, and she knew its absence by how little the memory distressed her. The crucial test was to give it a voice, and at last the time and the witness were right.

She'd been staring into the flames springing from the brush pile, almost shoulder to shoulder with Rex. He'd offered her a cigarette. He always did that even though he knew she didn't smoke. She thought it was kind of nice. She'd asked him something, she couldn't remember what, and he had started talking about Matthew and Gilda.

"Looking back on it," he said, "in some strange way, she needs his posturing and he needs her infidelity. Maybe she is more desirable if someone else wants her. I think there would be someone and he'd rather it was good old Rex. I'm where he can keep an eye on me. We three are a couple."

And, thought LeahNell, we four are a triangle.

Rex stretched out and leaned back on his elbows. He stared into the fire. "This can't be much fun for you," he said. "But you'll be leaving in a couple of weeks."

"I'll be back. I'm coming back after graduation."

He digested this for a moment. Then, "Why?"

"Why? I like it here. I like psychiatry; I like living here." But would being employed and accountable be as much fun as being a student? She wanted to work with new patients, and she hoped she wouldn't get stuck someplace grinding, like Clinic. "I want to go to school some day," she said. "I can live on the grounds and save my money." Get a paycheck. And be a sister to Ellen.

He was looking across the fire to where Cleo, Francis, Hopkins and Stella were a ring of shoulder blades, tipping their cigarettes to a communal match. As if in sympathy, Rex took a long drag. "You and I would be pretty good together. You wouldn't come back here on my account, would you?"

No, she wouldn't, even if Gilda were out of the picture. But it wouldn't be nice to tell him so. While she deliberated, the moment stretched to a significant length. She realized he was watching her.

At last he said, "What was that all about, with Patsy? 'The bravest thing' you ever saw."

"Why, standing up in front of God and everybody and admitting she'd let Hopkins have her. It was the only way she could shut him up." She took a breath. "I could never have such courage."

Rex waited, and she recalled that only yesterday she'd asked him if he would be her therapist. She'd gotten over that. She parried. "Do you think you can train yourself to fall in love with the right person?"

He laughed. "Ask me a question, any question, I'll give you a dissertation. How's this? We think falling in love is something that 'happens to us,' without any responsibility on our parts. We drift through life letting people wash in and out of our senses. This is passive, childish, magical thinking. We should cultivate love: search out a suitable candidate, focus our light through a lens until something bursts into flame."

He snubbed out his cigarette, tossed it into the fire. "Wondering why I don't practice what I preach?"

She fumbled for a safe entry. "Not you. I'm attracted to the wrong people. Life seems so simple for everyone else. They want what they're supposed to want. When I try to be like everyone else, I get into trouble. I don't fit."

"Does this have anything to do with Patsy?"

"I don't know. Maybe. I'm an egghead and I guess I'm a prude. I learned to swear and I tried to smoke and drink, but I didn't fool anyone. If I ever stood up and said I wasn't a virgin, no one would believe me."

"Are you apologizing because you're a virgin? Or because you're not?"

She sucked in her breath. He was so quick. "Yes."

"Yes, what? Are you?"

"No. Or, yes ..."

"That sounds like being 'slightly pregnant.' Forgive me for laughing. It seems to me you're talking about two or three different concepts. Clinical, technical virginity. Or innocence, a psychological, spiritual quality Matthew claims Francis has lost. Reputation seems to be the issue with Patsy." He pulled out his pack of Camels, offered her another one which, declined, he took for himself.

She was grateful for the clinical language. He wasn't going to make her wallow in it.

He lit the cigarette, cupping his hand around the flame against the wind. "I would guess that if you're not intact, you are still inexperienced, innocent. For future alliances, you can translate that however you see fit. You don't have to answer to anyone."

Oh.

After a moment, he said, "Floyd?"

She shook her head.

"Had you been drinking?"

She nodded.

"Then you're giving yourself too much credit -- blame -- for what happened."

Then he said something startling: "How refreshing. I haven't known a girl to be concerned about her virtue since I was in graduate school. Seems to be going out of fashion. Around here, the only concerns are rape and pregnancy. As illustrated by the way we spent our morning, with Rochelle. You come from a different world, LeahNell."

What did I expect? He's an institutional psychologist. He deals with real trauma, real abuse. She pulled out of her slouch and looked up into the bowl of night sky.

She recalled how she had shrunk away from Victor, Dr. Reamer, when, afterward, he had reached across her to unlatch the car door, his jaw sagging at the sight of the ruin that must have shown in her face, the momentary breach of his bluster when he said, hoarsely, "Get yourself an icebag."

How on trembling legs she'd crossed the yard lit by a cold, indifferent moon, turned the nails clamping the window screen and lifted it, raised the window, and lowered herself soundlessly, painfully into her basement room.

How in the dark she had pulled off the mother-crafted turquoise formal gown, pushed it crumpled into a corner of her closet and, barefoot and shivering in her bathrobe, felt her way up the stairs to the small kitchen, opened the refrigerator door to a blinding blaze of light and drawn out a tray of ice cubes.

How, closing the blinds against the chilly light of the moon, she'd put herself to bed in the dark cave of her room with the icebag, so cold that it was indistinguishable from wet, anesthetizing her wound for the rest of a sleepless night.

How, evenings, she'd sat in the communal smoking room letting wash over her all the raunchy stories, the raucous laughter, the whispered confidences, the snide asides, and the plaintive recitals of the other students, whose perceived moral laxity she had held herself above, her sisters under the skin whom now she was no better than.

How little, finally, her own misstep mattered. Not the calamity she'd blown it into, not the defining moment of her life. Just ... armor, her excuse for not making decisions, not resisting.

Only what? a year and a half ago? It seemed like twenty. She'd been vain, foolish, trusting. Her younger self. Then.

This was now.

After final exams here, which prospect she relished, she would return to Boise, to Trinity Hospital for the three months until graduation and one more to make up sick time.

The last months of the senior year were traditionally a time of privilege -- daytime only with no split shifts on the floors of one's choice, the prestigious position of assistant head nurse, recognition by the doctors, relaxed censoring, and the gaping admiration of younger students. She guessed that she, though, would be assigned again to night duty. It was all right with her. She had not ingratiated herself with the head nurses, had never taken orders blindly, had asked too many questions and volunteered too many ideas about how to do things better. If anyone bothered to consult her, night duty would be her choice.

Nights were free of interference, and priorities were crystal-clear. The night nurses were autonomous, resourceful, beholden to no one, loyal to each other. They had their own folklore and brand of humor.

She doubted that she'd be denied the night off for the senior prom. She would rescue from ignominy in the back of the closet the ill-fated turquoise formal gown. Astonishingly, it had been not only intact but unbloodied, and she had stuffed it into a large paper bag and waited for an opportunity to surreptitiously incinerate it, an opportunity which never materialized. The dress had languished while the intensity of her revulsion cooled. It would be fun to dress up and sashay into the gym and kibitz, watch her classmates and their dates sneak out to their liquor stashes, marvel at the antics of doctors and head nurses with class barriers down for a night.

And she'd always wondered what ever happened to her moccasins abandoned under the Douglas fir. Maybe she'd go for another midnight swim in Dr. Fiddler's pool. In the back yard of Dr. Ambrose's apartment. Alone this time... Would that seem too forward?

And when the four months were over, yes, she would come back to The Farm. Her parents would be disappointed. Her mother had the insane notion that their house could be turned into a nursing home. Daddy just plain wanted LeahNell to come back to Little Wood. But she didn't, couldn't, live in Daddy's world any more. And Daddy's world had never been as it seemed.

She used to think of Daddy as her own guardian angel, who walked her to school that first, awful, barely remembered autumn and helped her see that there was not a troll under the bridge; who'd defended her against her mother's irrational expectations; who'd played duets with her on Grandmother's old Steinway. Who'd shared a bed with her mother; who'd discharged his husbandly duty twice in order to give life to her and Keith ... That he more than slept with her mother behind that door, closed at night and on Sunday afternoons, was a possibility she had never let past her mind's censor. How astonishing that even the Oedipus Complex hadn't opened her eyes.

And then to realize, those few weeks ago, that her mother hadn't been the only one. He was the father of Ellen. He had slept with -- "slept" with -- made love to, had intercourse with. Had *fucked*. Not only her mother, but *Mrs. Quill*. She had told it to herself like a story from beginning to end, repeated it, rehearsed and rehearsed, and by the ninth telling it had lost its shock value, its capacity to thrill, and then it dawned on her that she resented Mrs. Quill's claim on Daddy less than she did her mother's.

She wondered if that was another facet of Oedipus Complex. Or was there some forgotten association from her childhood? Early childhood. But not that early, because she'd been five when Mrs. Quill -- Mary-- left, and she remembered a lot of things before that.

The ratcheting sound of the old doorbell. Playing in the attic under the surveillance of the great white eyes of the round dormer windows. Pulling treasures out of trunks; hiding in the trunks; playing dress-up in Grandmother's old-fashioned frocks. Daddy had taken a picture of her at two and a half years old in a dress of white muslin with the entire length of the skirt trailing behind her. Sitting between Daddy and Grandmother in their pew in the little Episcopal church kitty-corner across the street, she mesmerized by the trio of stained-glass windows above the altar. Trotting along behind Daddy pushing Grandmother there and home again in her wheelchair. Grandmother had stopped going to church after ... after ... After something LeahNell's mind won't recall.

And she remembered a day under a canvas roof, with water streaming down outside a tiny window while she jumped and jumped on a bed and no one stopped her. Daddy was there and old Salvador and maybe someone else.

But she didn't remember the fire or the hospital. She had dreams of fire, no: *a* dream of fire, the same dream, off and on most of her life up until, oddly, the night of Victor Reamer. Not quite a nightmare, but as if she were watching herself wandering through a city in flames. No, she didn't remember the fire or the hospital or Mrs. Quill.

No longer overhead, the moon was edging toward the west, throwing shadow across her path back to the picnic site.

The Jeep was loaded, the campfire snuffed. Whitaker had helped Matthew before crowding with his friends into Mr. Wheeler's station wagon now moving just ahead of Rex's car to the farm road. Matthew was in the driver's seat of the Jeep, door still open, apparently waiting only for her.

Suddenly, he erupted from the car, waving his arms, she supposed to hurry her on.

"They're gone!" he shouted. "The keys are gone! The bottle's gone. Stella found the bottle." He spun around and waved his arms. "Rex, stop!"

Uncertain whether to join the futile pursuit of Rex's car, LeahNell watched Matthew running up the ramp.

After the blue Chevrolet had disappeared around the curve, he slowed, sagged, and started back, shoulders slumped, hands jammed deep into his pockets.

"Bastard saw me," he muttered. "I know he saw me. All right -- we walk."

He glowered at LeahNell. "Yes, the keys were in the ignition. I always leave them in the ignition, daytime anyway, except on campus. The Jeep wasn't fifty yards away. Why would

I take the keys with me? I'd probably lose them."

He turned and cast a baleful glance into the dark that had swallowed the car. His foot slid off the ramp and he landed on the other foot twisted under him. He got up, wincing, then step-hopped to the Jeep. He tried his weight on the foot, fell backward onto the car door.

He looked up at LeahNell. "Can you find your way home by yourself? I don't recommend it. The dogs'll rip you.to ribbons." He twisted around and pulled out the load of blankets. "Come on, help me. It's going to be damn cold."

Everything was happening too fast for LeahNell. Was he planning to stay here all night? Just the two of them?

Did she have a better plan? She took the bundle from him and carried the blankets, corners trailing, to the site of the campfire, now extinguished and branch-swept away.

"Drop them," said Matthew. "Right there is the warmest place we'll find. Now we bundle up and hope for a rescue party. This is our bed for the night, and we'd better get into it before the ground cools."

The wind whipped her hair across her face. She shivered and hugged her elbows close to her side. "Can't we burn the cowflops?"

"I don't smoke, you don't smoke, they have the matches. Me Tarzan, you Jane. Your chastity is not at stake. Adultery is not my style and if it were, you are not my type."

He grasped one end of a blanket and flipped it out. "One to lie down on, while the ground is still warm. Two blankets for you and two for me. Now, down you go and cover up. No, not over there. Right here. Next to me."

She edged closer to him, careful not to touch. She pulled the blankets around her up to her chin. Mercifully, the ground was softer than she'd expected.

They lay on their backs, and after a few minutes, Matthew put his hands behind his head and began to speak. "That bottle was almost full. Chivas Regal. Which probably doesn't mean anything to you. Now maybe Rex will believe she's alcoholic. Not to mention narcissistic, which is the bigger problem."

"How did she know where to find the bottle?"

"Hopkins provided her with a veritable plethora of clues. While you were otherwise engaged. From there, she waited for opportunity and had her beach bag ready. Staged her hysterical vignette -- what a performance. She carried it off just long enough to convince Gilda and Rex.

"They'll believe me after Stella does whatever she's going to do, which I believe will be spectacular. And I will be vindicated, but the damage has been done."

"You couldn't lose your job over this, could you?"

"Not likely. The damage I had in mind is domestic. Gilda."

But wasn't Gilda's affair with Rex "damage"? Even if Gilda accepted Stella's version of what happened, wouldn't a dose of retaliation from Matthew balance the score? Too, what of Gilda's mysterious reference, only yesterday, to taking a little trip to Pocatello.

"What will happen to Stella?"

"Depends on how the drama plays out. Don't *you* get any notions about curing her. Look, I know you think you're coming back here. Don't do it. You can't change anything. The work is demoralizing -- processing a never-ending stream of patients into a downhill slide.

"I most regret Driscoll, whom I can't seem to help more than temporarily. He's a good man, until he goes back to his old cronies. He can't resist the old habits, and soon, here he is again. Stinking. Disheveled. Mortified. I'm beginning to hope the little Spanish lady will make him want to stay here."

"It's people like Driscoll who make me want to come back. They need a place like this. A sanctuary."

He snorted. "The Farm is more like a leper colony -- stack them away and forget them. We are expatriates, with all the implied isolation, the narrow-mindedness and intellectual inbreeding."

"You sound as sociological as Rex."

"I've been here too long. I'm beginning to think the way he does. We spend too much time together -- we have so little in common with anyone else in this squirrel cage."

"But Rex goes into the wards and talks with inmates and attendants. He *finds* things in common with people."

"Well, that's Rex. Saint Rex. I'd rather be among my own kind. It's time for a change."

Matthew wouldn't leave here, would he? "What kind of change?"

He shook his head. After a moment, he said, "The Spanish lady -- I understand she's from your hometown. Do you know anything about her?"

"Her name's Ynez. I've read what's in the admission document, which didn't tell me much. She came here -- was committed -- in 1935. I know that Mrs. Quill sponsored her for years. I kind of remember her in Little Wood, when I was little, before I started school. I know I should remember Mrs. Quill and sometimes I get a little glimmer, but then my mind shuts down. Then I have dreams ..."

Would Matthew be interested in her dream? If she knew what the dream meant, could she remember what had happened? She'd secretly yearned for a *Spellbound*, *Gaslight* revelation of hidden trauma -- the building of events to a fully orchestrated crescendo -- and how it would release her to be confident, accomplished and *happy* evermore. Matthew, in his first lecture, had dismissed that scenario as pure melodramatic drivel. But the dream was her only clue. Mrs. Quill had told her what happened, but it was not the same as knowing. And what had taken place before the fire? Why had she been there?

Matthew bunched part of his blanket into a pillow and turned on his side toward her. "Speak to me of women, that I might understand your species better. Tell me anything but don't be surprised if you hear it at our next soirée. You know how loose-lipped I am."

She was silent.

"Perhaps I could phrase that more delicately for your virginal ears," he said. "We mustn't waste a rare opportunity for intimate disclosure. How little I know you, LeahNell. If I hadn't been told you were a nurse, I would never have guessed. You're not the type -- ruddy-cheeked, hearty, bucolic, not to say bovine. *Nor* my type, or have I already told you that? You're not mean enough."

Not mean enough? Not as mean as Gilda.

"Do you deny it?" he said. "If you possess even an

ounce of meanness, you keep it to yourself."

"And if *you* are anything but mean, if you have an ounce of sentiment, you never let on." *So there, Matthew.*

"Sentiment? I'm so sentimental I slosh." His voice came from far away. "I may be a congenital smart-mouth, but I do love Gilda. I will do anything on this earth to hang onto her. Lie, commit mayhem ... "

Drowsy, she willed herself to dream of the fire.

She dreamed the reservoir was under a foot of ice, which broke up into floating islands that dissolved and evaporated into cotton candy clouds.

The sun rising over the sand dune insinuated itself under her eyelids and she could feel Matthew's arm slung across her waist on top of the blanket. She heard the distant hum and then dull rumble of a car approaching over the marshy ground. She startled awake. The rescue party.

She sat up as Rex's blue Chevrolet came over the top of the dune, down and off the ramp, and skidded to a halt a few feet away. The car doors popped open and Francis and Cleo, the sun throwing sparks off her pink hair, stepped out, still and silent, and surveyed the cozy campsite.

Cleo broke the spell with a jutting hip and a mock glove strip and twirl. "Aren't you the shady lady? Looks like we're crashing your party."

"Oh, come on, Cleo. How do you expect them to keep from freezing?" Francis looked away from LeahNell, as if he were willing himself to believe it.

Matthew took his time waking up and crawling out of his blanket cocoon. Finally he glared up at Francis "Well? What are you doing with Rex's car?"

"Cleo insisted that we look for Leah," said Francis. His manner made it clear that for all he cared they could have been becalmed in the dunes forever. "We couldn't find Gilda. No one answered the door at Rex's, but his car was there... " He paused to let that soak in. "... and we borrowed it."

"Did Rex leave the keys in his car?"

"No. I hotwired it."

"I had no idea you had such talent. Too bad you weren't here when I tried to start that bucket. Sit down. You make me nervous towering over me."

They sat down and some of Francis's moral superiority dissipated. "You missed the fireworks," he said. "Jep and Ollie's leave was up at midnight, and when we walked them up to Men's Intermediate and Mr. Wheeler let them in the door, Casey was there.

"Turned out that when Jep and Ollie went missing, Dr. Swenson called him. There he was with a big, greasy, cat-eats-the-canary grin while we tried to explain. Because he was on duty, he outranked every one of us. He decided to let Jep and Ollie cool their heels in locked cells overnight. Separate cells."

Matthew whistled. "Casey separated Tweedledum and Tweedledee?"

"He tried to. They caught him by surprise, knocked him over and ran. Right out the door and disappeared. We finally found them, Casey and Dr. Swenson and Cleo and I. In the old tunnel system."

In the tunnels with Casey. LeahNell shuddered.

"I don't know how they got in there, but I think Casey knows. He cornered them, and Jep snarled and tried to fight him off. Ollie wet his pants. The most pathetic thing I ever saw."

Francis swallowed hard. "Don't bother telling me you told me so. Casey packed them off to Men's Violent. He and Swenson were talking about electroshock. That's all I know."

Matthew's grimace as he got to his feet made it clear he'd forgotten about his ankle. He stood by as LeahNell folded the blankets and returned them to the Jeep.

"What about Stella?" Matthew sounded exhausted.

"Stella? Rex drove her back to Admissions. We were riding with Mr. Wheeler. What about her?"

"That's what we've got to find out. I have no car keys. Help me start the Jeep, Francis."

18. Dr. Quill

It was past midnight when they returned the station wagon to Dr. Swenson's driveway and the house was dark except for a first-floor window. No question of disturbing anyone within, thought Dr. Quill. Mrs. Quill's daughter was staying the night and was surely asleep. Tomorrow would be soon enough to report on Rochelle's whereabouts.

Mrs. Quill put the car keys in the glove box and they exited. It was a short distance to her gray Plymouth in front of the administration building and to his apartment beyond. They strolled, as was their due at the end of a long, eventful day. He felt alert, good for a few hours yet, reluctant to quit her company. No need for talk; it was enough to walk beside her, her long stride matching his.

Too soon, they reached her car. He walked her around to the driver's side and opened the door. She turned and touched his arm, looking up as if to speak, withdrawing her hand just as he touched her elbow and as instantly released it. "Good night, Dr. Quill," she said and slid behind the wheel.

"Good night, ..." *Good night, Mary.* To call her Mrs. Quill now, he thought, would be ironic. He closed her door and walked briskly to his apartment building.

In the hall, he could hear a phone ringing, the sound amplifying as he approached his door, and cutting off just as he opened it. Who would be calling him at this time of night? If it was important, they would try again.

There had been no room at Pocatello General. They went on then to Twin Falls, where admitting Rochelle to the hospital had been complicated. It was a short-staffed Saturday and the on-call physician was an orthopedist reluctant to take on a schizophrenic patient or accommodate her attendant in the same room.

The hospital chief of staff was found at the golf course and the superintendent was called away from a family wedding reception; and at last, credentials were established and protocols observed. A cot was brought into the patient's private room for Alma Duffy. Dignified and presentable in non-institutional clothing, she would spend that night and several more mediating the unfamiliar milieu in Rochelle's behalf. A late supper tray was brought to Alma in the room.

Mrs. Quill and Dr. Quill were served a warmed-over dinner in a corner of the otherwise darkened dining room. Then, after conferring with the hospital chief of staff, who had himself come in to admit Rochelle, and making a final check on the patient and her attendant, they were free to go.

They retraced their steps through corridors to the ambulance entrance and found the door locked. They back-tracked to the front entrance past the half-dark admitting desk and waiting room, around the building to the back, where the station wagon had baked for hours in the sun. Windows and vents open to the breeze, the car with Mrs. Quill at the wheel crept through the streets in the summer dusk to the span across the Snake River canyon and the open road back to Millennium and The Farm.

For five years they had addressed each other in formal roles. Now, even with their recent pattern of suppers with Ellen and LeahNell, where he less participated than was entertained, he felt ill-equipped to speak with Mrs. Quill on personal terms. At last he ventured, "You're an easy, able driver. I hope you won't be offended if I say that you drive like a man."

"How does a woman drive?"

"*Touché.* Since I don't drive at all. Over-generalizing of course, women are said to be tentative and unfocused. At odds with the machine."

She nodded. "They'll make a wide sweep left before turning right. I learned to drive, bought a car, when I came here. Out of necessity. One of the inmates who worked in the farm shop taught me the rudiments of driving and I practiced, evenings, on the road to the reservoir until I got it right."

Yes, that was the way she'd do it. "Your car's a forty-one, isn't it? How do you like driving a station wagon?"

"Not much. It's too big. And sluggish. And automatic transmission -- I feel as though the car is driving *me*. I like to feel the road through my feet."

They rode on in silence, through miles of sagebrush and fragrant fields of alfalfa and beans. The occasional farmhouse and barn with pungent corral approached from afar, accelerating as they neared and whizzing by as they passed. Mailboxes. Gravel roads disappearing down lines of poplars and Russian olive marking homesteads. The rumble of railway crossing. Daylight faded to a dim glow behind them to the west, until the moon just past full arose ahead of them.

Outside Pocatello, she pulled into a gas station. He excused himself, and when he returned from the restroom, the station attendant was holding the hose at the lip of the gas tank, his unblinking stare fixed on the meter. Still behind the wheel, Mrs. Quill was leaning into the door post, eyes closed. Neon colors from the station sign etched stripes across her face.

That she was asleep he didn't doubt. Under the wing-like flare of eyebrows, the contours of her cheekbones were soft and the corners of her lips drooped into an odd half smile. He was transfixed.

He wondered if in studying her face he was violating her privacy.

It seemed not. Even in sleep she looked vigilant, with no parting of the lips, her slightly arched neck supporting her head. Still, he knew or could surmise more of her past than she of his, giving him an unfair, unwanted advantage.

At last the station attendant withdrew the hose. He snapped on the gas cap and wrote out the requested receipt. Dr. Quill paid the man, pocketed the ticket and got back into the car. He shut the door and she did not awaken.

"Mrs. Quill?" he said, and she did not stir.

In the cup of his palm, her shoulder was firm, warm.

"Mary," he said. And then her eyes were open wide and curious, not knowing who or where for a long moment.

She sat up and stretched. She looked at him and smiled, then reached for the key in the ignition and turned it.

"Shall I drive?" he asked. "I haven't for years but I guess I've still got the old reflexes."

"Thank you, but I'm all right now."

They were on the highway again, headlights seeking the median stripe, as the moon was now to their right.

"Why do you not drive?" she asked.

"I haven't needed to drive -- I have nowhere else to go. I quit driving five years ago, before I could hurt someone. Alcohol. I'm an alcoholic." There. He'd said it.

At first, she made no comment, and he thought, What did I expect? Few came to The Farm without cause, and he already knew hers.

"You've known a lot of grief then," she said.

An odd way to look at it. Charity he hadn't earned. "I *caused* a lot of grief."

"Are you cured?"

"There is no cure. You can only quit. I quit five years ago."

He told her about Boise. About Trinity Hospital and the delivery that went bad. The flight east. The stopover in Little Wood, how he had nearly stayed. "A bartender by the name of Wellcome, formerly Sheriff Wellcome, helped me quit. I think you knew him. I'm assuming you are Dr. Flower's nurse, who left town after the fire."

"Yes. Oh yes," she said softly.

She was silent for a long moment, then suddenly she laughed. "What a trail I've left. That falling-down barn near the railroad siding. 'Quill's Feed.' And I thought, who would ever find me in the state asylum? Who indeed. Alma. Then LeahNell, who didn't even know about me until she and Alma and Ellen -- until we all came together at that ballgame. And now I have no more secrets.

"But oh, that little town had secrets. So many buried connections among people, so much under the surface." She was driving slower now. "It's the way of small towns, I suppose. I was there only three years and I could have lived there the rest of my life without knowing ... "

He waited.

"There were odd ... dislocations I couldn't penetrate until one day I discovered that LeahNell's grandmother, who was wheelchair bound, wasn't crippled at all. After that, little by little, everything began to fall into place. Until the fire. Dr. Flower and the hospital -- just gone. I can't bear to think of that land reclaimed, another house there."

"As of five years ago," Dr. Quill said, "the shell was still standing. Wellcome took me to see it. He told me the old lady who owned it, dead now, wouldn't have the hospital torn down, wouldn't sell it. When I saw it, all that was left was a two-story lava-rock hulk, no roof. It was shrouded with vines, blackened tree stumps crumbling into the ground."

He paused. "The owner, Mrs. Thorel, Wellcome called her. Would that be LeahNell's grandmother?"

She nodded and he went on. "The old ruins is a local legend, kept alive by ghost stories. You know how kids love a vacant building -- they don't go near that one. I did see an old man poking around in the weeds. Old, but lean and fit, grizzled but clean-shaven. Lantern-jawed. Basque, I'd say."

"Salvador," Mary breathed.

"Someone you know?"

"Leonard Thorel's father. As it turned out. Eleanor's father wouldn't let her marry a Basque. He forced her into an arranged marriage. Salvador is also father of Ynez -- the Basque woman with Driscoll at the ballgame. And he is LeahNell's grandfather, although I doubt that she knows it." Her breath caught. "And Ellen's grandfather."

He had a moment's sinking sensation of loss. A life in Little Wood had nearly been his. He could have known these people. "The way of small towns," he murmured.

The road curved and Millennium swung into view, dark except for the neon "Olympia" and one lone dim light inside the depot.

He took his time getting ready for bed. He removed his shoes, poured a glass of milk, and sat down and put up his feet. Years ago, his nightcap had been a splash of bourbon over ice which evolved into splash after uncounted splash, not bothering with the ice. He didn't miss it any more. He did wish he had some saltines to dunk.

He regretted not having shared the driving with Mrs ... with Mary. Surely, handling a car would come back as easily as the techniques of surgery. Perhaps not as naturally -- he'd never particularly liked driving a car, but it was a useful skill.

Ah, but surgery. His fingers still knew the way of the

scalpel. He recalled the morning's pleasure in the resistance of good tissue to the thrust of the instrument and the sudden, plummy acquiescence, then the forgiving way it embraced the restoring suture.

On the side-table, the phone clamored. He lifted the receiver and responded. For a moment, he heard nothing, then Mary Quill's voice, faltering, came to him. "My house has been entered, and I don't know what I should do."

He sat up straight, gripping the arm of the chair. "Are you all right? Is someone in the house?"

"There's no one here. Now. I've looked everywhere. The door to the porch ... fresh wood splinters on the floor. Nothing's missing that I can tell, but someone was in Ellen's room. Her underwear drawer ... Someone has been lying on her bed."

He thought fast. They had no security personnel other than the attendants on duty or on the grounds. The county expected them to police their own problems, which to date had involved only minor infractions by inmates or patients, usually alcoholics.

"Stay by the phone," he told her. "I'll get help. Mr. Wheeler is just down the hall. Don't go outside. Not even to your car. Especially not your car. I'll call you back."

He hung up and the phone rang. He picked up. "Hello!" he barked.

"Dr. Quill, I'm sorry to disturb you, but we've got a problem ..."

"Mr. Wheeler, I was just about to call you. Let me go first."

Mr. Wheeler listened, then said, "My car's out front. I'll tell you about my problem on the way to Mrs. Quill's."

While Mary finished packing for her and Ellen's move to a staff apartment, the two men moved a radio-phonograph cabinet to brace the breached porch door. Mr. Wheeler checked locks on the windows and the remaining outside door. Dr. Quill leaned against one of the colonnades flanking the entry and surveyed Mary's house, a further clue, he thought, to her character, though it might take some time to decipher.

The only other living room he'd seen in the past five years was the Swensons', wherein all the seating, with lamp tables, was lined up around the walls. There were no book-shelves. Traffic patterns were defined by packed-down paths across the wall-to-wall blue shag. The curtains were opaque and floor-length, rose-colored, and they were called "drapes." Floral still-lifes between the windows. Tasteful, he supposed, but it felt institutional.

In contrast, this carpet was frayed and the furniture, with non-matching woods, was arranged in a group that took in the center of the room, leaving the walls for built-in book-shelves. Colonnades marked the transition to dining room, where one end of the table was given over to a dictionary, a   short stack of books, writing materials, a pot of ivy, and a cribbage board. A space for living.

The only embellishment was a large print of Shoshone Falls, to which natural marvel they'd been as close today as two miles. He'd seen its like ornately framed in many a bank.

He walked along the bookshelves, reading titles. One shelf was given to phonograph albums, 78 RPM. The standard classics, and some Bizet, Debussy. Several Rachmaninoff. On the shelves below, the Encyclopedia Britannica, three volumes of Durant's history, Steinbeck, Maugham, Mann, Tolstoi...

A textbook of anatomy and physiology, charred along the spine. On an impulse, he lifted it out. The back cover was scorched and split. He opened the fly leaf to the bookplate signature in precise, rounded script: "... Flower 1889." He closed the book and slipped it back into its niche.

"I guess this is the best I can do." Mary Quill stood in the hall doorway, a suitcase on each side.

She still wore her uniform, reminding him that she'd had no sleep since yesterday -- day before yesterday, it being now well past midnight. He would welcome a shower and bed himself. First, get Mary settled, then see what he and Mr. Wheeler could do for Jep and Ollie, how bring Ronald Swenson to reason.

They locked up and left, Mary and Dr. Quill in her car, Mr. Wheeler following in his.   At the staff apartments, Mr. Wheeler awakened the manager and got keys to a suite on the second floor, two doors down from the one Mrs. Quill had vacated some months before. The two men left her to her night's sleep and set out for Men's Violent.

They crossed the parking area and Dr. Swenson's large bland face loomed into the light as he came around his station wagon to them. He glanced briefly at the senior attendant, then gave Dr. Quill a collegial nudge.

"Don't we wish our charges would stage their crises during week days?" he said. "We've got a couple of backsliders in need of electroshock, but they can wait until morning."

"Jep and Ollie?" said Dr. Quill. "I'll want to check on them tonight."

Dr. Swenson shot Mr. Wheeler a sharp glance. "As you wish. Another little situation has come up. Patient name of Driscoll over on Admissions says one of the women tried to lure him into a binge -- claimed she had a bottle of finest Scotch -- and now she's disappeared."

"Stella," said Mr. Wheeler.

"Stella? Yes, I believe that was her name. Wasn't she the one who went to the picnic? Did I give permission?" A look of alarm flickered across Ronald Swenson's face.

Dr. Quill was fascinated, watching the crumbling of his superior's façade. "Had she left the grounds without consent?"

"No, she was given leave. Against my better judgment, since the request didn't come from a department head. But I didn't think much of Dr. Ryder's objections, and the interns' argument was ... persuasive. After all, a voluntary -- a *patient* -- doesn't need to be isolated from ..." He seemed to be sifting the possibilities for justification. "After all, she's not an inmate ... she's free to leave any time she wants ... but where did she ...? Were they serving ...? Were people *drinking*?"

Aha! Someone to call on the carpet. "As I understand it, this was a private party," said Dr. Quill, "and she wasn't exactly invited. All staff members there were off duty."

"Then our hands are clean, aren't they? All we have to do is find the young lady before the damage is done."

Before the damage was done? Dr. Quill thought it was a little late.

Dr. Swenson fumbled about in his jacket pocket, pulled

out his pipe, with a can of Prince Albert from another pocket. "It was a long day, and then I was called out after midnight. Field this one, would you, Angus?"

"Yes, of course. And it has been a long day."

"Um, yes. You did some surgery, didn't you? Tell me about it tomorrow. Perhaps we can meet at breakfast. Dinner time, at least." Sucking on his unlit pipe, Swenson shrugged and turned away. He seemed to have forgotten about Jep and Ollie, and Dr. Quill did not remind him.

He and Mr. Wheeler made a quick stop at Men's Violent, where Schwartz, as shame-faced and sorrowful as if he himself had perpetrated Jep and Ollie's misfortune, had been called back on duty. The two inmates, by Dr. Swenson's order sedated nigh unto oblivion, were sleeping it off in separate cells. By Dr. Quill's order, Mr. Wheeler would escort them back to Intermediate first thing in the morning, restoring all privileges.

The concrete-block wards and red-brick buildings were conspicuously situated around the loop of driveway. The old admissions building was set back, beside the ballfield, near the canteen and the rec hall. Its isolation served to shelter the newly admitted, salvageable souls from the inmate denizens of the back wards. A two-story lava-rock structure, it was the original housing for the asylum, serially modernized. With its porches it retained a sprawling aura of welcome, which Dr. Quill had felt did not extend to the likes of him, associated as he was with the practice of (so perceived) medieval tortures. Now, in the deep of night, the miasma of ostracism seemed to have lifted.

As he and Mr. Wheeler entered the nursing station, Driscoll, tousled and rumpled in t-shirt and jeans, waved and broke off discourse with the wiry blonde night nurse, Lucy Amity.

Driscoll's account was brief. Stella had come to his shared room on the second floor after midnight and awakened him, then waited in the dim hall while he dressed. With no explanation until he had followed her into the day-room, he realized that her breath was scented with liquor.

She waved a bottle two-thirds full of an amber liquid and, pulling off her blouse, beckoned him to a sofa in the corner. He backed off and there followed a whispered dispute. He refused to engage with her in any way -- sex or drink -- and tried to take the bottle away from her. She shoved him to the floor, clutched the liquor and ran.

"Where do you think she went?" asked Dr. Quill.

Driscoll had no idea, but Amity thought perhaps the tunnel. "That was Casey's idea. That's where he's looking."

So Casey too was having a busy night. Dr. Quill half hoped Casey wouldn't find Stella. She was in enough trouble. "Is anyone else in the search?"

"Not that I know of. We're stretched pretty thin."

Dr. Quill looked at Mr. Wheeler. "It seems that there will be no sleep for us tonight. How about you, Driscoll, are you game for some adventure?"

Driscoll was, and they were three on the hunt for the missing Stella.

"I don't think she's in the tunnel," said Driscoll. "We don't use them. I'd try the ballfield, and the bushes around the buildings."

They considered splitting up, but lacking a signal that wouldn't wake the whole campus, it seemed best to patrol in a group. Except for the cottonwood grove, which they scouted quickly, the ballfield lacked the kind of shelter where one could hide.

In a widening spiral out from the dark administration building, the three men covered the perimeters of the inmate and staff residences and the associated offices and services. Beyond lay only the canteen and the rec hall, which had no cover of shrubbery. The three men set out across the field.

Driscoll began to ruminate. He couldn't figure out why Stella had offered to share with him, unless, considering the consequences, she wanted to take someone down with her.

"It was powerfully tempting," he said, "and not for the reason you think. My thirty days are up and I don't want to leave. But I don't want a bad record here."

"The Basque lady?" said Dr. Quill.

"Yes. She won't leave The Farm. And if I get myself incarcerated for drinking, she won't have anything more to do with me."

"You can sign yourself back in," said Dr. Quill. "Have

you not been properly apprised of your rights?"

"Register with Personnel," said Mr. Wheeler. "Stay on as a patient until a job opens up."

The canteen was dark and the interior, as viewed from the windows, revealed nothing. They went on to the rec hall, which was backlit by the moon. The door was open wide.

The hall was almost bright in the moonlight. On the bandstand, two figures stood out in sharp relief. On the floor, one of the two rested on hip and hand, legs curled to the side in the feminine attitude Dr. Quill had found so pleasing at the ballgame. Her head in profile, her free arm described a lovely arc, palm upward in a gesture of supplication. The other actor loomed over her, holding her shoulder. In his other hand he held aloft what appeared to be, as Dr. Quill drew closer in the shadows, the coveted bottle.

For a long moment, Stella and Casey seemed frozen in a tableau, then she broke the spell with a mewling cry. "Give it back. It's mi-*ine*. I *want* it."

Casey pushed Stella down in a motion that twisted her onto her knees, nose to the floor. He slid an arm under her waist and lifted her sagging to her feet. Still holding the bottle away, he released her. She dropped to her knees again and wrapped herself around his leg, clutched his thigh, clawed his zipper.

He flung her away. "Slut! Don't touch me. Get your filthy hands off me."

She clung. Casey upended the bottle and poured the remainder of its contents onto her head.

Tired beyond reason, to Dr. Quill the episode seemed to occur in slow motion, so theatrical that his impulse was to applaud.

Not so Mr. Wheeler, who strode into the light of the bandstand and knelt beside Stella. His curiously nasal voice was audible over the rise and fall of her wailing. "Stop it. Both of you. Get up and come with us."

She got unsteadily to her feet. Mr. Wheeler looked at Dr. Quill. "Where to?"

Casey grasped Stella's arm, and now Mr. Wheeler's measured tones were no match for her operatic shrieks, among which only the words "Bastard!"and "Mine!" were intelligible.

She flailed and kicked Casey, Mr. Wheeler and Driscoll without discrimination. Casey, jaw set, eyes glinting, locked her wrists behind her. She continued to struggle and managed to connect a hard thrust to Driscoll's shin before Casey immobilized her.

Dr. Quill came alive. "Driscoll, go ask Nurse Amity for an icepack for your leg," he said, "and, Mr. Wheeler, get some IM vitamins B & C from her medicine closet and bring them over to Women's Violent. Better get a couple of five c.c. vials."

He took one side of Stella, Casey the other, and they walked her, sticky and stinking, and surprisingly docile. Under the streetlight as they crossed to the ward building, Dr. Quill saw that Casey held her arm twisted behind her. He didn't seem to be exerting undue pressure. Dr. Quill decided to let it pass, but regretted the necessity. She'd have come quietly with Mr. Wheeler if Casey hadn't interfered.

Without releasing Stella, Casey selected a key from the clanking bundle at his belt, and let them into the building.

Upstairs, in Mrs. Brunt's absence for her weekend off, two women attendants hustled Stella off to the shower.

Dr. Quill dismissed Casey to go home, then wrote admission orders. Mr. Wheeler arrived with the vitamins for injection, and Dr. Quill filled a large syringe with the bright yellow liquid. They waited.

One of the attendants, an immense redhead with aquiline features, sauntered into the station and plopped down onto the remaining chair. "We're putting her in a cell. Fighty little twist she is. Gave us a lot of lip, gave Miz Harper a bath. *She's* going to need a change of clothes -- scrub gown I guess -- to finish the shift." She picked up the chart. "Okay, what have we got here."

"Locked room, no restraints," said Dr. Quill. "Hydro daily and as needed. Absolutely no sedation. Five cc's of B&C IM daily. I put one ampoule in your medicine closet, should last the weekend. I'll give her the first dose now and then I'll be on my way."

"Five cc's -- whoa. She's not going to take that without a whimper."

"She'll feel it."

The sky was lightening in the direction of the farm

buildings, and a duet of roosters exhorted the sleeping to rise as Dr. Quill and Mr. Wheeler trudged back to Admissions. The grass was wet with dew, the air cool and redolent of alfalfa.

The aroma of fresh coffee greeted them in the dimlit nurses' station where, mugs in hand, Driscoll and Amity faced each other across the desk. Amity pointed to an array of mismatched mugs on a shelf. "Help yourself," she said.

Dr. Quill did. Mr. Wheeler declined but took a seat. Slightly pale, he was still immaculately groomed, his uniform unwrinkled.

Balancing his chair tilted on two legs and an icepack on his shin, Driscoll was speaking. "Lost my job when I was sentenced to The Farm again. When I dried out and graduated, I went back to Boise and started working as a waiter. Quite a comedown, but I rationalized it was good background for the Great American Novel."

He shrugged, lip awry. "I got a job at the country club. I was just what they were looking for -- suntanned, muscular. Impeccable manners, knew how to lay on the charm, knew when to quit."

Nurse Amity propped chin on hand. With fatigue, her habit of avoiding eye contact, unsettling to Dr. Quill, was more pronounced. Hair draggled free of her blond ponytail and the laugh lines from her eyes and mouth sagged. "Driscoll, would you please stop the balancing act? You make me nervous."

He set his chair down. "Could I have a little more of that coffee, Miz Amity?"

"More *coffee* -- you need to go to bed. You've been up all night." With a severe maternal look at him down her nose, she lifted the percolator off the single electric plate and half-filled his mug.

"Thank you, Ma'am. It's been years since I saw the sun come up. And this time I'll be sober."

He went on: "Didn't know what to do with my time off. What was I supposed to do -- go to church? One night, I met up with one of my old buddies, who'd disappeared from the party scene. He pointed me to the local AA. Nobody to talk to and antsy, finally I went."

He sipped from his mug, held it away and stared at it.

"Damn, Amity, you make a fine pot of coffee. How come you're still single?"

Which praise Nurse Amity let go by without a change of expression. Dr. Quill supposed this was not the first time she'd heard it.

"You sit in a circle," said Driscoll, "and you introduce yourselves: I am so and so and I am an alcoholic. You spill your guts ... every awful thing you've done in the name of drink. Some people cry. They cry and keep telling.

"It came around to me, and I realized it was either head for the door or talk: My name is Tom Driscoll and I'm an alcoholic."

Driscoll grinned. "So I said, 'My name is Tom Driscoll and I am an alcoholic and I can quit any time I want.' I started laughing. Couldn't stop. Nobody else thought it was funny. When the time was up, I couldn't get out of there fast enough. Even so, I figured I'd go back, but the next week there was a late party at the club, another the week after that. Good, easy money, couldn't turn it down.

"That weekend, I was called in for a special job -- they wanted Mr. Perfect for a stag party. The smell of the booze made me reel but I stuck it out. Afterward, I was cleaning up, and one of the older men came back in and poured me a shot. I backed off, then I thought, Hell, I'm bone-tired; one drink and I'll go home and sleep like a baby. I don't have to tell you how that story ended. My name is Tom Driscoll and I am an alcoholic and I can quit any time I want. I still think that's funny."

His grin faded. "What will happen to her? Stella."

Dr. Quill considered. "She'll dry out in Violent, the locked ward. This is the end of her career as a voluntary patient. She'll be committed. By law."

"Not for long," said Nurse Amity. "Her daddy'll take care of that."

"We'll see." Nurse Amity was probably right, but not if he could help it.

"Would she go to AA here? If we had a group? Why don't we start one?"

"Are you kidding?" said Driscoll. "Right here?"

"Go to bed," said Amity. "You're getting testy. Yes,

right here. Do you have a better idea?"

Driscoll stood, parked the icebag on the desk. "All right. I know when I'm not wanted."

Don't let it die, Angus Quill. This is the chance you've been waiting for. "That's the best idea I've heard since I've been here. Let's do it."

Nurse Amity studied her fingernails. "I suppose only patients on this ward would be eligible."

Mr. Wheeler had sat motionless and silent for so long that he seemed to have fallen asleep. Now he stirred. "Only the elites? If the patients can play baseball with inmates, why can't they get together and help each other? Alcoholism is no respecter of rank. Here's an opportunity to dissolve some barriers. Patients, inmates, anyone who needs it."

Amity looked doubtful. "Could staff participate?"

"Anybody."

Dr. Quill looked at her.

No eye contact. She shrugged. "I know somebody who might be interested." She and Driscoll exchanged glances, then each looked down.

Well, what do you know. Nurse Amity. Dr. Quill was beginning to feel right at home.

"In an institution, alcoholics are stuck in a revolving door," said Mr. Wheeler. "Here and gone and here again. We can help. What have we got to lose?"

"What do you mean 'we'?" demanded Driscoll.

"I don't think you can sustain such an effort without help."

"All we need is a room with a door to close."

"But how will you keep out the merely curious? The troublemakers?"

"You need some supervision, Driscoll," said Amity.

"And that's exactly why it won't work," said Driscoll. "It's a pipe dream. Allow me to quote from Hemingway: 'But isn't it pretty to think so?' It's a Sunday School, tea party approach."

"Do you think we are insincere?" said Mr. Wheeler.

"I think you're naïve. How would you get that idea past Dr. Swenson before all the life was sucked out of it? He'd have it regulated beyond recognition."

Amity waved him away. "We don't have to have his permission, do we? We don't need anything. We've got space. I'll bet one of our doctors would offer an office."

Driscoll drummed his fingers on the desk. "Alcoholics Anonymous in an asylum? We're as *anonymous* as butterflies impaled on pins, on view for all to see. Even our little psyches are probed. We have to account for everything from tic to toilet. What do you think 'asylum' means, anyway? I'm going outside to see the sun break over the reservoir and then I'm going to bed. Don't wake me up for breakfast."

He turned away, turned back, lifted his forefinger. "To quote ..."

Mr. Wheeler sat bolt upright. "Allow *me* to quote from Thomas Paine: '... ye that love mankind! Ye that dare oppose not only tyranny but the tyrant, stand forth! ... Receive the fugitive and prepare an asylum for mankind.' I'll tell you what 'asylum' means."

Driscoll's pedantic forefinger wilted. What a treat for Dr. Quill was the sight of Driscoll eloquently speechless.

Mr. Wheeler's eyes flashed bright blue in the dim light. "'Asylum' means refuge, secure retreat. From the Greek, it means sanctuary. Traditionally, churches, hospitals, monasteries all gave asylum. Poorhouses and orphanages gave asylum. Your narrow pejorative is a modern corruption of the word.

"And I can tell you that, whether we are locked up or carry the keys, most of us are taking asylum for one reason or another. Miss Amity, Dr. Quill, I myself. We are all taking sanctuary."

Indeed, thought Dr. Quill, astonished. While he had foreknowledge of Mr. Wheeler's personal burden, it had not occurred to him that Mr. Wheeler might, intuitively, have an inkling of his.

For a long moment, no one spoke or stirred. Then, "Go tell it on the mountain," said Nurse Amity. She stifled a yawn, stretched. "So what do we do now?"

"Dr. Swenson would require a professional leader," said Dr. Quill. "I could sponsor a group."

Driscoll tilted back in his chair. "With all due respect,

Dr. Quill, it doesn't work without absolute trust, absolute confidentiality. You don't have either if you have to answer to anyone outside. No leaders, no sponsors, nobody any better than anyone else. It falls apart unless we're all in the same boat."

Amity nodded. "It takes one to help one."

Which was not news to Dr. Quill. "I think you will find that I am well-qualified," he said.

Sunday morning. The air was unusually still and the grass steamed. It would be a warm day. The sun was well up when the two men went their separate ways, Mr. Wheeler to Men's Violent to escort Oliver and Jepson back to their home ward, and Dr. Quill to his apartment.

He doubted that he'd be able to sleep. He was full of himself and, yes, *intoxicated* with the possibilities.

He expected Ronald Swenson to be pliable regarding the proposal for an autonomous group for alcoholics, since he was in no small measure answerable for the night's events.

Beyond the administration building, Rex McFall's blue Chevrolet pulled to the curb, the intern Francis at the wheel, Cleo and LeahNell passengers, all emerging. LeahNell waved. Dr. Quill waved back. He smiled with wry remembrance of their introduction in the hydrotherapy room, she half-soaked, and the surprise stirring of his manly effulgence, signaling that all might not be lost.

Manly effulgence indeed.

His priapic splendor.

Indeed. Would he ever come out from behind his cloak of words and take a risk?

It didn't seem impossible.

Maybe he'd sleep after all.

See Ronald Swenson in the morning. It *was* morning. Suppertime, soon enough.

When see Mary?

Driscoll. Nurse Amity. Group. Takes one to help one.

My name is Angus Quill. I am an alcoholic.

19. <u>Casey</u>

They'd taken Rochelle away. They hid her away then took her to Pocatello. When he found out about it -- his buddy Miz Chisel told him in the canteen Saturday night -- he knew right away who was doing it to him: the Quill witch.

Decided he'd drop in for a little visit. Unannounced and not by way of the front door. Make the acquaintance of her daughter while he was at it. But there was nobody home, so he'd just made his mark and left. Best thing now was hole up and wait for his chance.

Then in front of his apartment building he'd met up with Dr. Swenson, who was looking for him. On a Saturday, as if he was on call, as if they owned him. Which they didn't, not until Dr. Swenson quit *talking* about making him head attendant and made it official.

"Jep and Ollie are missing," said Dr. Swenson. "Your co-worker Whitaker signed them out and they should have been back by ten."

That didn't sound like any of Casey's concern, until Dr. Swenson said, "I can't locate Mr. Wheeler either." *That* got Casey's interest -- a chance to show up the Great Healer.

So he'd gone along with Swenson, told him he'd wait for them to come back; he'd handle it. One more star in his crown, as his old Sunday school teacher used to say. Every time he one-upped Healer, he was a step closer to being in charge.

And he'd made Healer squirm. Couldn't do a thing to stop him from giving that sissy pair what was coming to them.

Until they up and got away from him. Knocked him down and ran away. That surprised him. He didn't know they had it in them. Getting too big for their britches and when he found them hiding in the tunnel, he let them know who was boss. Set them up for shock in the morning.

Then come to find out Healer turned them loose. He'd better watch his back. Yeah, it was a bad night and somebody was going to pay. That snotty slut Stella for one. All he had to do was wait until the time was right.

Casey waited. Watched and waited. Scraped his keys together.

For three days, every morning, eight-thirty sharp, Miz Moody would phone Miz Crack. Would Casey please come up and escort Stella and her attendant to hydrotherapy?

Seemed one female attendant wasn't man enough to do the job herself.

Miz Crack would send Casey up to Women's Violent to walk the ladies down to the tub room in the basement. Stella'd take one look at the size of him and go without a fuss.

Three days on Women's Violent to clean her up, flush the poison out of her system. Hydro and vitamin shots. All they'd let her have was a toothbrush and a hairbrush, but even in the muslin sack and scuffs the lockups had to wear, you'd still turn your head for a second look. The hip-switching walk, that red-blond hair.

In the steamy, echoing hydrotherapy room, the tub would be filling, one pipe clanking with a load of boiling water, the other pipe diluting it to a uniform temperature through a thermostatic mixer.

Casey'd turn his back while they undressed her and got her into the hammock in the tub and strapped down the heavy canvas cover. There she'd soak in warm water with nothing but her head free. Yeah, he'd turn his back, perfect gentleman, but it took more than a shapeless sack to hide the goods from Casey. He knew what was waiting for him.

She was skinnier than he liked his women. She was lean as a colt and that was the way he'd take her. Break her, ride her.

Afternoons, there'd be another call from Miz Moody as she was leaving for the day. Stella was tearing up the place, would Casey please come and take her downstairs? And then, change of shift, only two attendants on the ward and KC going off duty anyway, they'd bless him for bringing her back by himself.

The fourth morning, Wednesday, at eight-thirty, Miz Crack hung up the phone and told him, "They won't be needing you today. She's going back to Admissions, soon's her daddy bails her out. She's all dressed and ready to go. Turned up her nose at having breakfast, gonna get herself a BLT in the canteen."

If she went back to Admissions, he couldn't touch her.

"Hold the fort," said Miz Crack. "I'm off to Staff meeting."

He held the fort. Waited. Scraped his keys together.

At nine-thirty, Miz Crack came back from Staff. Early. "Get yourself upstairs, Casey. Daddy washed his hands of her. She's chewing nails and spitting grenades. They've got her jacketed; go take her down to the tub."

Miz Crack opened the medicine closet, began setting up pills and syrups. "If she calms down, take her to Women's Intermediate afterward. If she doesn't, she goes back upstairs."

Arms crossed in the jacket, strapped to a wheelchair, Stella screeched all the way to Hydro. Without taking off the muslin sack she wore, the RN and Casey slid her into the watery hammock. Casey held her down while she flailed, and the nurse tied her in and fastened the straps of the canvas cover.

Finally, Stella lay in her tub of tepid water with only her head free to roll, teeth gnashing, mouth spitting saliva and dirty words. Casey's shirtsleeves were soaked to the shoulders from the dousing Stella gave him. All the way back to Men's Violent, he could feel the starch melting out of his sleeves and sticking to his skin.

They kept her all day. At Hydro closing time and the end of his own working day, Casey got the call. Come and get her.

She was dressed and waiting, hair around her shoulders in damp ringlets. Her fingers were dimpled from the long soak.

"Mrs. Moody said she could go to Intermediate if she was behaving herself," said the nurse. "You're gonna be a good girl, aren't you, Sweetie?"

Stella was quiet, but Casey could see she had a certain look in her eye, the snide kind of look an unbroken horse would throw you just before its lip would curl and he'd nip a chunk out of you. Casey figured she'd resist *him* enough to make her worth the trouble.

The nurse turned her back on them, began cleaning the drained tub. "Well, she's ready. You can take her."

Yeah, she was ready as she was going to be. Sweet and

cleaned up. Not sloppy-drunk and stinking like a barrel of vinegar. Not eager and grabbing for his crotch the way she did. He had the slut right where he wanted her. And he wanted her all right.

He flashed her a big smile. "Come with Casey."

The basement clinic was closed for the day and the hall echoed. The yellow walls and fluorescent lights seemed brighter in the silence.

As Casey and Stella passed the doors -- Dental Clinic, X-ray, Insulin Therapy, Electroshock, the door to the stairs, then the unmarked tunnel to the kitchen and laundry and shops -- she focused on each of them. At the door into the main tunnel, she watched him thumb his keys until he got the right one and inserted it into the lock. Staring at everything as if she was memorizing them.

Or as if she was seeing it for the last time. *That* thought made Casey grin -- he wasn't going to *kill* her.

He opened the door and let her go in first. At the fork, he turned them into the hall curving away to the east. He could smell the old tunnel before the barricaded entry came into view. He took a deep breath of the damp, swampy, warm air. She was going to walk right by, but he took her arm and stopped her.

"Where are we going?" Her smile was poison-sweet.

"Short cut."

He nudged her around the barricade, inched by after her. The ceiling was dripping, and so low that he avoided the sloping sides. The only light was one flickering bulb down the way.

Stella's voice was small, quavering. "I don't like this." Her foot slipped. "Oh, I don't like this at all. I can't see. My feet are getting wet."

He took hold of her arm. "Hang onto Casey. It's not very far now."

Just beyond the flickering light was the old partial cave-in that was his burrow, dark, soft. Casey pushed her into it. She toppled and he dropped on top of her.

She fought meaner than he'd expected, with teeth and fingernails. Under the rough dress, she wore nothing but panties and he ripped them off. His bundle of keys jammed in his zipper. He shoved them out of the way and got his pants down over his hips. When he pulled up her dress to her neck and tried to ram himself into her, the keys gouged him in the groin. He unclamped and yanked them off his belt.

She was still fighting him but now it was different. As he thrust into her, he could feel her fingernails digging into his back, holding on. He plunged into her and she pumped her hips. It was over almost immediately.

Spent, shuddering and groaning, curled a little onto his side, he felt her sliding out from under him, the sack of dress pulling away with her. Then the dress came down over his head, slid under his neck and was jerked tight. He reared to his knees and slammed his head on the ceiling of the burrow.

Dimly he heard her feet slipping, the keys clattering, and through the sack he saw the light flicker off for a moment as her form passed. He pulled the sack from his head and stumbled to his feet. He tripped on his pants and hit his head again. Holding up the trousers with one hand, he lurched out of the burrow.

The back of his head was sticky-wet, trickling down his neck. The light hurt his eyes. He could think only, *Slut took my keys. Got to get them ... Slut took ...*

He pursued her back the way they came, through the tunnel. He knew where she was by the sound of doors closing. She didn't lock up behind her until she got to Hydro.

There was light under the door. Water running. He grasped the knob, shook it. "Open the door, slut. I know you're in there." His tongue was thick, filled his mouth.

He waited, rubbed his fingers together, his phantom keys. She had to come out sometime. The light was bright, made his head throb.

He rushed the door with his shoulder, hit it hard.

His head pounded fit to burst. He staggered back to the wall and backtracked to the old tunnel. He didn't need keys to get out. He knew that maze like he'd dug it himself, all the way back to the door that had no lock.

It was daylight outside, but he made his way unseen to his apartment. No need to break in. Just lift the door a little off its hinges.

He stripped off his clothes, left them where they lay, and soaked under a cool shower. Dizzy, he leaned on the wall. His head stopped bleeding.

He toweled himself dry, dropped the towel on top of his clothes.

Nothing in the fridge but a quart of milk. He drank the whole thing, from the bottle. The light hurt his eyes, made his head pound. He shut the door and felt his way along the wall to his bed. He'd rest for just a minute, get dressed and go back and get his keys.

The phone jarred him awake. He reached over, pulled back his hand. *Don't answer it. Must have fallen asleep.*

His apartment was dark as a cave. He turned on the bedside light. It exploded in his eyes in a fireworks cascade of red and blue and white-bright yellow.

He turned it off, reached for his uniform and got to his feet.

Slut took my keys. Got to get them back ...

20. <u>Mrs. Quill</u>

Staff meeting was early this week -- Wednesday, since Dr. Swenson would be out of town on Friday. It seemed to Mary Quill that he'd been making a lot of trips. She wondered if he was looking for a change.

She arrived early. It became apparent that certain individuals as they entered took more notice of her than usual, spoke to her, simpered and stared: Mrs. Carson of Men's Violent, Mrs. Chisolm of Infirmary, Mrs. Doyle of Women's Intermediate, Mrs. Frickes from the Clinic, and the old nurses from the back wards. Mrs. Moody, head nurse of Women's Violent merely gave her a brief questioning glance, then attended to her papers.

Rex McFall and Matthew Ryder flashed her warm glances when they arrived with Sarah, the head nurse on Admissions. Then Angus Quill took his customary place at the foot of the table, and the nurses gazed raptly from Dr. Quill to Mrs. Quill and back again.

She could understand their attention to him, after his heroic deed on Saturday, but what had *she* done to merit such scrutiny? He was apparently oblivious, focused on the doorway through which Ronald Swenson, flanked by business manager Mrs. Stone and Mr. Peters, the social worker, would presently enter. Down the hall, one door and then another opened, closed, and the trio appeared.

Without a word or a glance, the administrator lowered his frame into the one padded armchair. Mrs. Stone sat on his right. He proceeded to fill his pipe and light it with the match provided by Mr. Peters.

While all other eyes dutifully followed the lighting ritual, Angus Quill exchanged a long look with Mary. A familiar, unwelcome warmth rose from the back of her knees and flooded her chest, her neck, her face. *What a time for a hot flash.*

Dr. Swenson waved aside Mrs. Stone's summary and

went straight to his agenda, announcing first the creation of an independent Alcoholics Anonymous group for patients and inmates. Interested staff ... (He paused with a conspicuous clearing of his throat) could inquire of Dr. Quill ...

The flush ebbed, and Mary Quill felt the hour of the morning, when she was ordinarily asleep.

"... I scarce need mention our gratitude to Dr. Quill for his handling of the emergency surgery on Saturday night." Having accomplished his scarce mention, Dr. Swenson turned to the social worker. "Mr. Peters ..."

Mr. Peters aligned a sheaf of papers, cleared his throat. "Owing to an unfortunate incident Saturday night, the status of a voluntary patient on Admissions, Stella, has been challenged. Her father, in a letter received last night, rescinds further responsibility for her. By law, she is now committed to this institution as an inmate. In the presence of Mrs. Moody, I spoke to her moments ago in Women's Violent, where she has been temporarily assigned."

Mrs. Moody noted, "She's fairly tearing up the place." She nodded toward Mrs. Carson. "We need to get her down to Hydrotherapy."

Mrs. Carson's chair scraped the floor as she pushed it back and stood. When the door closed on her, Dr. Quill raised his hand and did not wait for permission to speak.

"Some problems arose on Saturday night that could have been avoided if there were a more direct line of authority to cover weekends, and after normal business hours.

"I'm speaking of, first, the ease with which a patient acquired alcohol, and, second, of the lapse that allowed an attendant to terrorize a pair of harmless, long-term inmates. We have heads of department and supervisors, but no clear line of responsibility and authority regarding the attendants who are the mainstay of inmate care on every shift every day of the week. I suggest that a charge attendant be appointed."

Dr. Swenson had been listening with jaw clenched to his pipe and an appraising stare. Now he put down the pipe and spoke in a drawl.

"It might be a good idea to delegate. I shouldn't have to be on call to solve all the problems around here. ..."

A moment of stunned silence gave way to murmurs of approval around the table. What is he up to? wondered Mrs. Quill; it isn't like him to give in so easily.

"... And so, I propose to appoint Casey Cochran."

Wake up, Mary. She leaned forward, braced her hands on the table. "May we please put it to a vote? I nominate Mr. Wheeler."

Dr. Swenson took his time turning his head to look at her hard. With a smile that stretched his lips, he said, "Yes, by all means, let's put it to a vote. A show of hands, please, for Casey."

Mrs. Stone's and Mr. Peters' hands shot up.

"Unless the rest of you are abstaining, let's see it for Mr. Wheeler." The edge in the administrator's voice was unmistakable. "All right, you can put your hands down. But remember, the decision is mine."

Maybe, thought Mrs. Quill, if he doesn't care that we all resign.

"And if that's all the urgent business ..."

Dr. McFall leaned forward. "I requested an item on the agenda."

"Tabled," said Dr. Swenson. He pushed back his chair, stood and strode out the door. Mrs. Stone and Mr. Peters scrambled to collect their papers and follow him.

She knew well the nature of Rex McFall's "item": an application for Alma Duffy's discharge and employment in the psychology department. Mrs. Quill suspected that Ronald Swenson would ultimately grant both, but would hold out and make Rex sweat.

She shivered, and drew her sweater close around her shoulders. The day was warming, but she felt a breeze on the back of her neck. Curious that pivotal times in her life were often ushered in by a phantom sense of a change in the wind. And now the ascendancy of Mr. Wheeler to full professional status. In what way would his promotion affect the tone and working of The Farm?

She could think of no better word than humanizing. No more abuses or exploitation of inmates. A step away from the traditional asylum, although Mr. Wheeler himself had defended the use of the word.

Certainly Ronald Swenson had been comfortable with the concept, in theory bowing to modern practices while retaining the hierarchy of the old. How gracefully now would he bend to a realignment of power?

The answer might be in why the change was being allowed to happen. The back of her neck prickled with the conviction that Dr. Swenson would not be around to preside over the new order. Relinquishing that much control, ceding territory was not consistent with his character and prospects. Mary Quill guessed that he had simply, in his own estimation, outgrown his job and would leave.

Who would replace him? She prayed it wouldn't be Dr. Quill. She believed he'd be an able, generous administrator, but she doubted he'd be happy.

Was Angus Quill's happiness any of her concern? Did she trust him? Would she take a chance on an alcoholic? If her intuition was right, he seemed to be taking a chance on her.

Though she missed her home just beyond the campus, she was glad to have only half a block to walk to her bed. Ellen would be out for several hours yet helping Julie Swenson, who could still be counted on to keep Ellen occupied while her mother slept. When LeahNell's classes were over for the day, baseball with the Mossbacks would occupy both girls.

Mary Quill arose from her day's sleep to a quiet apartment and, outside, shouts and the crack of ball against bat. Tousled, half-dressed and wrapped in her old dressing gown, she would have toast and a cup of tea to sustain her until supper time. In her tiny kitchen, while the teakettle heated she sat at the table by the window overlooking the ballfield. Below she saw LeahNell, under the nearest cottonwood with Cleo, turn and look up at her. Where was Ellen? LeahNell waved and started up the sidewalk toward the apartment.

Mrs. Quill waved back and, ashamed at being caught in such disarray, ran for her hairbrush. She released her hair from its crown of braids and brushed it, white and rippling to her waist. The buzzer sounded and she laid down the brush and opened the door.

LeahNell, alone, entered talking. "Ellen's babysitting Roland and Rita. Mrs. Swenson took the older kids shopping in Pocatello."

The teakettle whistled a three-note chord, then a full-throated five-note, not to be ignored.

"Come sit down and let's have tea," said Mrs. Quill. And toast. Cinnamon toast?" A rare opportunity to talk with LeahNell by herself.

LeahNell sat at the table, rushed on. "... Becky and Elspeth don't babysit anymore. They're too busy with Evans and Johnston. Hopkins is still in ... futile! pursuit of Patsy. And Cleo broke up with Francis. I don't know why. She won't talk about it."

She paused for breath and her voice slowed, softened. "And we're all going back where we came from. Ten days."

"But you're coming back?" Mary turned off the burner, removed the kettle while she tamped black leaves into a teaball, dropped it into a homely brown pot. She filled the teapot with steaming water, popped on the lid, looked at her watch. "Help me remember four minutes." She put two thick slices of dense white bread into the toaster, pushed down the lever.

"I'm coming back," LeahNell said. "I do hope I can talk with Alma again before I leave. How long will they be in the hospital?"

"Rochelle's healing fast. Dr. Quill and I'll bring them back this weekend. Would you like to come along? Ellen might or might not."

"I'd love to. I won't be in the way?"

"Not at all."

"When I come back to The Farm, I won't be a student anymore. I'll have a fixed assignment, which I hope won't be Infirmary. I like working nights. Can I work with you, Mrs. Quill?"

"I've no idea what's available, but I'll certainly put in a good word for you." She set out white hospital-issue plates, cups and saucers. "Don't you think it's high time you called me Mary? You're an adult and we know each other too well to be formal."

"Mary." LeahNell looked pleased. "Oops -- it's four minutes." She got up and fished out the teaball.

Mary stirred sugar and cinnamon together in a bowl and, when the toast popped up, spread it edge to edge with butter and topped it with the dry mix. "I could do this better at home, where my oven has a broiler element. Here, I must work fast and hope it melts."

They sat with the plump brown teapot and fragrant toast on the table between them. "I haven't had cinnamon toast since the last time I went home to Little Wood," said LeahNell.

She pressed a dry sugar patch deeper into the buttered surface, took a large bite, chewed at length. "Imagine having a window right onto the ballfield. I hope I get an apartment on this side. But I'll bet you miss being at home. Is it true Casey broke in? That's what everyone says."

She didn't wait for Mary's response. "I love your house. It reminds me of home -- our house -- Grandmother's. The colonnades and everything built-in."

"Not by accident," said Mary. "I decided I would never buy my own house unless I found one in the style of your grandmother's. I didn't think it could ever happen. I'd walk or drive by this one and admire it, and then last year there was a 'for sale' sign. It's much smaller than yours, of course."

"Our house is too big for the four -- now three of us. My mother hates it, or says she does. She plans to move them into something modern and leave the big house to me for a nursing home. As if I would *ever*."

"What does your father think of that?

"She tells Daddy what she wants and he listens and says, Yes, of course, Olive, if that's what you want. And then she argues all the fine points and little by little, she talks herself out of it. As he knows she will. And then she goes around looking put-upon and self-sacrificing, and tells everyone that Daddy would never be happy in another house. They go through this at least once a year. And it's true -- he wouldn't be happy anywhere else, but he lets Mother talk herself out of it."

Yes, that sounded like Leonard. Mary thought that in spite of the difference in their ages, he and Olive understood each other pretty well. In most ways.

LeahNell was looking at her as if in invitation, but Mary kept her observations on LeahNell's parents to herself. Perilous territory. It occurred to her that the girl was as eager -- and as ambivalent -- as she herself to breach the delicate questions.

The moment passed and LeahNell broke the silence. "I wrote that letter to my old boyfriend on Friday? Monday night my mother called. Absolutely hysterical that I'd broken the engagement. Today, I got a letter from Daddy. He says she'll get over it. It's just that she really likes Floyd."

LeahNell gazed into her tea and stirred. "Or what he stood for, what that marriage would mean: me stuck in Little Wood living *her* life all over again -- church, bridge, study club, Eastern Star, good works, children. Daddy wasn't keen on Floyd -- though he never said so."

Mary refilled their cups half-full, and the pot dripped its last onto her dressing gown. She stood and dabbed it with a towel. "I've never had much use for aprons," she said. "Comes of wearing uniforms, I guess."

"Mother always wears an apron in the kitchen. She sews them out of flour sacks and old tablecloths and even patchwork. Frilly little organza when she entertains. She was horrified when I told her what a nurse has to do without ever soiling our precious uniforms. Blood. Excreta. Emesis." LeahNell paused. "Do you ever wish we didn't have to wear uniforms -- white?"

"No. I never have to decide what to wear. I was almost forty before I developed any sense of style. Which I learned from your mother. Do you dislike uniforms?"

"I don't mind. I like white. Funny though, when the other girls come off duty, the first thing they do is take off their shoes. Then they unbutton their uniforms, strip off the stockings and garter belts. They'll sit around -- all of them -- barefoot, their uniforms at half-mast, but they don't take off their caps. Melba wore hers into the shower one time, and we still have to remind her to take it off when she goes to bed."

Mrs. Quill nodded. "It's what the cap stands for, isn't it? They issue uniforms to everyone, but you have to deserve the cap. So it's the last thing you take off."

"Not me." LeahNell shook her head. "It's not more than a couple of ounces, but the weight of that thing still gives me a headache. Earning the cap was the hardest thing I've ever done. Four months of insomnia and stomach aches and migraine, and even then it didn't end. It wasn't enough to do everything just right. It wasn't enough to put the patients ahead of your own welfare. You had to have a certain attitude, which I couldn't figure out until I just quit caring and started talking back. I thought they'd kick me out, but they didn't. Isn't that crazy?"

"That's the way of bullies. They test you until you ... show your mettle."

Mary put down the towel, sank onto the chair and looked into LeahNell's face. "Oh my dear. I've been thinking of you only as Leonard's daughter -- his and Olive's daughter. The girl who grew up with two parents, for whom everything was easy ..." She leaned toward LeahNell and touched her on the cheek.

"You were such a dear child with your little piccolo voice, sitting on Dr. Flower's lap and playing with his ring, riding the elevator with your daddy, following Ynez around her garden ..."

She'd never had a chance to tell LeahNell about that last day in the hospital with Dr. Flower. The public health officer from Boise: polite, almost apologetic, avoiding eye contact. Just doing his job, whether he liked it or not. Dr. Flower asking no questions, betraying no surprise, complying with the request for an interview. The closed door to his office, the emergence an hour later of the two men, both sober and ceremonial in their deference to each other. Dr. Ambrose, that was his name, the doctor from Boise.

His son, along for the ride and a fishing trip afterward. Twelve years old, self-contained, would be a concert pianist, he said. Left-handed, as revealed in the charming exchange between him and five-year-old LeahNell, whose eyes never left his face. Mary Quill recalled thinking then: *She's going to remember this boy.*

Dr. Ambrose's parting words: "I'm through here. Let's go, Nick."

Then Dr. Flower pale and silent, emptying his drawers of records, carrying the stacks downstairs to the furnace. The furnace pipes partly disassembled. Glowering, maybe psychotic

Antonio and handy-man Mr. Flinch arguing about how to put the pipes back together. The fire.

And LeahNell didn't remember the boy. Or Dr. Flower or the fire.

"But it hasn't been easy, has it?" Mary withdrew her hand, uncertain of LeahNell's feelings.

But the girl's face warmed and flushed, and she caught Mary's hand and held it. "It used to be easy. I never had to work hard for anything. Until nursing school. I was soft."

They sat unmoving, holding hands, and finally LeahNell spoke. "Is your name really Quill?" Her free hand fluttered, birdlike. "Everyone is saying ... Oh, the stories are flying. That you're married, that you left him ... the reasons vary ... and he searched for you and found you and followed you here and tried to win you back and you just ignored him for five years ... And now you see what a worthy person he really is."

Mary laughed, then sat up straight as a schoolgirl. "There's a barn near the railroad on your way into town. It's falling-down old and the broad side is painted: 'Quill's Feed.' It's where the train stops to take on water and you'd see it only if you were on the right side of the train... I stared at it for fifteen minutes fifteen years ago and it felt like a good name for me. It still does. I've become quite attached to it. Until Angus Quill came along, I'd never known another soul by that name."

LeahNell sighed and took an audible breath. "I don't know what -- whether -- to tell Daddy. Or if you want him to know. Where you are. About Ellen."

"You might tell him we met. I think you'll know by how he responds... whether he asks for more."

And what if Leonard did want to know? And want to meet Ellen -- which was his right, his moral right if nothing else. How could that happen without heartache? Ellen and LeahNell had already made the most of the challenge, but they were young. They had the thrill of discovery, like finding out there was human life on a distant planet.

"Be careful, LeahNell. Consider the consequences, for your mother especially. Once you speak, it's out of your hands."

Of one thing Mary Quill was certain. She was running no more.

In the administration building, dark except for the nursing office, the evening supervisor gave a sketchy report and was eager to be gone. She lived in town and had a husband at home, so Mrs. Quill was sympathetic. But something didn't fit.

She scanned the ward rosters, found nothing amiss, and at last said, "It seems that all is quiet."

"Yes, for a change. With Rochelle and Alma gone, and now Stella, even Women's Violent was business as usual." The younger nurse took off her flaring, black-banded cap, tucked it into her locker and took out her purse.

Mrs. Quill frowned, tried to sort it out. As recently as this morning, Stella was on the rampage and being taken off to Hydro. "Evidently, the tub quieted her down. Did she go to Intermediate?"

"I suppose so."

"She isn't here. She's not listed in Intermediate ..." She flipped the page. "... nor in Women's Violent."

The young woman sighed, put down her purse. Mrs. Quill picked up the phone, dialed.

Mrs. Brunt in the violent ward was sure Stella had transferred to Intermediate, whose charge attendant was as certain she'd gone back to Violent. Perhaps Stella had simply returned to her old ward, Admissions? A call to Miss Amity demolished that hope.

Though she regretted the necessity, Mrs. Quill awoke the hydrotherapy nurse, who was presumably the last person accountable.

The Hydro nurse's response echoed the lethargy her treatments were designed to induce in the inmates. After the third statement of the problem, she said, "Casey came and got her. Took her to Intermediate."

Casey did not answer his phone.

The evening nurse studied her feet, shoulders slumped. "Go on home," said Mrs. Quill. "We'll take it from here." The young nurse flashed her a look of gratitude and was gone.

We? This was not the time for heroics. Mary wanted help she could trust. Her first, unparsed, thought was Angus

Quill, but she wondered at her motivation. Mr. Wheeler, though unaware of his impending promotion, was the obvious choice. Not to mention that as charge attendant, he would now be forever on call.

He was as alert and focused as if he had been sitting by the phone. "Let's start where she was last seen," he said. "Don't go by yourself. Meet me at the door to the basement."

She gave way then to impulse and phoned Angus Quill before setting out for the clinic basement, where Mr. Wheeler was waiting for her.

They hadn't far to look. A thin edge of light showed under the door to Hydro and Mary could hear water running. She tried the door and, finding it locked, advanced her key, but some premonition stayed her hand. She stepped back and looked at Mr. Wheeler. He took her keys and unlocked the door, swung it open.

In the bright-lit hydrotherapy room, they faced the row of tubs, tap ends nearest, sloping head ends farthest from them. At first, she could see only that the near tub was full of water, overflowing and pooling on its way into the floor drain underneath.

They approached. On the tile, a pair of dirty white canvas scuffs pointed away from the tub, toeing in girlishly. Underwater, her head at the tap end, Stella faced them. She lay on her side, one arm flung upward toward the faucet, eyes wide open, a look of curiosity on her face, visible beneath her floating red-gold hair. The water was pink-tinged, though no marks were apparent on her body, which was blue-white and waterlogged.

Mr. Wheeler lowered his head, his lips moving as if in prayer. Absurdly, Mary could say only, "Oh, the poor thing. Where are her clothes? We've got to get her out of the water."

She reached for the plug, but Mr. Wheeler said, "No. She's obviously dead. We can't help her. ..."

Down the hall, a door opened, closed.

"... The sheriff will want her untouched." He turned off the tap and went for the door, where his path crossed with Dr. Quill's coming in.

Angus Quill's white hair was sleep-tousled, shirt stuffed in unevenly, his thin-soled shoes carelessly tied. "Sheriff? Yes, you'd better call them." He joined Mary tubside and for several moments surveyed the scene, his eyes coming to rest on the floor. "Whose keys are those?"

On the floor by the faucet pipe lay a bundle of keys splayed around a ring, the only collection, to Mary's knowledge, larger than her own. She gasped. "They're ..."

Less a noise than a sensation of moving air turned her to the doorway, where Casey stood, his head tilted to one side, seemingly tracking her with one eye, which came to focus on the keys now in her hand. He lurched into the room, advanced on her, his thick-rubber-soled shoes making no sound.

"Mine. Gi'em here."

As his big face loomed, she noted that his eyes were unevenly dilated -- one pupil wide, the other almost pinpoint -- and there was a large hematoma on the back of his head.

He lunged and she tossed the keys into the tub, ducked out of his way. He grabbed at her as Angus Quill pulled him away. Casey spun, flailing, and Angus, now the target, lost his balance on the slippery floor.

Casey was upon him in a second and punched him high in the stomach. Down went Dr. Quill, breath knocked out of him with a *whump*.

"*No! Angus!*" Mary's arm whipped around with all the force and momentum her words had released. Her fist connected with Casey's jaw and he toppled backward, his head smashing into the rim of the tub.

Had she killed him?

Angus lay on his side, emitting harsh, deeply guttural sounds of agony as his scoured lungs strained to fill. Mary was on her knees on the wet floor trying to comfort him when Mr. Wheeler rounded the corner into the doorway.

"The sheriff's on ..." He halted. "What happened?"

"Casey came after his keys. I'm afraid I've killed him -- Casey."

She held Angus as his breath returned, frayed but even.

"Casey?" Mr. Wheeler swiveled, turned back to her. "Where? There's no Casey here."

21. <u>Asylum</u>

A waning half-moon followed the man until daybreak, and then the rising sun threw his long shadow ahead as he trod down the middle of the railroad track. He limped, and raised his left foot to clear each cross-tie. He had tripped twice and fallen once. His white pantlegs were shredded at the knee.

Millennium was several miles behind him now. Once at a highway crossing, car lights had flashed on his blind side and a horn blared three times. He'd kept going and the car crossed the track behind him.

Although the night was cold for June, the man's shirt was unbuttoned. His black tie, noose-knotted, hung askew to his waist. From his black leather belt, a nine-inch steel chain dangled. Without ceasing, he rubbed the end of the chain between thumb and forefinger.

Every few steps, he raised his free hand to flick off a fly worrying the ooze from a three-inch purple lump under his thin blond hair. The ooze glistened in the sunlight, drawing another fly and then another. His white shirt darkened with sweat between his shoulder blades.

The track swung to the southwest and became littered with cinders. The man's black shoes were soon coated with ash. Just ahead loomed the water tower on its spindly legs, and in the distance, a train whistle crooned, was silent, then sounded three short blasts. The track vibrated and sang, and shortly, the train rumbled into view.

Unseen by the engineer and unheeding of the engine with its headlamp still lit above the fan of cow-catcher, the man shambled on as it approached. The train, with a dozen boxcars, a line of empty, bouncing flatcars and a jaunty red caboose, slowed to a stop, chuffing, at the water tower. A man in blue-gray-striped coveralls and billed cap leaned out the high window of the engine waving his fist at the man on the track. "Hey, you crazy or something? Get offa the track."

The man in the stained white shirt and knee-shredded

pants raised one foot to clear the rail, hand-lifted the other to follow, and kept moving, beyond the water tower and onto a stubbled field to the south. He followed a line of Lombardy poplars for a hundred yards, then left its shade for the shelter of a falling-down barn in the middle of the field. He walked past the closed double doors, and skirted the building until he came to the Dutch door on the shady side. It was locked. He lifted the door off its hinges and it opened to him.

In the cave of the interior, the only light came from gaps in the ceiling, filtered through the sagging timbers of the loft. The air was warm and damp with the rich, fruity aroma of well-rotted manure and fermented straw. He breathed deep, sighed. *Home.* He dropped where he stood into the fragrant loam and was asleep within seconds.

The day passed and a night. Not long after sun-up, the man rolled over, groaned, put a hand to the back of his head. He was sitting up, scratching and coughing, when one large barn door creaked open letting in a wall of daylight and then an overall-clad, straw-hatted farmer.

The man in the barn flinched against the light and turned his face away.

The farmer, narrow-shouldered, wide-hipped in rolled-up pantlegs, sidled around to look at the man, who remained unmoving with his eyes closed. After a moment, the farmer tilted the straw hat back on her head, releasing a straggle of curly gray hair.

She spoke in a tinny, musical voice. "High time you was waking up."

The man shaded his eyes, looked at her, his head turned to one side.

"Pee-yew-ee! What a stink," she said, "If you ain't a sight. Looks like you got the short end of a fight. You been riding the rails?"

The man said nothing.

The woman shrugged. "Well, stand up and let's get a look at you."

The man hoisted himself up, stumbled, caught himself, braced his feet.

"Hmmm. Big bruiser. Bet it took half a dozen to bring

you down."

He fumbled, found the chain at his belt.

"What's your name, big fella?"

He stared at her aslant. His lips moved without sound. He cleared his throat."Kee." His voice was gravelly.

"What?"

"Kee."

"Keith?"

The man watched her lips, slowly nodded.

She squinted at him for a long moment. "I had me a cousin Keith. Don't know what ever happened to him." Her nostrils flared and her voice took on a harsh note. "Probably dead at the end of a rope."

The man stared, rubbed the chain between thumb and forefinger.

"Got someplace to go?"

He shook his head.

She toed a circle in the spongy footing, looked away to the small brown house at the far end of the poplars, turned back to him.

"Looks like those clothes used to be white. My sakes. They'll take some scrubbing. The washboard'll take the skin offa these old knuckles. Rheumatiz."

She glanced at him sharply. "Mind you, you got to earn your keep. Place needs a lot of work and the food don't drop into my lap." Her voice softened. "Ain't got much. Just one old cow, yard full of chickens. Corn, beans coming on. Taters. Apples. Good apples. Trade 'em with the neighbor for sugar and flour."

He swayed.

"Don't fall over now. Reckon you need some food in you. I'll give you a plate of eggs and biscuits, and then we'll get you into the washtub. How's that sound? Then some clean clothes. Got some old overalls you can wear. Way too short for you, but they'll do until your pants're dry."

She studied his face. "Little bit cockeyed, are we? No matter. Just watch that old rooster don't go for the bad one." She looked him up and down. "Don't guess you want to sleep in the barn again. I got a nice, soft bed, and a warm body'll be welcome."

The grin spread her waxy, cherry-red lips. "Won't that be nice?"

Matthew's car was the first to arrive at the depot on the mid-June Sunday morning. The back seat of the Jeep had been removed to make room for the girls' bags. Melba and Cleo sat on top of them, clutching the front seatback for the jolting ride. In the front seat, LeahNell was secure, though the window had jammed open admitting wind and rain.

Matthew overrode the curb and stopped the Jeep under the depot overhang, then stood by, tossing his car keys hand to hand while his three passengers unloaded their luggage.

"Forgive me for not being the gentleman," he said, "but I am handicapped." He had finally allowed Dr. Quill to x-ray the ankle, as a precaution, and was still Ace-bandaged and limping. "Where's a porter when we need one?"

"That's all right," said Melba. Her electric hair all but sizzled in the rain, and her signature, off-one-shoulder peasant blouse betrayed not a single goosebump. "Heavy lifting is our specialty."

"Speak for yourself," muttered Cleo. "What have you got to be so cheerful about? Your admirers didn't even show up to see you off. Shows you how much ..."

"They'll be here."

As if bidden, Mr. Wheeler's station wagon rounded the corner and thumped to a halt at the curb. The doors popped open and Jep and Ollie, followed by driver Whitaker, bounded onto the platform.

"Go back and close your doors," Whitaker told them.

He joined Matthew and the girls sheltering under the overhang. "Sorry we're late. They've been jumping up and down all the way, just sure the train would leave before we got here. I swear, they were going to make me follow the train all the way to Boise."

Ollie and Jep, simmered down now, returned and stood in the rain beaming from one girl to the next, alternating with nods to each other. Melba, nod. Cleo, nod. LeahNell, nod. Melba, nod, nod.

"Get under the roof, you two," said Whitaker.

"You ladies had better get your tickets," said Matthew. "Jep and Ollie and I will guard your bags."

Whitaker went inside with the girls and hung back with Melba. On the phone, the agent paid them no attention.

Cleo turned her back on them, and twisted her curly pink forelock while she spoke in a hurried tone to LeahNell. "I shouldn't have said that to Melba. Ever since I broke up with Francis, I can't seem to keep from mouthing off. I can't take this. I'm tired of acting like a silk purse. I just want to get back to Boise and my old friends."

She lifted her chest, gazed into the middle distance. "Make some new friends even. Wonder if that doctor, what's his name? ... still lives in Dr. Fiddler's apartment."

"Ambrose?"

"Yeah. Dr. Ambrose."

"Nick," murmured LeahNell. "Nick Ambrose."

"How would *you* know that? Well. We can stage another little party there. And this time I *will* go swimming. In my new swim suit. Which Francis thinks shows too much of me." She paused and thrust out her jaw. "And then we'll see."

LeahNell sighed, slumped a little.

"I always said I wanted to f... " Cleo glanced aside at LeahNell. "Well, you know."

"You also said you wouldn't give Dr. Ambrose a second glance if you didn't know he was a doctor."

"I don't have much choice. All the other doctors are married. No, wait. Unless he and that RN in surgery have tied the knot, Dr. Reamer is still available. Now *he* would be worth going after. He is. So. Tall. Muscular. Sexy."

"You'd try to compete with Berry? Showgirl-gorgeous Berry? And redhaired with a temper to match."

"She doesn't own him. Far as I know. I'd like to give her a run for her money. She owes me."

"What for?"

"I alibied her once ..."

The railway agent tilted back in his swivel armchair, holding the phone in one hand, the receiver to his ear with the other.

Melba and Whitaker joined LeahNell and Cleo at the

ticket counter. "He's hardly getting a word in edgewise," said Whitaker. "He must be talking to his wife."

The agent scowled at him from under his dark green visor, spoke a few curt words into the bell and dropped the receiver into its loop.

Three tickets in hand, the quartet rejoined the baggage guards outside. In their flat treble voices, Ollie and Jep were recounting their testimonial duet at the week's staff meeting. Matthew was listening with a look of studied patience.

"No doubt about it," he said finally. "Couldn't have run Casey off without you two. You're a legend."

"Yeah," said Ollie. "Dr. Swenson says we're ..."

"... heroes," said Jep, "but he won't let us leave."

They turned to Melba. "It looks like we're still ..."

"... gonna be here when you come back."

"You'd better be here," said Melba. "This place needs heroes."

The two round faces brightened, then drooped. "But we don't get to work ..."

"... in the kitchen anymore. We have to work ..."

"... in the canteen."

"The canteen? That's wonderful. You'll get to see everyone. The patients and the nurses and ... Everybody goes to the canteen."

"Any-old-body can work in the kitchen," said Cleo. "You have to be responsible to work in the canteen. That's a promotion."

"Really? Well then."

Matthew slouched over to Whitaker and said in a low voice, "What's the story here? Did they really take the sheriff through the tunnels?"

"They know the old tunnels better than anyone else," said Whitaker. "And they knew where Casey took Rochelle. Mr. Wheeler went too, of course. They didn't find a trace of Casey."

A grin spread on his earnest moonface. "Those two were all for sealing the tunnels, bricking them up then and there. If Casey was inside, too bad. 'Bury him alive!'"

Six feet away, Oliver and Jepson carried on. "... Serve him right!" said Oliver.

"Yeah," said Jepson. "Everybody knows ..."

"... he killed Stella. 'Course, we can't talk about that."

"Mr. Wheeler says not to talk about Casey and Stella, so we don't."

"But everybody knows ..."

"I haven't heard them talking about anything else," said Whitaker. "*I'd* like to blame Casey. But he couldn't have done it. The Hydro door was locked and his keys were on the floor. You can't leave and lock that door without a key."

"So where is Casey." It was not a question.

"Yeah. Maybe we'll never know, and I'm keeping my back to the wall. My guess is, he hopped a freight."

"And where's Mr. Wheeler? Did you steal his wagon?"

"He's on the ward. He's showing our new attendant the ropes. Casey's replacement."

A spasm flickered across Whitaker's face. He moved away, leaving Matthew and LeahNell a company of two.

"So you think you're coming back?" said Matthew. "You won't recognize the place. A new superintendent, from Minnesota. Medical school classmate of Dr. Swenson's. Our soon-to-be-former boss lost no time replacing Casey. The more things change, the more they stay the same. You've seen the new guy around? Hard to miss."

"I've seen him. He gives me the creeps."

"That surprises me. He's handsome, ..."

"Too handsome."

"... ingratiating, ..."

"Slimy. He has bedroom eyes. I hope Mr. Wheeler can rein him in." LeahNell laughed. "*Rein* him in. He prances like a stallion. Flicks his hand as if he's carrying a riding crop. Yes, the more things change ..."

"I had no idea you were so perceptive. After all the time I've spent in your company, how little I know you."

"You had your chance," she murmured.

He backed off, impaled her with his ice-blue gaze. "There's something provocative -- seductive even, in your attitude. Have I underestimated you?"

"He's just not my type."

"What is your type, LeahNell?"

She didn't answer.

"I always hoped Rex would be your type."

"I know."

Another car arrived at the curb. Rex's blue Plymouth, Francis at the wheel, Ellen in the passenger seat. Ellen lost no time seeking out LeahNell, but Francis advanced slowly toward Cleo, who glanced at him and whipped her head away.

Matthew edged over to Francis, now standing alone, downcast and silent.

"Where's Rex? Did you hotwire his car again?"

"No, I borrowed it." Francis's face was drawn, white around the mouth. "I begged for it. He's on the wards with Alma -- Miss Duffy. And Dr. Quill."

"Quill?" Matthew's head jerked back. "And you've been on the wards with them?"

Francis nodded.

"Traitor. Turncoat. So what are you doing here?"

Francis said nothing.

Matthew stroked his chin, gazed at the young man from under his brow. "You, estranged from your lady love, can't tear yourself away from the last sight of her disappearing into the far yonder."

Francis jammed his hands into his pockets and looked away down the track, then back at Matthew, his face a rictus of despair.

"Go to her," said Matthew. "She's right there -- go to her. Throw yourself on her mercy."

"But I don't understand her."

"You'll never understand her. Women are a different species. Appreciate her. Trust me. I *know*. Where's the damn train? I'm freezing."

Matthew turned his back and nudged his way close to LeahNell, drew her attention away from Ellen. "Speak to me of furnaces, tropical islands."

That small shift removed one obstacle and Francis inched closer to Cleo. When finally he stood at her side, both stared straight ahead, silent, for a long moment. Then as one they turned and walked together, not looking at each other, to the end of the platform.

"Isn't that sweet?" said Matthew.

LeahNell followed his gaze.

"Romance is in the air," he said. "Where are your other classmates? Where are my other interns? *Cherchez les femmes?*"

"Yes. The girls from Pocatello went home yesterday. The boys went with them."

LeahNell put her arm around Ellen. Matthew studied them, left eyebrow raised. "Did anyone ever tell you that you two look enough alike to be sisters?"

Ellen looked him in the eye. "Yes," she said.

He swept off an imaginary hat, bowed deeply and whirled away to focus on Melba and her admirers.

Ellen laid her head on LeahNell's shoulder. "I'll miss you awfully. I won't have anyone to talk to. All Richard talks about is going to med school. When he wants to talk at all. Mostly, he tries to get us off by ourselves and he keeps trying to kiss me. Rowena told me they're moving to Boise so Richard can attend a better school. He's changed, and I've never gotten along with Rowena.

"And Mother -- I don't know how to talk to her anymore. She's so... distracted. If she and Dr. Quill... They don't have much to say, but it feels as if they know what the other's thinking. They're always making eyes at each other. It's embarrassing. Yesterday, I said ... I wasn't thinking ... it just popped out, 'If you two got married, Mother wouldn't even have to change her name.'

"He looked at me kind of sober, and her face got red. I felt so silly. I just went out on the porch. Then I heard him say, 'How about it, Mrs. Quill?' And she didn't say anything that I could hear. It was so quiet I was afraid to look.

"Why don't grownups act their age? He must be at least as old as Mother."

"I've wondered the same about Daddy. Our father and your mother. I guess we'll never know what that was all about." LeahNell hesitated. "I guess I don't need to know. But if they hadn't... Well, you wouldn't be here. And I'm glad you're here."

"I just don't understand grownups at all."

"Sometimes I don't either."

The waiting room door opened and the agent appeared.

"The train's at the water tower. The engineer just telegraphed. They'll be along in a few minutes. Be sure you've got your tickets and your bags." He glanced down the track at Cleo and Francis, wrapped around each other. "If she's going anywhere, she'd better get back here."

Ellen broke free. "Be right back," she said. She pulled her collar up around her neck and walked swiftly down the platform.

Matthew watched her go. "So. You're leaving. My last chance to do you some therapy."

"You're too late."

"You're all cured, hmm? Set for life." He fidgeted. Shifted from one foot to the other and back again. Stroked his nose. "Did I tell you, you won't recognize the place? More than you know. Rex and your old teacher Alma Duffy will *be* the psychology department for a while. The new Department of Humanistic Psychology, he calls it. He can call it what he likes. I won't be here."

"What do you ... you won't be here?"

"Utah State at Logan. Not the big time, but it's a start. Anyone who sticks around here when they have options has the psychology of a leper. Or a missionary."

He drew a deep breath. "Gilda regrets that she is unable to see you off in person. She's busy throwing up." His jaw went awry in something like a smirk. He sobered, threw his hands up. "She's pregnant."

LeahNell sighed.

"You don't seem surprised," said Matthew.

"She said something a couple of weeks ago that made me wonder."

"Oh? What did she say?"

"I don't remember. It wasn't so much what she said as how she said it ..."

"She says she's not going to waddle. Whatever that means."

LeahNell looked up at him, her lips puckered into a question. He laid a finger on them before she could speak.

"I don't know," he said, "and I don't care. As far as I'm concerned, the kid is mine."

"I don't understand you three at all."

"You don't know enough to understand us. But you know that I'm making of Rex an honest man."

In the distance, a whistle sounded three short, muted blasts. The track vibrated. Matthew was still talking, unheard, as the engine rumbled into view, headlamp burning a blurry aureole in the rain.

Ellen, clutching her arms around her chest, and Cleo and Francis clutching each other dashed under the roof.

On came the train, arriving in a rush of steam and a grind of brakes, metal against metal, momentarily paralyzing the line-up under the overhang before their reflexes hauled them back and flattened them against the wall.

Francis, waving, ran alongside the track until the caboose passed him. When she could no longer see him, Cleo, face flushed, lips puffy, closed her eyes and settled back in her seat.

Across from her, Melba and LeahNell watched rows of poplars, fields and farmsteads reel by as the train approached the water tower without slowing.

Suddenly LeahNell leaned onto the window. "There it is. The barn."

"Look," said Melba, "a scarecrow in the field."

LeahNell squinted at the plaid-shirted, straw-hatted figure in knee-length overalls.

"I don't think so," she said. "Scarecrows don't move. I saw it move."

They watched until the apparition was out of sight.

"And scarecrows don't wave."

*Willa Perrine lives in
Northern California.
She is the author of*
Telling the Bones,
a chapbook of poems.

www.ingramcontent.com/pod-product-compliance
Lightning Source LLC
Chambersburg PA
CBHW031217020726
47499CB00002B/620